W9-AVS-333

Sea Music

Sara MacDonald

Sea Music

ATRIA BOOKS
NEW YORK LONDON TORONTO SYDNEY

ATRIA BOOKS
1230 Avenue of the Americas
New York, NY 10020

This book is a work of fiction. Names, characters, places and incidents are products of the author's imagination or are used fictitiously. Any resemblance to actual events or locales or persons, living or dead, is entirely coincidental.

Previously published in Great Britain in 2003 by HarperCollins*Publishers*

ISBN: 0-7434-8212-3

First Atria Books hardcover edition May 2005

10 9 8 7 6 5 4 3 2 1

Manufactured in the United States of America

For Milly

Who says, the past is gone.
The present is what matters, and the future.

Acknowledgments

I am very grateful to Hannah Collins for her time and help with matters legal.

To my son Toby, for firsthand stories of the Balkans.

To Jane Gregory, Lisanne Radice, Broo Doherty and Susan Watt.

To Tim, for unconditional love, support, and patience. This book is also in memory of his mother, Pam, to her house full of sunlight and a time we shared.

Lastly, I am deeply indebted to Milly, who inspired this book and to John, her husband with whom she now shares another happy life.

Sea Music

Prologue

It is not cold here in this land of blue sea, but shafts of ice reach out to pierce my skin with memory of coldness. Sometimes I dream of snow and the muffled silence it brings. I dream of snow with the sun glistening on its smooth surface, catching tiny particles of blue ice, incandescent and blinding.

I wake in the dark in a strange place of fierce storms and I remember what horror can lie beneath the silent beauty of snow.

I listen to Fred breathing beside me, his body warm. He is far away in sleep and the faces swoop down at me in the dark, their voices hover in the air, like distant whispers I cannot capture.

I get out of bed, go downstairs and wander about the little cottage, afraid that this life is only a dream and I am about to wake. I sit in the corner chair by the window and wait for the sun to rise out of the black water.

I will hear Fred wake, I will hear the bed creak, then his bare footsteps coming down the stairs. He will come to where I sit and he will reach out gently to stop me rocking. He will fold me in his arms, then he will pick me up as if I weigh nothing, throwing his hair out of his eyes, as he carries me back up the stairs to bed.

He will hold me tight to him and I will breathe him into me. This is my life. I have this life now, here with him. I can feel him smiling into my hair as he tells me about the plans for our new house across the garden.

How can this beautiful man love me? But he does. He does.

I will not always be this in-between person who walks on the sand dunes above the glittering sea, watching my dark shadow move ahead of me as we walk together, the girl I was, the woman I am now.

The house is almost finished. We live here in the cottage all the time now. No more long journeys at weekends. The house is wonderful. Light is everywhere; it fills every corner, it slides across the floor and colors the rooms in buttery sun. Great windows open up and let the untamed garden into the house.

I am so happy I tremble. I kiss Fred's hands because I cannot speak. I run through the empty rooms laughing and Fred leans in the doorway, his long legs crossed, pushing tobacco into his pipe, watching me with those dark eyes that hold love and amusement.

I make myself walk into the village. I am afraid at first. People stare because I am foreign. Sometimes, in the shop, they stop talking. When I am nervous I forget my English. Then, slowly, people begin to talk to me and I learn their names.

The farm workers in the fields behind the house bring me vegetables and creamy milk from the farm. Fred laughs at me—he says I flirt atrociously—but it is not, as he teases me, because I am a floozy, it is only because I am so thin.

The builders' rubble has been taken away. At last we move in. I can plan the garden. It is going to be perfect. One day Fred comes home with a little mixed dog and we call him Puck. I love him. When we walk on the beach, people come up to me and they ask, "How is Puck? How are you?"

Summer is here, the fierce winds are warmer, but I am ill and cannot bear to go out. Fred is pale with worry. Suddenly the doctor tells me I am having a baby. I cannot believe this, I have to keep saying it over and over. After all we have been told, Fred and I are having a baby.

Fred says I must not hope too much, it is early days, I must be careful. But I know. I know this child will be born.

When Fred goes back to London to work for his finals and he cannot see to worry, I dance round the garden and sing because of the happiness of this incredible miracle.

Christmas comes and then the New Year. I lie in my bed, or in a chair that Fred places by the window in the sun. I am careful, waiting. Waiting for spring and my baby.

Our child, a boy, arrives safely on March 18, 1951. He weighs 6 lbs. 2 oz. We call him Barnaby, after one of Fred's favorite uncles. Barnaby. Such an English name.

Small shoots spring from my feet and take hold in this light, sandy soil and root me here in this extraordinary foreign place filled with blue sea and sky. The past is gone. Marta is gone. My future is here. Is now. I am Martha Tremain, the doctor's wife. This is who I am.

Chapter 1

Lucy finds Abi dead under the cherry tree. The little cat has crawled away to her favorite place and still feels warm to Lucy's fingers. She knows it is stupid to feel so upset about an old tabby cat, especially when people are being killed all over the Balkans, but this one small cat has been with her most of her childhood.

She digs a hole to bury her deep next to Puck. She does not want her found and dug up by badgers or foxes. The cat is still loose-limbed and floppy, and Lucy places her in the hole cradled by roots as if she is still sleeping in the sun, but she cannot bear to push earth over the little feline face.

She picks bluebells and mint and garlic flowers and lays them over Abi's eyes and head, makes a cover between the cat and the rain-soaked earth. Then she takes the spade and buries her. As Abi disappears from view Lucy suddenly sees herself under the ground too, a cold and literal walking over her grave.

Barnaby appears from the house and takes the spade from her, makes good the small grave and chats about what flowering thing they can plant on top of Abi. Lucy tells him about the horrible sensation and wonders if it is an omen. Barnaby says, smiling in that comforting way he has, "Lucy, remember when you and I went to pick her up from the farm? You were only six and that little cat has been a part of your childhood. You have just buried a chunk of your life, that is all."

Lucy knows he is probably right. Barnaby has been central to her childhood. He has given her security and unconditional love. He has never let her down, ever.

She turns, shading her eyes from the sun, and stares back at the house. In the conservatory her grandparents are moving around each other aimlessly. Fred is looking for his newspaper and Martha, despite the warmth of the day, is clothed in many woolen garments. It is like looking at a bizarre backdrop to some surreal play.

A lump rises in Lucy's throat. She is deserting them. She is leaving Barnaby with *this* and she has not even had the courage to tell him yet. She feels torn and suddenly apprehensive of the future. For Barnaby, for Tristan and for herself. These are her grandparents and she should be here for them. Lucy turns away, bends once more to the small grave and pats the earth flat.

Barnaby is watching her. "What is it, Lucy?"

"Tristan has just been posted to Kosovo."

Barnaby sighs. "Oh, Lucy, I am sorry." He picks up the spade and pulls her to her feet, putting his arm round her as they walk back to the house. "Tristan will be all right, Lu, I am absolutely sure of it."

Martha is waving vaguely at them. Lucy does not think her grandmother has a clue who they are, but she and Barnaby both wave back, smiling.

Gran. Lucy feels again a lightning snake of sadness. She wants to protect and keep everything in this house safe, as it has been all her life, and she knows it is impossible. She has no power over her grandparents' old age, state of mind or eventual death.

Barnaby locks the church door and stands on the porch looking out to where the sea lies in a semicircle round the churchyard. The tide is in and the estuary lies black and full, silhouetted by small, bent oak trees.

Barnaby walks past the ancient gravestones towards the water. He is reluctant to make the small journey across the road back to the house. He stands looking towards the harbor, listening to the throb-throb of the boat engines in the evening air as the small, colorful fishing fleet makes its way carefully over the bar and back to the quay.

Barnaby longs to spend this spring evening with another adult, a woman, if he is truthful. The familiar feeling of wasted years shoots through him briefly and painfully. It is not just loneliness that accentuates his single state; it is the slow, tragically funny and innocent return to childhood of both his parents, as if they have mutually given up being adult together. There is no one but Lucy to share this with: to laugh with, so he does not cry.

Lucy has been wonderful, rarely impatient, always concerned and tender with her grandparents. But she is another generation and she cannot share his memories. She has Tristan, her own life to lead.

There is Anna, but his sister does not want to accept what is happening to her parents. She is, as always, heavily involved with her career, and a husband. Anna, normally so practical, is in denial.

Barnaby turns away and makes his way down the church path and across the road to the house. Martha is peering out of the hall window, watching for him, or someone she recognizes, within the fuzzy haze in which she now lives.

He opens the door and calls out, "I'm home."

His mother dances towards him on tiny feet. "How do you do? I'm Martha Tremain," she says graciously.

Barnaby takes her small hand. "And I am Barnaby Tremain, your son." He smiles down at her, watching the bewildered expressions of doubt pass over her still-beautiful face.

Martha sees the laughter in his eyes and she laughs too, a little burst of relief. Of course. It's *Barnaby.*

"Oh, darling," she says. "How silly! I'm going quite dotty, you know."

"Rubbish," Barnaby says, kissing her. "Where's Fred?"

"Fred?" Martha shrugs eloquently. She does not know, her face is blank again, but Barnaby can see his father and Mrs. Biddulph out on the lawn. His father has Eric, the ginger tomcat, on a lead and is trying to get the cat to sit. Eric is not finding the lesson in the least amusing and Homer, his little Lab cross, is sitting on the grass, looking puzzled.

Poor Mrs. Biddulph looks cold and ready for home. Barnaby opens the French windows and calls out to his father. The old man's face lights up and he moves with surprising agility towards his son. Mrs. Biddulph unclips the lead from Eric, who stalks off into the undergrowth, his thin tail twitching with indignation.

Mrs. Biddulph is not pleased. "I've been trying to get Dr. Tremain inside for at least an hour. He hasn't had his tea yet."

Barnaby gives her his best smile. "Never mind. Whisky time, I think, Dad?"

"Good idea, old chap. Sun's over the yardarm."

Barnaby laughs and takes his father's arm. "It is indeed. Mrs. Biddulph, thank you so much. Will we see you tomorrow?"

"I can't really say. Mrs. Thomas has taken on new staff. Young girls won't stay *five minutes,*" Mrs. Biddulph says scathingly. "I'm surprised she didn't ring and tell you."

Barnaby prays there is not going to be a stream of indifferent girls to confuse Martha even further. Mrs. Thomas, who runs the Loving Care Agency Barnaby uses, is universally unpopular with her staff.

"She pays crap, expects the earth and buggers everybody around," Barnaby was told by an efficient, purple-haired girl who lasted a week.

Once indoors Barnaby closes the French windows. Mrs. Biddulph puts on her shapeless wool coat, a garment she wears winter and summer.

"I might see you tomorrow or I might not, Vicar. Good night all." Mrs. Biddulph departs at speed, already thinking about Mr.

Biddulph's tea, the bus, and getting home in time for the *Antiques Roadshow.*

Barnaby gathers both parents up, herds them into the sitting room and pours whisky into their familiar heavy tumblers. They watch him like expectant children and take their glasses greedily.

"Thank you, darling." His mother raises her glass to him and smiles her sweet vacant smile.

"You having one, old chap?" his father asks.

"Indeed I am." Barnaby sits tiredly in the armchair and looks at his parents fondly. All so normal. All calm and Sunday eveningish. If he closes his eyes for a moment he can almost believe he is twenty again and spending another soporific weekend with his parents, comforted by routine but restless to be away.

"What's Hattie cooking for supper, I wonder." Martha's voice wavers against his closed eyelids. He opens them. His father is staring at his mother.

"Hattie isn't here anymore. She died, didn't she?"

Martha's eyes fill with tears. "Oh dear, shouldn't we have gone to the funeral? Shouldn't we have sent flowers?"

Barnaby takes a long deep drink from his whisky glass. "Mum, Hattie retired about ten years ago, then sadly she died. You did send flowers, and you did go to the funeral, so that's all right, isn't it?"

"Oh, yes, darling. Sometimes I forget things. How silly."

"I'm going to finish this drink, then I'll start your supper. Cheers! Here's to summer."

"Cheers, darling."

"Cheers, old chap."

There is silence as they drink and watch him. A blackbird sets up a squawking in the cherry tree, which is about to explode into blossom.

"Naughty, naughty Eric cat," Martha murmurs, and Barnaby smiles and begins to relax.

His mother gets up and wanders round the room. "I'm rather

hungry, darling. I'll just go out to the kitchen and tell Hattie to do us all an omelette."

Barnaby sighs, gives up and gets to his feet. "I've just told you, Mum, Hattie is no longer here. It's just me tonight. You'd like an omelette?"

"Why isn't she here? I didn't give her the day off. It's too bad."

Moving to the door, Barnaby hears his voice rising, although he is trying hard not to let it. "Hattie is dead, Mother. Look, I'll put the television on for you. I think it's the *Antiques Roadshow.* Sit and watch that with Dad, and I'll be back in a minute with your supper."

As he closes the door he hears his mother say, "I didn't know Hattie was dead, darling. When did she die?"

"Oh, ages ago, M., ages ago," his father says. "Think I might have another drink."

Barnaby stares into the middle of the fridge, fighting an aching tiredness. He cannot see any eggs and an overpowering depression suddenly overtakes him. He hears the front door open, then the glass inner door shut with a bang that makes him wince.

"Hi, Barnes, it's me," Lucy calls out unnecessarily. He hears her making a run for the kitchen to see him alone before Martha hears her and dances out of the sitting room to see her beloved granddaughter.

"Help me, Lucy. What on earth can I give them for supper? The fridge seems empty."

Lucy claps her hands over her mouth. "Oh, bugger, I forgot. I told Mrs. Biddulph I would do the shopping. She will get things she likes and Gran and Grandpa hate."

She opens the door of the freezer and pulls out fishfingers and chips with a flourish. "Here we are! Gran loves them."

Barnaby looks doubtful. "She seems to live on them. I'm not sure your grandfather is so keen."

"Darling Barnes," Lucy says briskly, "they both ate a huge

roast lunch. I keep telling you, honestly, they don't need two cooked meals a day. You just make work for yourself."

"I know, bossyboots, but food is their one comfort and distraction. Look, there is some cheese at the back of the fridge; that will do for Fred."

"I'll eat chips with Gran."

Barnaby raises his eyebrows. "If I remember rightly, you too had a large Sunday lunch, or was I seeing things?"

Before Lucy can answer Martha flies in. "Lucy, Lucy, how lovely . . ." She lifts her cheek up for her gangly granddaughter to kiss and Lucy hugs her.

"Hi, Gran. I'm about to cook you fishfingers and chips. I'm going to pig out on the chips with you."

"Darling child, how lovely!"

Barnaby lays four trays out three times. Martha, longing to be helpful, promptly puts them away three times.

"How can I help, darling?" she keeps saying to Lucy. Lucy brings her alive in a way even I cannot do, Barnaby thinks, in a way the young spark the old with their energy and cheerfulness.

They have supper on their knees in the sitting room. Barnaby sits next to Fred and shares his cheese and biscuits.

"Barnaby and Gramps are both going to dream their heads off, darling, whereas you and I are merely going to get porky," Lucy whispers to Martha.

From across the room Fred looks at his tiny wife and his tall, skinny granddaughter sitting beside each other on the sofa.

"I am extremely concerned," he says drily, "that my antique sofa is going to give way under all that weight."

He regards them so seriously from over his half-moon glasses that they all burst out laughing.

Glimpses, Barnaby thinks, small, joyous glimpses of people you love, swinging back.

Chapter 2

A northeasterly wind blows in from the sea and hits the cottage head-on so that the small house shudders. The storm has gusted and rampaged around the coast for days, taking roofs and everything it can lift and hurling them around the gardens. It blows itself out in the first light of day and returns again at dusk. Trees bend and tear in the wind, their branches strewn across the road like broken limbs.

Lucy tosses and turns in the night to the mournful cry of curlews down on the estuary; wakes abruptly and lies anxious in the dark, feeling as if she is poised, waiting for some nebulous disaster that is edging her way.

She sits up, shivering. The church beyond the window looms out of the dark. The dawn sky is lightening to a faint pink above the gravestones which rise eerily up like small tors. She gets out of bed and pulls a pullover over her childlike pajamas. She misses the warmth of Abi jammed into her back. She goes downstairs to make some tea, switching on all the lights in the cottage. Carrying her tea back to bed she sits on the window seat in her bedroom, clutching the warm mug, listening to the wind begin to drop.

As a child she sat here so many times in the holidays, feeling relaxed and happy to be with her grandparents, listening to the church bells and the seabirds. Waiting for the first light when she could pull on shorts and T-shirt and run across the road, down the narrow path by the church to the beach.

When she was small, Fred and Martha still occasionally rented the cottage out, but when Fred retired he needed the spare room of the house for a study and they kept the cottage free for Barnaby or Anna and Lucy to stay in. If Lucy came alone she would sleep in Fred's study. The room always smelled comfortingly of tobacco and leather, but the cottage was where she was happiest. It was like having her own den. She would walk with Anna or Barnaby across the garden to have breakfast with Martha and Fred at the round table in the conservatory surrounded by Martha's geraniums.

Lucy and Tristan still often walk across the garden for breakfast, but it is Barnaby, not her grandparents, who cooks the bacon and makes the toast now.

Lucy suddenly longs for Tristan. Kosovo looms as foreign and unpredictable as another planet.

She jumps up. The only way to lift this mood will be to go out and walk. She pulls on jeans and two sweaters and makes her way downstairs again. Homer, who spends the nights with Lucy, opens one eye, but does not move. Lucy lets herself out, blowing across the road in the tail of the gale. She climbs the steps over the Cornish hedge into the silent and dark churchyard. She has never been afraid here; it is as familiar to her as Martha's garden.

The sun is slow in rising and she is across the golf links and down on the beach before it emerges, a beautiful gilt curve, like the edge of a plate over the horizon. There is a high tide running and she sits on the rocks and watches the sun rise up, orange and gold over the harbor, glistening the surface of the water.

Lucy does not want to leave. This place, her grandparents and Barnaby have always been home. Now, suddenly and subtly over the past months, the responsibility has changed. The caring, the childlike dependence has shifted. Martha and Fred are slipping away from her into old age and the dread of one of them suddenly dying, of her not being here when it happens, feels unbearable.

Lucy shivers despite her two sweaters. This anxiety is not just about her grandparents. It is about Tristan too. And the teaching job. And living in London on her own.

Anna will be in London, but Lucy is certainly not going to let her mother know she is nervous and afraid of failing. Anna would tell her she has spent too long in Cornwall, and this is what happens when you drop out, even for a short time.

She can hear her mother's voice and she grins suddenly, thinking of Tristan, who would say the same thing but in a different way.

"You're just in a panic because you got a bloody good job when you didn't expect to, Lu. Come on, you didn't do languages to wait on tables, did you?"

Lucy sighs and jumps off the rocks onto the sand. She is not accustomed to being melancholy and she turns slowly for home. Now she is up and wide awake she might as well sort out her things. She has accumulated so much crap. She will have to go up into the attic and see if there is any room to store all the childhood stuff she cannot bear to throw away.

Lucy climbs the ladder up to the attic and pushes open the hatch. She feels vaguely guilty, as if she is about to trespass. She should really have asked Barnaby before she came up here.

Using her torch Lucy finds the light switch on her left, and the dim bulb swings slightly, catching the dust. There is plenty of room up here. Most of the floor has been professionally boarded and Lucy wonders why her grandfather has always had a thing about people coming up here and falling through the ceiling.

The room smells of mice and dust and a world that no longer exists. There is an old gilt mirror, mottled, the frame rotting. Heavy, old-fashioned golf clubs. A box of little pewter mugs, relics of school cricket matches. A box of books. A huge grim picture of a fast-running gray sea. A faded, frayed hat with paper flowers. Leather suitcases neatly stacked one on top of another.

Rolled carpets, a broken wicker chair, and a disintegrating box of crockery and vases.

Lucy swings the torch round in an arc and sees a hardboard partition to the left of the hatch opening. Big enough to house a water tank, it has been eaten by mice and is beginning to disintegrate. There is a crude door into it with a small latch.

She heaves herself over the ledge of the open hatch and crawls over to the door. She pulls it cautiously and it falls away, completely rotten round the hinges. Kneeling upright she drags it carefully away from the partition and pushes it aside. Shining her torch inside the darkness she sees an old school trunk. Nothing else. No water tank, no hidden electric wires or pipes.

Moving inside the hidden room, Lucy sees that over the years the trunk lid, with her grandfather's initials on the top, has warped, and documents have slid to the floor below. A rusty padlock lies broken in the lock. Lucy pulls it out and opens the lid. Mice have been in and made nests; there are droppings and small mounds of eaten paper. On the top lie cardboard files of deeds and medical journals; letters in bundles, some stored in plastic files.

Lucy shines the torch downwards into the trunk and pokes about with her free hand. Why has Grandpa made a room to hide this trunk? Under her fingers Lucy suddenly sees a faded pink box nestling under letters and old documents, pushed carefully to the bottom of the trunk, underneath diaries and ancient ledgers.

She leans over and moves the bundles of letters carefully so that she can pull the box out and she places it on the floor beside her. The box is tied with colorless ribbon and the writing on the lid is faded and in Polish. Lucy's fingers hover over it.

Gran's box? Her heart is thumping. In that small second of hesitation Lucy's intuition tells her she should stop and put the box back in its hiding place, yet she is already sliding off the ribbon and lifting the lid.

Letters. Browning letters in a foreign hand. A large envelope with typewritten German: *Social Welfare Department of the Municipal*

Administration of Warsaw. It is not sealed. Lucy opens a creased and faded piece of paper within a small cardboard folder like an identity card.

The document is torn and flimsy, almost in pieces. This writing too is in German. It seems to be some sort of crude birth certificate: "Anna Esther . . . Born 8 February 1941, Warsaw, Poland." The surname is indecipherable, as if it has been rubbed out.

"Mother. Marta Esther . . ." "Oweska" has been added later, obliterating the name underneath. "Father . . ." The paper is watermarked and conveniently torn.

All that is left on the card in which the paper is folded is some sort of German official stamp and the date, 1943. The rest is illegible. What does it mean? Her mother was born in London in 1945. Gran and Grandpa have told her so. *This piece of paper would make Anna four years older than she is.* It does not make sense, and why have the surnames been rubbed out?

Lucy shivers. With shaking fingers, she pushes the documents away from her, back into the box. *She does not want to know.* She replaces the lid and puts them all back into the top of the trunk. Clumsily she moves away backwards, anxious to be out of the attic. There is nothing she can do about the rotten door.

She closes the hatch with a bang, pushes the ladder back to the ceiling and, blanking from her mind all possible implications, she runs across the garden to go and dress Martha before she starts her breakfast shift at the hotel.

Chapter 3

Coming out of court Anna congratulates herself. She was unsure she could win this case, but she was assisted by an overconfident Junior Counsel for the Prosecution who had not done his homework.

She stands for a moment, a tall figure in a navy suit, blinking in the early evening sun. Her fair hair blows away from a face with high cheekbones and startling blue eyes. People glance at her as they pass, turn for another look, as if she might be someone they should know.

She looks at her watch: it is rush hour, too late to walk back to chambers and get involved with postmortems. She hails a taxi, without any difficulty, much to the annoyance of two businessmen, and climbs in. She will make her way to the Old Vic. If she is early she can have a drink while she waits for Rudi.

As she sits in the early evening traffic, Anna's mind returns to the man she has just defended. His solicitor rang her at her chambers. He was not from the usual firm who instructed Anna, but he told her he had a client who had insisted he contacted Anna, as he had been told she was the best QC he could have to defend him.

The solicitor had apologized, knowing Anna's list would be full, but he had promised his client that he would approach her. Anna was immediately interested when he mentioned the name of the firm involved in the fraud case. The solicitor also came from a prestigious law firm it would be useful for Anna to have instruct her in the future. She arranged for a conference with Counsel for the one hour she had left that week.

The client had come to her chambers on his own as his solicitor was in court. He had thanked her for seeing him and was visibly distressed.

"I have nothing to lose by asking you to help me." He held out an envelope to Anna with shaking hands. "Would this be enough to retain you?"

Anna was amused, but she also admired his courage and determination in wanting her to defend him. She was aware she had a rather alarming reputation. She went over the case with him, then asked her long-suffering clerk to juggle her list so she could take on the case. Something in the man's blind faith in her had made her sad. She rang the man's solicitor and asked him to look into legal aid.

The Prosecution Counsel tried to prove that the defendant's ignorance of the deception going on within his own firm was pure fabrication, a callous and calculated fraud. Anna's defense rested on the fact that he was totally ingenuous and had had a steadfast but misplaced trust in the honesty of his business partner.

That fraud, operated on the vast scale it had been, would have been beyond him. She was forced to make him seem stupid in court, but it was part of her job. He'd paid dearly for blind trust. She worked for a fraction of her normal fee and, against all the odds, she won.

She takes her mobile phone from her bag and telephones Alice, her clerk. They chat for a moment about the case, then Anna asks her to return her client's savings minus a derisory amount for her fee, and to tell him that legal aid had covered the costs. That small, rather pathetic man, without an ounce of malice or bitterness, has lost his wife, his house, and every penny he possessed.

Before she rings off, she checks on her morning mail and her appointments for the following day. She has an unusual meeting in the afternoon with the CPS, who want her advice on the possibility of prosecuting an old Nazi living on a housing estate in Dorset.

Anna stretches tiredly, feeling herself coming down from the high she always gets when she wins a case. Out of the corner of her eye, she catches the flash of a cherry tree about to explode into blossom and is reminded suddenly of Martha's garden. She wants to take Rudi down to Cornwall so he can see it in the spring. Like a lot of Germans he has romantic notions of the west coast.

Barnaby seems to be making rather a meal of looking after Martha and Fred. After all he does have outside help, and he has Lucy. Cornwall is too far away for Anna to see Martha and Fred as much as she would like. Holidays have to be planned like a military campaign.

Not wanting to dwell on her parents' senility, Anna hastily picks up her mobile phone again to speak to Rudi. His secretary tells her he has just left for the theater. Anna leans back in the slow moving taxi and closes her eyes.

She still has trouble believing her luck in her late and happy marriage. Rudi, a financial consultant for a Swiss bank, works long hours himself, so accepts her workload and ambition as perfectly normal.

As a child, Anna felt Martha and Fred's disapproval if she was too competitive. She had learned that to be openly ambitious at home was considered *pushy. Not very nice.* It was not that her parents ever articulated this sentiment, it was something she instinctively knew.

In the long nights away at boarding school she would sometimes daydream she had been adopted or sent home with the wrong family at birth. She would lie imagining Fred's wealthy, sophisticated family somewhere out there in the dark wilds of Yorkshire, beyond the windows, longing to meet her, so alienated did she so often feel in the holidays, with Martha and Fred and saintly little Barnaby.

Her parents bent over backwards to appease her, and she had felt furious with them for being so patient, so bloody understanding.

She felt her power, the sheer force of her own personality at a very young age.

She would get a surge of satisfaction in knowing Martha and Fred would do almost anything to pacify her, keep her sweet, because the alternative would be a pervading atmosphere that upset the whole household.

Yet imposing her will on her parents brought her a sharp loneliness and sense of loss. All through her childhood she had looked for something to anchor her to Martha and Fred, to the place where she lived.

Later, as a teenager, her fantasy changed and she would search in her mind now for a figure who would immediately recognize that she was far cleverer than these very average parents living in their insular, West Country world.

This person—usually in her daydreams a young and handsome man—would whisk her away from total obscurity in the country to her rightful position, center stage. Like the place she effortlessly occupied all her school life.

Yet, something in her ached for the place Barnaby held in her parents' hearts. Martha and Fred told her continually how proud they were of her, but Anna was sure they wished her kinder, gentler, other than she was. They seemed as puzzled at the way she had turned out as she herself was.

Coming home from school in the holidays, Anna would immediately see Barnaby and be consumed by a frightening rage of jealousy of this placid baby, this good small boy, who had had her parents' undivided attention while she had been away.

She would spend the holidays slyly making him cry. After he too left home for boarding school and she started university she still verbally bullied him. Once he was steeped in the timeless and barbaric ways of public school, he never told, *never blabbed.* There was something soft but intransigent in Barnaby that still irritated her to death.

As the taxi filters out of the traffic, Anna sees Rudi waiting for her outside the theater. He waves, his face lighting up when he sees her. His eyes dwelling on her face. He moves forward to pay the taxi as she gets out. She feels the familiar surge of excitement and pleasure in him.

They met at a conference in Zurich. After a seminar she had given she overheard him muttering appreciative and complimentary remarks about her to a colleague, not realizing she was fluent in German and understood every word.

Rudi had told her that he had been so bowled over by *that beautiful English barrister,* it had been like walking into a door. She was giving a series of lectures to clever, noisy delegates that weekend and it had been a challenge to keep them engrossed and silent.

They strolled through the parks of the city together. They went to the opera, talked of their failed marriages, their work and themselves. For the whole of that weekend Anna spoke only German and it was a strangely liberating feeling. She felt comfortable in her skin, in the country, and with Rudi. It had been like waking from a long, lonely sleep. That weekend was also the beginning of a successful international lecture she was establishing as a consultant. Rudi was seconded to the Swiss Bank in London the following year and he took a lease on a flat in Chiswick. His sons flew out regularly for holidays. They were adolescent and enjoyed London and all it had to offer, so they were polite to Anna. She found them much easier to handle than Lucy, who had always been an enigma.

Anna and Rudi married a year later, when their respective children had got used to the idea. Lucy begged to leave her Dorset boarding school and go down to live with Barnaby and her grandparents. She wanted to take her A levels at a sixth-form college.

After talking to her headmistress, Anna eventually agreed. Both she and Rudi tried to persuade Lucy to stay in London, believing that the standard of teaching would be higher, but Lucy was adamant. She did not want to live in the flat with Rudi, Anna, and Rudi's visiting children.

Anna was not surprised. Anything or anybody Anna liked, Lucy would dislike on principle. However, the flat was too small for three teenage children, and the thought of having Rudi to herself, except for his sons' visits, had been a huge relief. Lucy got surprisingly good A levels. She was as happy with Barnaby, Martha, and Fred as Anna felt distanced and irritated by them.

Anna feels a sudden relief that Lucy is now an adult. Life is so much easier. As Rudi bends to kiss her, she thinks how lucky she is. Rudi, having fulfilled most of his own ambitions, opted to forgo promotion and coast happily towards retirement in London to be with her. Anna knows she is happier than she has ever been.

Anna shakes hands with Rudi's Swiss guests and they make their way to the bar. Rudi's hand hovers courteously at the small of her back. It reminds Anna of the way Fred walked beside Martha, and she is touched. Somehow, it makes her feel secure, for Fred has been as constant to Martha as the changing seasons.

Chapter 4

Evensong is over and Lucy is helping Barnaby put Martha to bed. Fred is perfectly capable of managing himself, but he cannot manage Martha anymore and it upsets him. Her grandparents have single beds now, near enough to touch, to hold hands in the night, but not to disturb each other's sleep.

Martha always goes to bed first and Lucy will sit and hold her hands, check her hot-water bottle, give her her pills, talk to her and marvel at her still-beautiful face. Martha has always worn pretty linen nightdresses, and somehow, once she is in bed she relaxes, her face loses its anxious look and smoothes into a tiny unlined child's face. Suddenly coherent, she will tell Lucy long rambling tales of building this house, of starting the garden from scratch. Of meeting Fred in London. Of love at first sight.

Fred will appear out of the bathroom, bathed and immaculate in pajamas and dressing gown, and say politely but firmly to Lucy, "Good night, child."

It is her signal to leave them. She will bend and kiss her grandmother, who twines her thin arms round Lucy's neck. "Oh, my darling, how I love you!"

"I love you too, Gran. Sleep well. Good night."

She bends to her stooped grandfather. "Good night, Gramps. God bless."

"God bless, child."

Every night it is the same. Barnaby comes then to tuck them in, to stand at the end of their beds, to say a good night prayer.

"Good night, darling Barnaby," his mother whispers, eyes closed, half asleep.

"Good night, Mum."

"Good night, old chap," his father says.

"Good night, Dad. Sleep well."

The security of ritual. Barnaby shuts the bedroom door and leans against it. "Sans everything," he breathes. Fred will fall into a deep and heavy sleep, but Martha could get up a dozen times and wander about during the evening.

Lucy is pouring them both a glass of wine and they sit together in silence, drinking. All week she has wanted to ask Barnaby about the box she found in the attic. She has never had secrets from him, but she looks at his drained and exhausted face and is silent.

After a while she says, "Barnes, you can't go on like this. Sundays are hell for you. You need weekend carers now, not just old Mrs. B. for a few hours. You are going to need round-the-clock help soon."

She hesitates, then says miserably, "You know that interview I went up to London for, teaching foreign students? Well, I got the job."

"Lucy, that's marvelous." Barnaby leaps up and kisses her. "You clever girl. I'm *so* pleased for you. Just think, you'll be able to use your degree and earn some decent money."

"Well, the pay is not brilliant, but the best thing about it is that I can go and teach in Italy for three months. But how are you going to cope on your own? It's going to get worse with Gran." She gets up and pours more wine into Barnaby's glass.

"I don't start the job for a couple of months, but Tristan wants me to spend his leave with him before he goes. It means I would have to leave quite soon . . ."

"Lucy," Barnaby says firmly, "how I manage is not your responsibility. You've got your own life to lead." He is watching her closely. He suspects Lucy is anxious about leaving Cornwall and the security of this household. "It will be fun for you to live in London for a while; it doesn't have to be forever. It will be a great adventure and much easier for you and Tristan to be together when he gets back from Kosovo. I'll miss you enormously, you know that, Lu. You've been wonderful these last few months, but there is a world out there waiting for you."

Lucy bursts into tears. "I don't think I should go. I should be here, near my family. I don't think you dare admit you need more help with Gran and Gramps. I feel sick just thinking of leaving you."

Barnaby is startled because this is so unlike Lucy. "Then I've been very wrong and relied on you too much. I'd feel mortified if you thought you couldn't get on with your own life, Lu, or that you might be influenced by my needs or those of Martha and Fred. I understand how you feel about Cornwall, but there's always going to be a home for you here. You have your whole life ahead of you with a man you love, who thinks the light shines out of your bottom."

Lucy gives a watery grin, then giggles. "True. But, Barnes, will you please, please think about getting live-in help? It doesn't have to be through the agency. There must be retired nurses, people like that. You could move into the cottage, have a bit of space and peace. You need it."

"Lucy, round-the-clock care is very expensive. The only way we could begin to afford it would be to rent out the cottage again. Don't forget the cottage does not just belong to me; Anna and I share it."

"Well, Mother will bloody well have to help financially. It's about time she took some responsibility. Barnaby, you must have some life, somewhere to shut yourself away. You'll go mad with carers here all the time—"

"Lucy," Barnaby interrupts, "I am quite capable of looking

after myself. Just think what *you* want to do, what will make you happy, and do it."

The phone rings suddenly, making them both jump. Barnaby's heart sinks; he knows who it will be.

"That will be Anna," Lucy says, "with a guilty Sunday duty call. Don't let her get to you, Barnes."

But Barnaby is already tense, and listening to Anna's firm, confident voice puts him more on edge. She is about to take a short break and would like to come down with Rudi to see Martha and Fred. She presumes it will be all right if they stay in the house as she would rather not inflict the cottage and Lucy's lack of hygiene on Rudi.

Barnaby swallows his annoyance. "Anna, it's not all right, I'm afraid. The carers arrive early. There is chaos in the mornings with only one bathroom. You'll also find Martha and Fred very confused, especially with anyone they don't know. I'm sorry, but it's not fair on the carers, and I couldn't cope with two extra people in the house either. Could you come down on your own this time and stay at the cottage? It's some time since you last saw Martha and Fred and I'm afraid you will notice a difference."

Anna is annoyed and snaps back at him, "You are evidently finding it difficult to cope, Barnaby. You should have let me know. It's obviously time we thought about a home. We'd better talk about it when I come down."

Barnaby explodes. "We most certainly will not! I can't believe you are even suggesting it, Anna. Come down and see for yourself before you start making comments like that. I'll get Lucy to tidy the cottage before you arrive."

He waves at Lucy to be quiet. She is jumping up and down and punching the air, sticking her thumbs up to the sky.

"Of course I haven't any objection to you coming down with Rudi . . ." Barnaby takes a deep breath. "It's just that if you come down on your own, you could spend a little time with Martha and Fred, Anna. Have a holiday with Rudi another time.

Fred, especially, will appreciate you coming. Please think about it and let me know. Good night."

Barnaby finds he is trembling with weariness and suppressed rage as he replaces the receiver. Anna continues to be one of the most self-centered people he has ever come across.

Lucy is still hopping up and down. "She is such a totally selfish human being," she echoes. "Don't tell me it's wrong to dislike my own mother sometimes, Barnes. She makes me *furious.* Does she *ever* ask you how *you* are? Does she, *hell!* Thank God you stood your ground. She's got such a bloody cheek. Sorry, I'm knackered . . . Got to go to bed . . ." Lucy wilts, suddenly exhausted.

Barnaby kisses her good night. "Sleep well," he says drily. "Having a vicar as an uncle has done nothing to improve your language."

He watches her walk across the damp grass and disappear through the little gate to the cottage. How could Anna have produced this child he loves so dearly?

The curlews down on the estuary warble mournfully into the darkness. Startling himself, Barnaby admits suddenly that he too can actively dislike his sister. Not only does he wish her in Outer Mongolia, but he realizes he has always felt like this.

Martha's memories, so long suppressed and left behind, are beginning to surface slowly and slyly, like bubbles. Time for Martha has become meaningless. Past and present merge and blur. Voices and faces pass like shadows across her mind, throwing up long-forgotten lives. Those lives seem so real to Martha, so near, as if she can open a door and move into the rooms of her past life once more. Those far-gone lives of her childhood draw her back with long tentacle arms, to enfold her in their sense of nearness.

She reaches out to touch the fleeting sleeve of a dress, the rough tweed of a jacket. She smells fresh bread in the oven. She sees faces she loves bending to her, smiling, chiding her wildness.

With longing, she lifts her head to feel their breath upon her cheek, turns to catch the sound of faint laughter and the warmth of a hand.

She listens to the wind rattling the long windows so that the sound echoes through the house, shutting doors with a sudden click, moving the curtains outwards, lifting the rug in little tremors, like ghostly footsteps through the hall.

Mama and Papa are having tea with the German doctor and his wife. Marta and Mama and Papa have traveled from Lodz all the way to Warsaw by train to see him. Marta has been sent into the garden with the doctor's small boy and the nursemaid. The nursemaid is not watching them, she is flirting with the gardener.

Marta stares at the German boy with fascination. He has the whitest blond hair, very blue eyes, and white, white teeth. He is wearing lederhosen and a pale shirt, and his bare arms and legs are brown and smooth as apples. He stares back at Marta disdainfully. He does not like to be sent outside to play with a girl.

Marta stands on the terrace steps, wary and a little frightened, like a small rabbit ready for flight. The boy puts his hands on his hips and, coming closer, looks down at her.

"How old are you?" he asks.

"I am five," Marta says, trying to make herself tall.

The boy is pleased. "Well, I am older, I am eight. Mutti says I am going to be much taller than my father." There is a silence. Then he says in a bored voice, "Come, I am going to go and see the horses."

He turns and marches away towards the stables. Marta follows him. She is afraid of horses, but she is not going to say so.

The horses are standing looking out of their stalls, shaking their great heads against the flies. They are groomed to a shiny perfection, their manes shimmer as they toss their heads.

The boy goes to a big stallion. "This is Tylicz, my favorite horse. When I am older I will ride him, but at the moment he is too big and strong." He takes an apple out of his pocket and turns to Marta. "Here, you may feed him if you like. Give this to Tylicz."

He is watching her closely and he smiles suddenly. She is growing pale at the thought of approaching that huge mouth. He knows, he knows I am afraid, Marta thinks.

The boy places the apple in her hand and leads her towards Tylicz. Desperately, she tries to hang back, but the boy pulls her sharply forward, tells her there is nothing to be afraid of and lifts her clumsily towards the great head of the horse. Marta screams as his long yellow teeth reach out towards her. She drops the apple and jerks away. The boy loses his balance and lets Marta fall onto the hard stable floor.

He bursts out laughing; he can see she is not hurt and she looks so funny. Marta will not cry. She is angry. She picks herself off the floor, bends and takes the fallen apple, wipes it on the hem of her dress and breaks it into pieces with her teeth. She has remembered something Mama told her and she arranges the pieces on the flat of her hand.

She walks over to Tylicz and, trembling, stands on tiptoe and raises her hand up, up, towards the horse, keeping very still and balancing herself on the door of the stall with her other hand.

Tylicz looks down at her almost as if he is smiling and very slowly and gently he bends over the stable door, craning his neck down to her hand. He can only just reach the apple, only just brush her hand with his whiskery mouth. He tickles her open palm, his mouth velvety, as he scoops the apple up, and Marta laughs as he crunches it noisily.

She cannot stop laughing for the relief of not being bitten and the laughter lights up her face and fills her whole being. She is not afraid of this boy. She is not afraid of the horse.

When she turns round the boy is laughing too, and the look in his eyes is no longer scornful. Marta hears Mama calling and they turn together and run across the green lawn, back towards the house. Marta's head is held high and her back is stiff with triumph.

The boy's mother is standing with Mama outside the French windows. She reaches down and ruffles the thick blond hair of the boy. She is pretty, Marta thinks, and golden, but she does not smile. Next to her,

Mama looks tiny and far more beautiful, with her shiny dark hair and smiling brown eyes.

The German doctor comes out into the garden with Papa, and bends to Marta. "Your father and I are old friends, Marta. We studied together. I hope you and my son will be friends also, because your papa has agreed to come and work with me. He is going to build you a house on that land over there that backs on to the forest. Then, you see, he can help me run my clinic."

Behind the tall doctor, Marta is watching the boy. He is standing with his hands on his hips, feet apart, staring at her with those pale, intense, turquoise eyes. His mother reaches down and whispers something to him. He pulls away embarrassed, shrugs off her hand, and in a little lightning movement kicks out at a garden chair, which collapses with a clatter on top of a little dog, who gives a great yelp and dashes away.

The boy jumps. Marta does not think he knew the dog was there, but she is not sure. It is time to go. Her father takes her hand. She turns and looks over her shoulder. The boy is standing with his blond hair blowing in the wind, still watching her. He seems suddenly alone and strangely beautiful. Exciting. Marta shivers.

Chapter 5

Lucy wakes early and pulls on a T-shirt and tracksuit bottoms.

"Sorry," she says to Homer, as she lets him out into the garden for a pee. "I'll take you out later, but you can't keep up with me when I'm running."

Homer looks martyred and slinks back to his bed.

"Come on, don't be a drama queen." Lucy lifts his heavy old head and plants a kiss on it, but the dog is not to be mollified.

Lucy opens the front door and runs past the church and down the path towards the beach. The air feels warmer, expectant. Birds scuttle about in the undergrowth, flying low and gathering feathers and fluff, grass and twigs. She runs down the steps and jumps onto the sand. The tide has turned and she can just get round the point.

Lucy pushes herself, running steadily, jumping the waves that slide in and pool round her feet. She can feel herself beginning to relax. The beach is deserted, stretching long and colorless in early morning light.

Happiness flares suddenly, a joy in being alive. Lucy increases her speed, her hair flapping rhythmically as she gets into her stride. The lighter mornings always make her wake earlier, but it is not daylight that disturbs her sleep.

She has covered a great length of the beach fast; now she slows down as she feels her legs tiring, measuring the point she wants to reach. She pushes the thought of that small odd birth certificate firmly out of her mind. She will think of Tristan instead. She heads up the beach and collapses near the rocks, sweating and panting. In the distance fishing boats are coming out of the harbor, battling over the bar with the wind against them.

Lucy considers what it will be like to live away from the sea again—not just in London, but wherever it is that Tristan could be posted after Kosovo. She is unsure she can live for too long away from the coast. Worse, if they marry, what if he has another single posting and she is left on her own in some army quarter?

She squints up at the sky. She can hear skylarks in the dunes behind her. She and Tristan have never really discussed marriage; it is an understood thing. Tristan may be a lapsed Catholic, but his parents certainly are not.

Tristan and Lucy are firmly given separate bedrooms when they stay, despite his mother being quite aware that they sleep together. It is not done primly or critically and Tristan's mother had gently explained that she could not have double standards. Laura, Tristan's youngest sister, still lives at home and there was no way they could countenance her bringing a boy home and sleeping with him.

Lucy grins. Separate bedrooms were funny. Tristan, bringing her tea in the mornings, borrowed his father's silk dressing gown and cravat, inked a curly mustache with her eyeliner and did appalling Noël Coward impersonations, which sounded more like David Suchet playing Poirot.

Lucy wraps her arms round herself as she cools.

"Do I end up with a baby every year and a waist the size of a block of flats?" she asked him.

"Certainly you do," Tristan replied. "I have a weakness for waistless women." Then, hastily, in case she took fright, "Has my mother got fifteen children? Of course not. We will just use the rhythm method. Coitus interruptus." Seeing her face, he burst out laughing. "Idiot! I'm teasing." He picked her up and twirled her round. "Anyway, you might throw me over for a fisherman and settle forever in the place you love most, at the end of the world."

He was smiling, but his eyes were serious. *Tris.* She cannot imagine life without him. All this, all she has here, would mean so much less if he was not there.

She gets up and stretches, jumps up and down, loosening her limbs. She starts to run back, slower this time. The outgoing tide has left a line of foamy scum on the wet sand.

Tristan has made her grow up. He does not always say what she wants to hear, but she listens, especially about Anna. Her heart gives that anxious lurch again. *Like the moment you wake and know something is wrong.* She closes her eyes tight, banishing unease.

Anna sent her a little note in a card, congratulating Lucy on getting the teaching job. It is not the sort of thing Anna usually does. Lucy suspects that Alice, Anna's clerk, bought it, or Rudi. After the congratulations, Anna wrote, "About time you rejoined the civilized world. I think you will find it stimulating. Love, Mum."

Lucy tossed the card aside crossly, but when she told Tristan, he said carefully, "I think you are a bit hard on Anna, Lu. She sent you a card because she was proud of you. It doesn't matter who bought it."

"I'm not hard on her! Anna can never do or say anything that does not have a hidden barb. Not to me, anyway."

"Is it possible that she cannot do or say anything that you don't feel defensive about?"

Lucy was stung. "You don't understand. If I am defensive, it is because all my life she has been critical—"

"Lu, this is a circular conversation. We are not going to have an argument about the dragon in a wig. You're right, I don't know what it feels like to be her daughter. I don't know what it feels like to have had a working or ambitious mother. I think you are just very different people and it's a shame you don't get on. I am sure she is as proud of you under her fiery nostrils as you must be of her."

Lucy reaches the steps and stops again, the sweat pouring down her face. The bloody thing is she *is* proud of Anna. She remembers her coming to her school to give a talk on careers, just after Lucy had taken her GCSEs. Anna arrived looking stunning, immaculate. When she started talking you could have heard a pin drop in the hall. Lucy was fascinated. It was like watching someone she did not know. Anna the barrister in full stimulating flow, encouraging debate, challenging assumptions. Anna alive, doing what she was best at. For two hours she had forty girls and thirty boys from a neighboring school riveted.

Lucy pulls herself up the steps, panting. It was the same day that she told Lucy she was going to marry the German banker. In bed that night in the silent dormitory, Lucy thought: that is why she looked so beautiful, why she was so sparkling. Anna is in love.

Lucy had already decided she wanted to leave school and take her A levels at a sixth-form college. There was no way she was going to go back and stay in a small flat with Anna and her new husband. The thought was gross.

Barnaby was back from Northern Ireland and was staying in the cottage on leave. Lucy rang him and asked if she could go down and live in the cottage and take her A levels in Cornwall.

Barnaby thought she was too young to live in the cottage on her own, and her grandparents were too old to have a seventeen-year-old living with them permanently. Lucy argued that she had been staying in the cottage every holiday of her life and that it was ten steps to Fred and Martha's front door.

Both her grandparents thought it a wonderful idea. It was the first time Lucy saw Barnaby sad. He was leaving the army and seemed distracted. He took off on his own, went traveling. Lucy thought maybe he wanted to stop being a priest.

When Lucy was about to leave for university he came home. He had applied for a parish in Cornwall to be near Martha and

Fred. Martha was not very well, but no one knew what it was then.

Lucy reaches the cottage and bumps into Barnaby coming out of the gate. He bursts out laughing when he sees her. "Oh my goodness, look at the state of you! You haven't got any fat to lose, for heaven's sake. I came over because Homer was howling his head off."

"Homer is a spoiled brat," Lucy says, looking sternly down at the dog.

"Of course he is, he has lived with your grandparents all his life. He only transferred his affections to you because you go for longer walks and do not ration his biscuits. Are you coming over for breakfast or are you working?"

"I am coming over. Is Gran up? Are you cooking bacon and eggs?"

"Your gran is having breakfast in bed as usual and I am not cooking bacon and eggs. The logic of you running and then eating a cooked breakfast escapes me."

"That is because you are a man," Lucy says sweetly. "I am on a twelve-to-three today and I need sustenance to get me through."

"You might get a boiled egg. Spoiled brat," Barnaby says, turning and ducking through the garden gate, trailed by Homer. Lucy grins and goes to ring Tristan.

Chapter 6

The first thing Anna hears as she opens the front door is Maria Callas. *"Suicidio! In Questi fieri momenti."* She stands listening, leaning against the door. Evening sun catches the colored panes and flickers across the hall. She can smell the smoke from one of the small cigars Rudi smokes.

The moment is so perfect, Anna feels reluctant to break it. She goes up the stairs slowly. It has been an especially good day and she is home early. Her flat consists of two floors. The room off the hall at the front of the house she uses as a study or third bedroom. Adjoining it is a tiny breakfast room with a gas ring and small sink. It has French windows on to a tiny terrace garden, which she and Rudi use in summer. On the first floor there is a drawing room, two bedrooms, bathroom and kitchen.

Anna loves this flat. It contains everything she needs. She has lived here a long time and spent a lot of money, but it is now worth four times what she paid.

She pushes the drawing-room door open quietly and watches Rudi for a moment. He is sitting in the leather swivel chair, half turned to the window. *The Times* is spread over his knees but he is not reading. His head lies back against the chair and his eyes are closed as he listens to the music.

Anna stands quite still looking at him. The way his hair, gray-white, grows just over his ears. The way his face seems always tanned. The way the long fingers of his right hand hang over the arm of the chair. His mouth firm, with tiny vertical lines.

There is something sensual and intimate in watching someone with their guard down, watching the face of someone you love when they think they are alone. Her stomach knots with the strength of this love. It bites suddenly at her being, unnerves her so much she puts her arm out to the wall to steady herself.

The shadow of her arm makes Rudi turn, swing round in his chair, startled. He just catches the expression on her face before it changes into a smile. He holds her eyes and his own heart leaps. There is a depth to Anna he will never be able to penetrate. Yet that fleeting, powerful look that he caught on her face tells him everything he needs to know. She loves him with a passion that renders her vulnerable. *Someone once betrayed her.*

The moment passes. He smiles and opens his arms, gets up out of the chair. "Anna, how wonderful! Unexpected. You are home early!"

Anna laughs. "It's a miracle!"

They stand holding each other. The raw moment of exchange hovers between them, still there in the gentleness of their arms and hands resting on each other's back as the voice of Maria Callas flows round them.

"I thought," Anna says, leaning back to see his face, "that I would like to take you out to dinner. I booked a table at that new Italian place, because I thought we could walk, it's such a lovely evening."

Rudi breaks away to turn the music down. "Are we celebrating anything other than the fact you are home early, my darling Anna?"

"Well, I have just been told my name has been put forward again as a circuit judge."

"Anna! How wonderful. This is what you want? Does it mean more work? Less work?"

"Different work. It means traveling, but it would be promotion.

I would not have the huge casework I have now." She smiles and picks her bag up. "But I have refused before, and I think I will refuse again, I am addicted to the fight on the floor. It is just gratifying to be asked!"

They walk into the kitchen and Rudi gets a bottle of wine from the refrigerator.

"I start on the Piper case tomorrow—you know, the pharmaceutical negligence case I was telling you about? It is going to be a marathon. So tonight, I thought it could be you and me celebrating having a whole long evening together on our own."

Rudi moves towards her, tucks a tiny piece of her hair behind her ear.

"Have we time for a long leisurely shower before we eat, do you think?"

"I think," Anna says softly, "we definitely have time."

The silence of night swoops, closes and traps Anna in darkness. She can hear the distant, haunting echo of weeping. The landscape is bleak and stark—no buildings, only stooped moving figures silhouetted against fires that flare out into the blackness.

Hands hold her too tight, cover her nose and mouth so she cannot breathe. She wakes with a jolt and lies, heart pumping, as if a cold hand has suddenly shaken her.

The exposed shoulder of Rudi sleeping beside her is clammily cold at three in the morning. Anna, brushing against him, shivers. The window on her right shows a cold, clear night full of distant fading stars and the blurred shape of rooftops and willow tree.

She cannot remember what woke her, only that the memory of it is disturbing. She goes over next week's court case to see if there is something she has missed. She thinks about her appointments for the rest of the week and the lecture she is giving in Berlin on Friday, but there is nothing she can find to make her anxious or sleepless.

Martha comes into her mind; this slow, creeping senility of her parents. Has she just dreamed of them? Anna does not think so, but there is a growing problem down in Cornwall that she knows she is avoiding confronting. Round-the-clock care is available, but expensive. Presumably that is why Barnaby seems determined to shoulder most of the care.

Anna sighs. She hopes that Martha and Fred will not outlast their money. Fred has always worried about money and if he were forced to sell the house it would break his heart. There is going to be no easy answer. At least she tries to be practical about her parents' welfare—unlike Barnaby, who is just sentimental. He is too close to Martha and Fred. It is not healthy. He should be married, have children, be living in the plain but easy-to-run modern vicarage in his other parish. He should have his own life, *a separate life,* from his parents.

Anna feels a sudden pang of pity. If that little nurse he had been engaged to had not been blown up in Northern Ireland, Barnaby might be living his own life by now.

Her parents have always been poor. She hated this fact as a child and it has made her careful with her money. Fred always made it clear to Anna that he would have no money to leave her and Barnaby, just the house, the cottage and the plot of land that Martha made into part of her garden.

Anna and Barnaby grew up knowing that there had been a terrible disagreement between Fred and his parents after the war. They remained steadfast in their refusal to speak to Fred or acknowledge his family.

"But why?" Anna asked her father. "Why don't they want to see us?"

"It is me they do not wish to see, not you, darling," Fred said.

Martha, across the room, put down her sewing and said quietly, "That is not quite true." She looked at Anna. "It is me that they do not wish to see or acknowledge."

Fred turned and smiled at Martha with such love in his eyes that Anna said quickly, loudly, "Because you are Polish?"

"Because I am Jewish as well as being foreign, darlink."

Anna saw the hurt in her father's eyes and her heart hardened. She would not care about grandparents who made her parents sad. All the same, it was the stuff of fantasies. And Anna did fantasize.

The uncle whom Barnaby had been named after was also his godfather. He had come to Barnaby's christening and he and Fred remained close. He used to send Barnaby and Anna beautifully wrapped Christmas presents.

Once, when she was at Durham University, he took Anna out. The anger that he felt about Fred's banishment, even when he was an old man, was still in his eyes.

"They are only hurting themselves. They have missed out on the only grandchildren they will ever have." He grinned foxily at Anna. "Younger son a grave disappointment. Neither inclined to marriage nor to work."

Anna has always found it hard to believe that Fred could have been left totally without means. When people grow old they forgive. Lord and Lady Tremain would surely have wanted to make peace with their son before they died.

She remembers her father going to Lady Tremain's funeral the year she sat her O levels. He drove up to Yorkshire alone and did not return the next day as planned, and Martha was worried. When he eventually arrived home, he looked sad and defeated; muddy and disheveled.

He had walked for the whole of that lost day, round the grounds of his home, visiting people on the estate, reliving gentle memories of a happy childhood. Saying good-bye to ghosts. Trying, Martha explained to her children, to come to terms with the terrible waste, the pointlessness of his parents' endless stance.

The *deliberate* loss of a son . . . Martha could not understand it. As if Fred were really dead. Lady Tremain, old but still bitter, had refused to let Fred go to his father's funeral.

"So *cruel,*" Anna would hear Martha say to Fred over the years. "They are entitled to pretend I do not exist, even that our children do not exist, but not you, their elder and beloved son. I will never understand this. Never. I cannot."

Anna feels the familiar irritation, even now in the dark, at the flowery dramatic way her mother has of talking. Martha might think of herself as English, she might have incorporated all the small English mannerisms, but the way she uses phrases, the way she uses her hands and gently presses people's arms is not English. It used to embarrass Anna at school; she much preferred her father's soft, English voice.

If it hadn't been for a trust fund set up by Fred's grandparents for him, something even his parents could not legally deny him, Anna would have had to go to a state school. The thought often makes her go cold. She almost certainly would not be in the position she is today. The judiciary of her age group is still almost entirely made up of people who have been privately educated.

Fiercely loyal to Fred, and eavesdropping as a child, Anna can remember distant aunts and uncles passing guiltily through Cornwall to visit them. Fred sometimes went to London to meet old friends, to Martha's joy. But he never saw his parents again. The only time he returned to Yorkshire was to bury his mother.

Fred's brother is dead now too. What did they say to each other on the day of their mother's funeral? Why did they not become reconciled? Too much bitterness? Betrayal? Fred has never explained.

The anxiety is still with Anna. Will she wake Rudi if she gets out of bed to go to make tea? It is so rare for her not to sleep these days and she is afraid of disturbing him.

She thinks of Lucy. Lucy coming back to London is a very good thing. The cottage can be rented out at the going rate. Barnaby has steadfastly refused to take any rent from Lucy, and Anna is pretty sure she can afford it as she has been working in a hotel.

It would not surprise Anna if Tristan has been living at the cottage at weekends or when he is on leave. Rudi stopped her asking Lucy, pointing out that it would have cost them far more to have her living in London and that his sons were subbed on their visits, so it was important to be fair.

Anna let the matter drop. Rudi was right: she could be hard on Lucy. She shudders at the thought of what some of their friends and colleagues are going through, with children who sponge off their parents for as long as possible. Lucy has never asked for money; she has always been good about getting herself holiday jobs.

The day is lightening. Anna slides down the bed, hoping to sleep again. She cannot put off going down to Cornwall for much longer. She will have to discuss plans for the future with Barnaby. She must think about arranging power of attorney so she can see how Fred and Martha are financially. Barnaby can be bloody awkward when he decides on a course of action.

It would be much easier to have Rudi with her. Barnaby would find it more difficult to argue with her. Surely it is not because Rudi is German that Barnaby suggested she go down on her own? Fred was always too protective. She and Barnaby were always discouraged from discussing anything to do with the war in front of Martha.

It must have been terrible for Martha to have to leave her family at a young age and flee to England, alone. But it was all such a long time ago now. Life has moved on.

She has never thought about having Jewish blood. She is so fair, she has always identified with Germans and Northern Europeans, especially since she started lecturing. God alone knows what sort of throwback she is. Some Scandinavian ancestor Fred had in the family cupboard. She has that rare blonde hair that does not fade but stays a Nordic white. Anna has always been proud of her looks and a little vain, enjoying the attention she attracts.

Lucy is olive-skinned and dark, although she highlights her hair now in thin streaks of blonde. Still gangly and colt-like, Lucy is like Martha, except in height. She has the same creamy coffee skin and shiny blue-black hair that gleams in the light. And like her father, of course. The same eyes, the same way of using her hands.

Claudio was an Italian musician Anna had a short fling with and uncharacteristically got pregnant by. She briefly married him for form's sake and they parted in a sad but friendly fashion before Lucy was born. The only thing he asked of Anna was that his child carried his name.

Anna has absolutely no idea what happened to him. He just drifted completely out of her life, and it is something Lucy holds against her. "Everyone needs to know who they are," she will cry dramatically from time to time, but not very seriously.

Barnaby has been Lucy's father, brother and best friend. Lucy is pragmatic and inclined to make her own happiness. Anna has never felt close to her daughter, and perhaps one day she will try to find Claudio. When she has children of her own.

Anna never intended to have children and Lucy was left with nannies for most of her childhood, or with Martha and Fred. Barnaby would whisk her away in the holidays, when he was on leave. He would take her to France or Italy with a girlfriend and spoil her atrociously.

A surprise baby arrived at an awkward moment in Anna's career. She was junior counsel and fiercely ambitious. She wanted to be one of the youngest women to take silk. In your thirties you had to make good or you were lost to the young, mostly men, coming up behind you. She became a Queen's Counsel at thirty-six.

Rudi is snoring gently and Anna is still wide awake. She likes the warmth of his body in the bed next to her. Comforting. Yet this vague but familiar unease still lingers, like a half-heard snatch of conversation blown in at an upstairs window.

Anna's heart starts to thump painfully again. "Oh God," she whispers into the coming day. "Don't let me start these wretched nightmares again."

* * *

Barnaby sits on the battered old sofa in the conservatory, experiencing a tangible sense of timelessness, a brief lament for the years that have slid slyly by while his back was turned. If he closes his eyes he is once more that prep schoolboy curled up, dreading the end of the Easter holidays.

He used to crouch in this peachy-smelling glasshouse listening to the birds at twilight while the destructive wind brought in scents of cherry blossom, of wallflowers, and dropped pittsoporum seeds. Early pollen filled his nostrils, making him sniff and sneeze as he lolled there as dusk came, making the trees luminous in the dark.

He would listen to Fred read softly to his mother, his whisky glass perched precariously on the arm of the chair in Martha's dressing room, which led directly through glass doors from the conservatory.

T. S. Eliot, Edward Thomas, Siegfried Sassoon, Wilfred Owen—sad and brilliant dead poets. All his life snatches of lines have popped into Barnaby's head, and with those lines come the evocative smells that accompanied the words: sausages, flowers, cordite, dogs. House plants, whisky, dust, his own unwashed feet.

As the rise and fall of his father's voice soothed Martha's headache and reached him just outside their room, loneliness would descend out of nowhere. There was a close intenseness between his parents that excluded him without their realizing it.

In bed, in the dark, a haunting, animal keening would penetrate the cobwebs of his sleep. A cry, a whisper. Hushed voices. In the morning, loss real and enduring breathed and moved behind quick smiles.

Barnaby could not understand why his happy family life, full of love, did not make him feel as safe and secure as it should have done. Martha and Fred were never indifferent or uncaring. Warmth filled this house. Yet, Barnaby knew that the strength of what he felt was not imagined.

His childhood felt as if he were following a snatch of song down a dusky corridor, only to find when he turned the corner there was only a vibration hovering in the night air, no singer held the trembling notes he heard. The feeling of loss was searing. He was sure that if he could only capture that lingering echo he would recognize the singer and the haunting song they sang. Then his feeling of carrying a weighty sadness might end. Instead of his parents disappearing into shadow, they would remain flesh and blood to him.

Barnaby sensed a truth that was missing from their lives. A bewilderment of childhood where honesty is obscured, where secrets are kept.

Standing, bleak on the station platform as he went back to school, he would wait for Martha to hug him to her again and again. Fred would bend and kiss him. Always. Barnaby would board the train, would hurry down the corridor to the school carriage and jostle to the window to catch sight of them. Each time he would will them to see *him,* Barnaby Tremain, eight and a half years old. Not just another white-faced little schoolboy in school cap and blazer identical to hundreds of others with their noses pressed to the window on the school train for Paddington.

He knew they loved him, yet before the train even pulled out of the station they would turn once more to one another, their heads close together, walking away from him down the platform. His mother so thin and tiny. His father bent towards her, his left hand hovering protectively behind her back.

They never turned for one last wave although he always waited, breath held with longing, leaning out of the carriage window to capture that last glimpse of them as the train hooted and sidled forward. But they never ever turned to wave.

To them he had already gone. Their concentration was on one another. Barnaby would pull in his head before a master caught him, and collapse into his seat, concentrating on pulling his socks up, on not blubbing.

He always, always wanted to shout to his parents' disappearing backs, "I'm still here. I haven't gone yet. I'm still here."

Barnaby, sitting on the long-faded sofa, drinking his own whisky, whispers to himself now, "I'm still here."

For it feels sometimes that the piercing echo of his parents' secret song still hovers in the flickering shadows and movements of the house. As they reach the end of their lives, it seems to move nearer.

Chapter 7

BERLIN

He has not been to the Freie Universität for over a year. He used to lecture regularly at the Institut für Physiologie, then suddenly he tired of the young; wanted to travel.

Ulrich Scheffell rang him out of the blue, asked him to come to the Institut to discuss a European lecture tour he was trying to organize.

"Why do you ask me at my age?" he asked.

"You know very well," Ulrich replied. "You are one of the most eminent orthopedic surgeons in Berlin."

"I am a retired orthopedic surgeon."

"You are not too old to travel round the world. And you are not too old to lecture. Admit that you are interested."

"I will admit to nothing. But I will let you give me lunch."

"Hah!" Ulrich rang off, delighted.

He parks his car with difficulty, thinking: no one walks anywhere anymore. Everyone has cars. This is why we are growing as fat as Americans.

He walks into the Business and Environmental Law School. Ulrich asked to meet here, as his grandson, studying European Law, wanted Ulrich to welcome some visiting lecturer.

There are a lot of people milling about and he feels vaguely annoyed at having to hang around with a mass of students waiting for Scheffell. He turns and suddenly sees through a doorway a tall, striking blonde woman in a black gown holding a pile of books. She holds herself a little away from the group of people talking around her.

He stares at her. He knows he has never seen her before, yet she seems familiar to him. He goes on staring with a tight feeling growing in his chest. She has a focused beauty, a sort of detachment he recognizes. It is a clever, ambitious face. Shaken, he turns abruptly away.

Scheffell appears suddenly by his side. "So sorry to keep you waiting." He smiles. "She is very beautiful, is she not?"

They push past students eager to get into the lecture hall, and go out into the fresh air. He breathes deeply.

"Who is she?" he asks.

"She is an English barrister. Her name is Anna. She is married to Rudi Gerstein, a friend of my wife. Where did you leave your car?" Ulrich guides him across the grass towards his office. "We will talk, then I will take you out for a good lunch. I would very much like you on my team again. At the very least, I hope you will think about it."

It is Saturday. He turns the pages of the newspaper slowly. A little pulse beats in his left cheek. It is raining outside, a steady downpour that splatters against the windows of his flat, making the large panes rattle and a cold draft waft through the room.

There. There it is, where he knew it would be: a photograph of the smiling British barrister taken at the FU. He stares down at it; smoothes the creases in the paper. Her face jumps out at him. The piece tells him that she has just given a series of three-day lectures to a group of law students on corporate fraud and the differences in the British and German judicial systems.

The paper congratulates her on her perfect German, her intellect, her beauty and the possibility that she is in line to become a British judge. He looks down at the photograph and the strange feeling returns. Her eyes stare back as if challenging him. He shivers and closes the page. Those eyes . . . Those eyes remind him of someone else.

He goes to the window. The world out there is deserted. He is not a man accustomed to being lonely. There has always been someone. There has always been a woman.

He crosses to the mirror and stares at his reflection: eyes still the lightest blue, maybe slightly faded, body lean and carefully looked after. Women always think he is a decade younger than he is. He fingers the soft skin under his eyes. Lately he has begun to sleep badly and it is beginning to show.

Since Inga left the flat has seemed bigger, emptier. Of course he was expecting it. The age gap made it inevitable. It was not as if she even lived here permanently. She perched on the edge of his life, the few clothes and possessions she left here tidily placed in wardrobe and drawer so she did not take up too much room. Inga, patiently hovering, hoping for the more he could not give her.

He did not expect her to stay with him as long as she did. Sometimes he took her with him when he traveled. More often he preferred to be on his own.

"Are you not lonely?" Scheffell asked him at lunch, full of red wine. "I have often wondered why you have never married. Even at your age, I see women look at you."

"I am rarely lonely," he replied. "Nor have I had any urge to marry. This does not mean I do not like women."

He returns to the window. A squirrel is running through the rain, over the bench and up the tree outside his flat. It looks in at him, waiting. He goes to the kitchen for nuts, opens the sliding doors and puts them on the table.

Inga was still young enough to find someone to marry her and have children. He told her so.

"Have you ever really loved anyone?" she asked quietly and bitterly.

He replied, honestly: "I am very fond of you, Inga, but you knew from the very beginning that with me there would be no marriage and no children. I never pretended or promised otherwise." It seemed as he said these words that he had used them to too many women.

When he was young and, he hoped, as he got older, he gave the women who marched hopefully through his life a good time. But if they wanted to breed or settle or get monotonously domestic they would have to look elsewhere. That each one thought she would be different was not his fault.

He suspects that Inga will be the last woman in his life. He is too old now even to pretend not to be selfish. At half his age, Inga is the woman he was fondest of. He has always been fascinated by the strength of the maternal pull. Inga, he is sure, despite her feelings for him, wanted a last chance of a child.

The squirrel runs down the bird table, along the railings of his balcony and leaps away among the leaves of the tree.

He goes back to the paper and stares down again at the photograph. The room is silent, still—so still that something stirs within him: a remembered, haunting pain that no amount of traveling can entirely banish.

Disturbed, he picks up the phone and dials a number with fingers not entirely steady. A number he has dialed many times. For so many reasons down the years. Hans can find out anything about anybody. Living or dead.

Chapter 8

Fred is feeding the birds with Martha's breakfast crusts. There is no wind and the morning is mild. Barnaby has fixed a swing bird table on a branch of the old medlar tree, away from the aged interest of Eric, who can still produce a sneaky pounce from the shelter of weeds and bluebells.

Fred notices that the twisted branches of the medlar look as if they might be dying. The wind has caught the leaves and the back branches are too near the Monterey pine. What a pity. What were the three trees that were always planted together in his grandfather's day? Medlar, mulberry . . . Damn it, he cannot remember the third.

He moves across the lawn and looks down at the disturbed earth between the roots of the cherry. He and Martha buried Puck under the tree. Lucy and Barnaby have just buried her little tabby here. He smiles to himself. He lost count of the hamsters buried here, until Martha had the idea of placing the catatonic little bodies in the warming oven of the Rayburn as a test. It was alarming how many of the poor creatures had only been hibernating. Barnaby was stricken with remorse, sure that they must have buried most of his hamsters alive.

Fred cannot remember how the tradition of burying all their pets under the trees came about. Perhaps because the dogs always sat here, half in and half out of the sun. He looks out towards the shrubbery for the blackbird with the freak white tail, and tosses a crust into the undergrowth. There is always a danger taming birds with a cat.

It is such a beautiful day and he has no headache. For once his mind is clear. This is the best bit of the day, just before the day begins in earnest. His private communion with the garden. For a few minutes he can pretend . . . Is it pretend? Or just looking back? Like old men do when they get ancient.

He can pretend that he has woken to find Martha already in the garden, checking her seeds in neat little trays in the old wooden greenhouse. He would walk across the grass with a cup of tea for her and she would look up as excited as a child and point out what each tray held and where in the garden they were going to be planted out.

She was so organized. From rubble and rampant weeds the garden evolved and grew steadily every year. She kept track of things in a little red exercise book, marking carefully where things failed or had been planted in the wrong place. She drew little diagrams for borders of color and smell; made sure that in winter there were bright berries, shiny leaves and shrubs to look at.

Eventually, he had to employ someone to help her. At first she was reluctant—she was intensely possessive of her garden and her privacy—but Fred knew he must find someone who would not take over but who would understand the sort of garden she wanted to create.

They had two false starts and then Hattie suggested her nephew, a boy of sixteen. Neither Martha nor Fred knew anything about him, and that was just as well or Fred would never have employed him.

Hattie arrived one morning with a surly youth called Adam, who looked as if he had been frog-marched up the drive. Martha, pretending not to notice his scowl, sat him down in the kitchen, made him tea and gave him a huge slice of homemade cake. Then she took him into the garden, pointed out the things she hoped to do and asked for his advice on this and that. What did he think about a pond here? Did he think they could enlarge the terrace, so that it had steps coming down?

Fred, hovering nearby, saw Hattie's anxious face at the kitchen window. The boy was monosyllabic. Fred wondered what on earth Hattie was palming them off with. He was about to leave to go back to medical school, and was anxious too, but he trusted Hattie.

He returned from London the following weekend to find Martha had a willing and able slave. The scowl had gone. The boy's white face was beginning to tan and half a pond had been dug.

Adam and Martha worked together twice a week for ten years. They made a spectacular garden, through trial and error, both learning as they went along. The boy had a natural talent and when he was offered a job as under-gardener on an estate on the Helford, Martha made him take it. She never wanted to replace him.

Fred turns away from the bird table and takes a walk round the garden. The old wooden greenhouse fell down a long time ago and nature has reclaimed so much of the garden. There is no telling where the borders once were. Tulips and daffodils spring up everywhere through tufts of long grass and bluebells. The old pond lies choked in the corner, covered in green algae. The heavy Victorian statue of an angel Martha found in a junk shop still stands placidly facing the house, snails nestling in his arms in little clusters. Lichen grows on his face and body like an extra filigree robe.

Much later, Martha told him that Adam had been in constant trouble for his violent, uncontrollable temper. Hattie took him in when her sister washed her hands of him. All he had done at her house, apart from being bored and sullen, was read her gardening magazines. Adam told Martha that he had been beaten constantly by his father. If Hattie had not taken him in, he would have killed him.

Fred thought then how right it was that Martha and Adam had come together. This garden that they made out of nothing had for both of them begun as a replacement activity and became an obsession and an abiding passion.

He supposes he ought to go in. Must not hold Barnaby up. The one thing he did not want to happen has happened. He and Martha have become Barnaby's burden. So unfair. His head begins to throb. Damn head. Difficult to think sometimes.

Is he sacrificing Barnaby for Martha? No. No. Can't think like that. Useless. Barnaby would no more think of a home than he would.

He walks slowly across the grass back to the house and the ghost of Martha flits with him. He so much wants to remember the young woman full of life and joy, who could make an ordinary day special. The young woman who built a garden. The young woman who wept in the dark when the shadows came and reached out for him. The woman he held and made love to. Breathed in. Breathed new life into.

He looks up. An old woman is standing at the French windows in her nightgown, waving at him. *He could be Fred. He could be the gardener. He could be anyone.* Her beautiful face is vacant, contains nothing of their life together. This, Fred thinks, is the hardest thing I have ever had to bear.

The new carer, arriving that morning, makes something of an entrance. She has spiky dark hair, a nose ring, an ethnic sweater and flimsy skirt finished off with a tight leather belt and boots. When Barnaby has finished showing her around, briefed her on Martha and Fred's routine and left the house in a rush, she makes coffee and takes it into the conservatory.

She stands looking down at Martha as the cup of coffee she holds for her grows cold. The old lady is crying silently and the girl examines her wonderful high cheekbones and sees the tears falling from Martha's closed eyes. She is disturbed and touched by the smallness of the old lady and the isolation of her senility.

She bends to Martha. "What is it?" she asks. "What's the matter, Martha? Look, I've brought you a cup of coffee."

Martha opens her eyes at the sound of her name. She is going to say, "I am Mrs. Tremain to you," but when she sees the pretty girl whose anxious face is close to hers she is so pleased she smiles. "Hanna! Where have you sprung from? I haven't seen you for ages!"

The girl places the cup of coffee in Martha's hands. "My name is Kate. Is Hanna your daughter?"

Martha looks puzzled. "No, no, I don't think so."

"I'm from the agency. I'm here to help look after you."

"You're very pretty."

The girl laughs. "So are you."

Martha's face lights up. "I used to be, darling." In that small face suddenly alight, in the ease of that casual endearment, Kate is captivated. Fred lowers the *Daily Telegraph* he is not reading and smiles at her.

"Hello, Kate. Welcome."

"Thank you, Dr. Tremain. I'll just go and get your coffee."

She comes back and perches on a chair next to him. "The vicar suggested you might like a drive this afternoon. There is a little gallery at Newlyn? He said you both enjoy going there, and then walking or driving along the front past the harbor."

Fred looks up at her. "That sounds absolutely wonderful. Martha would love it. How kind. Mrs. Biddulph doesn't drive, you know."

Kate smiles. "So I understand. Are you both OK here, if I go and do a bit of tidying up?"

"Of course. Of course. We are both fine. Enjoying the sun."

Kate makes their beds and tidies the bathroom. She is intrigued by this strange house with its shabby sofas and beautiful furniture, by its fading elegance and enormous conservatory that throws sunlight everywhere. The whole house smells dusty, rather like a greenhouse, and there is this sense of waiting. Is it waiting, this stillness? Or is it a vague sense of sadness, of lives coming to an end? Kate is not sure.

The Loving Care Agency jumped at the chance of taking her on even though she assured them she would only be temporary, that she intended to move on. The pay is appalling, but Kate is used to working for peanuts. The only help she has accepted, from the aunt she was working for in London, is the cost of a few weeks in a hotel while she looks for somewhere to live for the summer.

Kate goes to check on the two old people. Dr. Tremain is sitting beside Martha and has taken her hand. They both sit looking out through the French windows to the garden. "'It was a perfect day / For sowing: just / As sweet and dry was the ground / As tobacco-dust. / I tasted deep the hour / Between the far / Owl's chuckling first soft cry' . . ." Dr. Tremain is reading aloud to Martha. Kate smiles. How wonderful.

She starts to prepare their lunch with the food Barnaby has put out for her. It is incredibly quiet here after London. She has a moment's dislocation, as if she has suddenly jumped lives and found herself in someone else's kitchen.

Edward Thomas? Of course it is! She studied him for A level. "And now, hark at the rain, / Windless and light / Half a kiss, half a tear, / Saying good-night."

Martha, suddenly restless, comes in and out of the kitchen asking the same question. "What are we having for lunch today?"

"Chicken and chips?"

"How lovely!"

Martha wanders off, circles the house again and comes in through the conservatory door.

"Hello. Who are you?"

"I'm Kate. I'm just getting your lunch ready."

"Lovely, darling, what are we having?"

"Chicken and chips. Is that OK?"

"My favorite."

"Good. It won't be long. Shall I come and put the lunchtime news on for you?"

"Thank you," Martha says vaguely.

Kate finds Fred has already turned the television on.

"Come and sit down, darling," he says to Martha, "and watch the news with me."

"I will in a moment," Martha says, "but I am worried about lunch. What—"

"Chicken and chips," Kate says firmly, pushing Martha gently down next to her husband. "I will be back in a moment."

She is beginning to wonder how the vicar has not taken to drink. It is taking her ages to get this meal ready and she feels dizzy with repeating the same thing over and over again. She puts both their lunches on trays and carries them into the sitting room.

The room is empty. The television is talking to an empty room. Kate cannot believe it. Fighting panic she rushes back to the kitchen and dumps the trays and runs round the empty house shouting for them. How on earth could they both disappear so quickly and quietly?

She bolts out of the front door and down the drive, shaking with anxiety. Why did this have to happen on her first day?

Barnaby comes from the church with a parent on each arm. He smiles at her as he crosses the road with them. "Lost anyone?" he jokes.

Kate, mortified, nearly in tears with fright, turns and rushes back into the house.

Barnaby settles his parents in front of the television with their trays of food and a sherry each and waits for the new carer to come out of the bathroom. He makes them both a cup of coffee while he waits.

When Kate returns to the kitchen, embarrassed, he says gently, "It's quite all right, you know. I was only joking. You can't have eyes in the back of your head and I don't want my parents imprisoned in their own home." He pauses, facing the facts. "It's becoming obvious that I'll have to have two people here soon; it's going to be too much for one person. I'm truly sorry you got a fright, Kate. I really am well aware how tiring looking after my parents is." He grins at her. "One dotty person is bad enough, two is a nightmare! It will be no discredit to you if you decide it's just too much."

"No way!" Kate says quickly. "I just completely misjudged the speed of your parents. I'm not going to give up after one day!"

Barnaby hands her a mug of coffee. "I'm glad. Go and have your lunch in the garden. Relax. It is like summer out there this morning. I'll sit with my parents for an hour. I like to do that if I have time."

Kate digs out a book and a sandwich from her bag and goes and sits against the trunk of the cherry tree under a great, sweeping arch of buds about to burst into blossom. She wonders what a good-looking, youngish vicar—young by priestly standards anyway—is doing unmarried and looking after senile parents on his own.

Barnaby tucks Martha into bed for her afternoon nap. Fred has gone back to his chair in the conservatory to try to do the crossword. Barnaby is puzzled by Fred. He wonders if his father has simply withdrawn from a life where his beloved Martha is now dotty. Sometimes Fred seems quite dotty himself; at other times Barnaby has the sensation he is merely hiding behind a supposed dottiness in order to avoid facing what is happening, as if a dark cloud of depression or loss has stunned him into a senility he does not really have.

Barnaby says good-bye to a more cheerful Kate and drives off to a parish council meeting in the village hall. Normally he dreads these competitive parochial monthly meetings, but today everyone seems united in their desire to raise funds to help the refugees in Kosovo.

Martha lies propped up on pillows watching the movement of wind through buds of pink cherry blossom. The tree is getting old and gnarled. The branches bend and creak, spread and arch. Soon fat fingers of blossom will trail almost to the ground in great sprays of pink hands that layer the lawn like confetti.

It reminds Martha of something. Of somewhere else. The feeling she cannot capture squeezes her stomach, as if her body

has recovered a memory her mind refuses to recall. She closes her eyes, tries to banish this disturbing sensation and is taken suddenly back to another garden, where the flowers are gone, and all is now laid with vegetables.

She sees Papa bend to pick a caterpillar off a cabbage, his face grave as he turns to Mama, standing in the doorway of their house.

"Esther? It is time we talked about sending Marta to England. I don't know how long we have."

"Paul, no! Please, let's wait . . . Don't be pessimistic. We have so many good friends here. You are respected by everyone. The patients and the staff love you. We have standing here, my dear, and financial means, if things get difficult."

Papa stares at Mama and shakes his head. "Esther," he says quietly, "I beg you not to bury your head. Things are not just difficult, they are dangerous. What is the good of money if we cannot keep Marta safe? Please, you must accept what is happening. Everyone is fearing the worst. Both Germans and Poles are jumpy and frightened. Everyone is looking out for themselves. You must not count on anyone except fellow Jews. You will see, our Polish neighbors and German colleagues will not want to know us if Poland is invaded."

They stare at each other over the space that was once a garden full of flowers and now contains only things they can eat. Marta knows her father is frustrated by her mother, who has never in her life faced hardship or loss, and cannot yet grasp what is happening. Cannot, or is reluctant to face the end of their way of life.

"Heinrich will see we are all right. Heinrich won't let anything happen to us. I know it. You are colleagues, Paul. You are friends. Our children have played together nearly all their lives."

Papa walks abruptly towards the house. He does not see Marta sitting up in the window, listening. "Esther!" he says angrily. "We are Jews. His wife comes from one of the old Imperial families. Do you really think that Heinrich can protect us from anything? What is the matter with you? Are your eyes shut? How can you fail to notice what is going on around you? Do you think our money can protect us against this rising tide of anti-Semitism? Do you?"

Marta's mother grows pale at her husband's anger. He is a gentle man who does not raise his voice. Esther is not used to people being unkind to her. She was a spoiled child and went straight on to being a sheltered and beautiful child-wife. "Our children have known each other, played together . . . all their lives," she repeats.

"That time is over. It is gone. They are children no more," Papa says firmly. "I don't want that boy, who has the makings of a dangerous little Nazi, anywhere near Marta."

His voice is sad: "Heinrich and I have known each other for longer than I care to remember. But whatever he privately feels about what is happening, they are Germans, Esther, and we are on the brink of war. Already the family are distancing themselves. At work I am being relieved of many of my patients, many of my duties. If the Germans invade Poland, I would be relieved of all of them. You must understand, Esther, I could lose my clinic, my life's work and probably all my money."

"You can't know that!" Mama's voice is full of panic. "England will stop the Germans, you'll see, Paul." She claps her hand to her mouth.

Papa says quietly, "I wish with all my heart I could protect you and Marta from what is coming, but I can't. I cannot leave. I am a doctor and will be needed. The only thing I can do is send you both to England."

Mama stares at him, suddenly very sure. "No, Paul, we stay together as a family. Whatever happens, we stay together."

Marta, sitting up in the window of her room, shivers. She looks down on her arms, which are covered in goose bumps as if a cold wind has suddenly sprung up. She runs down the stairs, past her mother and across the garden to her father and clutches his arms. "Don't send me away," she cries. "You're frightening me, Papa."

Her father holds her hands between his for a moment and apologizes for frightening her. He tries to change the subject, make her laugh. He calls Pepe, their dog, and as they set off for their evening walk together he tells Marta about England and his friends who live there.

"England is a very beautiful place, full of rivers and trees. In the towns there are parks to sit in the sun. People take their children and picnic and sail small boats in lakes. People mix freely, Matusia . . ." Marta's papa takes her arm. "A distant cousin of mine has offered to take you in. This is a great opportunity for you to learn, to extend your education. You are so good at languages . . . My dear child, I need to persuade your mama to let you go even if she will not leave me. You must trust me and help me to convince her that it really is the best thing to do."

Marta is silent, for she knows Mama is right: they must all stay together. The birds of evening are singing and fluttering, caught in the blossom of the huge apple tree at the bottom of the next-door garden, where she plays with the boy. Marta listens to the noise the birds are making and her fear is back. She shivers again, her father draws her away and they circle the wood and go home for supper.

Marta remembers that walk. It was the last walk she ever took with her father without fear, without the hated yellow armband with the star.

Coming into Martha's bedroom, Kate sees that despite the warmth of the room, Martha is shivering with cold, sitting upright in bed, her tiny limbs trembling. She looks in the cupboard and finds a pale blue mohair sweater, which she wraps round Martha. Then she helps her into her trousers, which she has taken off. Her legs are like sticks and slightly misshapen. Odd little legs.

Kate chats to Martha while she does these things, but Martha is a long, long way away and Kate knows in Martha's head there is a different scene playing.

Twenty minutes later Kate has both the old people safely in the back of her car. She drives out of the gates and takes the road towards Newlyn.

As they drive along Kate thinks about how she will cope once she parks the car. She must hang on to both of them without seeming like a sheepdog. She is not going to lose them twice.

She turns the radio on low and twiddles the knob to Classic

FM. Fred turns contentedly towards the sea as they reach the coast road. Frothy waves are bouncing off the sea wall and the sun glints on the surface of the sea in dancing sparks.

Martha does not see the sea. She is still somewhere far in the past. She is worrying about her knitting needle. Has someone stolen it? Her knitting needle is vital. Before she goes to bed she wants to poke it into the holes. She wants to poke out those revolting bugs that stop her sleeping.

"My knitting needle," she murmurs.

Kate looks at her through the car mirror. "Don't worry, Martha," she says comfortingly. "We'll find it when we get you home."

Fred folds her tiny hand in his large one and Martha is soothed. She looks out and sees the shimmering blueness of the sea and the bright fishing boats heading in and out of Newlyn, and is enchanted.

As they drive past the harbor with the heavy trawlers and sleek yachts crammed together, the wind catching their stanchions and making a wonderful clinking sound, Martha smiles happily.

"How beautiful," she says to Fred, turning to him. "How beautiful, darling."

Fred, seeing her lovely smile, smiles too, his heart aching with love and fear. All his life he has protected her, now the knowledge that he can no longer do so is slowly killing him. He brings her hand to his mouth.

"My beloved little Martha," he whispers.

Kate turns the car round at the end of the road and drives back to park near the gallery. Watching their faces, she realizes they don't get out enough. She will try and change that.

"What did you say?" she asks Dr. Tremain.

"I said, it's a long time since I was last here," Fred says clearly.

Kate smiles.

Chapter 9

Anna sits with her chair swiveled round from her desk, facing the long window of her study. She loves these early mornings. The stillness helps her think. She feels mellow and calm, as if she has not yet put up a barrier between herself and the coming day.

Wisps of pink cloud hang in a vivid blue sky. Anna is reminded of Cornwall where the day unfolds from a blackness over the ocean to slow unfurling ribbons of color reflected in the water. Even before dawn there was light behind the darkness, waiting.

She had forgotten, almost forgotten those Cornish mornings.

She closes her mind and breathes in the sky outside the window. Tries to remember the child she was with no demands or responsibilities, waking to a summer morning, running down to the water in near darkness. The acute shiver of loneliness and wonder in the sound and size of a huge sea rolling in to empty sands stretching all around her.

Lucy was the same as a child. Half the fun was getting outside with no one hearing you . . . She used to take Puck, the small Labrador cross Martha adored. Or was that later? Was she older when they got the dog?

Deep pink slashes of cloud are dispersing over the Thames, spreading across the city, blurring and smudging into the sky, like spilled water paints, tingeing the river and touching the buildings.

She hears Martha's voice: "Red sky in the morning, shepherd's warning, darlink."

How old was she before Martha said "darling" properly? Anna cannot remember that either. She always has trouble remembering the sequence of her childhood. She often thinks her bad memory is the result of being so bored most of her childhood. Nothing of note ever happened to pierce the monotony of those seemingly endless years.

She gets up, goes to the long window and looks out into the wide, tree-lined road, at the elegant Edwardian houses opposite. It is deserted except for the line of parked cars. Curtains drawn. People sleeping.

She must be getting old, she concludes, if a sly trick of memory can turn those endless Cornish summers into nostalgia. Yet for a moment she does not see the houses; she hears the bent palm in Martha's garden, hanging askew to the wind, rattling like dry fingers. She sees the glint of silver water and white houses illuminated on the other side of the harbor. She can hear the scream of gulls wheeling and circling above her head and feel the sensation of cold wet sand clinging to her feet. She sees Fred waving to her from the steps to the beach. She smells baking, and Martha, standing in that old-fashioned kitchen, pulls a chair out so she can lick the bowl.

Something rises up in her throat for what might have been. If she had been different. If they had. It is like fingering a bruise. She is sure her nightmares go back to her early years. She often thinks it must be because Martha was so often ill when she was small. When Martha took to her bed, or could not eat, it must have been an emotional illness, not a physical one. Anna does remember spending a lot of time with Hattie. Fear and sadness affect children. When she was little something about Martha frightened her. Easy to be frightened when you do not understand.

Only one thing sticks in her mind. She was furious with her mother and threw herself at her, clutching at her legs in a rage that consumed her. That is all she can remember: not wanting to let go of those legs. She cannot remember a face or arms or a voice. Just those legs trying to get away from her.

Anna pushes the image away, stretches and takes a deep breath. She can hear Rudi moving about upstairs and she goes back to her desk. For heaven's sake, she is supposed to be studying her brief. Berlin was a success, but exhausting. Now she is about to reconvene a complicated criminal injury case and she is tired. Her workload is frightening this year.

She goes into the kitchen and grinds coffee and puts the pot on the stove. Places her files and papers back into her briefcase. She will have coffee with Rudi, then grab a sandwich later.

Rudi comes in smelling of soap, and kisses her. "You seem to get up earlier and earlier. Two complicated cases at the same time. Are you worrying, darling?"

Anna smiles at him. "No, not really. I've got a good team. But so have they. I do need to be on the ball . . ." She reaches out and touches his arm. "Sorry if I bored you last night. I just wanted to run it past you."

"You never bore me. And I do know a bit about insurance companies."

"Well, I am still sure they, or the airline, are stalling, playing for time, and I am not sure why. My client will certainly never walk again. They cannot avoid liability. I expected the usual initial derisory offer of compensation, which would be unacceptable. Instead of which they asked for four days' grace to make inquiries about a matter 'vital to the outcome of the case.'"

"Which means?"

"Which means, either they have discovered something which makes the airline culpable and they will pull out, or something that I have not been told that makes my client responsible, or partly responsible, for his injuries." Anna puts down her half-finished coffee. "Anyway, this morning I will find out. I must go." She gets up and kisses him. "Why are you smiling?"

"At the glint in your eye. God help the opposition."

Anna laughs. "I shouldn't be too late home tonight."

"In that case," Rudi says, "I shall cook you something delicious and healthy."

Anna holds his face to her for a moment. "Wonderful."

By the time she leaves the house the pink sky has disappeared and gray clouds cover the whole of the sky. As Anna walks to the tube station she remembers a task she was set at school: *What is your very first memory?* On the blackboard the teacher wrote, "My very first memory is . . ."

Anna sat and sat in front of a blank sheet of paper. She was quite unable to pick up her pen. Eventually her teacher said, "Anna, come on, this is not like you. What's the matter?"

Anna had gone white and begun to shake. *She was not going to write. She was not going to. She could not think . . . beyond . . . before . . . behind . . .* For the first time in her life she fainted. Fred came to collect her, took her straight home. For some reason he was cross with her teacher. "For heaven's sake, Anna is only nine years old. I know she is bright, but I don't want my daughter pressurized."

"It was not Mrs. Poole's fault," Anna said to him in the car. "Dad, I can't remember anything before my nightmares. I didn't want to write about my nightmares."

Fred turned to look at her and for a terrible moment Anna thought he was going to cry. He tucked her up on the sofa and lit a fire in the afternoon. Martha, pregnant with Barnaby, sat with Anna by the fire, playing snakes and ladders, and then they baked scones together. That day I did not spoil . . . I must have been ill, Anna thinks wryly.

What was it I was afraid of remembering?

She flashes her season ticket, goes through the barrier and stands on the platform waiting for the tube. This is the worst bit. She has finally trained herself, with Rudi's help, to use the underground. But she hates the gathering moment before the train whooshes in and people prepare to rush and push. She can cope this early in the day, but she would not dream of traveling during the rush hour.

I suppose, she thinks, my childhood must have been happy. It must have been later, as I grew up and recognized the smallness, the limitations of their lives, that I grew bored and contemptuous. Maybe I was afraid I would grow up like them.

The train comes hurtling into the station and Anna gets in. She sits down and opens her briefcase. It is going to be a long day in court. She smiles suddenly at her reflection in the train window. She is far happier having an enormous caseload than maudlin and totally useless memories of her childhood.

Chapter 10

BERLIN

He drives into the city early. It is a beautiful spring morning and the city unfolds in front of him, glittering and clean.

Inga's travel bag lies on the passenger seat beside him with the last of her possessions. She has not wanted to return to the flat to collect them and has asked him to meet her before she starts work.

He drives along the Unter den Linden towards the Bauhaus Museum where she works. He had hoped to take her for coffee in Kreuzberg but she said she was too busy to leave the building.

He is not looking forward to this meeting. He hopes they can at least get back to the point of civilized friendship. They have mutual friends and he would like to establish an understanding to avoid embarrassment for everyone. Remembering her cold voice on the phone he thinks friendship, at this point, is unlikely.

He parks the car and carries her bag to the entrance. He has always liked the clear modern lines of the museum. It had risen from the ruins of postwar Berlin like a building newly washed.

Inga is standing watching him walking towards her. She is not smiling. He greets her with two kisses. Her back is stiff, her face cold.

"How are you?" he asks.

"I'm just fine," she says evenly.

"Are you sure that you don't have time to have a coffee with me? The museum does not open for two hours."

"My hours are nothing to do with whether the museum is open or shut, but with the artifacts. As you know."

"Of course," he says, smiling, "I know. I would like to have coffee and talk for a few minutes, if you have the time."

She hesitates. Sadness and the feeling he can still engender in her pass briefly across her face. It would be kinder if he just handed her bag to her and left, but something obstinate in him wants to leave this relationship tidy and finished. Without rancor.

She holds the door open for him, reluctantly. "Come in. I'll make you a quick coffee."

She fiddles with the filter machine in her office and he watches her. She is very pretty, he is very fond of her, yet he feels no regret. "Inga, I really do want you to be happy. You must have known, as I did, that if you got involved with a man much older than yourself this parting was inevitable?"

She pours his coffee and carries it over to him, places sugar and milk in front of him, but does not sit with him.

"It was only inevitable when you decided that it was. I suddenly bored you with a need for something more from you. I stayed the course longer than most, so perhaps I should be flattered."

He is surprised. "You made the decision to end our relationship."

Inga laughs without humor. "You ended our relationship. Look, I understand. You are incapable of emotional commitment. You told yourself I left because I wanted children. This is not true. I am not overtly maternal. I left because I suddenly saw no future . . . Nothing was going to change."

Her anger shows suddenly. "I deserve more. You are happy to be with me when you are a little lonely and equally happy to drop me when you are your normal self-sufficient self. Yes, we often had a very good time—you are an interesting and charming man to be with—but it was not enough. I wanted to live with you and you made it clear that you did not want me to. Too often you preferred to go away without me . . ."

She looks away, fiddles with her coffee cup. "You seem to need no one. I have some pride. I left because you were destroying my sense of self. I was losing confidence in myself and my work."

She looks straight at him suddenly. "I pity you. To avoid the pain of loving, you miss the joy. Like so many of your generation, you are dishonest about your motives, in everything you do and in everything you did."

They stare at each other. The coffee scalds his mouth. The words hang between them. Both their faces are shocked and angry. *Like your generation.* She has wanted to say this before to him, he can see that. It came out before she could stop it, startling her as much as him. Words that cannot be taken back. The meaning all too clear.

Silence hangs between them. He gets out of his chair and walks away towards the entrance. As he reaches the doors he hears her voice, softly this time.

"I know that you wanted to draw a neat line under us today. So much easier when we meet in public. Neat lines are not always possible. Real life is messy and it hurts."

He does not turn round, but moves steadily to his car. He does not see that she is crying as she watches his tall figure walk away from her. Ten years ago she was thirty-two. Young enough to be his daughter. She found him dangerous in an exciting and powerfully sexual way. He was a challenge she has lost. Her friends warned her. She knows him barely better now than she did ten years ago. She shuts the entrance door firmly so that she does not see him drive away.

The traffic is much heavier as he drives home. He taps the wheel impatiently as he sits trapped between two school buses, idly watching the people on the pavements, some hurrying, some stopping at the little Turkish café he used to wait in for Inga sometimes.

Your generation. His generation watched Berlin reborn from rubble. What the American and British bombers did not destroy, the Red Army finished. *His generation* watched as Berlin was carved up into four pieces . . . "YOU ARE LEAVING THE AMERICAN SECTOR"—the sign, which had you sweating in your sleep, that one wrong turning, one small error, would land you in the Eastern sector.

The traffic picks up speed and he breathes more easily as he heads out of town. Mutti moved sharply and wisely from her old family home in the east, ahead of the Red Army. She hated the British and American bombers, but she feared the oncoming Russians more.

He was sent back to Berlin at the end of the war with a medical unit. Berlin, about to fight for its life, left with only the old, the lame and children to defend it. Berlin had not been his childhood home as it had been Mutti's but the devastation was still shocking. He thought that Berlin could never be rebuilt.

Reaching home, he parks and lets himself into the flat. He is angry with Inga for reminding him of the past, his age, and the fact that her generation and her children's generation can never forgive or forget his. Because it is held in front of them, in books, films, or a left-wing challenge, by someone, somewhere, every single day. Her age group seem to have a monopoly on self-righteousness, while knowing nothing.

He lights a small cheroot and sees with a start that he has received the fax he has been waiting for. He has waited, restless, all week for Hans to get in touch. He tears the message off the machine.

What am I starting here? What am I doing?

Hans urged caution. Any hint of irrationality made him nervous. He left for London reluctant and tight-lipped. He knows only too well obsession can grow. Catch a glimpse, a smell, a memory and you want more. *The past you buried always surfaces.* Who said that to him? Suddenly, he needs to know what is shadow caused by faulty memory, and what is substance.

The fax is disappointingly brief; tells him little. The woman is, unsurprisingly, clever and ambitious. Hans lists her academic achievements at length. He details minutely the steady rise of her career. But there is little about her personal life. Is he doing this on purpose? Hans can find out how a man turns in his bed. How he makes love to his wife. What he eats for breakfast. He can find out anything he wishes to know. If he wants to . . .

This woman was born and brought up in the west of England. Head girl at some English boarding school. One brother. One child from a brief marriage to an Italian. Married for four years to Rudi Gerstein, a Swiss-German banker. She is an excellent linguist and so is her daughter.

Is this it? This barrister could be any middle-class English girl. Yet the one thing he needs to know Hans cannot possibly give him. He looks out of the window at the rain blowing sideways, obscuring his view, trapping him with ghosts that are rising like whispers out of the dark edges of the room.

The past is suddenly crowding in from all directions. In the long nights alone now he feels the horror of being overtaken by memories he believed he had firmly buried.

Chapter 11

Dancing against Martha's closed eyelids, **the sun. Light and bobbing colors, patterns and floaters. A thrush in the garden sings and sings. The rain has stopped and the smell of cut grass comes in the window on a faint breeze.**

In a moment Mama, or Hanna, their maid, will call up the stairs to make sure she is awake. Hanna, who is not much older than Marta, gets very cross with her because she will lie there ignoring Mama's calls.

Hanna is a thin, obedient girl, who comes from a religiously observant Jewish family who vaguely disapprove of the Oweski family. Papa says they are so poor it is no wonder little Hanna has no sense of humor.

Marta loves these mornings. She has secretly been out in the garden in the first light, running in bare feet across the deliciously cold wet grass.

She likes to lie without moving, her face in pale yellow sunshine, daydreaming. She loves the dancing colors behind her closed lids and the safeness of opening her eyes again to familiar background noises, the sounds of a household waking up. Marta would like to be a child forever and as she thinks this she remembers . . . she remembers with a jolt and her eyes fly open.

Fly open to an unfamiliar room of beige walls and white paint work. Beyond the long windows, lawns stretch into glossy-leafed shrubs and old fir trees that form a wall of green.

Martha sits up quickly, then, suddenly dizzy, hangs on to the edge of the bed for a moment. She goes slowly to the door and

listens. Hearing nothing, she turns the handle and goes out into a large flagstone hall that leads into a drawing room filled with hot afternoon sun, which has bleached, over the years, all the covers and cushions to a uniform beige.

No one is there, but in a corner of the room a television flickers with images. Martha looks out into a musty geranium-smelling conservatory but cannot see her parents or Hanna. She swallows a slow-rising panic that they have all been taken from her while she slept in this place she does not remember coming to.

She pads on small bare feet to the French windows and looks out into the garden. She can hear voices now. A man and a girl are planting something near the cherry tree. She has no idea who they are.

Confused, desperately searching her mind for a clue to anchor herself here, Martha turns back inside to the flickering movements of the small screen, which has the sound turned off. She sees columns and columns of people moving in a mass along a road. Walking, hobbling, being pulled on carts or tractors. A great wash, a tide of human misery, dragging themselves onwards to safety, moving like robots in stunned bewilderment and fear.

The camera pans in on haunted faces and Martha, transfixed, is back, back with the fear and the smell, and the movement like an endless surge of water. Vast masses of human beings being herded, displaced and hated, to a fixed end. She crumples to the floor, watching. Remembering.

She rocks for Mama, for Papa, for poor serious little Hanna, for all those she loves, her eyes glued to the small flickering screen.

An old man is suddenly beside her, calling her name. The television is abruptly switched off. He bends and helps her to her feet, sits her in a chair, talking, talking in that gentle loving voice she recognizes. Martha stares at him. It is Fred. Of course. *It is Fred. This house is her home.*

She smiles at him, closes her eyes with utter, utter relief, relaxes. She is Martha *Tremain,* an Englishwoman.

* * *

Barnaby takes Lucy to the garden center to buy primroses for Abi's grave. Little else will grow under the cherry tree. They buy six cream primroses, and a white cyclamen for Martha.

Barnaby looks at seed packets, wondering if he should buy earth so that Martha can plant seeds in trays in the conservatory. The greenhouse is now irremediable, having collapsed inward on itself, burying seed trays, pots, faded baskets of plant food and all things dumped there over the years. Vine and nettles have all but obscured where it lies.

Barnaby keeps meaning to do something about it, but time and tiredness, or perhaps a depression that he knows will descend if he starts looking too closely at all that needs doing, defeat him every time.

Lucy has wandered away and he finds her looking at the water plants.

"Be nice to clear the pool, wouldn't it? I loved the lilies and those water buttercup things that used to grow there."

They both look down, thinking of how the garden once was. Lucy says suddenly: "Barnaby, Gran left Poland in 1940, didn't she?"

Barnaby smiles. "Yes, she did. What made you suddenly ask that?"

"I was just wondering if Mum was born here in Cornwall or in London. I always thought it was London, but I can't remember anyone telling me that."

"It was definitely London. Martha and Fred lived there at the end of the war. They came down regularly, despite the journey, to stay in the cottage and check on the house, which was being built at that time."

"So . . . I know they met in London when Gramps was on leave, but when did they get married?"

"I gather, very soon after they met. In the war people didn't wait. They grabbed at happiness because no one knew what was going to happen next."

"So they would have been married in 1943?"

"Yes. Why the sudden interest, darling?" He looks at her closely. "Were you wondering if Anna was born before they were married?"

Lucy goes red. "It is just," she says quickly, "that when I was younger I used to ask questions about them meeting and although Gran always told me it was the best day of her life when she met Grandpa, neither of them seemed to like talking about that time, and Mum always seemed vague whenever I asked her things about London."

Barnaby laughs. "I should think she was vague. She was a baby in London and very young when they moved here, Lucy. Can you remember anything much before you were four or five?"

Lucy thinks. "No, I suppose not," she says. "I think my first memory is either you taking me to a fair at night. Or getting smacked by Anna for locking that horrible au pair in a cupboard."

"You were, let me see, about four and a half when I took you to that fair. You hated every minute. You were coming down with a bug and the crowds bothered you. The horrible au pair, I'm not sure . . . five, maybe six."

They make their way to the till. Barnaby grabs some small seed trays, two packets of Virginia stock and a small bag of compost.

"For Martha?" Lucy asks.

"Yes, I thought it might be something for her to do."

Back in the car, Barnaby says, "What you have got to remember, Lucy, is that Martha arrived in a strange country, younger than you are now, having left everyone she loved, to live with strangers. We have no idea of the conditions she left behind her. She had the rest of the war, frightened and lonely, to imagine what might be happening to her family. Knowing that they probably would not survive."

Barnaby glances at Lucy as he drives. "I do not know what

state of trauma she was in when she and Fred met. All I do know is that your grandfather never let Anna or me ask her questions about the war or about her life in Poland."

"I know. Anna told me she never knew anything about Martha's childhood. I can understand about the years just before the war, but I can't understand why Gran would not want to talk about her childhood if it was happy. I mean, everyone looks back on the happy bits of their lives, don't they?"

"When I was very young, Lucy, when I had fallen or had a temperature, she sometimes used to sing to me without knowing she was singing in Polish. As I listened, the sound always seemed to turn into a lament. She would stop suddenly and I would put my hand up to her face and she would hold it there, flat against her cheek, her own hand over it. Small as I was, I felt the enormity of her sadness without, of course, understanding why."

Lucy swallows. Cannot speak.

Barnaby goes on, almost to himself. Lucy cannot ever remember him talking to her like this. "When I was growing up I longed to know; felt Anna and I would be enriched by knowing. We only had tiny snippets: a recipe, a childish game. Fred would tell both Anna and me that we only had the right to know the things Martha wanted to tell us. Maybe one day she would be able to speak of happy times in Poland. If not, we would have to understand."

"Now," Lucy says slowly, "even if she wanted to tell us anything, she can't. It's not fair for Gran to end up like this. God is cruel."

"Life is cruel, darling. I often think—I may be quite wrong, of course—that Anna might often be . . . tricky—"

"Difficult, you mean, Barnes."

"Don't interrupt me. Anna might often be . . . difficult because Martha and Fred must have been adapting to each other, to life after the war, to all that had happened to them both, when she was born. Even when I was a child I can remember them being very wrapped up in each other, very concerned for each other's welfare."

"Were you lonely, then?"

"All children are lonely sometimes. Our generation had a different relationship with their parents. Fred and Martha were the most loving of parents, but there was more distance between us than your generation has, on the whole, with their parents. Boarding school, as you know, accentuates that distance."

They turn in the gates. It is early afternoon and Martha will be resting and Fred will be asleep under the paper. Mrs. Biddulph will be listening to *The Archers.* As they pull up in front of the house, Lucy knows this is the time to ask Barnaby about the documents she found.

She opens her mouth, and Barnaby says, suddenly, very quietly, "Maybe life is not so cruel. Martha, returning to her childlike state—maybe now she can remember happy times in Poland, memories she blocked because they were too painful to remember." He pulls the key out of the ignition and turns to Lucy. "Maybe the sadness now is mine and Fred's, because we can remember her when she was young and bright and full of fun. I am so afraid I will forget how she once was."

Barnaby's face. The line of his mouth held in a loss he feels every day and hides. Lucy leans forward and hugs him, her head pressed away, hard into his shoulder. For the first time she feels the sheer weight of his tiredness in caring for Martha and Fred, day in and day out, without reprieve.

"I am so glad we talked," she says into his shirt.

"So am I, darling." He kisses the top of her head. "Come on, let's go and get some bread and cheese while everyone sleeps. Then we'll put those primroses under the tree."

As Lucy waters the primroses on Abi's small grave she realizes it is the first uninterrupted conversation she and Barnaby have had for ages. Mostly they are both too busy or too tired by the time Martha and Fred are in bed.

She thinks of her own father, whom she has never met. Anna does not even know where he is anymore. Claudio Pedrazzini—she has a cloudy photograph of him standing squinting into the sun in Milan. She could bump into him and never even know. Barnaby says one day she will probably want to try to trace him. She has inherited none of his musical talent, but, so Anna says, much of his laid-back nature.

She wonders, as she presses the wet earth down over the roots, if he ever, in idle moments, thinks about her. She has been lucky; she has always had Barnaby.

Lucy walks across the garden to put the watering can back into the falling-down garage, full of ancient bicycles and rusty paint tins. She thinks that her first instinct in not telling Barnaby about the papers she found was right. Either Barnaby knows and it is some secret he thinks should be kept, or it would be one more thing about Martha to make him sad. It isn't her business. It is Gran's. If there is a secret, it is not hers to give away.

Chapter 12

Lucy, finishing her early shift at the hotel, drives slowly home. It is an amazingly beautiful morning with no clouds. Cold but clear. The trees are unfurling pale virgin leaves, like tiny fists. Spring is everywhere, and Tristan will soon be gone to a cold and hostile place where spring comes late.

She stops the car and fishes in her bag for her mobile phone. She gets out and goes to sit on the seawall, watching a fast sea swell and crash on the rocks below her. After she and Barnaby talked about Martha she felt better, for a while. When she is busy, she can push away the image of that strange piece of paper in the brown envelope, but her mind keeps returning to it.

What else lies up there in the trunk? What other shock lies in that faded box? At first, she did not want to know. But as the days slip by and leaving for London gets closer, she feels torn between wanting a glimpse of something that might settle her anxiety, and a longing and equal dread of knowing the truth.

She has not told Tristan. It is not something she can discuss on the phone. Talking about it will make it real instead of lying like a dark place on the edge of her mind. Lucy wants to believe there is a simple explanation. She wants to believe everything is exactly as she has always been told all her life. The story of Gran's arrival in England in the war. The romantic meeting and falling in love with

Fred. A rushed war wedding before his leave ended. Anna's birth at the end of the war.

She wants to go on believing this. Yet that small faded box was obviously not meant to be found, so why not burn the papers instead of hiding them? Lucy has thought about it a lot. It is hard, maybe impossible, to destroy your own or other people's identity or possessions. After all, it is who you are.

Lucy knows she would have had to block her mind too if the people she loved had been left behind, killed in the war or perished in a concentration camp. So why is her mother's birth registered in a German document dated 1941 with an identity card dated 1943?

Was Anna really born in Warsaw, not London? Is she really four years older than she thinks she is? Perhaps Martha came to London later. Perhaps Grandpa met her somewhere else and they had a baby before they were married. Maybe Martha and Anna had to have German papers to get to England. That would mean Grandpa . . .

Lucy shivers, suddenly afraid, as if Martha's past is about to cast a great shadow over them and they will be swallowed in darkness. Like Barnaby, she hates secrets: they surface unexpectedly and hurt.

She dials Tristan, looking down on the waves, feeling the cold spray on her hands. She hates the thought of him going to a place full of hatred, American bombing, and streams of refugees. She listens as the phone rings and rings, then Tristan's breathless voice comes on the line.

"It's only me," she says. "I know it's early, but I just wanted to hear your voice."

"Soppy tart . . . Phew . . . Hang on . . . got to get my breath back. Just got back from a run. Phhhew . . . It's an amazing day here."

"It is here too. Huge sea."

"Are you OK, Luce?"

"Yes. Just dreading you going. Tris, was it really necessary to flatten Belgrade?"

Tristan sighs. "Debatable. Luce, come on, I'm not taking off yet. We've got leave together before I go. This isn't like you, my little ray of sunshine. Is there something you're not telling me? Like you want to throw me over, not for a fisherman but, *quelle horreur,* a bleached and muscled surf guard?"

"You wish!" Lucy almost tells him what is worrying her, but it is not the time.

"Luce, I have to go. I've got to shower and get into uniform. I'll ring you later in the day. Be happy, sweetheart, it's such a gorgeous day."

Lucy drives home and parks in the drive. She sits for a moment looking across the lawn, listening to the morning birds. Gran's garden is a spring garden and everything is poised to explode into color. She shrugs her mood off, closes her mind. It is impossible to be unhappy on a morning like this.

Lucy lets herself into the house. Barnaby is dashing about with Martha's tray and he looks relieved to see her.

"Thank goodness, darling. Your gran has dressed herself for high summer and refuses to change into warmer clothes. She's in the bathroom at the moment, very cross with me. Fred is having tea in bed until the bathroom is free and I have ten minutes to get over to St Michael's for Holy Communion."

Lucy grins at him. "You've also got marmalade on your cassock, Barnes. Did you tell me we haven't got anyone coming in until later today?"

"Oh, yes. Sorry, Lucy, it's a training morning or something, I can't quite remember. Kate is not coming until midday, but Mrs. Biddulph has just rung to say she can relieve you at ten o'clock. Is that all right?"

"Yes, it's fine. What a pity, I'll miss Kate again. I'm back at work at twelve o'clock. I'm dying to meet her. What's she like?"

"She's . . . different—quietly capable, and she drives, thank God. I quailed a touch when I first saw her—nose ring, short spiky hair—but Martha and Fred did not bat an eyelid. Lovely face, rather like a young Audrey Hepburn. I might be wrong, but I'd say she was a bit overqualified to stay long term."

Lucy raises an eyebrow at him. "You noticed her then?"

Barnaby gathers up his books filled with small flaglike bookmarks. "Kate is not someone you can avoid noticing."

Martha emerges from the bathroom, looking stunning in a mustard-yellow dress, a cream scarf and bare legs in tiny smart court shoes.

Lucy claps her hands. "Gran, you look beautiful, utterly beautiful!"

Martha smiles at her granddaughter. "Darling, thank you," she says graciously, throwing Barnaby a baleful look as he heads for the front door.

"Bye. See you all later . . ." Barnaby is out of the front door, galloping gratefully to his car.

Lucy giggles, suddenly deliciously happy again. "Tell you what, Gran, put this coat on . . . there . . . Now I want you to see your garden—it's looking stunning—then you can tell me if you are warm enough in those clothes."

She peers round the bedroom door at her grandfather while simultaneously helping Martha into her coat. "Gramps? Are you OK? Barnaby's just left. Gran and I are just going to have a quick potter round the garden."

Fred puts his teacup down. "I'm fine, Lucy, thank you." He winks at her wryly. "I'm going to get up in five minutes. Take your gran up to the copse. The wood anemones are out under the trees . . . look splendid."

Lucy and Martha walk across the damp grass. The early sun seems warm, but the wind from the sea is not. Martha holds her coat close as they turn towards the trees where the wood pigeons nest at the far end of the large, overgrown garden.

They both gasp at the sight of the great circular cloud of blue, white and gold lying under the spindly saplings and old sycamore trees. Lucy goes behind Martha to shield her from the cold wind and twines her arms around her neck.

"Did you plant all those, Gran?"

"No . . . Fred planted more and more each year until there was a great carpet of them, which grew and grew. So lovely. Oh, so lovely."

"Everything is just coming out. Look at that yellow, and the pink there in the corner near that white prickly bush thing."

Martha laughs. "Quince," she says. "I think." Then suddenly, "I don't want this all dug up for vegetables."

"Gran, why ever should it be? Of course not."

"It happens." Martha shivers, and takes one foot out of her shoe and dips it in the long wet winter grass. Lucy opens her mouth to say she will get cold, then seeing Martha's face, says nothing.

Martha, leaning against Lucy, closes her eyes, pushes her old toes into the damp grass and for a moment the sharp cold sensation shoots her down the years to another place, another time. She smiles, savoring the birdsong, the flash of newborn, translucent yellow leaves, red-flowering camellias, closed bud of cherry. She raises her face to the smell of spring, the first exciting promise of summer, to being young and full of hope, with the whole of life shimmering before her.

"Gran?" Lucy whispers after a while. "Don't get cold."

Martha opens her eyes, expecting to see Hanna, sent by Mama to bring her inside. But it is . . . it is . . . ? "Darling," she says, "it is a little cold."

Lucy bends and fits Martha's small bent toes back into her shoe, and arm in arm they walk back to the house.

Fred is in the bathroom with the radio on and Lucy sits Martha on the bed and, fetching a towel, dries and gently rubs Martha's feet warm again.

Martha places her hand on Lucy's silky dark hair with the

streaks of gold. "Darling, what would I do without you?" she says. "You shouldn't be doing this for me."

Lucy looks up and says fiercely, "Gran, why not? All my life you have been here for me and now I am here for you."

Lucy's eyes fill with tears suddenly and so do Martha's; for what has been between them and is now gone. Lucy longs to say, "Oh, Gran, I found something I wasn't meant to in the loft. What really happened to you in the war?" But she can't. It's too late. A few years ago, maybe. But not now. The Gran of her childhood is gone forever, but the person she was is still here, burning with the same unquenchable spirit. Lucy takes Martha's small hands and holds them to her cheeks for a moment, closing her eyes against her loss.

When she opens them, she says briskly, "Right, Gran, I'm afraid it's woolly tights, passion-killer tweed skirt and shapeless warm sweater for you. You've done enough trolloping for one cold spring morning."

Martha giggles. "Oh, darling, it's *so* much more fun being a trollop."

Fred, coming into the bedroom shaved and immaculate in tie and clean shirt, looks at the two women and the array of clothing on the bed and snorts at them.

"If ever there were a couple of trollops, it's you two."

Outside in the garden, the very first bud on the cherry tree opens a fraction and NATO drops a bomb by mistake on a bridge full of Albanian refugees fleeing Kosovo.

Chapter 13

The rain has stopped and the Berlin night is quite still except for the muted sound of traffic out on the autobahn. He wakes in the dark and for a moment believes he is back in his childhood. He can smell the roses from his mother's garden, but stronger still is the smell of horses and things he does not wish to remember. He can hear his heartbeat loud in the dark and the overpowering silence closes in on him. Why, after all these years, do the memories come flooding back? He has buried the past. He has buried it deep.

That was that life. This is another.

He can remember the first time he saw the little girl clearly. She had long, shiny black hair he wanted to touch. She was tiny, like a little doll, and she was afraid of horses. But she was not afraid of him.

Mutti was furious with his father. She did not want him to go into practice with a Jew, and she stood in the garden that day, unsmiling and icy. She called him to her and whispered loudly, "Ugh! How I hate the darkness of them."

He pulled away from her. Kicked out at a garden chair because of the sickness in his stomach, and the gardener's puppy lying underneath shot out with a squeal . . . *I shiver at the memory of her eyes. Close my mind against the echo of her laugh.*

All his childhood Mutti told him stories, terrible fairy stories of a race who ate their own babies, who were inferior, but a threat to all good Germans. After he met the little girl his heart told him something quite else.

How lonely they were, he and that fearless little girl. There were no other children nearby and only a hedge and a lawn between them. He defied Mutti, refused to think of her as Jewish. He and the girl were friends. They were friends.

Although he was older, she was the one with the imagination. They made small dens in the rambling garden on the edge of the forest, like nests, with old horse rugs and straw as linings against the cold and damp.

They always made more than one den to outwit Mutti. The girl seemed to know exactly where his mother would send the nurse or gardener to look for them, and where, in a tangle of dried fir branches, close under the branches of overhanging trees, grown-ups never ventured, if you stayed very quiet.

He was the practical one, carefully lining the small floor of their tree caves with layers of warmth. Pinching food from the kitchen and old coats from the hook in the stables so they would not freeze. Tying torn pieces of cloth to the trees so that they would know which way they had come.

In the depth of winter, when it was too cold to play in the garden, they often hid in the little tack room in the stable block. It had a small fire, and they played board games or drew pictures or read. The groom and the stable boy used to warn them when Mutti was on the warpath.

His mother knew perfectly well he played with the girl and she hated it. He could not take her into the house when Mutti was home, and even when his mother was out or away, the girl was so nervous she jumped at every sound, hated being inside his house.

His mother could not ban the little girl from the house and garden. She could not stop them playing together or from being friends, because of his father. He adored the child. She amused him. He also admired her mother, who was gentle and extremely well read.

Mutti was much too clever to dislike the family openly or show her jealousy and prejudice in front of his father. She enjoyed the money and lifestyle that the new clinic engendered. Instead, she made life difficult for the children, and any social interaction beyond the polite interchanges between the two families impossible.

This was neither unusual nor a surprise. Initially, the two families knew exactly where they stood and the conventions were strictly adhered to, in front of her. Jewish families kept to their own, lived among each other, not with Poles or Germans. As far as Mutti was concerned it should stay that way. Behind her back, the boy visited the girl in her home and so did his father.

As the years went by Mutti's jealousy of the girl and her mother, combined with her prejudice, became all-consuming, obsessive. Fueled by politics, the papers, her friends, Polish and German, it seemed to his mother that she had waited all her life for the time that was coming.

As his father's marriage disintegrated, as Poland began to prepare for war and indigenous Germans waited for their chance to seize coveted houses and jobs, as houses became empty and the trains overflowed with refugees fleeing while they could, his mother would beat him with his horsewhip for even talking to the girl.

He and the girl were like brother and sister. Until he changed schools. Until the company of his peers became more exciting. Until he began to understand the threat to the purity of the German race. Suddenly, they were children no longer and it was not possible to be friends.

He was a German. She was a Jew.

I shut her out. I shut out the memory of those haunting dark eyes. I shut out what I did and what I became. I close my eyes against the coming day, the boy I was. Against the sick endless knowledge of my own betrayal.

Chapter 14

Kate found a small vegetarian hotel on the edge of the village. Her room faces the estuary and she opens her window wide to a thick airless afternoon. This will be fine until she can find somewhere to rent.

Away over the water purple clouds are amassing. There is going to be a storm and she is glad of it. Her head aches and she feels tense and vaguely apprehensive.

She thinks of Martha. Martha and Fred living in that one-story, timeless house that holds the faint resonance of a colonial era.

Restless, she makes tea she does not really want, then throws herself on top of the bed and closes her eyes. She hears the first distant rumble of thunder start like a mumbled threat and with it the strange anxiety surfaces.

She thinks she knows the cause of it. Entering that house reminded her of Dora. The reminiscent smells of an old house, where long-faded curtains and fabrics of sofas and chairs hold still the nostalgic memories of childhood. And of hope. *Another visit, one more chance of saying and doing the right thing.*

She thinks about that freak London storm that sent her here, which woke her from a dream of such joy that she tried to cling on to it. She did not want to wake up in her aunt's flat in the center of London where any moment the dull roar of traffic would begin.

She lay listening to the violent wind isolating her in yet another city, and felt an overpowering dislocation and a longing to change the course her life had suddenly taken: regular employment, city salary, punishing hours.

She knew she should be grateful. She should be enjoying writing travel features. She should be glad of decent money. But she was homesick for India, for a job she had loved, for her friends. For the person she had thought Richard was.

The knowledge that she could never go back, never return to that place and time of happiness was a sharp pain under her ribs. It had ended so abruptly that Kate knew she would never take joy or fulfillment for granted again.

Her brother, Luke, had phoned to tell her that Dora was dying, the same week Richard's wife had flown unexpectedly to Karachi to join him.

—I have to give it another try, Kate. I have a four-year-old child.

—Of course you do. I see that. I'll stay in England. I won't come back.

—It might be easier for us both. It would be awful to have you so near.

—Yes. I expect it would.

Kate stunned, in shock; Richard trying to keep the relief out of his voice.

Later, when she could think straight, she realized Richard must have known for months that his wife was coming. An estranged wife does not travel thousands of miles with a small child, just hoping they will be welcome.

Kate gets off the bed, picks up her cooling tea and goes to the window. Why did Richard, thousands of miles away, after months of silence, decide to ring her at that particular moment, in the middle of a storm, his voice finally ending a life she could not let go of. Somehow she knew it would be him. Kate believes in karma.

—Kate, it's me, Richard.

—Richard. Is something wrong?

—Darling Kate, I just needed to hear your voice. You don't even sound surprised.

—No, I'm not surprised. Not in the least.

—Kate, you sound so . . . cold.

—Not cold, Richard. Sensible. It is what you wanted me to be, wasn't it?

Silence, Then—You are angry with me. I've hurt you, Kate. I'm sorry.

Kate was not angry, she was furious.

—Richard, I lived and worked with you for two years. You told me your marriage was over. Definitely over. Your wife rings you out of the blue to announce her return, and you suddenly tell me you must try again for the sake of your child . . . And, oh, by the way, as you have to go back to England because your mother is dying, maybe, it is better, easier, if you don't come back. Isn't that how it was? Tell me if I have got it wrong!

—I thought you agreed it was the best thing, Kate. I thought I had to try once more . . .

—So why are you ringing me now?

—Because I miss you very much and because I don't know if I can make this marriage work.

—I see. You want to keep all your options open, in case you get bored trying to piece together a relationship for the sake of your child?

—For heaven's sake, Kate, you seem intent on twisting everything I say.

—No, Richard! I flew home because my mother was dying and suddenly things became very clear. I saw things as they really were, not as I wanted them to be. You never stopped for one moment to consider our relationship before you leaped back into your marriage. You never rang me once to see how I was or to find out if my mother had died . . .

Kate felt the tears behind her eyelids.

—I thought we were close friends, but I was only a stopgap. An aid worker passing through. Unimportant, or you would have told your wife that it was too late, you had met someone else who meant something to you. Anyway, anyway, it doesn't matter.

—Of course it matters . . . Kate, please, I'm sorry, really sorry. I have made a big mistake . . .

—Tough.

—Can I at least fly home and talk to you?

—No. It's much too late, for me, anyway. Just for once, think about someone else. Your wife and child. Make your marriage work. After all, it was important enough six months ago to end our life together. I hope it all works out. No! I don't want to hear any more. I am going to put the phone down . . .

She felt Marjorie's arms round her shoulders as her heart jumped painfully.

—Well done, favorite niece.

—I'm your only niece.

—True.

Marjorie threw two books of maps onto the table between them.

—Where is it going to be this time? Which country?

—You old witch. England. For a bit anyway.

They placed the map on the floor.—Close your eyes and point.

—Have I told you, you are absolutely my favorite aunt?

—I am your only aunt.

Marjorie turned the map round. Kate closed her eyes and randomly stabbed her finger somewhere. She expected to land in the sea, but when she opened her eyes her finger was right on the toe of Cornwall.

—Very apt, Marjorie murmured.—All the nuts land in the toe.

Now Kate gets off the bed and goes to the window. How do you ever know you have done the right thing? She is drawn to caring for strangers, when she could not reach her own mother in any meaningful way.

She is about to become peripheral, drawn into lives that have nothing to do with her. People living, not with actual death, but loss, all the same. A small sneaky death of the mind. Is this too soon after Dora?

Against the backdrop of purple sky a fisherman in waders digs for eels, seemingly oblivious to the coming storm. The tall figure of a girl walks slowly along the foreshore with an elderly-looking dog. Her dark hair, streaked with random blonde strands, is caught up in a slide. She is young, coltlike, with an innocent elegance. She wears a cropped black T-shirt with bare midriff and white cut-off jeans. She stops on the shingle, looking up the estuary, out to where white waves are gathering on an incoming tide. Seabirds wheel in the wind over her head and curlews swoop low, calling out, flying inland against the coming storm. How bleak and lonely it is out there, the weather turns so capricious, changing quickly and suddenly.

The girl stands very still for a long time, and something in the slight and vulnerable figure catches at Kate. She knows suddenly it is a leave-taking, a long silent good-bye. Sadness starts up inside her, a strange pull at her heart. The girl must be Lucy; Kate recognizes the dog.

It is as if she is watching a small private lament. As if she is watching herself grieving for something she cannot change.

Kate stands at the window like a sentinel, as motionless as the girl below her silhouetted against that violent collecting sky. Another rumble in the distance, far away over the sea, and a flurry of fat raindrops lands in gusts against the window.

The girl moves slowly, the dog gathers its legs and jerks upright after her and they disappear slowly together round the point, leaving Kate watching the empty foreshore.

Chapter 15

Berlin

He sits in his flat studying a street map of London. He stares down at the tiny row of houses where Hans has told him the woman lives. He circles the house, the law courts and her chambers in the city with a soft lead pencil.

He makes another little circle on his English map, right down in the toe of England where the woman grew up. Far from London, but London is not far from Berlin, London is only a few hours away.

He pours coffee, then goes to open the glass doors and sits on the small balcony. If he took up Scheffell's offer he would have a valid reason for going to London. A two-week seminar would be good for him, keep his hand in, stop his brain from atrophying.

He looks across the swath of park in front of him to the city glinting below. The faint roar of muffled traffic comes to him from the autobahn. He thinks of his working life, the years flying by too quickly, the time so easily taken for granted. That time when you are young and single-minded. Striving to get to the top of your profession. Strands of a life gathered up in careful calculated threads. Career, travel and women. In that order. Each thread separate, unless he wished it otherwise.

Academically fulfilling years. Exciting. Because of the power. Every surgeon becomes aware of the seductive power in his hands, the thrill of learning, teaching, becoming expert. Healing tired, diseased, and broken bones. Mending, stapling together, piecing like an intricate jigsaw smashed limbs. Devising new ways of operating and postoperative care. Becoming eminent. All this, behind him.

Every doctor, at some time, abuses that aura of godlike status. Not necessarily with his hands as he heals, but with his heart, as he so casually picks up and discards the people who pass through his life.

Women, you mean. He sips his coffee and watches the wind get up, filling the air with pollen. Is it not amazing the euphemisms one uses to delude oneself? A third-party detachment. A collective *every* and *we* to distance ourselves from our own responsibility.

I have spent my life distancing myself. How many women, young or old, professionally and personally, have I hurt by my actions? Theater nurses berated for a simple mistake. Patients and young doctors sycophantic to avoid my sarcastic tongue.

I sit here now, retired, no power—still a brain, thank God—and I wonder how many times we have to learn the same thing. We can spend a whole life running from what lies behind us, believing it all happened to the person we no longer are. *My generation, now retired.* How many like me will find that once they stop running the thing that lies behind them is still snapping at their heels?

All the women I loved briefly and well, because they were attached to someone else and never free. How I relished the chase. Loved beautiful things. Still do. Still enjoy clever women. I needed always the challenge of obtaining something that did not belong to me. Again and again. *As if, one day, someone might be able to touch me. That I might feel . . . something.*

It is not that I do not remember love. It is that I dare not.

It is cold. He goes inside and bends again to the map with unsteady fingers. To age on the outside and feel the same on the inside, for memory to exert such power, is humiliating.

He had almost forgotten the thrill of an alluring and clever face.

The past is rearing up like a tidal wave. He wavers in its path, fearful of destruction, fearing it will swamp him. He is afraid that the person he has become will disappear abruptly to leave him as he once was. It is a terrifying thought.

Why is he suddenly haunted by a forgotten face, an echo of laughter, an imprint of footsteps across a lawn? How is it possible in the stillness of this sleeping city to hear the sound of horses' hoofs galloping through the wet leaves of a forest? Or smell the pungent scent of rain on pine needles; feel a thin strand of blue-black hair blow back and whip his cheek? He aches for what he has forgotten. He buried the child he was. He obliterated the boy, the golden, fallen, unstoppable thing he became. He buried a whole life successfully, completely and forever.

He turns abruptly away from the map, back to the window, as if the city below him might suddenly crumble and topple into the smoking ruins of Berlin. He shuts the glass doors firmly. He will take up Scheffell's offer. He will go to London. He will see for himself the things that make up this woman's life. He could be a fellow lecturer. Or just a tourist. Anyone can be anonymous in a large city.

He is not going to be careless now after a lifetime of caution. The irony does not escape him. He merely wants to see her again. He needs to see her close to, in the flesh. To know exactly what it was in her face that triggered memory of something quite else. Another time and place. Another world.

Chapter 16

Fred took Martha to Florence when Barnaby was eight. He waited until he thought Barnaby was old enough to appreciate art without getting too bored. Anna went on a skiing holiday with her school.

It was quite a feat to get Martha out of the house and garden. He had to pretend that it was really an educational trip for Barnaby. They had never taken a holiday abroad and he wanted to prove to Martha that they really could go away, and the house, on their return, would still be standing.

Barnaby helped. His excitement was infectious. He repacked his small school suitcase at least fifteen times. They caught the train up to London the day before their flight and stayed in the Gatwick hotel because Fred knew Martha would be in agonies in case they missed their flight the following morning.

Barnaby had never flown before and his delirious anticipation touched Fred. He was taking a risk: Martha was still prone to terrible bouts of anxiety and sleeplessness that would be almost impossible to hide in a small apartment.

Barnaby had had a difficult first term at prep school. Telling him it would get better was no comfort. He was the sort of boy who should have been a day boy. If things had been different, Fred would never have sent Barnaby away to school.

On the airplane Barnaby never stopped talking. Martha had to keep saying, "Eat, Barnaby. Be still, darlink. You will upset your tray."

Fred knew that Martha too was excited. He hoped to show her it was possible and quite safe to extend the boundaries of her life.

The taxi from the airport dropped them outside the Duomo, the nearest he could get to their apartment, and as Fred lugged their suitcases down the Via del Calzaiuoli to their apartment, he saw that it was going to be all right. Martha dawdled, her eyes everywhere. She wanted to savor this, her first impression of Florence.

"Oh, Fred. So beautiful. Look, look, Barnaby, at the carvings on that door."

The apartment was three floors up and they dragged their suitcases, laughing and puffing up the steep stairs. The rooms were clean and airy. Fruit and flowers waited for them on a table. On the roof balcony they could look across Florence, and behind them lay the ancient abbey Badia Fiorentina.

They could look down upon the cloistered gardens and see lemons growing on small trees. They gauged the time by the bell tolling for Mass, night and morning.

Barnaby darted through the rooms, choosing where he would sleep. Martha walked up the steep stairs and stood on the roof in September sunlight, looking out across the city, her hands clutching the rail, her long hair, trapped with clips, flipped round her face in an evening breeze. She was still for so long that Fred, leaning against the open door that led onto the roof and absently filling his pipe, began to worry.

He was reluctant to interrupt her thoughts. He was learning to understand that she often needed to go to places he could not follow. He had learned not to ask where she had gone and why; only to be there when she returned.

He moved across the space between them and, standing behind her, put his arms around her and his face against hers. He felt her smile and she leaned back into him, placed her hands on his arms.

She said, still looking across Florence, "Mama loved travel books. She had a shelfful of them. I used to read them on wet days. Papa would send to England and Germany for them and she would sit there translating with dictionaries. But oh, Fred, you cannot get the real feel, you cannot see how the light falls, or how shadows change the color of buildings. You cannot smell lemon or mimosa, or cooking. You cannot hear the bustle of people underneath your window . . ."

She paused. "Mama was married at seventeen. She never traveled anywhere. She never left Poland."

Fred tightened his arms around her and stayed silent, as still as Martha, looking outwards at the sun dropping behind the buildings, coloring them pink, glittering off roofs, blurring the colors before their eyes so that everything was a kaleidoscope of sight, smell and sound.

She had given him, voluntarily, a little piece of her. The moment was broken by the sound of Barnaby calling from below.

One memory, Fred thinks, leads to so many down the years of our lives. That holiday was where I discovered how much I did not know about my wife. Or my small son. That first holiday together was a moving on, for all of us.

I discovered how knowledgeable Martha was about so many things. I brought the guidebooks, but it was Martha who knew the names of the paintings, artifacts, and statues, Martha who knew the history. She effortlessly imbued in Barnaby the wonder and awe of a city crammed with more beauty than it was possible to assimilate in one visit.

On Sunday they all went to Mass in the Duomo, the wonderful Cathedral of Santa Maria del Fiore . . . Martha showed Barnaby how to light a candle, offer up a prayer. The first full-blown Catholic Mass that Barnaby had ever attended was pure opera. The priest had a tenor voice like an angel.

The exquisite music filled the cathedral and swirled around them. Barnaby had been riveted, his eyes glued to the priest. He stood and he sat, and he knelt in time with everyone else. His attention never wavered from the service, his eyes turning from the altar boys, swinging incense, to the processional choir. Fred and Martha watched him, fascinated, out of the corner of their eyes.

As they left the cathedral he took a lire out of his pocket and lit another candle, solemnly prayed, and turned with that smile of his that could light up a day.

The day before they left Florence, as they sat at a pavement café, a very young German couple came to sit at the table next to them. They were clearly agitated, but speaking far too fast for Fred to understand them.

He knew Martha was listening, although she had her back to them. Her fingers were curved round a wineglass. Barnaby was concentrating on his ice cream; Fred was drinking beer and the glass suddenly felt cold in his hand.

The couple could not make the waiter understand what they wanted. They kept pointing under the table and they got louder and more guttural as they grew desperate. After a few minutes, Martha could bear it no longer. She turned and asked them in German what the matter was.

They stopped, startled, then smiled broadly, asked if she were German. Martha told them she was not. The girl lifted her skirt to show a nasty gash to her leg, which she had covered with a handkerchief. Martha looked at Fred. He left his chair to examine it. It needed stitching.

He told the couple that they should go to a local doctor or the hospital. They insisted they just needed a bandage, but the nearest pharmacy was shut. The German girl began to get tearful.

Fred went back to the apartment and got his emergency medical kit. He swabbed the cut with brandy, got the German girl to drink a glassful and stitched her leg while she stoically bit her lip.

The couple then departed, full of gratitude, but not before the boy turned back and asked Martha, "Are you Czech? Slavonic? Polish?"

It seemed to Fred that a whole minute passed before Martha answered. "I am English," she said. Then, looking straight at the boy, "I was born in Poland."

The boy held her eyes. "I am sorry," he said.

Martha answered, very pale suddenly, "You have nothing to be sorry about."

"I am still sorry. And thank you again for what you have done for my girlfriend."

"Are you all right, Mum?" Barnaby asked, when the couple had gone.

"Yes, darlink, of course I am," she said brightly. "Do you know, I am going to have some of that brandy. Then we will decide what we will do next."

As they sat on the roof that evening, Martha said, "I am fine, Fred darlink. Do not keep looking at me anxiously. It was only that it was the first German I have heard since the war and it was a bit of a shock. It was a good thing to happen. They were just children. Now, where is Barnaby? It is our last evening and we will go somewhere and celebrate. Yes?"

That evening, in their bedroom at the back of the apartment, with the light off and shutters thrown back to the night to reveal the tower of the monastery, Martha turned to Fred, her dark hair, free of the pins, flowing round her. She looked so young, leaning there on one elbow in the light coming in from the window. She leaned forward to kiss him.

"Fred, I love you so, so much. Thank you. Thank you for bringing me here to this such beautiful place. I have been so happy . . ." Again she kissed him and again and again. He pulled her on top of him and was buried under her hair. Their lovemaking that night was passionate and intense. She was telling him that she was no longer so fragile. Telling him that he did not have to be quite so careful with her . . . She would not break.

Fred, looking for some pills in his old medical drawer in his study, comes across two black-and-white photos of Martha, taken in Florence. The light is early morning, streaming through half-open shutters. He gazes down at a young, radiant girl, lying on the bed. In one her dark hair is streaming across the pillow. She wears a thin, linen nightdress, her body clearly visible through it. She is smiling at the camera, at him taking the picture. In the second photo she is propped up on one arm, the look in her eyes sensuous and intent, the invitation unmistakable.

Fred feels his old heart turning and jumping at the memory of what they did next. How breathtaking this girl looks, young and vital and achingly beautiful.

Martha has scrupulously, over the years, placed all family photographs in albums, clearly named and dated. But not these two photographs. These were just for the two of them . . . Fred smiles. What will the children make of them when they are dead? Two old dears who once had a sex life.

Barnaby knocks and puts his head round the study door. "I just wondered if you are all right, Dad."

Fred pushes the photographs back into the envelope and places them into the drawer. "I'm fine. Just looking for . . . paracetamol. Can't find any."

Barnaby looks surprised. "Dad, they are in the bathroom cupboard. They are always kept there."

"Of course. Of course. But you know how I am, I always have pots and potions in drawers."

Barnaby regards the pool of emptied drawer on the floor. He smiles. "Looks like you found everything but pills."

"Sod's law," Fred says, struggling out of his chair.

Barnaby goes to help him. "I'll get you some paracetamol from the bathroom."

"Is there any Nurofen, old thing? Got a bit of a head."

"I'll look. Dad, when did you last see Brian?"

"Oh, last week, I'm sure it was. I am perfectly all right. Probably need new glasses."

As they reach the sitting-room door Fred says, "Do you remember that holiday we had in Florence, Barnaby? Probably not, you were awfully young."

"I remember. Not everything, of course. It was the first time I flew. Our first holiday abroad, wasn't it?"

"It was."

Noises and giggles are coming from the bathroom, where Lucy is bathing Martha. As Fred sits in his chair, Barnaby says, "I remember that everyone looked at Mum because she was so stunning, even though the Italian women were beautiful."

Fred laughs. "Fancy you noticing at eight! Are you sure that memory is not a more recent one?"

"I remember the roof terrace. And I remember the two Germans sitting next to us, and you sewed her leg up and Mum went green."

"Yes. They were very grateful."

"But it was the Mass I remember most. In the Duomo . . . Fantastic! Do you remember that day, Dad?"

"I remember it well. You lit a candle, made a wish."

Barnaby laughs. "I made a prayer . . . Sorry, Dad, I'll get your pills. You are looking gray."

"It is called old age," Fred jokes, but his head is throbbing badly.

From the door, Barnaby says, "Do you know what I prayed for? I prayed that I could become a priest, just like the Italian priest taking the service."

Fred looks startled. "Good Lord, I didn't know you had Catholic leanings."

"For a while. I dabbled in my teens. Got stuck on the infallibility of the Pope, birth control, but worst of all, celibacy!"

They both howl with laughter, bringing Lucy and a damp Martha out of the bathroom, demanding to know the joke.

Chapter 17

Kate gets up early the next day and walks along the saltings towards the beach with the water swelling in a high tide. The stillness is incredible. The sea laps gently, full of a pale yellow light. She sees no one. It is like having the world to herself. She stands glued to the sight of a scarlet camellia bush shedding red blooms against the moving swell of water and into this space something moves. A sudden sensory thrill, a sharp intake of breath. Here. Now. This. I am.

A part of her that has not been calm for a long time is suddenly at peace. For a moment she feels part of the water, part of the color and texture and smell of spring. She is suddenly conscious of something unacknowledged in herself.

This is the place she wants to live for a while. Kate knows it without a doubt.

She walks on past the long leafy gardens of the Victorian houses, up the hill away from the estuary, then reluctantly turns back towards the hotel. She has to go to a training session the agency is running. She feels suddenly relaxed, as if, having found the place she wants to live in, finding a house will be no problem.

The woman who owns the hotel thinks it might be.

"Most people who have houses to rent do short summer lets. There's more money in it. Of course you'll find somewhere, but maybe not in the village." She smiles at Kate. "You could ask in the post office. Dave Pasco knows everything about everybody, often before they know it themselves!"

"How alarming," Kate says.

On the way to Penzance she stops off at the post office. Dave Pasco eyes her nose ring with disapproval, but she is pretty and has a nice voice.

"Not sure I know, offhand. I could make enquiries if you leave it with me."

"Thanks a lot. I'm staying at the Banyan."

"Leave it with me," Dave Pasco repeats. "If I hear anything I'll let you know."

It is the second of two short training sessions. Kate has had to bite her lip, acknowledging it would be a mistake to admit that she has a psychology degree and has run these courses herself. She buys maps, trousers and walking shoes and sends Marjorie a postcard. She studies the maps over a pub lunch and sees she can walk from the village along the coastal paths for miles.

Returning to the hotel, she sees the owner is amused by her practical new clothes. Kate has a flash of annoyance. She should be used to it, but she does not like to be categorized by the way she looks.

The sun hangs high in a clear blue sky and the pale, empty beach stretches before her, dazzling her eyes. She feels like a child, on the brink of a big adventure, holidays just starting, brimming with possibilities. She takes her shoes off and runs across the pale sand.

One life has ended, but the other has not yet begun. *She is between lives.* Kate listens to the larks in the marram grass behind her, singing and rising, singing and rising. She watches small fishing boats in the distance dragging their nets. Seagulls weave and scream high in the sky and she lies on her back in the sand and lets the hot afternoon steal over her like a massage.

Kate finds to her surprise she is crying without sound, a release like the sudden uncoiling of a tight spring. She wishes she had come here long ago. She wishes she had been able to cry like this for Dora. If she could have wept would it have dispelled Dora's fury at dying? Would it have dispelled her own resentment of expectations she could never fulfill?

She sits up abruptly. Unfair expectations do not stop you loving and hoping, the small child forever caught in an adult, longing to please. With death, the hope for acknowledgment and uncritical love is gone: no more chances, just an aching sorrow and regret.

Sitting here, swallowed by the vast beach, Kate knows she must move on. Dora's death lies like a sick place, corroding her insides. She is twenty-nine years old. She has no children, no partner, no family but Marjorie, and Luke, whom she never sees.

What is she doing with her life? What does she want from it? She has absolutely no idea. All she knows is that being here makes more sense than London, where she was aware every day of the superficiality of her life after India. She was earning in a month what her friends would make in a year, and it made no sense. There was no one to work hard for. She has never been interested in material things.

In India, she did not have time to dwell on the state of her life—or her relationship with Dora. How is it possible to feel this loss over a mother she never got on with? A mother who was perpetually disappointed in her?

Kate shivers at the awfulness of having to watch Dora's lingering death, powerless to give comfort or reassurance because her mother's eyes remained stoically on the doorway of the hospice behind Kate's head. Waiting for Luke. Concentrating on willing him, her beloved son, to her bedside.

Realizing that her presence meant so little, even at the end of her mother's life, tipped Kate's world dangerously. The place that had been resolutely hopeful in her died with her mother. She tried to do the right thing, to be in the right place, a place where she should be needed. She wanted to make peace with binding words. She wanted them both to acknowledge one another, even if they could not love. *You are my mother. I am your daughter. Let us not dislike each other in your death.*

But her mother's frail body and strong mind needed to concentrate exclusively on willing *her son* to her side. On willing herself to live until he arrived. There was no time or energy to waste on Kate, who had achieved little that Dora believed to be important. A daughter who was not interested in money, who appeared to have no ambition, and who had provided no grandchildren. A daughter who earned peanuts roaming the world for peculiar humanitarian aid organizations.

There was to be no last touching reunion, no grand finale.

Luke, having summoned Kate from the Third World, was not there for his mother's death. He disappeared back to France, protesting he was in the middle of some crucial business deal. Despite Kate's pleading telephone calls, he did not come in time. Dora died waiting, watching for the door to fly open. For Luke to call out—Where is the most beautiful woman in the whole world? And Dora Openheimer would melt.

Kate feels again the wound of her mother's sorrowful death, the waste of her joyless life.

She feels poised; teetering on the edge of her own life. Yet she *has* moved on. She made a decision and stuck to it. She has freed herself from the sort of life her mother would have liked her to have. All she has to do is let go the memories.

What was it Marjorie had said before she left?

"Don't carry the shadow of Dora around with you, Kate."

Kate stares out again at the expanse of blue sea and sees the young girl she saw on the foreshore yesterday walking her dog along the sea's edge.

Lucy sees Kate and waves. "You've got to be Kate."

"And you've got to be Lucy."

"Hi! You were looking rather reflective as I walked along. Are you OK?"

Kate laughs and meets Lucy's eyes. "I'm fine. All this . . ." she waves her arms, "makes you rather reflective. I was sitting here thinking about mothers. Mine died not long ago. I always disappointed her."

Lucy plonks herself down beside Kate and snorts. "Join the club! I am the biggest disappointment in the history of the world. My mother is a hotshot barrister. She is terribly clever and stunning-looking, despite her age. She got landed with me, one constant disappointment."

Kate stares at her. "You're joking! I ache to be tall and willowy with skin that tans in a blink of an eye."

Lucy is pleased. "My father was an Italian . . . or so the story goes!"

They grin at each other and begin to walk back along the beach. "Will you stay here, do you think? I heard you were only trying the agency out," Lucy says.

"I plan to stay if I can."

"I've got to leave Cornwall, you see. There's no proper work for me here and I'm really worried about how Barnaby will manage his parish, and Martha and Fred. I've been around on and off for so long . . . I just wish I didn't have to go . . ."

"Lucy, I've told the agency I definitely want to work with your grandparents. I can't say for how long, but—"

"For a while, anyway?"

"Yes."

"That's *such* a relief. Barnaby said Gran and Grandpa took to you immediately. They've only had old Mrs. B. and really young girls."

"Lucy, you have to have a life of your own."

Lucy shrugs. "My life is here. I would never leave, if it wasn't for Tristan."

"Your boyfriend?"

"Yes."

"You're feeling torn, aren't you?"

"Totally. I know I have to go away, use my degree, earn some money. *Grow up,* Anna, my mother, would say . . . but."

Kate smiles, liking Lucy. "But here is safe?"

Lucy makes a face. "What are you, a psychologist or something?"

"Yes, actually."

They both giggle, but Lucy is surprised. "Why are you doing a dead-end job? You certainly won't stay with that agency for long. They'll drive you to drink."

"Lucy, I don't like responsibility. I don't much like establishment jobs. But what I do is never dead-end."

Lucy is chastened. "I'm sorry . . . I didn't mean it like it sounded."

"I know you didn't. Tell me about your grandparents." Kate watches Lucy's face change.

She looks away for a minute, then says, "Well, I expect you have gathered that Gran is originally from Poland. When I was small, it was terribly funny because she thought she spoke perfect English and when people asked her where she was from, she could never understand why. She and my grandfather are the loveliest people in the world. I have spent so much of my life with them." She looks at Kate. "It is so hard to see them . . . suddenly diminished. Old age is the bloodiest thing."

They have reached the steps and climb up to the path and walk towards the church. "Gramps was a GP, a really good old-fashioned one, who still visited his patients at home. He worked hard and retired late, because his patients had hysterics every time he said it was time to 'hand over the reins.' Then, this with Gran. Awful. She was able to hide it for so long, I think, because she is vague and airy-fairy, like me, only Grandpa suspected."

Kate says, "If it is any comfort, I think your household is the happiest I have been in for a long time. I think you and your uncle are doing a brilliant job. I fell in love with your grandparents at first sight."

Lucy's face lights up. "Did you? The feeling was totally mutual. They love the days you come in. Poor old Mrs. Biddulph is rather like a sheepdog: kind, but determined to round them up and corral them where she can see them."

They both laugh. They have reached the cottage gate and Lucy says awkwardly, "I'd ask you in, but I have to go and help Barnaby with supper. Evenings are a bit of a marathon. Is that vegetarian place OK?"

"It's fine. Rather quaint."

"Are you vegetarian?"

"No. It was the views I went for and I can put up with roast lentils for a while."

Lucy grins. "Will we see you tomorrow?"

"In the morning."

"Great. I'll tell Barnes it's you. Good night."

"Good night, Lucy."

Kate walks slowly back to the hotel. The road is without lights and the trees make it seem darker than it is. There is something innocent about Lucy that is touching: an openness, devoid of self-consciousness. She wonders if Lucy realizes how rare she and Barnaby are to so willingly give to those they love.

She turns and looks back. The whole of that faded house is a bit like stepping back in time. The faint glow from lighted rooms flickering through the thick hedge is comforting. Kate imagines that nothing has ever threatened the steady beat of their lives, except this, their old age, cruelly sprung upon them, affecting everything. Affection and pride in each other will have always been given and taken for granted. Unquestioned.

Out on the mud seabirds warble, a little ripple, a wistful, sad sound that makes Kate suddenly aware of being alone.

Chapter 18

Dr. Saurer takes Marta's hand. They are watching the horses being brought out from their stalls. "You have already met Tylicz and he is the largest of all my horses, so you see you have no reason to be afraid."

Marta is doubtful. She looks up from the cobbled stable yard and Tylicz seems like a mountain.

Dr. Saurer swings himself up into the saddle and the groom moves forward to lift her up in front of him. Marta's heart thuds. She does not think she will like being that high. Then she sees the boy sitting on his horse, watching, waiting for her to show her fear. I will not be afraid, she thinks. I will not let him see I am afraid.

Marta lets the groom swing her up in front of Dr. Saurer and he takes hold of the reins, one arm each side of her. She does not think it is possible to fall off, but she cannot look down. She grips Tylicz's mane with her hands. Underneath her knuckles his skin moves, slides under her fingers like a rippling snake.

"We are going to walk slowly down the lane and into the forest, so that you get the feel of a horse. Just for ten minutes, that is all."

At first Marta cannot relax, she is stiff and hangs on to the thick coarse mane too tightly. Then slowly, as the horses walk under the dripping leaves, she begins to relax. She feels the soporific movement of the horse under her, listens to the sound of his hoofs squelching on the wet leaves. He is not going to run away with her. She is not going to fall off.

She looks around her. High up here she can see different things. She can reach up and touch the branches so that the rain sprays down on their heads in a cold flurry. She can see down the valley when they come off the track. She can see little houses below them and smoke rising from their chimneys in little arcs and puffs.

Dr. Saurer reins Tylicz in at the top of the hill and the boy canters past them. He turns, makes sure Marta is watching, then he raises his whip and is gone like the wind, galloping into the distance, under the trees, disappearing in a spray of water, leaving the earth vibrating to the sound of hoofs in the damp air.

Marta holds her breath, watches the place he has disappeared. Tylicz stamps his feet, shakes his head and she squeals, terrified he will follow the boy, take off, with her on his back.

Dr. Saurer talks to the horse softly, soothes him as if he is a little child. "Steady . . . steady . . . Not yet . . . Wait, boy . . . Good boy."

The galloping hoofs come nearer and nearer. Horse and rider come flying back over the hill towards them, and the boy reins in and stops a heartbeat away from where Tylicz stands tossing his head impatiently. The boy's face is flushed and excited, the horse is sweating and snorting, and Marta catches the thrill in the air round the boy and she thinks: I want to do that . . . I want to ride like that.

Dr. Saurer dismounts, then lifts Marta down. He gets back on the great horse and Tylicz hardly waits until he is in the saddle before he flies away, away in a great thunder of hoofs, prancing and shaking as if he is dancing, and the smell of horse is left in the air and Marta cannot take her eyes off where they have flown.

The boy laughs. "Are you still afraid? Will you learn to ride?"

Marta's eyes are fixed on the place where horse and rider have gone and presently she hears the sound of horse breath on the air and they dance back over the ridge with the sun behind them, looking as if they are swimming in gold, and Marta knows with every shaking piece of her she has to ride.

She has to learn to fly under the trees and across the fields, away, away, where no one can catch her. She has to ride like them. Then she too can be free. Just her and the horse galloping, galloping into the distance. Disappearing over the hill to be swallowed in sunlight.

Chapter 19

The trip to London was remarkably simple to arrange. He told Scheffell that he would make his own living arrangements. He wanted to find a hotel near the teaching hospital and accessible to Lincoln's Inn. He has been asked to give a series of four lectures over two weeks. Not exactly arduous.

He arrives in London a day early. He will be a tourist. He will do all those things in England he has not done for years. He asked Hans to organize a hire car and to his irritation finds he has picked a Mercedes, much like the one he drives at home. He would have preferred something smaller and easier to park.

On his first morning he gets up at dawn, studies his map and drives the car across London. At this time of day there is little traffic. He parks and walks a little way down the wide leafy street where Anna Gerstein lives. He stands and looks across at the row of tall terraced houses. Nothing moves inside the long windows of her house. The curtains downstairs are not drawn. All the houses in this street are smart, expensive, and well tended.

He goes back to the car and sits watching the sky lighten over the city. He does not expect, or want, to see her. He was just curious to see where she lived.

Before anyone begins to stir, he drives away and parks the Mercedes back in the hotel car park. He will not use it in the rush hour until he has familiarized himself with London again, but he likes to know he has freedom of movement.

After breakfast he wanders through Hyde Park and along the embankment. Before lunch he visits the Imperial War Museum and in the afternoon the Victoria and Albert Museum. In the evening he goes to the theater and mingles with the mass of German, American, Japanese, and French tourists. All the world is here. He is no different than any other visitor. He listens with amusement to Londoners making racist remarks out of the corners of their mouths, smiling at this particularly English hypocrisy. A nation who would deny being racist. A nation that bombs countries who ethnically cleanse.

The following morning a car picks him up at nine-thirty. He has almost forgotten how satisfying teaching can be. To pass on your own technical expertise to bright and receptive students remains amazingly rewarding.

At the end of his lecture it is gratifying to be asked intelligent and difficult questions—more than the time allows. He enjoys lunch with his English host and some hand-picked students. The conversation returns to a topic dear to his heart and one that frequently affected the recovery of his patients: traffic accident victims who are unnecessarily paralyzed because they are moved by well-meaning members of the public before paramedics can get there.

He wakes the following day tired but stimulated. After a late breakfast he orders a taxi to Lincoln's Inn. The court is a wonderful cathedral-like building. From the map he has studied carefully, he knows all the chambers are within walking distance of the court.

He walks slowly down the Strand, admiring the architecture. The chambers are housed in imposing gray stone or old redbrick buildings. They have high windows and are clustered within courtyards and tiny passages. The names of groups of chambers are pinned neatly outside the front of the doors. There is a fenced area of lawn and trees, like a small, private park. He stands fascinated, watching groups of black-gowned QCs and solicitors talking and laughing together.

Suddenly he sees her coming out of a courtyard and down some steps into the Strand, head bent, talking to a colleague. She is clutching a bundle of papers tied with pink ribbon and her white necktie is flapping in the wind as she hurries along followed by a small entourage.

He did not expect to see her outside the courtroom. He feels a strange and sick excitement. He turns and walks back towards the court. He need not have worried about drawing attention to himself, taxis glide endlessly past and the pavements are full of shoppers, and scurrying lawyers and their assistants, beating a constant path to and from the courts. Most are carrying bundles of papers wrapped in that strange pink ribbon.

By the time he has gone through the security check and is inside the court, she has disappeared. He is totally unprepared for the imposing beauty of the interior. He stands watching as people mill about looking at the court lists pinned on dark paneling or stand huddled in groups in the echoing entrance hall with their solicitors.

Her case is not for another hour and a half. He sits for a while on a bench just watching people. Then restless, he wanders around with other members of the general public. Walking up a stone staircase he finds the courtrooms, smaller than he expected, and situated off long corridors.

He catches sudden, fleeting glimpses of her disappearing through a doorway, sitting on a bench, head bent in earnest conversation. Grabbing fresh air by an open window. Sipping quick, polystyrene cups of coffee. Eventually, a middle-aged woman usher clutching a clipboard calls out, "Armed versus Miller. Court eleven." He follows a stream of people into a small paneled courtroom, many of them Asian. Anna Gerstein is QC for the prosecution. The case is an industrial inquiry. He knows from Hans's report that she specializes in corporate fraud, negligence and criminal injury.

Because she is fluent in German she is also a consultant on international corporate matters.

The defendant is a rough but articulate Northerner who employed very young illiterate Indian and Asian girls in his factory in Hull. A large percentage were found to be illegal immigrants. A faulty machine caused one young Asian girl to lose a hand. The defendant and his insurance company refused liability because she was wearing a sari and had been told to wear Western clothes. The girl and her parents were "persuaded" not to sue.

When Health and Safety officers and the police began to investigate they not only found faulty machines and an environment that broke all the rules but evidence of illegal human trafficking. The defendant was also accused of false bookkeeping, tax evasion and criminal negligence. The Asian girl was not the first to be injured. She was just part of an "invisible" slave labor force.

The case appears to be cut and dried. He listens, fascinated, as Anna Gerstein lulls the defendant into a false sense of security: how hard it must be to recruit labor these days? He must find it difficult with so many businesses, to know what was going on in each one? She begins very quietly, and although the defendant must know she is leading him to something, his brain works much slower than hers.

He is intent on shifting the blame squarely on his Indian manager. He is not listening properly. Almost casually, Anna Gerstein extracts from his own lips his racism, misogyny and greed.

The barrister for the defense is also quick and able, and hired for his sarcasm, which is used to good effect on the obviously terrified young Asian girls. Constant objections bat to and fro between the two QCs. Much jumping up and down. Many appeals to the judge on both sides about methods of questioning witnesses. The judge appears to be enamored of the woman QC. He positively twinkles at her, even when upholding an objection from counsel for the defense.

He is amused and fascinated. It is pure theater, but theater with the power to determine lives.

Layer by layer the enormity of the case is set out against the defendant. Anna Gerstein wears him down on seemingly insignificant things. On and on relentlessly, like a terrier. With the frightened witnesses, hardly more than children, she is gentle, turning to the translator again and again to reassure them.

The judge reminds the court, before they adjourn for lunch, that despite all the evidence, it has to be *proved beyond all reasonable doubt* that the defendant knew what was going on in that particular factory, which was managed by a man with a vested interest in smuggling immigrants into the country.

Was the judge saying it wasn't enough to know he did it? It had to be proved?

When they adjourn for lunch he goes outside. The sun is out and people are sitting on steps, leaning against walls, smoking or eating sandwiches. Anna Gerstein comes down the steps with colleagues and for a moment she stands quite near him. He fights down an urge to approach her. She bends in a little huddle, exchanging notes, then she disappears quickly back through the courtyard towards her chambers.

He goes to buy mineral water and a sandwich. Half an hour later she reappears and leans into a taxi, giving hasty instructions. Then, she is gone again, trailed by colleagues, in a flurry of black robes, hurrying along the pavement and back into court.

In the foyer of the court he sits near to a group of people, waiting for the case to resume. Someone seems to have lost a witness. Ushers scurry importantly about and talk into mobile phones. Eventually, a small, frightened man in a shiny suit is propelled up the steps to Anna Gerstein, as she emerges out of an anteroom. She throws her hands up in relief as he is bundled through the door. The court reconvenes.

The frightened man in the shiny suit is persuaded to give evidence. This takes some time. Then a tape of a conversation he had with the factory owner is played to the court. There is silence. The QC for the defense withdraws his case.

The defendant is found guilty. Criminal proceedings will be taken against him at the Old Bailey for the death and injury of at least four Asians. The prosecution had obviously been intent on getting him on the greater charge, which hinged on one witness.

Anna Gerstein gathers up her papers and, smiling at her colleague for the defense, they leave the courtroom together. This, then, is the hub and rhythm of her busy life.

He makes his way to the café to have coffee. By five-thirty the court begins to empty. He walks past the courtyard where he saw her come out. The afternoon fades and evening comes and still he feels reluctant to leave. He stands in the shadows of dusk as people come out of the buildings and go home. One little light in a window burns on.

He convinces himself it is her chambers. What is her need to drive herself so hard? The details of her working life laid out for him by Hans leaves very little room for anything else. He knows the answer. He understands the force, the fierce ambition and excitement that drives you onward. It is not quite enough to be good. There is a need to be the best. He recognizes in this woman a single-mindedness that gets you to the top of your profession.

He feels, at the end of this long day, strangely sad and empty. The feeling of familiarity he felt at the university is still with him, but, in this setting, in England . . . What on earth, in old age, does he hope to find?

He walks away to find a taxi, leaving that small lighted window glowing in the dusk, shining like a small beacon in the empty courtyard.

Chapter 20

It is Sunday. Lucy is packing her things and irritable because the weather is good and she wants to be on the beach or lying with her Walkman in the garden. She cannot possibly take all these boxes to London. The pile of things for the loft is growing and growing.

She has been reluctant to go back up the ladder. She still has not mentioned anything to Barnaby. She keeps changing her mind about talking to him.

Organ music from the church floats over the road. Summer is poised, waiting. It is the hardest time to leave, but it would be unfair on Tristan to stay. They have decided to get married when he's done his tour of Kosovo. The prospect has cheered them both up and she must earn some decent money.

Lucy hears Barnaby talking at the church gate and she leans out of the window, waving a large, thin beer glass, startling the two old ladies he is saying good-bye to.

"Barnes, I've poured you your gin. Tonic is cold. Plenty of ice. Lemon sliced. But you'll have to get a move on if we are going to finish the bottle before lunch."

Barnaby frowns at her, but the two old ladies merely smile at Lucy indulgently.

"If you think you can embarrass your uncle in front of us, young lady, you'll have to try harder than that."

"And I, Lucy Tremain, née Pedrazzini, am not above smacking your bottom as I did when you were a bit younger."

Lucy grins at the retired postmistress. "You'd be arrested now, Mrs. Pasco."

Mrs. Pasco snorts. "True enough, and the world is not a better place for it. Good-bye, Vicar. And good-bye to you, cheeky young madam."

"Barnaby," Lucy asks as he comes through the door, "can I put some of my things in the loft? I've got so much stuff. I can't take it all and if the cottage is going to be rented, I need to store it away somewhere."

"If there's room up there, of course you can."

"There's plenty of room. Barnes, when were you last up there?"

"I haven't been up there for years. Fred used to spend hours storing his old papers, bills, and redundant medical documents up there. He made sure it was always dry so your things should be safe. Anna and I were always banned in case we fell through the ceiling. Wait until I can help you, if you have anything heavy."

Barnaby looks at his watch. "Lucy, are you ready? I must rescue Mrs. Biddulph. She made it abundantly clear this morning that they had to beg her to come in for a second Sunday in a row."

"Mrs. B. just loves to be begged. Yeah, I'm ready. Barnaby, when I went up to look in the loft the other day, I—"

"Lucy, tell me later. I'll see you in five minutes at the car."

"OK. OK." There is *never* going to be a right time to talk to Barnaby, Lucy decides.

They are taking Martha and Fred out to Sunday lunch. It will be an exercise in love and patience, but her grandparents love it. Many of the locals were Fred's patients and much of Martha's life has been giving tea, sympathy, and practical help to people in the village. Fred and Martha are remembered fondly and made a great fuss of, even though, most of the time, they have no idea who they are talking to.

In the afternoon, Fred watches Martha sleeping and smiles.

Martha has always adored Sunday lunch. For her it has been a celebration of family life, of Anna and Barnaby being home in the holidays. Her enormous shopping expeditions before these lunches always amused him greatly. So did her long hours in the kitchen on Sunday mornings cooking *perfect* Yorkshire puddings.

Even when Anna and Barnaby left home, she still loved to cook Sunday lunch for him. "Sunday Lunch always seems to have capital letters for Mum," Barnaby said once, laughing. "Miss them at your peril."

Until Martha could no longer drive. They fizzled out then. Fred, settling himself in the conservatory, suddenly remembers the last day Martha drove the car.

He went to the gate and looked down the road for her because he was anxious. She had been gone far too long. He knew that somehow he had to find a way of telling her it was time she stopped driving, but driving was an independence Martha never took for granted and it was hard to deprive her of what was probably going to be a last freedom.

He was unsure whether Barnaby, just back from leave after that dreadful business in Northern Ireland, had taken in his mother's slow but sure mental decline; the bursts of sudden amnesia, the forgetting of everyday things; the names of people she knew well. Martha had become socially adept at covering up her confusion, but common objects, signposts, stop signs, roundabouts, were becoming a daily booby trap. Old age was a minefield in itself, without the dreaded first signs of Alzheimer's disease. Fred had no doubt this was what Martha had.

As he stood there that day, looking anxiously down the road, the little blue Peugeot came unsteadily into view. The power of his feelings caught Fred off guard: relief and an aching sadness. Life was so bloody unfair. Martha had gone through enough without ending her days lost and wandering in another terrifying landscape.

All his life he had guarded her health and protected her against any single thing that could threaten her security or happiness. Now he was totally powerless. Martha had no protection and Fred, standing at the gate of the house they had shared all their lives, wanted to howl.

Martha drew up beside the gates without attempting to turn in and tried to smile at Fred. She was pale and trembling. She had had a fright. He went round to the driver's side, feigning cheerfulness.

"Hello, darling, I was just wondering where you'd got to, that's why I was lurking in the drive. Shall I park for you? You look rather tired."

"Fred, would you?" she said gratefully.

As Fred helped her out, he could feel the tremors of her frail body through his fingertips. He was taken back fifty years, to her uncontrollable shaking fits, those nights when all he could do was hold her tight in the dark, talking, talking of inconsequential things.

"The car can wait a minute. Let's get you inside first, M. You've overdone it."

"So silly, Fred, I got completely lost. I thought I would never find my way home. Then when I tried to ask someone, I couldn't remember the name of the house. I'm going dotty, you know, I am going absolutely dotty."

"Rubbish! Darling, it's just old age. I do just the same, you know."

"Do you? My darling, thank goodness for that."

Fred sat her down in the drawing room and went to put the kettle on. Then he drove the car into the garage. As he put the keys beside her, Martha gathered them up and held them in her hand for a moment, weighing them, as she might hold something intensely precious.

She looked up at him and held his eyes as if perfectly aware of what might be happening to her. "I think, darling Fred, you had better keep these. My driving days are over." She curled his fingers round the keys, and Fred bent and kissed her forehead before turning and putting the keys in the top drawer of the desk.

He could only guess at her fear. It was the first hole opening up between them. Martha was beginning to leave for someplace Fred could not follow. She was going to be marooned on an island alone where he would not be able to reach her or give comfort.

Later that evening, when Barnaby was watching the news with Martha, Fred went into his study and got out his medical books. There were no answers, no rules. But he had to consider time scales. He did not want to leave Barnaby vulnerable. He could not expect him to run two parishes and manage Martha. A home was unthinkable. He shuddered at the thought of Martha with doors and windows locked, unable to move freely, to get out, to be alone. *Quite out of the question.*

Here, at the end of their lives, Fred felt he was going to let Martha down. He felt certain, somehow, that Martha would outlive him. He went into his files and dug around until he found the envelope with the tiny scrap of paper.

This was the past, buried deep and almost forgotten. Martha had suffocated all memory and embraced with passion a safe English life with Fred. Any inquiry meant she had to acknowledge that she was once part of another fragile, terrifying existence—that once she was a different person with a different family and a distant, almost forgotten culture.

Reclaiming a life meant you could no longer bury pain and death. Reclaiming a life meant you had to come to terms with the total annihilation of that previous existence. Martha's mental survival had depended on Fred and this life. This English life.

Fred looked at the frail and extraordinary poignant piece of paper. It had come with documents returned by the International Red Cross after the war. He had placed it in the flyleaf of a small medical dictionary. He had come upon it purely by chance as he'd stored away the battered pink box in which her childhood things had been placed. Written on it were the words "Dr. Oweski" and the name of a Swiss bank.

Martha had wanted to be alone when she opened the box. Fred

had hovered in the hall in case she should need him, but he'd known he must not go into the room unless she called him.

When her terrible lament began, the sound rising and falling, so foreign in this sun-filled house, Fred, unable to bear the sound, had gone into the garden. Standing, he'd held on to the cherry tree and felt the enormity of her loss all over again. And of his own.

He'd wanted to weep. There seemed nothing he could do. Love was not enough. He'd felt, suddenly, that there was never going to be anything he could do to help her heal or recover. The loneliness he'd felt then, as he'd stood with his fingers pressing into the bark of the tree, overwhelmed him. Much that was familiar, *known,* and comfortable had disappeared for him too.

He'd closed his eyes, breathed in to recapture the smell of the house he had grown up in. A bowl of flowers on the hall table. Dogs lying on the flagstones, their breath blurring the thick slate. The carved coatrack and brass umbrella stand. His mother's scent hanging in the air of the wide staircase. His father's pipe sitting in a large glass ashtray in his study. The huge mottled gilt mirror reflecting their lives, year in, year out. The small things that had been a part of his life—unremarkable, but taken as given.

A family in the drawing room of which he might have asked, What shall I do now? Tell me, is there something more I could do to help Martha?

He had gone and cranked up the ancient motor mower and made perfect lines, up and down, up and down the lawn.

After a while, Martha had come running out to him and thrown her arms around him.

"Fred darlink, I see your face from the window and I cannot bear to make you so sad. I go for long walk now with Puck. Please, please, burn for me those things that came. Not because they mean nothing, but because they mean too much. I cannot look back, it is too big black hole. I will be swallowed. You, Anna, are the future."

Martha believed Fred had burned her past, but he had not

been able to. The house here had a long low roof with little space and no headroom. He had had the loft in the cottage insulated and boarded for storage and he had placed her childhood diaries, few returned books, letters and private papers back in the old faded red cardboard suitcase in which they had arrived from Poland and hid them in the loft in the cottage. It was then that he had found the sad little record of Anna's birth.

Anna born again, with a crisp new English birth certificate, not difficult to obtain in those chaotic postwar years. Fred had always felt anxious about hiding the truth, but Martha had been desperate that the child, already traumatized, should grow up secure and English and unaware of the circumstances of her birth. How could he possibly have argued otherwise? This had only been possible because Anna had been so small and undernourished and had reached puberty late. She seemed to remember nothing. She had just blanked out those early years.

Fred had been afraid the box would rot or get eaten over the years so he had placed it inside his old school trunk with his own diaries and letters and documents from the war. Laid her past with his.

As children, Anna and Barnaby had always been forbidden to go in the attic, but Fred had a partition made with a padlock when he rented out the cottage. As the years went by, the box at the bottom of the trunk retreated to the back of his mind. Even when he placed more papers in the trunk, lugged boxes of old medical books up there, he could almost forget it was there.

Fred always hoped someday Martha would reach out for memory of her happy childhood, as she grew safe and secure with him. But she never had. After her time in the British military hospital she never spoke of those war years.

Fred understood. He understood the necessary silence that had descended, suffocating, like a velvet blanket, shutting out all sounds, so that none could touch her. A scream, a vivid nightmare, a ghastly memory of brutality, snuffed out quickly. Smothered in unbroken silence.

Something had made him take that one piece of paper with the name of the Swiss bank, to keep separately and safely in his files. He had thought it might become Martha's right and protection.

On the day Martha had to give up her car, Fred thought that day might have come. He picked up his pen and wrote to his solicitor.

Martha still sleeps with afternoon sunshine touching her face. Time has not been kind, yet Martha's face remains beautiful. Fred, wondering where Lucy is, heaves himself out of his chair, feeling the dull ache in his head begin. He will take one of his pills, even though they make him fuzzy. Then he might just see how the cricket is coming along.

Barnaby is walking Homer on the beach. Fred is watching cricket and Martha is sleeping. Lucy longs to be on the beach too, but Barnaby has evensong in an hour and he needs a break.

Lucy has come to dread Sundays. She adores Barnaby, but there is something intransigent in his insistence on trying to look after Martha and Fred without adequate help. It is wearing them both down and Lucy suddenly realizes she is looking forward to being free of these long and endless Sundays.

Freedom, though, will come in a city where she cannot run with white sand underneath her feet and a great curve of blue sea stretching ahead of her. Lucy still views the move with trepidation. London without Tristan is not going to be the same. She will have no daily telephone calls to look forward to.

Tristan is now on standby to fly to Macedonia to be ready when the ground troops move in to Kosovo. Lucy dreads him leaving, but the good thing is that she will be working so hard that she will have less time to worry.

She looks up to find her grandfather watching her in a way he used to when she was little.

"You're looking sad, darling," he says.

Lucy grins at him. "Only because I'm a lazy C.O.W., Gramps. I have to go and do a proper job in London and I am going to miss everyone like hell."

Fred smiles. "I used to love London. But you'll be back often, won't you?"

"Of course I will, whenever I can."

"I hope it's a job you want to do."

"Well, it's not exactly what I want to do, teaching foreign students, but I'm lucky to get it. I'm going to share a flat with an old school friend for six months. Tristan and I are going to get married when he gets back, Gramps, so I have to earn some real money."

"Good. Good. Is . . . is . . . um . . . your young man up in London too?"

"He's in the army, Gramps. He's about to go to Kosovo."

"Bad business, darling, very bad business."

"I know. Don't let's talk about it."

Fred comes over and pats her arm. "Shall I make you a cup of tea?"

"Let's make one together."

They leave the sleeping Martha and go into the kitchen.

"I worry about Barnaby," Fred says suddenly. "We are going to need more help here, especially without you, Lucy."

Lucy is startled. It is a long time since she has had a rational conversation with her grandfather. "I know, Gramps. I have told him."

"It is the cost, I think. It is the cost of it all that is worrying him, Lucy. Capital only lasts so long. Years ago . . . I think it was, I wrote to my solicitor. I could see it coming with Martha, you see . . ." Fred stops, struggling to remember. "He was awfully good, rang me up. Told me he had made inquiries . . . but no go really . . . Banks didn't want to play ball." Fred peters out.

"You tried to get a bank loan, Grandpa?"

"No . . . no . . . no, nothing like that." Fred gets agitated. "Martha has always been so against it. But I thought I must try.

After all, if there is money, it does belong to her." He stares at Lucy. "I really do want her to have the best medical care."

"Of course you do." Lucy pours water into the teapot and Fred gets out Martha's thin china cup.

"Martha will miss you," he says suddenly. "And so will I, very much, darling."

Lucy swallows hard. "Don't make me cry, Gramps. I just don't know what I'm going to do without you and Gran." She picks up the tray. "Grandpa, what were you saying? What money were you talking about?"

"Money?"

"You were talking about money, just now. You thought Gran might have money somewhere?"

"Well, I shouldn't have been . . . Forget it, darling." He stares at her. "The solicitor told me it was too long ago and no *individual* could claim . . . too much proof needed, death certificates, you know . . . of Martha's parents . . . Hopeless, banks wouldn't play."

"Grandpa!" Lucy puts the tray down again. "You are talking about *Swiss banks?*"

"That's it. She had a tiny piece of paper with the name of a bank on. Her father . . . Lucy, I don't want to talk about this any more. Martha would be very upset . . . Let's take our tea into the drawing room. Come along. I'm sure she will be awake by now . . ." He shuffles out in front of her in the small-stepped gait of the old and Lucy's heart aches.

Martha is awake, quietly watching the birds scuttle and squawk under the shrubs in the garden.

"Hello, darling," she says. "Tea? How lovely."

Lucy puts Martha's cup on the small table beside her and watches Fred looking at the television news and turning to pat Martha's hand. Sometimes her grandfather seems perfectly lucid and rational. His senility follows a completely different pattern from Martha's. Martha is no longer here as the person she once was. Fred always seems here, just a long, long way away where no one can quite follow him.

Barnaby dashes in with Homer and flies straight out again to evensong.

"Gramps?" Lucy asks. "Will you both be OK if I go over to the cottage for half an hour to do a bit more packing?"

"Of course we will, dear girl. Of course. Off you go."

Lucy walks across to the cottage with Homer trailing her. The last bell for evensong is tolling across the garden and Lucy can smell wood smoke. Someone has had a bonfire. She sees herself suddenly in her best blue school coat skipping and jumping between Fred and Martha as they hurry, laughing, late as always, against the setting sun, to evensong.

She wonders suddenly if Martha and Fred took her to church as a child every Sunday to give her a security she did not have with Anna, a place in village life. Maybe this was why Martha was so firmly Anglican too. It gave her the same roots as Fred. As English as cricket on the green. Garden fetes. Scrambled eggs and toasted soldiers after evensong.

She never doubted their belief. It was as obvious, if more understated, than Barnaby's. But once she was in her teens they didn't insist she should go with them, and did not always go themselves.

She remembers how she would hold on to Martha's small, crooked hands—*Too much gardening, darling*—turning and twisting the rings on Martha's fingers during the sermon to see them catch the light from the colored windows. Martha's hand would curl over Lucy's and she would feel a love so absolute for her grandmother that tears would well up in her chest. A childish foreknowledge, that with love there had to be loss.

Sometimes in the holidays, when Martha came into her bedroom at night to tuck her in, Lucy would throw her arms round her. "Don't ever die, Gran. Don't ever die and leave me."

Martha would soothe her and say, her face a little sad, "Darling, child, I have to die sometime. I am so, so much older than you."

Then she would quickly change the subject, make Lucy laugh or read her a story. When Lucy was miserable at boarding school, at night she would squeeze her eyes shut and pretend she was in bed in the house in Cornwall with the wind making the casement windows rattle and her grandmother sitting on the bed like a guardian angel.

Lucy lugs the things she wants to keep onto the landing. She pulls the ladder down and goes up to make a space for them. She switches on the light and stares across at the trunk. She hesitates and then crawls over to the rotten partition, lifts the lid of the trunk and takes out the faded box.

Startled by a sudden noise below her, she hastily climbs back down the ladder to find her grandfather standing at the bottom. He is out of breath and agitated.

"Just now," he says, "can't remember what I said. Get muddled. Probably not right. Take no notice."

Lucy hesitates, sits abruptly on a box among her sea of belongings.

"Grandpa. The other day I went up in the loft to see if there was room to store some of my things. I found a box and documents in that old school trunk. They were behind a partition which had rotted away. Is it to do with Gran and the war?"

Her grandfather has become very still. He stares down at her without smiling. He seems to be struggling for words. Then he says in a tone he has never used to Lucy before, "You have absolutely no right to go up there without permission. You will not touch any papers up there, Lucy. They are private and they belong to me and your grandmother. They are nothing to do with you. You will replace them in the trunk. Do you understand? Martha did not want anyone hurt."

Lucy is stung by his anger. "Grandpa, I wasn't prying. The partition had rotted away. The trunk wasn't locked, the lid is warped and it was half open, with papers falling out. Things have been disturbed by mice nesting . . ." Lucy takes a deep breath. She so wants Fred to tell her the truth. "There was an envelope with a sort of birth certificate inside. I did glance at it, but I didn't understand . . ." But he is not going to.

"Put them back, Lucy. Put them back and shut the trunk up again. Forget them. You must promise me you will make them secure again. Lucy . . . ?"

Fred is breathing heavily and reaches out to hold on to the ladder. He thinks: I promised Martha. I promised I had burned them, but I could not do it. They are all that is left of a whole life . . . She did not want to remember, ever . . . But I thought, when we are both dead, the past will make sense, perhaps to our children . . . But not yet . . . not yet.

He is so distressed, Lucy says quickly, "Gramps, Gramps, don't worry. I promise. I promise I'll make them secure again, I'll shut the trunk up, I promise."

She wants to cry out that this is wrong. Secrets are wrong. We are what we are and who we are, always. Nothing can change that. But she does not.

She takes his arm, reassures him again, changes the subject and talks of supper as they walk back across the garden in the dusk to the house. A dove coos high up in the trees, a fat, comforting sound Lucy always associates with this house and the happy bits of her childhood.

Behind the trees the tide is in, the deepest swollen pewter. Car doors bang. It is the end of evensong. In a moment Barnaby will be home. She will make sure that Martha's box is hidden again, but Lucy knows she will look inside it first.

Grandpa, the gentlest of people, is hiding something. It is to do with Anna, with the war. Lucy needs to know what it is that lies hidden up there. She needs to know the truth.

Chapter 21

He has always enjoyed driving round cities. Sometimes he will rise early, at other times he takes the car out in the evenings and drives round London. He has made himself familiar with the area in which she lives and works, and he has also visited the Swiss bank where her husband works.

Driving a car in busy traffic is challenging and gets the adrenaline going in the same way as taking dangerous jumps on a horse. There is just you in control, judging speed and distance. At home he will get in his car and drive around Berlin late at night. A city never sleeps. From the safety of a warm vehicle, with the rain washing the dark streets clean and the windscreen wipers monotonously moving to and fro, there is the illusion of comfort and safety.

Out there, there are other people walking and driving, eating and dancing. He is not the only one awake at two in the morning. He prefers this to the silence of his suburban flat.

His visit to London is drawing to an end. His lectures are finished. He has no reason to stay. Most days he has driven to Lincoln's Inn. Sometimes, just as other tourists do, he walks past the chambers, soaking up the atmosphere around the busy courts, as if he might, this way, get nearer to her.

On warm days clerks and solicitors are scattered on the grass in the courtyards, sitting on benches munching sandwiches, relaxing.

He imagines that in the summer the grass is covered with prone bodies. The environment is so English. There is a constant buzz in the air as the busy, important-looking black gowns fly to and fro.

He will look at the court lists to see if she is in court that day, then join a small group of people entering the room. Sometimes he takes a notebook. He could be just a faded hack looking for something to fill his column. Just one more gray suit among many gray suits.

It has been fascinating observing Anna Gerstein and the way the judicial system works. It is certainly different from Germany. She is consistent, concise, and very, very quick. She is also formidable as she bandies insults with an opposing QC or apologizes sweetly to the judge.

Today she is representing a baggage handler who had fallen from an airplane and was unlikely to walk again because of some technical reason with the luggage door he finds hard to follow. The insurance company for the airline is contesting the amount of damages. Anna Gerstein, with a theatrical flourish, brings evidence to prove that the airline had known about the faulty door and, either through negligence or human error, it was not put right. She gets maximum compensation, a five-figure sum for her client, a small nervous man, who constantly fingers his collar. He gets the impression she likes to take on the big boys. He is very sure that he would only want this woman to *defend* him.

There is a moment before she leaves the court when she glances his way. He realizes, that like an actor on a stage, she is not necessarily focusing on his face, but his heart jerks all the same. Something, a small toss of her head, her look miles away, a slight turn of the mouth, not a smile. Her expression, *I did it. I got them,* makes him feel suddenly weak and a little sick.

He comes out of court into a wet afternoon. People scurry, heads bent against the rain, hailing taxis, hurrying home. He longs suddenly to be back in his warm flat in Berlin. In a city he knows and understands.

As he reaches his car and is fitting the key into the lock, the woman runs down the court steps with another barrister. Their black gowns whirl about them in the rainstorm as they hurry along the other side of the road, heads bent against the rain.

He fights the sudden urge to run and pull the flying hair away from the woman's eyes, step back, stare into them so that he might judge for himself the arrangement of genes, the composition of bones, the height of cheekbone and texture of skin. Is it the creamy, pure, fair German skin, soft as a child's? How does the hair grow from her scalp? How does it lie about her head? The eyes would tell him all he needs to know, he is sure of it, if only he could get near her.

The need to approach her is painful and strong. He wants to run across the road and grab her, speak to her in his own language, express this compulsion to know what is obsessively filling his heart and his head, drowning out the present with voices and half-forgotten faces that clamor and fill his nights.

Almost as if she is drawn by the intensity of his feelings, again she half turns his way and shivers as if suddenly cold, and the barrister beside her holds his arm up over her shoulders like a black bat, as if to protect her against the weather.

He bends quickly and gets into his car. Hell is this. A strange wet country where he suddenly has no point of reference. No landmark. He cannot atone, appease, voice regret to any human being where it will have any meaning.

He grips the steering wheel. He cannot die before he tries.

This is perhaps his final selfishness. He knows if he disturbs the past he will affect both the present and the future of more lives.

Chapter 22

The small cottage is hot. Lucy throws the windows open to the evening. Way out there in the darkness, men fish and smuggle, with the swoop and shadow of seagulls in their wake.

She thinks of Tristan getting ready to fly to Macedonia. In the dark of nights does he feel fear? He would never tell her. Lucy imagines him up in Nottingham with his parents in that beautiful house with its huge windows and great paintings of fish, collection of reels, maps of rivers, stuffed fish, and beautiful light furniture and squishy old sofas.

She remembers how the light in his bathroom filters through heavenly colored windows, like bathing in a church. Nottingham is home to Tristan, as Cornwall is home to her. He will pad round the house and lie in his room touching base, hugging his mother, talking fishing to his father. Content.

The first time Tristan took her home Lucy was amazed at how close he was to his parents, how affectionate and proud and uncritical they were of him. No constant digs, no wishing he was other than he was, just an abundance of unconditional love.

Lucy smiles. It is why Tris is so nice. He has grown up in a happy, secure Roman Catholic family. She could have gone to Nottingham with him, but she knew in his heart he wanted to go alone, that his mother would want him to herself for a few days before he flew away.

She tries to imagine what his mother will be feeling at the thought of Tristan going out to try to keep order in a dangerous place where the rule of law has completely broken down and life has little value.

She wills Tristan to telephone before she goes up into the loft to stow away some of her things. Just hearing his voice always makes her feel cheerful, but the telephone remains silent and Lucy does not want to ring and interrupt their family evening.

She goes to the landing and pulls the ladder down and climbs up into the dark attic, switching the light on behind the hatch. She carries up two bags of stuffed toys, childhood books, and old A level papers, and pushes them into a space on the right of the hatch. Then she heaves herself onto the dusty boards and over to the trunk. The box lies where she left it. Looking up she sees a small glimmer of light in the roof; a tile must have slipped. She will have to tell Barnaby.

She lifts out a tied bundle of Fred's papers. There are cards, letters with MoD stamped on the envelopes and some of his diaries, dated 1940–45. She gathers the bundle to her. Then, pushing the trunk with her feet, she manages to move it away from the tiny gap in the roof and she shuts the lid firmly.

Lucy carries the bundle downstairs and returns for the box. As she closes the hatch she can feel her heart thudding guiltily. She gets a cloth, wipes off the worst of the dust and puts everything on her bed. She has a bath, gets into her thick childish pajamas, makes herself a mug of tea and climbs into bed.

Curlews warble in small rising songs like distant, far-off hymns.

Lucy sees for the first time that the faded box has an International Red Cross seal across the front. The brown envelope still lies inside on top of the Polish letters.

Lucy picks up Fred's diary dated 1944, but there is no mention of anything domestic, just brief troop movements and maneuvers and training. She lifts some letters held together with a ribbon and sees with surprise it is Fred's writing on the envelopes. Someone has returned his own letters to him.

27 January 1945
My dear Mother,

Please forgive my writing when I am so low, but I need to tell you both the horror I witnessed today. I do not want to believe what I saw. I keep thinking I will wake up and find it was only a nightmare.

Charles, the American intelligence officer, my 2IC, Peter Cohen, together with our driver, Cpl. Miller, lost the rest of our convoy, which was on an observer mission, and we ended up with a Russian unit. The Germans had emptied the camps ahead of the Soviet army and tried to destroy as much evidence as possible. They must have been trying to march the women away from the Russians. The Germans go on killing prisoners even when they know it is all over.

I was in a Land Rover with Charles, driving in miserable, freezing conditions. The Russian convoy was somewhere behind us. We suddenly came upon a huge pile of clothes dumped near a barn. We pulled up, wary, guns ready for any fleeing Germans. We got out of the vehicle and stood looking round us. We caught a movement and froze. Slowly, some rags moved, rose from the pile and swayed and staggered towards us.

At first we couldn't make out what it was. Then, I saw it was a human being. I could not move; none of us could. The hairs rose up on the back of my neck. The figure raised its skeletal arms towards me in a pathetic little plea for help and I saw the little stick legs under the sacking skirt begin to give way and I ran, ran to catch her as she fell. We all moved then. Soldiers ran to the piles upon piles of rags. Ma, they were all women, most were dead, but a few, just a few still lived and breathed. We picked up those living and ran with them in our arms—they weighed nothing—to the mobile hospital down the road. This moment will haunt me all my life.

• • •

30 January

I have been unable to post this letter.

The girl I caught in my arms, that tiny, starved bundle of rags, lies unconscious, ill in hospital. I visit her every day. They tell me she is dying. They found arsenic in her bones. I have not cried since I was eight years old. I cried today.

I want you to tell people, Mother. I want the world to know the savage cruelty that has been happening here. These terrible, terrible death marches away from the horror of the camps full of the dead. Men and women, shuffling in starving columns to be shot, burned alive or starved to death. Make sure people in England know what the Germans have been doing in this war.

Not long now and I will be home. It will be good to ride again with my brother, and breathe fresh, English air. I long to see everyone and hear all the news. I do hope all is well with you.

Love to you both,

Fred.

PS. Two weeks now since I began this letter.

The girl did not die. What a will she has to live. Today, she told me her name. "Marta," she said. "I am Marta Oweska."

Lucy sits motionless, her body icy. She stares at her fingers lying on the page covering her grandfather's words. She folds the letter. Her teeth start to chatter, she shakes uncontrollably and slides down into the warmth of her bed.

Her grandfather told her not to read. He was right. He was right. Lucy rocks and rocks, her arms wrapped round herself, whimpering in the silent, empty house.

Gran . . . Gran . . . Gran. You never got to England. You never reached safety. I didn't know. This is what happened to my flesh and blood. This was my grandmother . . .

Everything is changing, disappearing in the time it takes to read a letter.

I don't want you to be someone else, Gran. I want you to be You, as you have always been. I don't want you to have been a girl who suffered appalling things, things I can't even imagine. I want to think of you as I always have done, safe in London. Meeting Grandpa, growing happy again. I want everything to be as I have always been told. Please, Gran, I want you as you have always been to me.

But Lucy knows this is not possible. She lies in shock, huddled in the bed, staring blankly out of the window. She hears Barnaby come in and take Homer out. She hears him come back and call out. But she cannot move or reply.

She hears the phone going downstairs and Tristan's loud, cheerful voice distantly fills the cottage on the answering machine, but she cannot move, cannot rush to answer it.

Eventually, when all is silent, when deep night has crept into the room, heavy and suffocating as moth wings, Lucy gets up and pulls on Tristan's heavy leather coat and calls Homer and they go out of the garden gate, down the path onto the beach. There is a full moon and the sea is black and silent. Beautiful to her. Peaceful. Safe.

She stands for a long time listening to the night birds away to her right on the mud flats, listening to the soft smack and hiss of the waves, phosphorescent in the dark. Where the wind, ruffling the night sea like feathers, makes shadows and patterns of eerie, changing light, belonging not to this world but to some other mysterious existence below the waves.

Lucy has a choice to make: to read on or to return the box and diaries to her grandfather's trunk. To the past.

* * *

That evening Barnaby walks over to the cottage to give Homer his last walk and finds that Lucy must have gone to bed, but the cottage door is not locked and Homer comes stiffly out looking pleased.

"She really ought to lock the door," Barnaby says to him. "Your guarding days are long gone."

He meets Dave Pasco from the post office on the dark path down to the saltings, walking his aged boxer.

"Barnaby, glad I bumped into you. There was a girl looking for a cottage on a long let. I wondered if you were thinking of letting your cottage again, now young Lucy is leaving?"

"Probably, Dave. I can't afford to leave it empty, much as I'd like to."

"That's what I thought, what with Mrs. Tremain needing . . . Care doesn't come cheap, Vicar, I know that."

"What was she like, this girl?"

"Well . . . different. Bit alternative, if you know what I mean. Rings everywhere. But posh accent . . . pretty. Staying at the Banyan."

Barnaby tries not to laugh. Not too many girls like that around the village. So, Dave doesn't know everything.

"Thank you, Dave. If she is interested in that particular cottage, tell her to get in touch. You know my number?"

"Got it in the post office. OK, Vicar. Regards to the doctor, and your mum, of course. Good night."

"Good night." Barnaby grins to himself in the dark. Dave will have a crisis of confidence when he realizes he was the last to know Kate is working for him.

So, Kate is looking for somewhere in the village? It is very unlikely she will want to live next door to the job.

It is a wonderful evening. The estuary is on a flood tide. It is like being on the prow of a ship, the lights across the causeway glistening in white and yellow paths on the water, and the colors of the night changing rapidly as the moon sails in and out of the clouds.

Homer keeps stopping as if pointing out it is past his bedtime so Barnaby turns reluctantly for home. Perhaps Lucy has already walked him. He loves this time of night when nothing is required of him, when peace descends and night sounds crowd out the worries of the day. Often the loneliness will return, a wistfulness, a yearning for something more, but mostly he feels thankful he had been offered the parish here and not in some inner city where his spirituality would have struggled.

Where would he have been now if Martha and Fred had not needed him? If the only woman he had wanted to marry had been free?

He suddenly realizes he has unconsciously put his life on hold. He does not think: this is all there will ever be, but he cannot think beyond his parents at the moment, beyond the needs of the parish and keeping his head above water. He wakes many mornings and thinks: oh God, get me somehow through this day. But he also has complete faith that God will do just that.

As Barnaby pushes the old dog through the back door of the cottage he sees there is still a light on upstairs. He goes in and calls up the stairs.

"Lucy? I'm just bringing Homer back. Make sure you lock the back door."

He listens, but Lucy doesn't reply and, unwilling to wake her, he walks back across the garden. He peers in at his parents, but they are both sleeping. He showers, says his prayers and switches Radio 4 on low.

Rent for the cottage would be incredibly helpful. But it has to be the right person; the cottage is too near the house to make a mistake. He has, of course, always known that Lucy must leave, but it will be a wrench not to have her around the place.

The familiar ache under his ribs that is the sorrow of his mother's condition, the slow losing of her, swings darkly back: his last thought at night, his first in the morning. He hastily puts the radio up a fraction and listens to the late night short story which happens to be by P. G. Wodehouse and sends him smiling straight to sleep.

Chapter 23

On the plane home to Berlin, the unreality of the last few weeks overcomes him in a fit of mental exhaustion. He had nearly missed his flight. It was stupid to do that detour to hope to see her one last time. Utterly stupid. Yet, he has another image of her now, not in court, not flying about in a black gown. He has the image of a woman happy and elegant with the man she shares her life with.

He'd got in a traffic jam trying to get to Victoria. He was anxious to find the right place to leave the hired Mercedes. At Victoria the train was just leaving. At Gatwick he'd caught his flight with ten minutes to spare.

He immediately has a double whisky and, lulled by the warmth and hum of the plane and odd scraps of conversation that rise and fall around him, he sleeps almost immediately.

When he arrived in Berlin most of his friends were dead. He had no idea where Mutti was and he was unsure of his father's fate, although he believed him dead. The Russians were plowing, seemingly unstoppable, through East Prussia, driving their tanks over anything in their way, especially over the convoys of refugees flying desperately in front of them. Poland was next.

He was sent to Berlin because he was injured, could not hold a gun and was no good anywhere else—sent to join the children, the stricken and the old. He had medical knowledge and he was expected to patch and heal, to work miracles in the rubble.

Exhaustion and lack of sleep, hunger and the sheer unreality of a landscape wiped of known landmarks had the surreal quality of nightmare. Broken buildings smoked and loomed upwards. Children climbed over the rubble, looking for food, clothes, anything that would help them survive. People fought as they looted. Shops and houses were emptied of anything salable, anything that could keep them warm and dry.

Refugees poured in from the east. Houses like rats' nests were made in the rubble and ruins of Berlin. And still the bombers came. First the British, a pause, then the Americans.

A form of unbelief and hysteria settled. Despite the party line, despite the daily shooting of deserters, most no longer gave the salute. Those who did were sometimes spat at.

He no longer had the ability of coherent thought. He bound children's feet. He bandaged wounds with torn sheets. He did what he could for the injured and dying soldiers who stumbled off the trains. He tried to think what he would do when the Russians came.

Often he was so cold and exhausted he did not care if he lived or died. His arm ached where he had been wounded. He was afraid it would get infected. Some mornings he woke and, like the rest of Berlin, felt terrified of what was coming.

He made his way one morning to the flat Mutti had kept in Tiergarten. She had kept it for when they visited Berlin. The house had been bombed, the upstairs completely gone. A bed hung over the edge of an upstairs bedroom; ragged curtains blew from a window left in half a wall.

He climbed over the rubble and peered down at what had been their ground-floor flat. The door was buried, but there was a broken window through which he could climb down into the dark. He lit a match. The room was littered with broken glass and pictures, but was still discernible as a room he remembered: there, a chair, where it had always been. Mutti's small desk was covered in dust, but when he opened a drawer, there was her writing, neat and sure and slanting in ledgers and on envelopes.

He knelt in the dust and eerie silence and wept, holding her unsent letter tight in his hands, weeping for himself and a normality and order he had almost forgotten.

He crawled through a doorway and pulled a blanket from a bed covered in rubble. He looked for food, but there was none. A tap was dripping and he placed his bottle under it. Going back into the main room he wound the blanket around himself and slept. He felt hot and feverish and very strange.

When he woke it was almost dark. Hurrying, he left the blanket, grabbed his water bottle and tried to hide the broken window from outside. This was his place; he would return. It was somewhere recognizable in the middle of chaos. He made his way back to his post as fast as he could, not wanting to be shot as a deserter.

When he reached his post there was a rumor that the Red Army was only a day away. He looked around him at children with guns that had the wrong ammunition, took in the motley, pathetically inadequate little army of old men, young boys, and injured soldiers like him who could hardly hold a gun.

His injured arm probably saved him. The next day he was full of fever, almost delirious. The sky was dark with planes. The Russians were bombing Berlin in readiness.

An old doctor pulled him off the rubble as he was trying to clean his gun. "You are useless here, you cannot even hold a gun. Get to the hospital, where at least when the fever has gone you can be of some use."

As he stumbled off, the doctor called, "Get rid of your uniform, boy."

The plane circles for landing. The lights of Berlin twinkle below him. Welcoming. He is glad to be home. He feels that edge of . . . not sadness exactly, more a sense of being alone and returning to a house in darkness. It is a time when he would have rung Inga and asked her to supper. She is quite right. In the morning he would possibly have made it clear he had things to do.

They land with a bump and he thinks suddenly, startling himself: should I have married? Had children? Would the feeling of loss, of missing something fundamental in life, have tied me to a woman in gratitude, an intimacy I have never experienced? Would love for a woman who was the mother of my children have been different?

He gathers his things together, smiles briefly at the air stewardess. He will never know.

Reaching home, he slides the glass doors back and stares down at Berlin below him. Beautiful, modern, vibrant. To him, anyway. He had watched it built anew, divided into four pieces, then divided by a wall. The seams no longer show. Just a few bricks left in a road, a constant reminder.

Did I make a life? A small random gene which survived all, to become successful and clever and procreate a chromosome of me in her turn, that I might live on? That my life might have some point, some meaning?

Is this to be my last vanity? The last ultimate cruelty which makes up the sum total of what I am?

Chapter 24

Anna sits at the large oak desk in her chambers and looks out at the plane tree whose leaves are just beginning to unfurl. Telephones ring at regular intervals in the building. She hears the soft voice of her clerk talking to the typist next door.

She loves this room with its high ceilings and cornices, its great rattling windows and soft colors. She found the desk at an antique sale years ago and the size and solidness of it, taking up the space between her and a client, is reassuring and comforting.

In the old days, when she was a young barrister, the anxiety, the terror, the hopelessness of the people sitting with their solicitors on the other side of her desk would disturb her. All their hopes were pinned on her and she needed the solidity of oak to make a distance between the smell of their anxiety and her clinical and detached judgment.

She has kept the room uncluttered. The wide pine floorboards are polished and covered with rugs. There is one small armchair in the corner by the large fireplace. In the bottom cupboard there is a kettle and some Earl Grey tea bags. When she has clients Alice brings coffee in on a tray.

In the top cupboard she has a small mirror, a bright blue papier-mâché bowl Rudi bought her, containing a lipstick and moisturizer, and a stand with her wig on it. Sometimes, when she is alone she places the wig on her head and looks into the mirror and knows how she will look when she is old, when her hair is totally gray, the texture of it no longer soft to touch, but springy and wiry. She will take it quickly off her head and replace it on the stand, irritated by herself.

Anna has a contempt for useless vanity, but she is aware she has held back those invisible years, when suddenly without warning a woman disappears. One day you can be walking down a street in spring with a lilt to your step and people turn or smile at the picture you make, the way your hair bounces, the slimness of your figure, the femaleness that is you. Then suddenly, it is gone. You can wear the same clothes you wore yesterday, your hair is just as newly washed but no eyes follow you. You have vaporized, never to be uniquely remembered as *you* again. You have disappeared into the next generation overnight, without even realizing it, because you feel just the same.

Anna has always been stunning. She still is. She is *not* invisible. The job she does, the power she wields make this impossible. But she is aware that the years are beginning to be held back with difficulty. She no longer thinks of her body as taut and as perfect as she can make it. The slackness of her skin depresses her. She has less time to play tennis.

Before she met Rudi it did not seem to matter so much. She did not really think about her body, as women with good bodies can avoid doing until middle age. Ambitious and work-driven, her mind had never dwelled on the trivia that goes with being female.

A wisp of something an older friend once said to her comes swinging back.

"What was so frightening, Anna, was, here I was, a professor, eminent in my field, well thought of, always spoiled and lauded because I was pretty as well as clever. Well, as my looks faded, so did my confidence. It dived in a terrible spiral. Yet, I was just as clever, just as worthy. Nothing had changed, only outside the lecture hall I wasn't fancied anymore, and I despised myself for minding so much, for letting my confidence ebb away into space.

For realizing that despite my cleverness, I perceived myself with men's eyes."

Anna gets up from her desk and bends her head to the heavy scent of narcissi sitting in a vase on her desk. She is waiting for Rudi to pick her up on his way back from a meeting. She has promised not to work late tonight and starts to put the case file she is working on into her briefcase. The buzzer goes on her desk and the receptionist's tinny voice tells her that Rudi is in reception and should she send him up?

"No, I'm on my way down," Anna says.

She pulls her suede jacket off the back of her chair as Alice comes in.

"Anna, you're looking tired. I hope you're going to relax while you're away."

Anna smiles. "I'll try. I'll switch my mobile on in the car, so don't be afraid to ring me, and I've left my number on my pad. If the CPS get in touch about my letter, let me know . . ."

She laughs suddenly at herself as she watches her clerk's face. Alice has been with Anna for eight years. She is totally competent to deal with anything that might come up in twenty-four hours.

"OK, OK, I'm going . . . I'm going."

Rudi turns and smiles at her as she comes down the stairs, his face crinkling with pleasure. Anna experiences one of those rare moments of pure contentment. She is looking forward to getting out of London. They walk together to the courtyard where Rudi has parked his car. Anna gets in and fastens her seat belt. As they pull away from the curb, Anna notices a green Mercedes pull out behind them. She has seen it before, parked on meters near the court.

"Do you think it's the Mafia, that green Mercedes?" she asks Rudi. "Perhaps my timid Mr. Brown is really a Godfather!"

Rudi doesn't smile. He has noticed it before too. "Have you mentioned it to Security?"

"Darling, I was only joking! You know all Mercedes owners notice other Mercedes."

When they pull up at lights Rudi reaches for a pen and jots down the registration.

"You're not really worried?" Anna wishes she had not said anything.

"No. I'm just cautious by nature. It comes with being a banker."

Rudi does not tell Anna that his own security people have told him someone had been making discreet inquiries about them both. Or that he has seen the car near the house. He knows with the sort of cases Anna excels in she is bound to have made enemies and there is the security of his bank to consider.

As he negotiates the heavy evening traffic, Anna says, "I've got an adjournment for a couple of days and as I've got a meeting in Bristol tomorrow, I thought I might stay the night and then drive on to Cornwall to see my parents."

"Good idea," Rudi says.

Without taking his eyes off the traffic, he reaches out to touch her hand. "The break will do you good. You're working too hard, Anna. Shall we eat out?"

He looks in his mirror. The Mercedes swung away to the left long ago, but he feels unaccountably anxious.

"Just drive carefully tomorrow. The weather is about to break. They have gales down in the West Country and there will probably be heavy rain. Anna, maybe you'd be better driving this car all that way. It's heavier."

Anna laughs. "Rudi, I love my car. I am not swapping my zippy little Merc for this great heavy tank. Let's try the Italian. It shouldn't be booked midweek."

"Have you rung your brother? Does he know you're going?"

"No," Anna smiles. "I thought I would surprise them all."

Chapter 25

In the stillness of the night Lucy peers at the fading, browning photographs of a Polish family she knows nothing about. As she turns them over, she sees they have names, these people, written on the back of the photographs. There are dates, and places she has never heard of. "Slovakia 1823." "Uncle Karel's fourth birthday." "Frieda and Marik's wedding, 1917." "Mary in the garden in Lodz." "Marta and cousin Anya aged two and three, Krakow 1926."

Lucy sits up and turns to the light. Two little girls, Marta . . . and cousin Anya, muffled up in coats with big buttons and scarves and stout shoes, standing outside a door in the snow. The photograph is so old, their faces are blurred smooth of features, but they have a likeness, belong to a family Lucy never knew existed.

Lucy turns to a small bundle of letters addressed to Marta Oweska, all written in Polish. She puts these aside. There are another three letters with Marta's name on, tied with a faded ribbon, but with no address, as if they had been delivered by hand.

Carefully, Lucy undoes the ribbon and eases the first letter out of the envelope. They are written in German, which Lucy reads with difficulty because of the fragile state of the paper.

My dear Marta,

I write this letter with great reluctance. You have brought much joy to me and I will always think of you as I would my own daughter. You know, of course, that your father and I have been friends since we were students. That time is over. It is dangerous for both our families.

My dear, you know why I write. You really must not meet my son again, even if he asks you to ride with him. Life to him is a game in which you could lose your life. He is at the moment in Berlin with his mother. He will come back believing himself omnipotent. I am sure your papa does not know that you still have contact with him. If you can, keep the happy days in your heart. Look after your parents, be strong for them, Matusia.

Heinrich Saurer.

Lucy folds the letter in its old creases and replaces it in the envelope. The next envelope has the address scrawled out and has been returned to sender. Two different pieces of writing paper fall out.

The first letter is almost unreadable: the ink has run; the German is halting and stilted.

Dr. Saurer,

Do not worry. I have stayed this side of the hedge for many weeks now. It is quite impossible for me not to realize what is happening to fam . . . like ours, Jewish families. The world is closing in. We are losing everything. My father is trying to . . . for me to join Aunt Rena in England, so you see you . . . not feel responsible for me. I have grown up very quickly. I realize that even having been friendly with Jews will be dangerous for you and y . . . family.

We have known your family all our lives. But our life has ended and we can do nothing. Do you know that I cannot go to school anymore? Do you know Papa cannot practice any longer, anywhere, as a doctor? Do you . . . the shops are not allowed to serve us? Of course you know. Papa gave up everything to work in the clinic with you. He trusted you.

I do not understand. No one does. I remember your friendship

> *and your kindness but I am no longer the child . . . once knew. I am forced to watch my parents shrivel with humiliation and lose every shred of dignity, everythi . . . they have worked so hard for all these years.*
>
> *I am no longer Marta, your friend. I do not exist for you and you do not exist for me . . .*

The letter trembles in Lucy's hand. It is not her parents' humiliation Marta writes about, this teenage girl, but her own, and the bitterness of the child/woman burns into Lucy as if it has just been written, not folded and fading with the years in a trunk in an attic in another country.

The second piece of paper, undated, states baldly in German:

> *I return your letter. Do not contact my family in any way. Do not ever presume on my husband's friendship. Both my husband and son are serving the glorious Third Reich.*
>
> *Frau Saurer.*

A breeze brings, through the open window, a scent of summer, a heavy musty smell of creek mud and flowers. Lucy slides down the bed, holding on to the box. She feels heavy with a sadness that seeps into her bones in an ache, like the onslaught of fever.

A discovery once started cannot be abandoned, but the unfolding of it will leave her changed. She remembers at school asking the history teacher how it was possible that people in England did not know about the concentration camps. She remembers watching old black-and-white newsreels avidly, because Gran was Polish. She was always proud of having a Polish grandmother; it made her different. She had told people her grandmother had escaped from Poland to safety and met her grandfather in London. It was a romantic story.

It is almost impossible to take in that this girl who wrote these letters is Gran. It is as if her grandmother has become someone else. The comfortable, funny grandmother of her childhood, so terribly English in her ways, was once a girl in a brutal, unknown landscape, who suffered unspeakable things that she can never talk about. Gran was not safely in England. She was a part of history captured in those harrowing newsreels that Lucy watched in an English classroom.

Gran is someone else, and she must be too. For she, Lucy, is the result of what became of her grandmother. She, Lucy, is the end of the story.

Half asleep, Lucy goes on turning and peering at the dark serious faces of this large extended Jewish family. Did they all perish? Were they all wiped out, leaving her grandmother quite alone? The thought seems insupportable in its horror. It is beyond her imagination.

She thinks about Barnaby, and her mother and her grandparents and her friends and people in the village just disappearing, never to be heard of again. It is beyond her imagination.

She lies with her fingers touching a photograph of a little girl, sitting on a stool in a garden, hands on her knees, beaming out at the photographer in that serious, happy way small children have at the importance of their likeness being captured forever. She is without a care in the world.

The writing on the back of the photograph is faded and almost unreadable. Once it stated in a proud and joyous hand, "My Matusia, 1928."

Lucy imagines the young parents who wrote on the back of their little girl's photograph, proud and happy, believing a whole life was before them. She sees them older, defeated. Unable to protect that small life they had brought into the world.

She folds the letters and puts them away with the documents. She fingers the box and the yellowing pages, afraid they will crumble and disappear like the silenced lives, burning behind the haunting photographs.

Chapter 26

They gallop and the horses' hoofs are muffled by the soft wet pine needles on the floor of the forest. Overhead, early sun slants sideways from the moving green sky, flickering and catching, flashing dark and light, dark and light.

They gallop neck and neck on the track, and Marta bends over the mare's neck as the low branches reach out like slim fingers to catch her face, pull her hair loose. She glances at the boy and laughs. She is going to win this morning, she is going to win.

The boy's face is set as he crouches over his horse's neck. He cannot bear to lose, and Marta feels the laughter bubble up inside her. She smells the sweat of her horse, the damp leaves, and the scent of her hair, which Hanna washed for her last night in rainwater and lavender.

She grips the mare with her knees as she stumbles. She urges her forward, faster and faster as she sees the edge of the forest and sunlight ahead. The leather saddle under her squeaks as she leans over the horse's neck and then they are out, out into sunlight and she has won. She has won.

She wheels the horse round and the laughter bursts out of her as she sees his furious face.

"You cheated!" he shouts. "You had a head start. You know perfectly well you did."

Her hair is wrapped around her face; she has lost her ribbon. She jumps off the horse and gives her her head and the mare immediately dips her soft mouth to the wet grass.

Marta holds her hair from her eyes and peers up at the boy to see if he is going to remain sulky. After the trees the sun is warm, and she lifts her face, closes her eyes against his cross face, trying to swallow the laughter. He needs always to win.

When she opens her eyes again, his face has changed. He dismounts and stands staring at her. Marta smiles but he does not smile back, just goes on looking at her with that strange intensity. His eyes turn a deeper blue, full of specks and stars. He moves nearer and she hears the sound of his quick breathing, feels it on her cheek. The hairs of her arm, where they almost touch, tingle.

She is very still. Behind her in the forest, only the sound of leaves falling. She is afraid of the suffocating feeling in her chest, the sudden awareness of her body, the tightness of her bodice as her breasts press against the material. She shivers suddenly and steps back as the blood comes to her face. She lets go of her hair and it flows like a shawl around her, hiding her face, and she is grateful.

The boy moves then and grins suddenly, takes a piece of string out of his pocket. "Here, let me tie your hair out of your eyes or you will kill yourself riding home."

Marta turns her back and he plaits her hair down her neck like he plaits his horse's mane. She feels his fingers on her neck and she shivers again and those fingers stop and move for a moment up into the warmth under her hair and stay there, cold for a second, still.

Then he goes on plaiting and as he ties the string to the end of her hair they hear what sounds like distant thunder. It rumbles across the valley, yet the sky is blue against the rising sun.

She feels his hand freeze on the small of her back and he moves away, staring down the misty valley, squinting into the distance. The noise is moving towards them like a swarm of bees. Marta looks upwards and sees wave upon wave of planes in the distance. They fill the sky with their noise, flying east and southwest, and the shadow of them blots out the sun.

Without turning, he says softly, "Get on your horse! Get on your horse and ride for home. Quickly!"

She stares at him, unable to move. He turns abruptly and lifts her, almost throws her onto the mare. "Ride back the way we came. Don't stop for anything until you reach home."

Marta looks down at his face. It is frightened and strangely excited.

"Why? What is happening? Why aren't you coming back with me?" Marta knows what those planes mean, but she does not want to believe it.

The boy's eyes blaze. He stares at her, distant, withdrawn, no longer with her. "I ride to my friends. I must be with them for this moment." He hesitates, then suddenly his voice is hard and cold, the way he can be sometimes. "When you get home, tell your father the Germans are invading Poland . . ."

He turns her horse round and brings his whip down hard on its rump, and her head jerks as the horse leaps forward and Marta clings on as they fly back under the dark green trees, sunlight flashing and catching, flashing and catching. Back over the thick pine needles while foam collects round the horse's mouth and sweat forms on her shiny neck like a white necklace.

Marta thinks she will fall off from fright. She throws the reins at the groom and flies across the lawn and over the hedge and across her own lawn where Papa is watching for her. He sees her coming and throws open the door and pulls her in, holds her tight to him.

"The Germans . . . the Germans are invading Poland," Marta whispers, ashen and shaking, collapsing against him.

"I know. I heard the planes, but they are nowhere near Warsaw, Marta. Thank God. Marta, you must never, ever creep out of this house alone again . . . Your mother must not know . . ."

Why isn't Papa angry? She has disobeyed him. She did not believe him about the boy. She did not believe that the Germans would invade Poland. Marta is trembling. All she can think is: he left me alone. He left me to ride home alone. A bitter sense of betrayal fills her.

Papa is watching her face. He knows.

He says quietly, "The outside world will be closed to us. Your childhood is over, Matusia. It ends here, today." He takes her hand, pulls her into a chair, his face gray and urgent, and Marta is afraid.

"I have sheltered you for as long as possible against all that is happening. It has been easier because we live in the country and you have not had to be confronted daily with the sights on the Warsaw streets. But you are not blind, you are not deaf. Hanna talks to you. Now you have to grow up quickly and face the truth. We are Jews, my child, and that means the collapse of friendships and many more betrayals . . ." He turns Marta's hands in his own. His eyes, as they meet hers, are full of sorrow but firm. "The house next door no longer exists. Germans are not permitted to be friends of Jews. Never put them to the test again, Marta."

Marta is very cold. The boy whistled to her from a cold dawn, the long low whistle that meant he had the horses ready and waiting. Marta could not resist the smell of rain, the sound of the horses outside or the boy her father mistrusted. They were friends.

That day was the last day she laughed for the sheer joy of being alive, of being free in the soft blue beginning of a new day . . .

Lucy opens the door softly and peers in at Martha. Martha has been restless all day. She is asleep but the sheet and blanket are mangled round her legs and her eiderdown has fallen to the floor. Lucy tidies the bed and tucks Martha's legs back inside. She pulls the eiderdown up over her slight body, tucks it round her shoulders.

She watches Martha's face. She is not sleeping peacefully and she begins to toss and turn as Lucy stands there. Lucy sits on the bed and strokes Martha's hair. After a while her breath seems more even and her body becomes still. Lucy tiptoes out, shutting the door carefully.

She goes into the garden and listens to the bell ringers. In a week she will not be here to check up on Gran, to calm her on the bad days when Martha is unable to follow the sequence of a day and becomes anxious and frightened. Will Barnaby have time? Will he remember?

The sky is purple. The clouds hang low and heavy, trapping the air. All her life, since she was a tiny child left with feckless au pairs, overstrict nannies and horrible boarding schools, she had only to pick up a phone and hear her grandmother's voice to know nothing bad could really happen. The gentle voice would flow on and on like soothing music until it had comforted and healed.

There has always been something unsaid between the two of them. From her birth her umbilical cord led back to Martha, not Anna. And now she is leaving her. There is a possibility Martha could die while Lucy is away and the thought is unbearable. Lucy makes a run for the cottage as the first burst of rain slants suddenly from the violet sky.

Chapter 27

At breakfast the owner of the hotel hands Kate a piece of paper.

"Dave Pasco rang. He says if you are still interested in renting a cottage in the village to give the vicar a ring. His niece, Lucy, is going to live in London and the cottage might be free." She stares at Kate, "I thought you . . ."

Kate grins. "I do work for him. I didn't know the cottage was going to be rented. Thank you."

"You will have to talk to the vicar, find out what his plans are."

See if he wants me in the cottage, you mean, Kate thinks.

"It needs a coat of paint and you'll have to like the sound of church bells." The woman smiles at Kate and moves away.

Kate's fingers curl round the piece of paper. She feels a surge of excitement. That little cottage is practically on the beach . . . She reins herself in. Things seldom fall into your lap just like that. The vicar might not want her so close. She walks through the village towards the church. She does not know the best time to approach Barnaby. She does not know the hours vicars work and she does not want to catch him at a bad time. She will go and look at the cottage first.

Kate is wearing pale yellow jeans, a multicolored jacket she bought in Bombay and her new light walking boots as she plans to walk on along the coastal path.

This morning she noticed her short hair was starting to grow again and her pale face was turning brown in the wind and salt air. She is beginning to feel different already. The compulsion to chop her long brown hair off after Karachi, after Dora died, is gone. The defiant, childish impulse with a group of friends at Glastonbury to have a nose ring has somehow faded.

She stands inside the church gate, looking across the road to the cottage. The small windows are thrown open to the day and there is the soft thud of music from inside. The windows and door do need a coat of paint but it does not detract from the small but perfect proportions of the cottage and the surge of pleasure she feels at the sight of it.

She lifts her face to a pale yellow sun, sighs, doesn't even realize she is smiling. She cannot tear herself away and stands there in a patch of sunshine, leaning against the church gate, looking across at the house.

She does not hear Barnaby come out of the church and walk down the path towards her until he is at the gate. Startled, she turns, meets his amused brown eyes and is embarrassed at her transparent joy.

"Good Heavens! You must be the person interested in renting a cottage in the village. How do you do?" Barnaby holds out his hand solemnly. He is laughing at her and Kate feels her face redden.

"Yes, it's me," she says, suddenly self-conscious to be found lurking outside the church.

"Dave is going to be mortified at losing his grip on the village hierarchy." Barnaby looks down at Kate's hand: it is small and very feminine with shell-pink nails. The touch of that hand makes Barnaby feel a pleasure he has almost forgotten. It is a young hand.

"Would you like to have a look inside?" he asks. "It's quite small."

"There's only me," Kate says.

Barnaby pushes the garden gate open against some overhanging branches.

"I must cut this back," he mutters, and turns and holds the branches back so that she can pass. "I warn you, Lucy is packing, so heaven knows what it's like inside . . . Lucy?" he calls. "Lucy, are you there?"

He guides Kate through the back door and they stand in a small quarry-tiled kitchen. There is a flurry and a crash from upstairs and a loud "Oh, shit!"

"Lucy!" Barnaby calls severely, but Kate can tell he is neither shocked nor cross. "Can you come down? We have a visitor."

Lucy appears disheveled and flustered, and Kate sees immediately the timing is wrong. She makes a deprecating face at Lucy, who doesn't smile back.

"Kate is looking for somewhere in the village to rent, Lucy."

Lucy stares at Kate without expression and Kate says quickly, "I'm sorry, I didn't mean to barge in. I was going to wait, ring later, but the vicar—"

"Barnaby," Barnaby says.

"—found me out there leering at the cottage and I think he felt honor bound to do something about me before I was carted away. Sorry, Lucy, it's obviously the wrong time."

Lucy relents against such honesty and sniffs. "Well, it's got to be done. Someone's got to move in. It's just I think of the cottage as mine and I can't bear the thought of anyone else living here."

"I don't blame you. I wouldn't either. And I wouldn't like anyone looking round while I was still here."

Barnaby, watching Kate, thinks she is handling Lucy perfectly.

"Lucy, could you show Kate round while I dash back to the house to get my briefcase and have a quick word with Mrs. Biddulph?"

Lucy, who is wearing faded jeans and a not very white sweatshirt, is looking at Kate's wonderful jacket. She would like to dislike her for even thinking of moving into the cottage, but she can't quite manage it.

"This is the kitchen, very small as you can see, but it's OK.

Hall . . . downstairs loo there . . . and beyond, the porch to the front door, which we never use. Here's the sitting room. This is great because it's so big—obviously two rooms knocked into one . . ." Lucy is galloping Kate around as quickly as possible.

She bounds up the stairs with Kate behind her. The landing is full of boxes and bags of rubbish. "Excuse the tip . . . Bathroom, badly in need of something. I've just got used to it, don't notice. Biggest bedroom looks out over the garden. It's where Anna sleeps when she's here. Right, here is my bedroom, not so big, but I can see the sea from my bed and I can hear the creek birds in my sleep . . ."

Kate can tell Lucy is near to tears and turns quickly away to look at the view. Beyond the church spire, blue water shines, and Kate aches, almost trembles with wanting to live here.

She turns back into the room as Barnaby calls out and comes up the stairs. She is just in time to see Lucy move a box sharply with her toe so that it slides underneath the bed and out of sight.

"What are you going to do in London, Lucy?" she asks.

"Teach. English and foreign students. Then I'm going to Milan for three months on an exchange."

"Lucky you."

They go back downstairs and Barnaby makes coffee, and Kate asks Lucy where she is going to live and extols the virtues of Notting Hill. Tells her of her own love of London and what fun it can be.

"So why did you leave London if you love it so much?"

"Because I've lived in cities for too many years and suddenly I needed a change."

"What did you do?"

"I worked for various charity organizations, mostly in the Far East. Then I worked on a travel magazine for a few months in London. Nepotism. My aunt was editor."

Lucy is impressed. They carry their coffee out into the small secluded garden framed by a large escallonia hedge that hides Martha and Fred's house.

Kate looks back at the cottage with its slate overhang. It is a pretty shabby gingerbread house and she loves it. It seems to her it is just crouched, waiting for her.

"What is the history of the house?" she asks Barnaby.

"My father was left the huge house you can just see through the trees by his grandfather. It is an exceedingly ugly house and very dark. Fred sold off the house and kept the grounds to build a house for him and Martha. They wanted to position it so that it got the sun all day. That is why everything is so faded!"

"Gran made the garden out of nothing," Lucy says.

"My parents moved down from London as soon as they could after the war. They lived here in the cottage, which was part of the estate, while the house was being built, so the cottage has lots of happy memories. It was their first real home together, but too small for a family, and my mother feels the cold. The cottage does not get the sun all day." He smiles at Kate. "They met in London during the war. Martha, who, as you know, is Polish, was living there and Fred was on leave. Love at first sight, I believe."

"How wonderful. Were you born here?"

"I was born over in the house. My sister, Anna, was born in London, before they moved down, but Lucy was very nearly born here. Anna insisted I drove her back to London to have the baby because she was booked into a private clinic. However," he grins at Lucy, "Lucy was such a horrible baby, she was soon back in the cottage, with a fierce nanny."

"I've spent more time in this cottage than anywhere else." Lucy's face is suddenly sad.

"Even when she was small she always wanted to sleep over here, rather than in the house," Barnaby tells Kate.

"The graveyard didn't worry you?"

"No, I'm rarely spooked."

"I hope I'm not holding you up," Kate says to Barnaby as he flicks quickly through his diary. She is holding him up—he should be in Penzance— but he doesn't mind. He needs to be sure before he offers her the cottage.

"I think you'll be bored," Lucy says. "You're used to the bright lights and things. Nothing much happens down here. It can be lonely unless you've grown up here, you know."

Kate smiles. "Are you trying to put me off?"

For the first time Lucy smiles back. "No, not really. Just curious about why someone should come so far, and why here?"

"I don't know, Lucy. Perhaps I shall find out."

Lucy stares at her, surprised, for this makes perfect sense. "What do you think of the cottage, then?" she asks.

Conscious that Barnaby has been watching her closely, Kate says, "I think you know what I feel. I dare not even think about living here because I want to so much."

Admiring Kate's honesty, Lucy laughs suddenly, throwing her hair back, her eyes lighting up, her mouth open to show almost perfect white even teeth. She is very pretty and it is like the sun coming out. Kate feels again that little surge of fear for her, a sense of wanting to protect her. A sort of innocence Kate feels she has lost. The joy of a moment.

"What do you think, Barnes?" Lucy asks provocatively, knowing perfectly well it is something that should be discussed privately. "I think if we *have* to let the cottage, Kate should have it. It makes perfect sense." She turns to Kate. "This cottage belongs to my mother as well as Barnaby. She would have liked to have charged me rent. Now I'm going, she will be over the moon because Barnaby has no excuse not to rent it out."

"Lucy, you are the end," Barnaby says mildly.

Kate hands Lucy her empty mug. "I must go. Thanks for the coffee. Thanks for showing me round, Lucy."

She turns to Barnaby. "I know you'll need to think about it, but could you let me know sort of soon?" She meets his eyes, trying not to show too much hope, which could be off-putting.

Barnaby is amused and touched by her longing to have the cottage.

"As far as I'm concerned, it's yours to rent if you would like it.

But, I'm afraid I would have to ask ninety pounds a week and I think you should be sure you want to live right on top of where you work, Kate."

Kate's face lights up. "I'm sure." She laughs. "I'm quite sure. I don't need to think about it."

"Then it's yours," Barnaby says. Kate is standing close to him and she smells of lemon grass, and her happiness is wonderfully contagious.

Kate says good-bye and moves quickly to the garden gate, the branches of the overhanging tree catching her hair as she passes out into the road. She runs to the beach and up onto the dunes and walks fast for nearly a mile before she slows down, exultant. Oh, that cottage, that blissful little cottage. How bloody perfect life is.

Chapter 28

BERLIN

The day is mild and still. He drives out to the woods to walk. Squirrels dive up and down trees. It is early on a weekday and quiet—just the sound of birdsong. Walking always calms him. He used to come here when he was a student.

The brain hoards isolated moments of seemingly unimportant data, like photographs pushed into a desk and forgotten. Conversations surface, filtering upwards, as though through cobwebs.

He was fourteen when Mutti took him back to Prussia to visit relations. She drove him to the house she had grown up in. He found it as austere as the surroundings and people. He was quizzed by distant cousins about his activities and his loyalty to the Führer. He was put on huge horses and made to practice baton charges with a sword as if he were a Mongol from the Steppes.

Something in his Prussian cousins' fervor had been catching. He suddenly yearned to be that fearless. And he began to understand why his mother was so proud of the family she rarely saw. And why she was so prejudiced.

When he was small Mutti had always seemed beautiful and strong, almost perfect. She brought him up to believe it was possible to achieve anything. He only had to reach out and success and power could be his.

Unlike his father. Mutti considered his father weak; whispered to him that he must be the man of the family. Told him he was like *her* father. Like her. Told him time and again how proud his Prussian grandfather would have been of him, to remember always that he had aristocratic blood. Much was expected of him. He must not let her down.

His mother was a beautiful woman who became bitter. She hated to be reminded she had Polish blood. She had adored her father and disliked her poor mother, who, as far as he could tell, died early to get away from them both, leaving them her money and her Polish home.

By the time he died, his Prussian grandfather, who was fervently anti-Polish, had spent his wife's fortune and left his mother with little, except the house in Poland, which had been neglected and managed by a Polish family. His grandfather had refused to allow any of his wife's money to be wasted on her Polish property.

After his death his mother moved to Berlin where she met his father. He has seen photographs of her at this time. At eighteen, she was amazingly beautiful. His father had money. His family had been shipped out at the beginning of the century to populate annexed Polish territory with German blood.

Like her father, Mutti was very good at spending. At first, he supposes, she must have been happy and grateful that his father poured money into the estate and set up a thriving clinic on the edge of the woods. But she was bored easily. She loved the house but missed the city. Ideally she would have liked her lifestyle transferred to Berlin.

If Mutti had not reminded him at every turn that the family next door were *Jews,* another species altogether, might he have behaved differently? In memory, has he mitigated, chosen to forget his own adolescent love of power, his excitement and vanity as he strutted about exercising it? A power that grew and swelled with the invasion of Poland and his mother's idolatry of Hitler.

She encouraged him to laugh at his father, to despise his father's *love of Jews.* When he was young he could never have admitted to her he admired the Jewish family next door. They were interesting, educated. They had European books, American literature, medical books even his father had not heard of before they came to Warsaw. He liked them. Especially the girl.

Her laughter is what he remembers most, the infectious ripple as it rose and fell over the garden that rolled to the edge of the forest. Playing hide-and-seek with her, jumping out at her under the great spreading branches of the apple tree.

He remembers when they were small how his mother would sit disapprovingly under that apple tree, watching as they rode down the drive, he and his father and the little girl. That girl was fun and wild, ahead of her time. He sees that now.

Strange, she was the nearest he ever came to having a female friend. He introduced her to her passion for horses. She loved the freedom, the speed, the excitement and danger of riding.

She was the one person he could not frighten. She grew used to his moods, stared his cruelty in the face until it grew pointless. Guessed, perhaps, that Mutti beat him for playing with her so often. The girl accepted him as he was, while they were young.

Later, as she slowly grew beautiful, blossomed, her body swelling and curving, the passing touch of her hand would make his adolescent limbs shake. But it all came to an end . . . He had to make her into just another Jew—all that family. Not human, nor desirable but dirty, subhuman, dangerous. He had to.

There are always choices, he thinks. Your father chose one way and you another.

It is these things, these small snapshots, that constantly take him back to the garden of that Polish house. He can hear Mutti's voice, his father's and *hers.* Voices whispering in the dark. They have always been with him. There are a hundred ways of shutting them out. Drink. Working too hard. Women.

It is not that he does not know himself. He knows himself only too well. Now, it is hard to recognize the boy he was, terrifying to recall the cruelty of him. It has become impossible to tell what was truly venomous in him and what was abject fear for himself. Like a schizophrenic he has separated the boy from the man. Before the war. After the war. A line. A door shutting.

Mutti became a bitter old woman. Defeat of the Fatherland. End of her love affair with her Führer. He once heard her called Frau Hitler by some laughing youths.

She did not live to see the new prosperous West Berlin. Money poured in from the West, a safeguard against Soviet communism. Theater and music thrived. Industry was regenerated. In the fifties she frowned at the freedom, the chance, of his generation to be young again. To ride their bicycles round the woods and swim and picnic by the lakes.

She would have loved the theaters and art galleries and museums that sprang up. Berlin was split, but everyone could walk easily between the two, enjoying the culture of both. But Mutti was no longer young and beautiful, so perhaps she would not have gone.

She walked along the Unter den Linden at the end of the war, down the avenue where the embassies and official buildings of the German Empire had been, and wept at the ruins of it all around her. The world had moved on, but Mutti could not.

She did not live to see him qualify as a doctor or made a professor at the Freie Universität. She died in her half-renovated flat, her drawer full of Hitler memorabilia.

When he buried her, he wished he had known when and how his father died. He always imagined him lying in the snow and being left there to die.

He wishes his father could have known that he became a doctor, as he had always hoped. He pledged to do good and to heal the sick. He wishes he could have told him that he meant it. He spent his whole working life specializing, perfecting, finding new ways to knit broken bones together.

But he knows himself, knows the coldness in him is inherent. It is not caused by the war, it lies deep in his psyche. It has always been there.

Chapter 29

Lucy wakes to insistent knocking on the back door of the cottage. Finding her mother on the doorstep she is startled and furious.

"You've no right to descend without letting us know. You could easily have rung to say you were coming. You were just trying to catch me out, I know you were, Anna."

Anna sighs. "You may not believe this, Lucy, but the world does not revolve around you. I had a meeting in Bristol yesterday afternoon so it was logical to drive on down." She drops her overnight bag in the hall. "I'm only here for a night and I don't want to argue. Lucy, I don't have to ask your permission to stay in my own cottage."

She moves past Lucy into the kitchen. "Is Barnaby taking a service? There's a light on in the church. I didn't like to go to the house in case I woke Martha and Fred."

"Barnaby's taking Holy Communion. He always does on Thursdays."

Anna leans past Lucy to switch the kettle on. "Is there any hot water? I'd like a shower, Lucy, then I'll make us breakfast."

"Plenty of hot water, go ahead," Lucy mutters. "Don't know what the bathroom's like."

"I'll take these upstairs with me, then." Anna smiles at Lucy drily and picks up a cloth and cleaning fluid.

As she goes up the stairs, Lucy says sulkily, "I don't eat breakfast. I don't even know if there's any bread."

"I've brought croissants and cereal and fresh coffee."

Lucy glares at her mother's back. She hates the way Anna manages to take over a whole house in a matter of minutes, commandeer it as if no one else had a real right to be here. She knows she is behaving childishly. Every time she is away from her mother, Lucy swears to herself she will not let Anna get to her, she will behave in a cool and grown-up manner that will irritate Anna much more than her childishness. But she never quite manages it.

She goes upstairs to get dressed. The shower is running in the bathroom and resentment seizes Lucy again. How like her mother to intrude, violate her space, ruin her last few days here. With a start she sees she has left Martha's box out again and looks for a place to hide it.

She has not finished going through it. She is unable to read any more. She just can't. She has had time to talk to Barnaby, but she does not feel like talking about it anymore. She does not want to share this with anyone. If it wasn't for that strange birth certificate, Lucy might have asked Anna if she knew about the contents of the box, but Lucy's instinct is that Anna knows absolutely nothing.

Lucy goes to her childhood hiding place in the window. It looks like an ordinary window seat with heavy coats of gloss paint, but there is a little spring that releases the wooden lid and Lucy has always hidden her treasures here.

Fred made it for Lucy when she was about eleven or twelve and keeping copious diaries. Lucy was outraged because she thought Anna was going through her private things, so Fred, who was decorating at the time, devised this secret place for her. Anna was convinced Lucy had got in with undesirables in the school holidays and Fred suspected she did sometimes look through Lucy's things.

The day is dark and brooding, and reflects Lucy's mood exactly. She pulls on a sweater and jeans and takes Homer out. Barnaby is coming down the church path and she sees by the expression on his face that he has seen the silver Mercedes in front of the cottage. His face is closed. She waits by the gate until he reaches her.

"Guess what? Anna had business in Bristol so she kept on coming."

Barnaby is struggling with himself. "Anna has every right to be here, Lucy."

"I know," Lucy says bleakly. "But I just know everything will be awful by lunchtime. She will have upset the carers and made us both feel thoroughly guilty for things we haven't done, or have forgotten to do, or should have done . . ."

Barnaby laughs without humor. The familiar dread of always being found wanting by Anna invades his bones too. She will make him feel once more the inadequate younger brother, the non-achiever, the bumbling vicar to be patronized for the limitations of a small and narrow life.

He stops this line of thought abruptly before it undermines him. "Lucy, it really isn't like you to be this down. You've been gloomy for days. Cheer up, we're going to need to pull together—" He stops, his words sound in his own ears like Jack Hawkins on the brow of a frigate in a black-and-white war film. Ridiculous. "Do you know how long Anna is staying?"

"Only a night," Lucy says. "Thank goodness. I'll see you in a minute, Barnes. I'm going on the beach with Homer."

"Toast on the *terraarce* in twenty minutes?"

Barnaby tweaks her hair affectionately.

"Two pieces." She smiles wanly.

Lucy runs down the path to the sea. She can feel rain on the wind and another storm is brewing, vivid, luminous clouds gathering over the harbor. She has an awful dread of this coming day, of leaving next week, of the new job. Of what she has discovered. She does not want anything to change and suddenly her safe life is turning into a different shape from the thing she has always believed it to be.

People should always tell the truth, then you know you have not got the fear of catching them out. She feels sudden tears behind her eyelids as she reaches the sea and walks along the shoreline. The water is extraordinary just before a storm, the colors bright as migraine colors, too bold, too bright. Pressing on her eyelids. Bruising like thumbs.

The day is going to explode and rip the sky, churn the water and disturb and unsettle. Elemental and alien, its power cautionary and alarming. Bright fishing boats turn and scurry ahead of that threatening black sky. Tankers make for shallow and sheltered waters. At the first splatter of rain, Lucy turns and runs back to the house, with Homer lolling behind her.

There is a crouching fear in her that is as lonely and disturbing as the unnatural colors of the day. She knows she is behaving badly, but she feels totally unequal to facing her mother. She runs past the cottage. Inside, she can see the back of Anna sitting at *her* table having breakfast.

She runs up the drive to the house. Martha is waiting by the window and Lucy flies in and hugs her fiercely, her tears full and fast as she clutches her grandmother.

Worried, Martha tries to brush away Lucy's angry tears with her small, crooked fingers, but she has no idea what they mean.

"Oh, darling," she says. "Darling, are you hurt?"

"No, no, just stupid, Gran. Have you had your breakfast?"

"I don't think so."

Barnaby calls, "In here, Lucy." He has set the table in the conservatory and there is the wonderful smell of toast. He sits Martha down with Lucy next to her, hands his niece a tissue without comment and puts hot buttered toast in front of them both. He calls Fred, then sits and pours them all tea from a big red teapot.

Lucy knows this is how Barnaby copes—being gentle when he does not feel kind, so that the gentleness will win and he will not hate himself. She sees the way his fair hair is receding and his tired open face is touched with broken veins. All his life Barnaby has protected her and she is unable to protect him from anything: life . . . Anna . . . the grim old age of his parents . . . loneliness. Who will look out for him when she leaves?

Lucy clamps her mouth round her toast to stop the tears starting again.

Anna washes up her breakfast things, clears the bits from the sink, tidies the kitchen, then turns to the cottage, which is indescribably dirty and chaotically full of Lucy's packing. Thank God the girl is getting back to London where she will have to hold down a job and get a grip. Barnaby has spoiled her—he always has, ever since she was a baby.

She feels the familiar depression of being home, and the weight of being a child again swings back. Cornwall. The endless grayness of so many long holidays. The envying of other girls whose parents could afford to go and find the sun. The interminable boredom. Each day following another like Grandmother's footsteps.

Her mother gardening in a large hat for hours and hours, oblivious to all, in her own little world. Sitting on the beach with a battered paperback while Barnaby dug castles and moats in the sand.

The slowness of everything. A particular kind of parochial smugness, of a people happy to live by the sea and let the world whirl by without them, has always had a disastrous effect on Anna. She cannot understand this muddling along, this happy disorder. In the fast and frenetic life she and Rudi lead, it is vital that they are organized. Now, here she is confronted by Lucy's chaos and Barnaby's wishy-washy sentimentality.

She lights an illicit cigarette and wanders into the sitting room. Lucy's computer squats there, taking up most of the table. A headline lying on top of curricula and sheaves of information on Milan stare out at her. Curious, she sits down and starts to read what Lucy has downloaded from the Internet.

HOLOCAUST SURVIVORS WIN PAYOUT
SWISS BANKS TO SETTLE SUIT FOR $1.25 BILLION

Copyright 1998 • Houston Chronicle News Services

NEW YORK—Representatives of Swiss banks and Holocaust survivors announced a settlement Wednesday in which the banks agreed to pay $1.25 billion in reparations to victims of the Nazi era. The money will be paid out over four years and will include dormant account claims against two commercial banks. Tens of thousands of Holocaust victims deposited money in Swiss banks as the Nazis gained power in Europe, expecting to retrieve it later . . . but bank officials stonewalled survivors and their heirs after World War II, claiming they could not find accounts, or demanding death certificates.

Why is Lucy looking up this stuff? The page goes on to give the views of aged survivors who will probably be dead before any settlement is made. Anna feels strange, as if there is something she should remember, a familiar ache that wants to surface. She gets up and looks out of the small windows at the sky. It is purple and glowering. It threatens and so does her memory.

She sees herself suddenly at about ten, bored on a wet summer holiday. The cottage was between tenants and empty. Fred used to throw the windows open to air it, especially if he had been painting in there. He would leave the front door wide so that the sun could reach the hall.

She liked to go in there and sit in the chairs, walk round in the little dust motes caught by the sun, sneezing in the musty air. The old cottage always had a still, heavy feel, as if it were listening or waiting for something. She would come in here with a book or some drawing and sit in the window seat. No one disturbed her; she could be quite alone.

Fred knew she came, understood, especially when she was very young, that she needed to be on her own. He did not expect her to talk or explain why she loved the feel of the empty house. Sometimes he left biscuits or a drink on the kitchen table for her, like an invisible friend.

That September afternoon she went upstairs and the wooden loft ladder had been left down so that the paint on the ceiling could dry . . .

Anna pulls herself over the ledge and crawls inside. She shines her pocket torch around the musty room. One half of the roof has boards placed across the beams for storage and access. The room is full of dead spiders and one small dead mouse. There are two gas masks lying ominously on the dusty floor like hollow faces, and the debris of war. Blackout curtains, tins of old army rations, an army greatcoat with brass buttons, now the bitten home of mice. There are leather suitcases with faded and torn labels, ration books and a straw hat decorated with roses that Anna thinks she remembers seeing Martha wear in a photograph.

She turns and shines the beam around into the corners and notices what looks like a secret room, just behind her, in the darkest place of the attic, almost hidden by the opening hatch. Curious, Anna crawls forward carefully, making sure she places her feet on the boards, not between the beams. Using her torch she looks for an opening in the hardboard partitions and finds under her excited fumbling fingers a latch that opens one of the panels like a door.

Inside the little room there is just a trunk. Awkwardly, she moves over the boards to reach it. She shines the torch. It is an old school trunk belonging to her father. Beside it are cardboard boxes of documents and a brand-new padlock. The trunk looks as if it has been recently opened and more papers added to the carefully packed stuff already in there.

Anna lifts out two brown envelopes from the top of the trunk and turns towards the light from the open hatch. In one are photographs of Fred's childhood. Fred riding a pony, with a groom leading the tiny child against the backdrop of an enormous house. Family groups on large stone steps that lead down to granite lions. Fred with his brother and little girls in white. Fred with his mother and father. Fred with a nanny.

Anna is fascinated—overawed. She knows the story. Her grandparents would not hear of her father marrying a Polish Jew. Just think, she could have been spending her holidays in that grand house. She could have been born to privilege and money. She could have swanked to the girls at school. Instead she is just a scholarship girl, the daughter of a struggling GP. If only her father had married someone English, he would not have been disinherited. Putting that envelope aside she moves to the next one. It is large and contains old and tattered documents. She shakes them out. At the bottom of the envelope an armband with a yellow star falls out and a necklet thing. Anna is very still. They are eerily familiar. A fearful dark thing reaches out and grips her. She shivers violently.

Memory, like a deep fog, stirs but will not lift. Slowly, as if they have a life of their own, her fingers reach out towards the yellow star. She lifts the armband like a sleepwalker and puts her long thin arm through it so that it lies on her forearm. Rests there.

From far, far away, a voice calls her. In the attic the dust whorls gather in her nose and the air is still and thick and foreign. Anna takes the armband off quickly and places it in the dust.

She turns to the velvet neck band and instinctively turns the velvet inside out. Tiny crumbs drop out with a crumpled piece of cardboard. In a trance, she wets her finger and places it, trembling, where the crumbs have dropped into the dust and droppings of the attic floor. The finger is halfway back to her mouth before she comes to with a start.

Somewhere below, his voice nearer, her father is calling her. Scrabbling and guilty she hastily pushes the documents back into the envelopes without looking at them. One tears as she tries to hurry. Anna starts to refold it so that it goes into the envelope and sees her name suddenly on the strange piece of paper.

"Anna Esther . . ." She opens it and stares down. Her name is Tremain. Tremain. She licks her finger once more and rubs at the name that is not hers, rubs until the old paper crumbles nearly into a hole and her spit falls onto the paper in her haste, blotting out . . .

Her father's voice is under the hatch now and angry. He is coming up the ladder and his head will appear through the hatch any moment. Anna hastily throws the envelopes back into the trunk and moves quickly to get to the other side of the partition, skinning her knees as she hurries.

She is afraid. Coming up here is forbidden. As her father appears she peers down at him, her pale hair sweaty and dusty, falls into her eyes. He stares up at her.

"Come down, this instant, Anna."

He goes back down and Anna climbs down the ladder after him, covered in dust and dirt.

"Wait there and don't you move," he says, and climbs back up the ladder and pulls his legs up. Anna hears him replacing things, shutting the trunk up again. She hears the click of the padlock, the scrape of the partition being put back.

He comes back down. Anna has never seen him so angry.

"You will never, ever go up there again. It is dangerous and you could have fallen through the roof. Do you hear me, Anna?"

But he is not angry about the roof. Anna knows this. He sees suddenly that she is shaken and pale, her blue eyes bright at his anger, and he bends to her, brushing the cobwebs and dust from her Aertex shirt and shorts.

"You will forget this afternoon, Anna. You never went into the roof. You never opened anybody else's private things, because that would have been terribly wrong, wouldn't it?"

Anna nods her head, numbly. Her father leads her out of the house.

"Let's go and have some tea. Your mother has made a cake. What have you done this afternoon? Did you go to the beach? Have you played in the garden?"

The child that is Anna catches on fast. "I collected shells all afternoon, I was down on the beach all afternoon."

But that night she dreams of a dark girl with a drawn, thin face who holds Anna to her for a moment before she hands her over to a man in a sort of uniform. The girl, who wears a yellow star on her coat, is crying. Crying and holding Anna tight. Anna is pulled away into darkness, down, down into darkness. She cannot breathe. She tries to get away, but she cannot move. The terror inside Anna overwhelms her and she screams and screams.

Fred comes and holds her, rocks her in the dark and she clings to him, crying. The only time she has ever clung, will ever cling.

"Just a dream, darling, just a horrible, horrible dream. Soon, it will be morning."

"You are my father. You are my father," Anna cries over and over again.

"Of course I am your father, you silly little toad. And you are my beloved child. Now go back to sleep."

In the morning Anna has shut it all out. It is a facility she has for unpleasant things. She was never in any old loft. She collected shells all afternoon yesterday, down on the beach. She fills a jar with them to prove it, to prove to herself, that is what she had been doing, and she writes the date in thick laborious lettering on a jam label and sticks it on the side of the jar.

Chapter 30

Anna bends under the arch of trees to get out of the small cottage garden. The little wicket gate is open and she walks slowly into her parents' overgrown garden and stands looking at the lawns full of daisies and the shrubs and trees all grown into one another. It is not unattractive, this rural chaos. It looks a bit like the Lost Gardens of Heligan without the history.

Quite unsuitable for an old couple. The place is a time warp, the upkeep of the house and garden far too much work. Anna stands under the brooding sky and quickly calculates what the house with large garden and a cottage with sea views might fetch on the open market. A great deal, she imagines. Property is going up.

Anna is shocked at how shabby and dilapidated everything looks. The garage doors are practically falling off. The roof of the old hen house has caved in. The lawns look like wildflower meadows. Up to this moment Anna has believed her parents should stay here, but now she sees it is obvious that the house and garden need a lot of money spent on them. Money Martha and Fred do not have. It is only a matter of time before neglect will lower the value of the property and they will all lose out.

Could she and Rudi buy Martha and Fred out? This would release money her parents are going to need. It would make a good investment. She could settle them in a small bungalow near here

with a manageable garden. Martha and Fred have lived here all their lives, but it boils down to their best interests in the end. They would have some capital. Heaven knows what it costs to run this rambling place in winter.

At least they would all be prepared for when one of them died or had to go into a home. There would be money for their care. It really did make sense. Even as Anna thinks this, she knows Barnaby would put up every objection under the sun. He has always loved this place, is sentimentally attached to it in a way she never has been.

Although he did not know it at the time, the best thing Fred's grandfather did for Fred when he died was to leave him the small manor house here in Cornwall, which his own father had bought on a whim for golfing holidays. Fred had planted a great sheath of rare and valuable trees to screen the house from the rest of the garden. Now, they were huge, beautiful and established, with a tree preservation order on them.

When Fred sold the manor off he built, on land that had once been tennis courts and kitchen garden, a unique and slightly odd colonial-type house that he and Martha had designed together. Martha loved the idea of large airy rooms that caught and held the sun all day.

A few years ago Fred's solicitor suggested he make a deed of gift to his children to avoid death duties, so Fred made over the cottage to Anna and Barnaby at the same time as Lucy started to live down here permanently.

Barnaby must realize, surely, that Fred's money will be dwindling away. The only income Fred has ever earned is as a country GP. Even if his relations left him small amounts, his finances must be finite.

The sensible thing, Anna thinks, is for her to act on power of attorney—not because she wants to annoy Barnaby but because she is better able, because of her profession, to see clearly their needs. She can stand away and make clinical judgments that Barnaby isn't able to.

Anna circles the house, crosses the lawn and bends under the huge sweeping fig tree, which showers her with heavy dew. She sees the heads in the conservatory sitting round the circular table under the grapevine and stands and watches them before they see her.

They seem so close. A curious, unfamiliar feeling of wistfulness—childish jealousy?—is fleeting and gone in a second. She is on the outside of this family looking in. She always has been. Anna knows, as if she is watching another person, she is going to disrupt that comfortable family tableau. She cannot help herself.

The large leaves of the fig rustle as she moves forward and Barnaby sees her. She watches his face fall before he quickly, briefly, smiles and calls out to her. Lucy moves her mouth in acknowledgment but cannot manage a smile. Fred gets up and goes to her.

"Anna, darling, how good to see you."

Anna kisses his cheek. "Good to see you too, Father."

She turns to her mother, who is looking at her blankly. Anna is unprepared for this. It feels like a sharp slap in the face.

"Mother?" she says bleakly.

Fred goes round the table quickly. "Darling, it's Anna. Isn't this a lovely surprise?"

Martha is still staring at Anna as if she has never seen her before. Anna goes closer, tries to take Martha's hand.

"It's me, Anna, Mother."

Martha looks at her bent fingers in Anna's groomed, neat hand, then peers up at Anna's face and says politely, "You are not my daughter. You are Frau . . . Frau . . ." She turns to Fred and whispers, "Who is it, darling? I can't remember."

Anna looks down at Martha. "If I'm not your daughter, Mother, I am not sure who I am." She laughs in a brittle bark, tries to make a joke. It is painful.

Barnaby touches her arm. "Anna, come into the kitchen, I've just made some fresh coffee."

Once there he turns to her. "Some days she's more confused

than others. It's just a bad morning. She'll remember you in a moment. Sorry, sorry about that."

"Why are you apologizing?" Anna snaps. "It's not your fault, is it?" She looks at Barnaby accusingly. "I had no idea she was so bad. Why on earth didn't you let me know she was like this?"

Barnaby sighs and hands his sister a mug of coffee. "Anna, it's nearly a year since I told you Mum has Alzheimer's. You've made one flying visit. You haven't seen her for nearly nine months, surely you must have realized that it's a progressive disease?" He adds gently, "I have tried to explain her deterioration to you on the phone, you know."

Anna looks at him. "Whenever I've spoken to her on the phone she sounds vague, but more or less normal."

"It is rather like Pavlov's dog. Mum can make the normal social responses, ask people how they are, answer normal inquiries, just out of habit. But she won't remember who you are or what you've said one second after you have put the phone down."

Anna is, surprisingly, silent. She is more shaken than she would ever admit to Barnaby by the deterioration in Martha. It is shocking. She is unsure what she expected, but her mother, always small, seems to be shrinking. Those great dark eyes and quick smile that lit up her face are fading and blank, the intellect behind them gone. Anna did not expect to feel this surge of loss, but she does.

Barnaby sees that Anna is deeply upset, but doesn't know how to comfort her without getting snapped at. He searches for something to say that she will accept and not find patronizing.

Lucy has gone with Martha to help her get dressed and Fred has disappeared to the lavatory with the *Daily Telegraph,* as he always does at this time of day.

"Anna, Mum could have a perfectly coherent conversation with you later. Not for long, but—"

"How are you going to cope without Lucy?" Anna asks suddenly. "I mean, the whole thing is going to become impossible.

Fred doesn't seem too bad, but it's not fair on him. Maybe seeing Mother like this is affecting him. Have you taken expert advice? Have you ever considered a home for her, Barnaby?"

Barnaby's face closes. "We have excellent carers. We're slowly building up a rota of people Mum likes. I can get more help as I need it. Fred and Martha have never been apart. I just don't understand how you can even suggest it, Anna. We are managing perfectly all right."

"For how long?"

"I've just told you, when I need it I'll get extra nursing care. Martha and Fred are not going into a home, singly or together. There is no need for it."

"Maybe not at this very moment, but soon there is going to be a great need for it. You are just not facing it, Barnaby. What about when Mother becomes incontinent?"

"I will deal with that problem when it comes." Barnaby makes himself unclench his fists. Only Anna can make him this angry. "Why on earth, if I am coping, are you so keen to have them in a home? I'm mystified. You know perfectly well what most homes are like. They would both just curl up and die."

Anna is watching Fred's slow progress across the garden to the bird table. The rain is coming and he is about to get soaked. His trousers hang loose and he has an old man's shuffle and an air of filling the day.

"Would that be such a bad thing?" she says under her breath.

Barnaby follows her eyes. He is chilled, as he often is, by Anna's cold and pathological hate of disorder, of uselessness. He turns to her, furious.

"Go home," he snaps. "Go away, where you can't see and be offended by the old age of your parents. It need not affect you. I haven't asked you to contribute financially. You don't have to be in any way involved. I will just write to you when they have both died. How does that suit you?"

Anna finishes her coffee and puts the mug carefully down on

the table. "Stop being dramatic, Barnaby. You're so entrenched with looking after them on a daily basis, you can't or won't see the long view or what might be best for them, medically or psychologically. Of course I don't mean any old home. I mean a really good one, which would cater for all Martha's needs as she deteriorates."

"Which presumably, in your view, would mean selling their home to pay for it?"

"How else could we afford it?"

"Would that also mean that you and Rudi might take it off their hands for what you would consider a generous sum?"

Anna flushes for once, outmaneuvered. "Not . . . necessarily. Of course it would have to be valued and go on the open market."

Barnaby makes for the door, his face grim. "I have a funeral to organize. I'll see you at lunchtime."

At the door he turns. "I don't want to have this conversation again, Anna. The subject is closed. Please, please try not to upset the carers. It is extremely hard to get good people."

"Barnaby?" Anna calls after him. "Perhaps you should question your own motives. Is it natural to give up any hope of a life for yourself, for two old people who have had theirs? Or is it that you are incapable of living an independent life away from Martha and Fred? Whatever . . ." she waves her hands, "this is a pretty sad existence, don't you think?" She gives that nervous little triumphant laugh he used to hear in his childhood sleep.

White-faced, Barnaby says, "Anna, I don't think I am the one with the problem." Then he shuts the front door.

Lucy comes flying out and puts her head in the car door. "I heard a bit of it. Don't let her get to you, Barnes. Please don't take any notice. She's always like this when she's upset or guilty, you know that. Something gets inside her. She can't stop herself. We've just got to struggle through this day somehow. Please, please don't be sad. I can't bear it."

"I'm all right, darling." Barnaby pats her hand. "See you at lunchtime?"

"I'll be there, don't worry. I'm going to hover. Kate's on today and I don't want her upset. Gran and Grandpa adore her, but Mum is going to have a fit about her nose ring and her butterfly tattoo and say she is unsuitable. Oh God . . . pray this day goes quickly."

Lucy flies back into the house, hair and lanky legs flying and Barnaby laughs to himself, cheered. Thank God for Lucy. Sensible Lucy, who recognizes it is guilt that guides Anna's tongue.

Chapter 31

Mama has a book, a beautiful bound book of brown and tan leather with gold lettering on the spine. It is a privately published travel book written by an Englishman who traveled through Poland in the early 1900s.

It had been translated painstakingly into Polish by Marta's grandfather, Mama's father, and faithfully reproduced with the beautiful watercolors and pencil sketches he did on his travels.

Before Marta is allowed to touch it, Mama makes her wash her hands and sit at the table so that she will not mark the pages or bend the spine. Marta cannot read yet so Mama will sit, tenderly lifting the thin tissue pages that protect the paintings, her face flushed with pleasure as she turns the pages for Marta.

This book is special to Mama because Marta's grandfather was killed taking part in an insurrection against the Russians. Like countless other middle-class Poles, noblemen, and Catholic clergy, he fought bravely, dreaming of an independent Poland.

This book was his last gift to his wife. The small paintings jump out at Marta because of the bright and wonderful colors of the clothes and the sadness in the Polish faces.

Mama tells her the faces are serious, not sad, but Marta does not think so. The melancholy within these people stares out of their eyes as if they are silently weeping.

Marta is fascinated by this world that is gone. Here a bride in a headdress of bright reds, yellows and blues. A white blouse with gathered cuffs and lace at the throat where a red jewel lies. A bodice of great splendor and a full skirt that is covered in flowers. Over her shoulders she has thrown a great multicolored cloak. Her hands lie still and lifeless in her lap. There is a little curve of dark hair showing under the headdress. The skin is smooth and sallow, the eyebrows heavy and arched, the nose straight, the line of mouth tight.

It is the eyes that haunt Marta. They look down and away, not at the artist who painted her. They hold such a depth of sorrow that Marta feels a lump rise to her throat, for the hands in the painting mirror a hopelessness too.

This sadness is replicated in all the paintings of Polish faces.

"Why is everyone so unhappy?" she asks Mama yet again.

"It is what the artist captured. This is what he saw. This is the overall impression that he came away with. It does not mean all the people in the paintings were unhappy. But the somberness of the times they lived in is captured in their faces." Marta doesn't understand.

In this book are the long-forgotten names of places, of cities that have disappeared or changed names, and places that are still part of her world. Zakopane . . . The Tatry Mountains. There is a beautiful shadowy picture of the Stare Miasto, Warsaw, tiny people beneath. Color-washed figures muffled in bright cloaks and headdresses, faces unseen, lighting candles in churches, crowded into markets.

The words, when Marta has learned to read, spring out with the names of long-gone princesses and kings, emperors and conquerors, a world that has disappeared into history books. Marta particularly wants to take this book away to read herself, but Mama will not let her read it on her own.

One afternoon, when Marta is older and she cannot go out to ride because of the frozen ground, she takes the book down carefully and sits at the table and starts to read it properly. Hanna has lit an early fire and the cold winter day is banished as Marta opens the pages randomly to the paintings she loves, for the first time reading the description that goes with them.

Everywhere, the English traveler's words describe with love the color and beauty of the countryside. The goodness, sincerity, and patience of the Polish people, the difficulty of Russian bureaucracy, the architecture of the buildings. Then, he comes to "the Jewish Quarter." With a sudden burning shock Marta takes in the words. "Everywhere," he writes, "Jews. Sinister . . . black . . . dirty . . . obsequious. Dishonest. Beautiful buildings ruined by trading Jews . . . Squalid, noisy and crowded streets. Awful, hanging ringlets . . . I have a horrible shrinking fear of being approached, touched by them . . ."

Shrinking fear. The words spring out of the pages and cover Marta hotly, making her fingers holding that frail protective tissue shake. Like Frau Saurer. She always looks at me as if I am dirty. Always. She never ever talks to me directly or meets my eyes. She makes my heart thump with her distaste.

Mama and Papa come breezing into the room in their winter coats, come in laughing, bringing a blast of cold air with them. They see Marta's face and her fingers holding the book and their laughter stops. Because they know that she has already experienced that feeling within the pages, but that it is a shock to see anti-Semitism so boldly written, making it real and somehow startling against the beauty of those little paintings.

Papa takes the book from Marta and returns it to the shelf.

"Why," Marta asks, "are we hated?"

"Perhaps feared is a better word. By people prejudiced, who do not understand us. Because Jews are successful as a race and we seem to be everywhere," her father says.

Mama comes and sits beside Marta. "Your grandfather could have left those chapters out of the book but he wanted his readers to see what is written about Jews." She smiles at Marta, takes her cold hands in her own. "About people like us, ordinary Polish Jews." She squeezes Marta's hands. "Don't look so sad, little one. The world is changing, getting wiser."

Marta is still young, but she watches her father's face as he stands looking at her and she knows what Mama says is not true. They are not ordinary Polish Jews. They are not poor, like Hanna and her family. They do not have to haggle on the street or crowd into the Jewish Quarter in damp tenements. Nor do they have to live in the same area as other wealthy Jews.

Mama is gentle. She cannot bear unpleasant things. She will hide the truth in the world outside, from Marta and from herself.

Her father loves her mama, Marta is sure of this, but their marriage was an arranged one. She was seventeen. Papa was thirty. Maybe her mother looked like the mournful, helpless bride in the book on her wedding day. Yet their marriage is so happy that her mother forgets it was arranged. All she remembers is their first meeting and the joy of remaining loved and safe.

Yet some days Marta will catch her mother's face turned to the forest and to the hills. She will see her face wistful and her hands restless as they sew. She will see that the walls of the house confine her and her heart turns to a world she will never know.

Mama is clever and good at languages. Twice a week she teaches Marta English, partly, Marta thinks, so she does not forget it. She could have been successful in her own right, she could have done so many things, but she never got the chance. Even a large family is denied her. She fell from a horse as a child and damaged her back. Papa told Marta she nearly died giving birth to her, so there were no more children. Here in the walls of her kingdom she is safe from the world outside. But Marta knows there is another world her mother lives deep inside her head.

I will never be trapped by walls or by marriage, Marta thinks fiercely. Never. Mama, the eyes in your book haunt me. They are your eyes. They are mine.

Chapter 32

Barnaby drives through the village and tries to put the conversation with Anna out of his mind. She could not have arrived at a worse time. He could have done without an argument with her today. He is driving to Edith Ash's house to meet her distant, ever-absent niece, to arrange the old lady's funeral. Barnaby is going to have trouble sitting on his righteous anger or minding his own business.

Miss Ash has been devotedly cared for by Molly Treen, one of Barnaby's parishioners, for at least ten years, and Barnaby knows that the wealthy Miss Ash changed her will just before she died in favor of this niece. Barnaby knows because Miss Ash asked him to witness it.

"My niece is always so kind and helpful on the phone, Vicar. Such a busy girl. She sent me these photos of the children—aren't they beautiful? She says of course I must look after Molly, but a thousand pounds is quite sufficient and Molly will be very pleased."

Barnaby, about to give Miss Ash Holy Communion at home, said, "Edith, you do remember that Molly gave up her own little cottage all those years ago to move in and look after you? You told me how desperate you were at the time for someone to live in. You also told me you had made her a promise that, in return, you would look after her financially. 'Make sure she was all right,' I think you said. She will never be able to afford to buy another house in the village now. You must know that."

Edith Ash looked at Barnaby with her shrewd little brown eyes. "Blood is thicker than water," she said finally. "I did mean Molly to have the house. She has been a good friend to me over the years, but my niece and her husband are against the idea. He seems to think Molly was always after me leaving her everything. They are family, you see, Vicar."

Barnaby, shocked but not surprised by her callousness, had wanted to snap, "Who finds you when you fall, Edith? Who visits you in hospital, feeds your cat, cleans your house and goes to the shops for you and listens to your constant moaning?"

The theme was depressingly familiar: "She is the best daughter, friend, neighbor, in the world. I am so grateful to her, Vicar, but it is my son, daughter, nephew, you see . . ."

Barnaby knows he should be used to it. He has been part of the heartbreak of so many family funerals. He has witnessed too often the shock of the death followed by bewilderment held like a sour taste on the tongue. He has listened helpless to the disbelieving little laugh that covers unexpected betrayal. He has watched closed faces and trembling hands clutching alcohol at funerals, drinking in stunned desperation.

Middle-aged, unmarried daughters, caricatured in sitcoms but real to him, nursing a parent with unflinching love and patience. Giving up all hope of a life of their own, only to find, on the death of the parent, the promised house is shared or the money to run it goes to an absent sibling with energy, time and money to blow in and charm once in a blue moon.

He has seen sons who toiled faithfully, beyond any sense of duty, putting their marriages at risk, sometimes neglecting wives or children, only to find some cruel clause in a will that left them struggling. He has watched bitterness in all its chameleon forms throbbing like a tic beneath the surface of the skin: the pretending it did not matter and the guilt that it mattered a lot, because it was not just about money and possessions and houses. It was the suffocating sadness and anger that something given unselfishly, unflinchingly, had simply been taken for granted. Barnaby will never get used to the casual cruelty, the malevolent selfishness of the old, who wave their wills like banners when frightened or alone, then, familiarity breeding contempt, the carers are abandoned in favor of absent family, gathering like carrion crows.

He turns into the drive of Edith Ash's house. Outside the neglected but imposing granite house sits a large new Volvo and a small removal van. From the bottom window the small figure of Molly clad in an apron waves a duster at him, her honest open face smiling and welcoming.

The worst thing, the very worst thing, Barnaby thinks, will be seeing Molly's bent head in church next Sunday, praying for her own wickedness in disappointment after her childlike trust of a promise. *Miss Ash gave me her word, Vicar.*

Barnaby closes his eyes. He is never prepared for the power of his own fury, like the flare-up of a fever or hitting a wall at a hundred miles an hour. Where has Molly's goodness, her belief in a loving God, got her?

The front door opens and a tall, beautifully groomed woman comes out and stands on the top step to welcome him. Coldly gracious. The house already hers. She reminds him of Anna.

"Get thee behind me," Barnaby mutters as he gets out of his car.

Kate enters the house and is startled to find a tall and striking blonde woman standing in the hall. The woman doesn't smile or introduce herself and Kate stands awkwardly, not sure whether to pass Anna and go on into the house. She hopes Lucy will emerge from somewhere pretty damn soon.

"I'm Kate," she says eventually. "From the agency? I've come to take care of—"

Martha comes dancing into the hall, her face lighting up when she sees Kate. "Darling . . ." She goes straight to the girl and kisses her. "How lovely to see you. Where are we going today?"

Before Kate can answer, Lucy comes into the hall.

"Sorry, I was in the loo. Kate, this is my mother. This is Kate, Mother. It's brilliant because Kate can drive and she takes Gran and Grandpa out in the car, which they love."

"How do you do?" Anna says stiffly, nodding but not putting her hand out to the girl. Good grief, what is Barnaby thinking about? This girl looks like a traveler and probably is one with her disgusting nose ring, her spiky hair and overbright clothes. She is surprised her parents have accepted her in the house looking like this. "What happened to Mrs. Biddulph?" she asks.

"She still comes. We have a rota of two carers and one on standby, but Kate is the only one who drives so it's great for Gran and Grandpa."

"You have insurance, I suppose, for driving my parents about?"

"Of course. The agency arranges all that."

Anna gives Kate what is supposed to be a polite smile. She is not easily going to forgive this ragbag girl for being acknowledged by Martha when she has not been.

"What qualifications do you have for working with people like my mother?"

Kate stares at Anna with puzzlement and growing dislike. "Well, the agency sends you on a short course on dealing with the elderly and mentally frail and one night's practical training on lifting. Then they give you a certificate and proclaim you trained." She pauses, enjoying the triumphant look on Anna's face. "However, I did a degree in Psychology at Bristol and I hope to do my doctorate next year at Exeter," she lies.

Lucy tries not to laugh. Good for Kate. That's shut Anna up for two seconds.

However, Anna suddenly asks, "Where do you live, Kate?"

Kate hesitates, meeting Lucy's eyes. "In a hotel . . . at the moment. I'm hoping to find somewhere to rent soon . . ."

She tries to move out of the hall with Martha hanging on to her. She can feel herself getting angry. It is nothing to do with this woman where she lives. Why is she getting the Spanish Inquisition? What does the woman expect for £3.95 an hour, for God's sake?

Lucy, trying to make things better for Kate, says, "Kate is going to rent the cottage, Mother. It's all arranged."

"Is it indeed?" Anna says quietly. "We'll see. Barnaby has said nothing to me."

Kate has had enough. She turns abruptly away and says to Martha, "Where is Dr. Tremain this morning? Still feeding his birds?"

"No, I don't think so," Martha says clearly. "I think he is reading his newspaper in the conservatory."

"Let's go and get some air and see if he's ready for coffee."

As they disappear, Lucy says furiously, "Why? Why do you always have to do that to people? You always have to put people down. Does it give you a buzz or something?"

"Don't be silly, Lucy. Doesn't it occur to you that in the short time I'm here I need to ensure your grandparents are being looked after properly?"

"God, Mum, if only you knew how pompous you sound. Presumably you mean Barnaby and I are incapable of judging who is good and trustworthy with Gran and Grandpa?"

Anna waves her hands irritably. "I am not going to pursue pointless arguments with you, Lucy. What happens now? Obviously we can't take Fred or Martha out. This storm is about to break."

She lifts her hair from her neck and Lucy sees little beads of sweat on her top lip. Anna seems tired.

Outside it is growing darker and darker and there is a low rumble in the distance.

"When the weather is like this," Lucy answers grimly, "it's a bloody long day, I can tell you. Kate, or whoever is on, has to find Gran little jobs to keep her occupied and feeling useful, like helping clean the silver, or putting things away in the kitchen. She watches television in the day now, I'm afraid, but she sleeps quite a lot if she doesn't go out. If it's a good day she and Grandpa sit and talk, or have circular conversations, anyway."

So, this is what her parents have come to. This is what old age means, Anna thinks bleakly. And Barnaby dares to have the vapors at the mention of a home. At least there they have singsongs and their hair done and entertainment.

"Fred," she says to Lucy, "seems to have aged out of all proportion, but he doesn't seem gaga to me."

There is an enormous clap of thunder, which sends Homer rushing, sliding and slipping on his old legs into the hall. Lucy grabs him. "It's all right . . . calm down, Homer. It's only thunder. That's it, you go under the table."

Lucy rushes to close the French windows, which are caught by the sudden wind. Kate is hastily bringing Martha and Fred out of the conservatory into the sitting room and they shut the doors against the pummeling of rain on the thick glass roof.

They turn and watch the sky spreading violet and yellow like an angry wound and are awed by the lightning streaking silver over the trees. Anna bends and pulls all the plugs from their sockets. It is ages since she has seen a storm like this. Usually they build up during the day and let fly at night.

Martha, looking anxious, sits on the sofa far away from the window. She hates storms and Lucy goes and curls up next to her.

Fred slips out of the room and goes to his study and sits in his comfortable old leather armchair. He wishes he still smoked sometimes. The storm will clear the air. He feels hot and agitated. There is something he should have sorted out, he is sure of it, but he cannot for the life of him remember what it is. Only that it is important. Anna is here and he has a feeling she might have been able to help him if only he could remember. Was it something to do with money? He isn't sure.

Anna. He sighs. This means trouble, someone upset. He has always been able to handle her better than Martha or Barnaby. Little Lucy is quite adept, he thinks. He always hoped as Anna got older and more successful her quick, hurtful tongue would give way to fulfillment, if not happiness.

Fred sighs. Martha has always believed Anna was her cross for surviving. The child that was Anna hugged her secrets to herself. She wrapped silence around her like a cloak and peered out of it at a world that could never be trusted.

Martha understood this, tried so hard, but could not get near the child—a strange, damaged little girl who metaphorically bared her teeth when Martha approached.

Those first years of Anna's life are locked deep inside her head, and Fred and Martha have always known that they are the key to her innate insensitivity to other people. Her cruel streak.

You cannot make anyone talk about things they can't bear to. Martha told him how Anna came to be. Once. It was never discussed again. Fred has the bones of Martha's life, but not the flesh—jigsaw pieces, small chunks told randomly in the dark of those first years of married life. He has had to guess the rest, try to accept he can never fit all the pieces together. For Martha and Anna, silence is a wall and each brick vital. Martha will never, ever talk to him cogently again and it seems at times unendurable to Fred that there will always be gaps in the life of this woman he has loved all these years.

As Anna puts her head round the door Fred remembers suddenly the box in the attic. Should he have burned every single thing of her past as Martha wished? Or was he right to hide them, for someone else to piece those hidden lives together one day? He doesn't know.

"May I come in, Father?"

"Of course you may." He looks at the beautifully groomed

woman in front of him. What a far cry from that pathetic little bundle he first set eyes on.

"How are you, Fred?" she asks, sitting at his desk and swiveling round to him.

"Getting old and forgetful." He smiles at her.

"What about Martha?"

"Not so good, as you can see. Some days are better than others. We couldn't manage without Barnaby."

"Are you happy with the care?"

"Most of the carers are wonderful with Martha. We are very lucky."

"You don't think Mother could get better care with professionals on hand round the clock, Father?"

Fred looks at her warily. "You mean a home, don't you?"

"Not any home. A really good one with excellent medical facilities."

Fred smiles again, wryly. "Do they exist, Anna? Because in all my life as a GP I have rarely come across one. I have come across dedicated people running homes with poor facilities. I have come across expensive clinical homes run like concentration camps with dodgy private consultants. Why would you want to put your mother into a home?"

"I don't. I just want to take the stress off you and Barnaby. It's not going to get any easier and I want to be convinced she is getting the best care she can. Has she seen a specialist?"

"Brian brings the geriatric chap round every now and then. Anna, there is no magic potion, only drugs to help your mother. We are all bumbling along as best we can. This is the best we can do in the circumstances, believe me. Martha and I have never been parted and she will go into a home over my dead body."

"That's likely to happen, Father," Anna says coolly. "You look very tired."

Fred stares at her. He wonders why she comes. She seems deaf to both his and her mother's real needs. Her need to control, to be in charge of every situation, to pigeonhole, is pathological—always has been. He remembers her bedroom as a child, like a surgical operating theater. Anna had to have order, everything in its allotted place, or she threw a wobbly. It was her way of coping. It still is.

His head throbs. He wants her to go; he will have to take some more morphine soon.

"I suppose," he says slowly, "one of the reasons you came down was to get power of attorney?"

Anna is startled at his shrewdness and her face gives her away.

"I am not ready for that yet, Anna. When I am, I will know it and have one drawn up. But as Barnaby is here and has to cope with the running of the house and the bills, it is more logical to give him power of attorney, don't you think?"

"I think you should give us joint powers, so it is not open to abuse."

Fred fights a wave of pain. He closes his eyes and presses his head back against the leather chair. He speaks firmly in a tone that takes her back to her childhood. "Anna, but for Barnaby we would probably both already be in a home—at the very least besieged by social workers. Every day of my life I thank God for Barnaby. Please . . . I must rest now."

Outside the rain starts in great bursts and hits the window. Thunder still rumbles on in the distance. Anna looks down at the gray face of her father. He suddenly looks very ill.

"What is wrong with you, Father?"

"Apart from being old?" He tries to smile.

"Fred, what is it?" Something is stirring inside Anna that feels like panic.

Fred opens his eyes and looks at her. "I have cancer, darling. A brain tumor. Inoperable."

The endearment and the words make tears spring to Anna's eyes. Fred is startled and touched.

Unable to bear the pain in his head any longer, he whispers, "Top drawer, Anna. Please hand me that little medical bag."

Anna opens the drawer and passes it to him. His hands are trembling and she goes to help him open it. Inside is a syringe.

"Morphine," he says quietly. "Sometimes I get the dose wrong."

"God! You shouldn't be doing this. You should be getting proper medical help."

"Just help me, dear . . . the syringe, that's it, put . . . Open the sterilized needle . . . Thank you."

Fred takes the needle and with trembling hands injects himself, then with a sigh falls back in the chair.

Anna is appalled. She feels entirely vindicated in her original assessment of her parents' needs. They both need caring for professionally. Fred's eyes open. His eyes are clearing and his color is better.

"Anna, I don't have long. I don't want to go into hospital and leave your mother. Neither do I want to be kept alive by steroids or chemotherapy. Barnaby does not know about the morphine. I wanted to wait until Lucy had gone to London. These are my last days with my granddaughter, please don't spoil them. You've come at an unfortunate time, otherwise you wouldn't have known. Please, please don't spoil the time I have left."

Fred feels so weary. Anna's poisonous jealousy of Barnaby, her need to upset and hurt him, smash and spoil anything he has, or does, has always been relentless. It seems he and Martha have failed her.

Anna is silent, staring at him. Fred smiles at her, forging a cheerfulness he does not feel. "We'll manage, you'll see."

Anna's face has gone ashen, bloodless, and he sees again that thin little traumatized child that lives on inside her.

"I love you, Anna," he says under his breath, so he does not embarrass her. "I always have and I always will."

Anna is crying. She nods and abruptly leaves the room. Fred closes his eyes, leans back against his old battered leather armchair and murmurs, "'It seems I have no tears left. They should have fallen—/ Their ghosts, if tears have ghosts, did fall—that day/ When twenty hounds streamed by me, not yet combed out.'"

Anna hurries out of the front door and back through the dripping garden to the cottage. She has sneered at her family all her life; never thought she could feel this overpowering sorrow at how their lives are ending. As she reaches the gate she realizes she has always loved Fred more than her mother. Loved him without ever even thinking about it.

Chapter 33

Mutti took him to Germany to hear the Führer speak to the Hitler Youth. It was there he experienced the astonishing, unforgettable thrill of his first Hitler rally. He was fascinated and repelled at that hysterical voice, embarrassed at his mother's glowing eyes and pink cheeks.

The heightened tension of so many people made him afraid, yet he was carried away by those seductive, persuasive words as if they were meant only for him.

". . . but in you, Germany will live on and when nothing is left of us you will have to hold up the banner which some time ago we lifted out of nothingness." Applause. "And I know it cannot be otherwise because you are flesh of our flesh, blood of our blood, and your young minds are filled with the same will that dominates us." Applause. "You cannot but be united with us. And when the great columns of our movement march victoriously through Germany today I know that you will join these columns. And we know" applause "that Germany is before us, within us, and behind us . . ."

When he and his mother returned to Warsaw his father moved out of the bedroom he shared with Mutti. Quietly, without fuss, he removed his silver hairbrushes and old-fashioned shaving brushes to a small back room that overlooked the garden. In their place stood the highly polished silver photograph frame with the picture of Hitler that his mother had taken from her dressing room and placed on her chest of drawers. It was only later when he was older that he realized the significance of the two things.

Mutti bustled in with a defensiveness in her stiff body that he learned to know well as he grew up. She patted the top of his head.

"Just you and me. You and me, my son, my good little German."

Years later, when the Jewish doctor was forced to leave the practice, when he lost all his money, his father had withdrawn from both his mother and himself. He did not bother to argue with Mutti, he just distanced himself. The boy suspected he used to go off and treat Jews, in the way he always had done.

He loved his mother. He loved her and listened to her because she said what he wanted to hear. Yet, when he was young, despite Mutti, he still wanted his father's approval. He loved the times his father put aside to ride with him. He liked sitting in his father's study, poring over his old medical books. His father had traveled widely in his youth. He had trained in England and America. He came from a family of doctors, liberal in outlook, well read and academic. He and Mutti had as different a background as it was possible to have. Mutti rode beautifully but hardly ever read a book. She was unable to debate rationally or hold a cohesive argument. She just lost her temper, spouted party tracts or left the room.

He rarely heard his father criticize his wife. He was always polite to her in front of him. Before he grew away from his father he knew perfectly well, in some deep unacknowledged place, that his father was a good man and far more intelligent than his mother. But at the time it did not suit him to acknowledge it.

He never met his paternal grandparents. Like the girl, he had a father much older than his mother. His father had been approaching forty when he met Mutti in Berlin.

When his mother was happy, when she got her own way or liked someone, she could dazzle and charm. It needed no imagination to see how charmed his father must have been with a girl of twenty-three.

There was the time his father took him to Lwow. He wanted to attend the funeral of a cousin. He showed him the house where he had lived for a short time as a child—a town house, with peeling window frames and a front garden full of flowers.

His father was amused at his face. "It is now a little dilapidated, but it was a house full of character. We never stayed anywhere too long; my parents were always on the move. My father's money went into traveling to improve his medical skills to bring home. Every time we returned from our travels, we bought a house somewhere else. My father was like a sort of roving surgery. He went where people needed him, regardless of race or creed. He taught me to value each individual, no matter who they were or where they came from."

His father put his hand on his shoulder. "My grandfather and my father inherited wealth from properties in Germany. They used it all their lives to help those less fortunate. It was fortuitous that I met your mother when I did. In helping her, I found the ideal place to build a clinic in peaceful surroundings, for my patients.

"I saw your face. It is not big houses that count, my son, but whether you use wealth for good or ill."

What amazed him on that trip was the wake after the funeral. Everyone piled into a large room and sat debating the state of the world and the fate of Poland in particular as they drank vast quantities of vodka.

The majority of men there were Poles. There were, of course, ethnic Germans like his father. And there were Jews.

They all sat round a huge polished table and argued excitedly with their arms, getting pleasantly inebriated. The drunker they got the ruder they got about Mr. Hitler. He had never seen his father so happy or relaxed. The women of the family came and hastily took him away to eat, before the men were under the table.

It did not occur to him at the time because he was too young, but when he looked back he had realized how lonely his father must have been, and why he wanted the Jewish doctor to come and run the clinic with him. They had trained together in Warsaw and had both been doing postgraduate studies in virology at different hospitals in England. His father needed an intellectual equal. The girl's mother had been educated and was well read too.

There were things you never told Mutti. Who had been at the funeral in Lwow was one of them. His father regularly visiting the house next door was another. And anything to do with the girl. The girl he also kept secret and separate from everything else in his life.

He became involved after school with other ethnic German youths. They reveled in this new upsurge of fascism. There was a heady feeling coming from Germany that things were changing. He was encouraged by Mutti, but he did not need any encouragement.

Soon, Poles would no longer be able to monopolize the good jobs, the best houses. When Poland was invaded, when war began, they were ready—these bored, excited youths—to be a willing part of Hitler Youth. He had his photograph taken for propaganda. He appeared in films exhorting good ethnic Germans to be just like him, patriotic and loyal.

He felt wonderfully powerful. In love with the image that was portrayed in the posters of German manhood: uniformed, buckled and helmeted, booted feet wide, arms outstretched, bearing pointed shields like wings, with the Nazi insignia. Guarding women, children, and the precious Fatherland.

Slowly and insidiously he grew to enjoy the nervousness he could engender in people. He became intoxicated with the knowledge that his father, some of the doctors and nursing staff, and many of the servants grew afraid of what he might report.

He was riding in the forest with the girl when they had heard the drone of German planes on the horizon—hordes of them, like flocks of migrating birds, flying on reconnaissance in the distance.

He remembered the Führer's voice: "And when the great

columns of our movement march victoriously through Germany today I know that you will join these columns. And we know that Germany is before us, within us, and behind us."

He thought his chest would burst with excitement and pride.

He had turned his back on her and galloped down the valley towards the sound of them, to his German friends, and the *"Fahnenlied"* had risen to his lips in strange exultation and defiance.

Unsere Fahne flattert uns voran.
(Our banner flutters before us.)
Unsere Fahne ist die neue Zeit.
(Our banner represents the new era.)
Und die Fahne fuhrt uns in die Ewigkeit!
(And our banner leads us to eternity!)
Ja, die Fahne ist mehr als der Tod.
(Yes, our banner means more to us than death.)

He closes his eyes as he remembers the girl's ashen face as he threw her on her horse. He trembles for what he still cannot come to terms with in himself. Until that moment he had been unable to exclude her from his life. She was the child he had grown up with. She was the girl he . . .

It was twenty-seven days before the German army finally marched into Warsaw, but he sang "The Banner Song" louder and louder into the clear morning air to banish forever all that had been in his heart moments before, as his hands lay on the soft whiteness of her neck.

"Unsere Fahne ist die neue Zeit . . . Ja, die Fahne ist mehr als der Tod."

He shivers as he remembers. So many betrayals. He feels as if he has a virus poisoning his bloodstream. The life he has, the life he had, is not the same. He is no longer the man he was. He has caught a glimpse of what could have been. What might have been. Of some yearning he could never admit to. Some hope of childhood he suffocated in such fear of what he knew was forbidden. His coldness, his cruelty, has always been his escape against weakness. Mutti beat him too often for *Rassenschande* for him not to believe it was wrong . . . despite his father's example.

I must stop these thoughts. This is no good . . . no good. I must stop this.

He feels dislocated, as if he has suddenly returned from a long journey and can find nothing familiar, nothing to relate to anymore. He looks out of the window of his flat at the neat formal gardens where a woman sits on a bench and holds her arms out to the squirrels and they feed from her hands.

It is dusk and the light is dying. He thinks of a woman in a pale leather jacket: her face is turned, laughing, her head just so. The angle familiar. Known.

He gets up and shuts the sliding glass doors. Placing his fingers on the light switch he makes the room spring suddenly into a warm glow and for a while the darkness is banished.

Chapter 34

Unable to get Fred's face out of her mind, Anna makes herself a pot of strong, fresh coffee. As it brews she looks out of the kitchen window where the huge copper beech rises up over the hedge. The wind is still ruffling the leaves but the storm is dying and the sky clearing.

Anna longs to be back in London. There is really nothing she can do here and anything she does do will be resented. She switches her mobile phone on, hoping Alice might ring. She has an odd case coming up for which she has applied for a judicial review. She would rather be working than standing here in the tail of a storm watching the rain.

She sees Lucy bend under the overhanging trees to get through the gate and a wave of irritation floods through her. Why don't they cut the branches back, for God's sake, instead of ducking and getting a face full of rainwater?

Nothing gets done here. Every time she comes it is all exactly the same. The same overgrown garden, the same broken hose pipe lying in exactly the same place. Doors and windows that never get painted. Always an air of gentle neglect, of genteel poverty. She cannot bear it.

Lucy comes in through the open back door. She too looks depressed.

"Gramps looks awful today." She slides onto a chair without looking at Anna.

"Coffee?" Anna asks.

The smell of fresh coffee is too good to refuse.

Anna hands her a mug and sits in the other chair. Lucy waits for some barb but it does not come. Her mother seems subdued and says after a moment, "Fred is ill, Lucy."

Lucy looks up. "He gets terrible headaches. Sometimes he seems on another planet. I'll make a doctor's appointment."

"He won't go. He knows exactly what's wrong with him. One of the reasons he's so often on another planet, as you call it, is because he's taking diamorphine to kill the pain. Fred's got cancer, Lucy. He's asked me to do nothing. He's terrified of being taken away from Martha."

Lucy's head jerks up, shocked. "Oh God! He's not dying?"

"Lucy, I don't know how much time he has."

Lucy stares at her mother, her face ashen. Does Barnaby know? Has he kept this from her? A dull pain presses down on her chest. Anna too is visibly distressed. Her face is still beautifully made up and composed but for once her feelings show. She suddenly dives into her bag for cigarettes. Lucy has never seen her smoke before. Anna waves the packet without apology.

"Very rarely. Rudi doesn't know."

Lucy wants to cry. "Can I have one?"

Anna pushes the packet over. "As long as it doesn't become a habit."

She fidgets for a moment with the lighter. "Lucy, why are you downloading information from the Internet about Holocaust victims claiming from Swiss banks?"

Lucy had quite forgotten she had left all that stuff in the sitting room. She hesitates. There will never be a better time than this to tell Anna, but something stops her. She cannot make the words come. "It was something Grandpa said. He told me he wrote to his solicitor a few years ago. He was obviously worrying about money. Gramps seems to think that Gran's father got money out of Poland during the war and into a Swiss bank. But Grandpa was told that he needed lots of evidence—family birth certificates, death certificates of parents and so forth. And even if he found all this proof, his solicitor apparently told him that at the moment Swiss banks were not prepared to consider any claims from individuals."

Anna is silent for a moment. "I should think Fred is just very muddled. He is taking morphine, and other drugs, for all I know. But I do know a colleague who has been involved in cases by Jewish claimants. I think it would be impossible in Mum's case. Documentary evidence would definitely be needed and she was not a direct victim. What's the matter, Lucy?"

"I must have some air. I've been cooped up for hours. I'll walk Homer."

"Lucy?"

"What?" Lucy turns at the door.

"Do you know if Fred still stores all his old papers up in the loft? He used to."

Lucy goes hot and shrugs. "I don't know. He keeps an old trunk up there full of stuff."

She turns and bounds down the path. Anna has always known when Lucy is lying. Or feeling guilty. She wonders why.

She goes and pulls the ladder down, climbs into the loft and switches on the light. There is a mass of Lucy's things lying everywhere and marks in the dust on the floor where cases have been pushed about and things moved. The partition has rotted away and the trunk seems nearer the roof hatch than Anna remembers. She moves forward and kneels to open the lid.

So many old photographs. Moments caught forever and frozen in time. There is a fluttering, painful feeling in Anna's head. She hears her father's angry voice and the feel of thin paper tearing and a small piece of cardboard falling out as she hurriedly fumbles to place the documents back in the envelope.

Below her the phone blares out into the cottage, making her jump. She moves away, backs down the ladder and answers it. It is Rudi.

"Anna?" he says. "I have to ask you something. That case you are preparing for the CPS. Have you come across the name Dr. Kurt Saurer?"

"No, I don't think so. Why?"

"It's just . . . someone of that name hired that green Mercedes you saw outside the court. I've seen it near the house too. I did a private security check on him. Anna, a Berlin firm of solicitors have been asking questions about you and your work. I think he probably was following you."

"But why, Rudi? Are you there? Don't go silent on me. Why do you think it is to do with the CPS case? People make inquiries about solicitors or barristers all the time."

"Because Saurer was once a Nazi."

A wave comes in and swamps Anna. A faded red box, a gas mask, an old leather coat, a broken chair. A piece of paper, *a name.* Memory flies. She makes it fly.

She takes a deep shaky breath. "Rudi, no one has any reason to follow me. The case is unlikely to even get to pretrial. There is not enough evidence for a safe conviction. It is too long ago. Too many witnesses are dead. I am only advising the CPS because most of the evidence is in German.

"I don't take criminal cases as a rule and it's only because I've been involved in some very long cases that I've been asked to advise at all. Look, I get cranks occasionally—it comes with the job. Yes, I did notice the Mercedes, and I know I joked about it following me, but even if someone connected with the CPS case was checking up on my reputation in court, I am not in danger. If someone wanted to get to me, Rudi, they have had ample opportunity."

She pauses, takes a deep breath and says more slowly, "Please stop worrying, darling. I'll be home tomorrow. I'll talk to you then."

"Anna, you are all right? You sound . . . odd, not yourself."

"Rudi, I'm fine, just tired. Things are tricky here. Very depressing. I'll explain when I'm home."

"Take care of yourself, Anna, please." Rudi has never heard Anna sound so low.

Standing in the empty room, Anna feels a pervasive fear. She feels cold and her hands start to shake. She moves back to the ladder, feeling jerky and uncoordinated. She makes herself go back up into the loft and she throws open the trunk. Frantically, she riffles through the heap of papers, looking for a large envelope . . . documents . . . a box. There is nothing. Just Fred's life and his memories lying on wood shavings.

There is no dark thing creeping my way, it is just my imagination. I am tired. I am tired.

Anna knows the danger does not lie outside herself. It lies with the crouched thing inside her. Like a shadow, like a part of herself. As a child she was terrified that if she turned too quickly she would catch sight of the shape and horror of it just behind her. She knew it lay waiting and that it could hide anywhere. Neither darkness nor daylight was safe. Her mind would throw up a sharp snapshot of a face. She would hear a poignant, fleeting song, an unfamiliar note of music she could hum.

She shivers. When she was little the only thing that helped was to have order. If you were tidy, if everything was neat and in its place, it was harder for the thing to creep up on you.

What is your very first memory? Here, here is my first memory. The cottage. I was a baby in London . . .

Something else lies beyond that. Something you cannot . . . Remember when you were small. You woke surprised you were here . . .

Here was strange. Voices. Nothing made sense. You curled up, shut everybody out. Waited, silent for them to move you on again . . . terrified of the uni . . .

No. No. No. No.

Anna slams the trunk shut. If there were any of Martha's papers here, they are not here now.

Lucy comes into the hall with Homer as Anna is shutting the hatch and pushing up the ladder. She stares up at her mother. Anna is deathly pale. She looks old and—Lucy's heart gives a leap—her mother's face is haunted by something. It is a face she does not know.

For a moment they stare at one another. Then Anna says, her voice unsteady, "I want to know if you have taken anything from the loft. Moved anything from there, Lucy."

"What are you looking for?"

"Things like Martha's birth certificate. Any old papers of hers. If I am going to check on this compensation thing, I need . . ." Anna is clasping her shaking hands together.

"I think Grandpa keeps those sort of things in his safe." Lucy cannot take her eyes from her mother's shaking hands. Anna is frightened. What has happened while she has been out? Anna knows or remembers something she is afraid of.

Lucy has never seen her mother like this. Should she say something? Lucy quails. Now is not the time to rake up the past. Anna is *terrified* of it.

As her mother comes down the stairs, Lucy says, "Grandpa has always forbidden us to touch anything in the roof. He hated me even putting my stuff up there."

"So you haven't removed any papers or documents from the trunk?"

"No," Lucy lies, and the lie feels wrong, catches in her throat. But she has to. Look at the state of Anna. She must talk to Barnaby first. Oh God, she doesn't know what to do.

"Mum, I'm sorry if you can't find things because of all my stuff. If you tell me what you're looking for, I'll help you."

Anna swings round, away from Lucy, holding her hands up violently as if to cut off Lucy's voice.

"I don't know what I am looking for," she suddenly screams. "I don't know!"

Lucy jumps, shocked by Anna's loss of control.

"Anna," she whispers, "what's happened? What's the matter with you? Half an hour ago you were perfectly all right."

Something snaps in Anna.

"All right? Perfectly all right? With Martha senile, Fred dying? Don't be *stupid,* Lucy. They should both be in a home. I can't keep coming down to this . . . this godforsaken place to check up on them. I have two difficult cases coming up. It's just ridiculous, the whole setup. Irresponsible. One word to Social Services and they would back me to the hilt."

Anna is working herself up to a totally disparate and displaced anger. She goes and pours herself a whisky.

"My God, unmonitored, probably illegal use of diamorphine, a vulnerable old lady in the care of a girl with a ring in every orifice. An inadequate vicar, who sees only what he wants to see. I would be totally vindicated by doing something about this before I go." She rummages in her bag for her cigarettes.

"Anna!" Lucy cries. "You can't. You can't play God in Martha and Fred's lives. You have already told me Grandpa asked you not to. You agreed."

"A dying old man, Lucy, who does not know what is best for him or Martha."

"If Grandpa doesn't know, I don't know who does." Lucy makes for the back door. She must go and find Barnaby. "I don't know what the hell is suddenly eating you. Go home, Mum, if we all offend you so much. Go back to work and just leave us alone. We are coping perfectly all right without you."

Anna is pouring herself another drink. Lucy does not want to watch her mother drink like this. She goes down the steps into the garden.

"Lucy," Anna follows her to the back door, "don't think your beloved Barnaby has a final say in the welfare of Fred and Martha.

They are my parents too, and I intend to do something about them, believe me."

"What do you mean?"

Anna's face is closed, icy and irrational. "I haven't made my mind up yet. I will either get in touch with the relevant geriatric department, or—" her eyes go past Lucy to the overgrown garden—"I will sell my parcel of land. I had almost forgotten that Fred left me the plot of land over there. He knew Barnaby would want the house, and the parcel of land made it fair. If I sell I could afford round-the-clock care. Barnaby can rejoin the real world and I can be satisfied Martha and Fred are getting the best care available."

Lucy turns, white-faced, and walks back towards Anna. "If you sell that land, Martha will lose a huge chunk of her beloved garden. Someone will immediately build a horrible bungalow. All Gran and Grandpa's privacy and feeling safe here will go. You know Grandpa only meant you to sell that land when he was dead, in case you or Barnaby ever needed money. Anyway, you can't sell. Barnaby would never let you."

"He wouldn't have a choice, I assure you. I drew up the agreement. We *do* need the money . . . for care."

Lucy, furious, loses her temper. "What's your problem, Anna? A row with Rudi? Work? Well, don't bloody well take it out on the rest of us. You don't have to keep coming to this *godforsaken place.* We are much better off without you."

Anna says quietly, "I intend to make some changes around here before I leave tomorrow, Lucy. I shall certainly be making some phone calls."

Lucy stands there terrified. Anna could start something irrevocable that will tear Martha and Fred apart. She seems to be on some sort of hysterical roll that is becoming out of control.

"Why, Anna? Why do you want to hurt everybody? I don't understand. Is it because Barnaby is coping so well without any help from you? Is it because your power doesn't extend down here? Or because you can't bear Barnaby to give his time and love to Martha and Fred willingly? How can you possibly think Gran and Grandpa would be better off with paid carers than Barnaby, who loves them? You're mad!"

"Because," Anna replies coldly, "I have to make sure the law is not broken and that old people like Martha and Fred are cared for in an expert way, with all the practical help professionals can give them."

"Even if Gramps asked you not to? Even if you might split them up and break their hearts?"

"Hearts do not break, Lucy. He might even thank me."

In a panic, Lucy screams at her mother. "You know what you are? A power-crazy control freak. Don't you dare tear their lives apart, don't you dare!"

"Someone has to make unpleasant decisions around here. I am merely doing what I believe to be right."

"No, you're not! For some reason you want to get at Barnaby. You always do. You want to blow his life apart too. You are nothing but a nasty-minded little fascist, Anna. I feel sorry for you. It's in your blood, isn't it? In your very genes."

Lucy's words carry over the damp garden and seem to hover in the air as she runs weeping away from Anna through the gate.

It's in your blood, isn't it? In your very genes.

A cardboard suitcase with a little handle and a Red Cross seal. She is clutching it as she sits at a railway station between a man and a woman in uniform who speak a strange language.

Anna whimpers, wraps her arms around herself. Sits on the cold steps, rocking.

Chapter 35

Martha does not like the storm or the atmosphere in the house. The day seems to hover, without moving on. The dread will not leave her. It gathers in the stillness like thunder, growing until the weight of sadness seems unbearable, the pressure of coming darkness absolute.

When Martha was a young wife she used to cry silently inside herself. Voices and faces moved beside her like shadows. In London, in the postwar crowds, she would catch a glimpse of a face and her heart would leap with hope. She would run to touch an arm and the person would swing round to show her a stranger's face.

The weight of her loss would press down on her, hideous and threatening.

The smile she showed to the world, in those early days, and the words she used often had nothing to do with what she was really feeling. This awareness of the duplicity of human beings formed an unbridgeable chasm in Martha's mind; the consciousness that no one could ever truly know what was in another person's mind and heart, even Fred's, was isolating.

Martha hid so much that even the closeness of love could not always protect her inner self from fracturing into a million pieces. Fred understood this. He tried to help her avoid the unpleasant all their lives, without daring to tip the balance in too many attempts to confront the cause of this living anxiety; this overpowering sadness that swooped in and shadowed Martha's days.

Now, this awareness in Martha is almost gone, but the anxiety goes on breathing in Martha with a life of its own.

In the afternoon, when the storm has gone, Barnaby, Fred, and Martha sit outside under a brave watery sun. Eric, the cat, lies on the lawn, stretched like a long ginger sausage in the semishade of the cherry tree, where the thin branches and fluttering leaves make dappled and moving shadows over him.

Martha sits very still, waiting for she knows not what. Fred and Barnaby are reading their papers. Suddenly, over the hedge flies the sound of harsh angry words. Loud and bitter, they hover in the air and Martha trembles. Fred and Barnaby stop reading. Lucy comes wheeling round the trees with Homer and walks towards them. Barnaby touches Fred's shoulder and gets up.

"I'll go and make some tea, Dad."

As Lucy reaches them he puts out his hand and Lucy clutches it. She is trembling. Martha gets up too, relieved to see Lucy.

"I would like to go back to bed."

"OK, Gran." Lucy smiles into Martha's worried face. "Would you like a hot-water bottle?"

"Yes, please." Martha has a hot-water bottle summer and winter, day or night.

"I'll do it," Barnaby says. "Lucy, have you had lunch?"

"Barnes, I'm not hungry, but can I have a cup of tea? I'm really tired. I think I'll have a rest with Gran."

"All right, darling. Take your gran to bed and I'll bring it to you."

Lucy is very pale. She turns and looks at her grandfather, and Fred knows Anna has told Lucy what he asked her not to. He holds his hands out to her and she goes over to him, bends down and winds her arms around his knees. Fred, knowing she is overwrought, says nothing, but strokes her dark, tangled hair with the odd, fair bits for a moment before she gets up and flies away indoors.

Tucked up in bed Martha says to Lucy, "Draw the curtains, shut out the day. I don't like it."

Lucy draws the curtains. This horrid day is shut out, but glimpses of light through the curtains make her think of the sick bay at school, that strange sensation of going to bed during the day.

She lies down in the dark beside her grandmother.

"Darling, how nice." Martha is nearly asleep and she pats her granddaughter lovingly as she pushes away a dark memory that is creeping inexorably towards her.

WARSAW GHETTO, 1943

"*Raus! Raus!* Out! Out!" The Germans come suddenly at dawn to catch them asleep. They batter the doors with rifle butts and people spill from the houses, blinking and confused like sleepy, frightened animals.

"Shoes!" Mama cries. "Matusia, you must put on your strong shoes." It is hot but she makes Marta put on layers of clothes one on top of the other, then her winter coat on top.

They are rounded up, pushed and hurried to the square. Marta watches women cling to their children, clutch their babies, lug and trail bags and coats. She shivers. She was only just in time.

They are herded together and marched forward. Soldiers shout at them to move faster, prod them roughly with rifle butts. People who are sick or old, or who fall, are shot. Marta takes Hanna's hand as everyone is pushed on towards cattle trucks that lie waiting in a siding, rows and rows of them. They all stare at them in disbelief. Thousands of bodies behind Marta press to see. Suddenly, the soldiers drive them forward again, yelling abuse and herd them into those trucks using their whips.

Mama whispers, "Someone has made a dreadful mistake."

They are being penned and crammed inside like cattle. The soldiers use dogs to bite at their heels, to make everyone run inside, flee up the ramps in terror.

People fall in the chaos, lose their cases and bundles. Women scream out as a child is lost, as clutching, desperate fingers are pulled apart. A last old man is shoved and kicked inside Marta's truck by a soldier's boot and the doors are slammed shut. Marta stares at his startled and terrified face. He has dropped most of his bundle of possessions and he weeps.

The train begins to move slowly, jerkily forward, then gather speed. A dreadful wailing starts. It rises and falls like an endless refrain with the miles. The sound of despair covers everything, clutches them all. The truck is so full it is not possible for everyone to sit so people take it in turns to rest.

In one corner there is a bucket of water. How long will that last? Marta thinks. Just one for all these people. In another corner there is a bucket for excrement. It is not empty for long. It overflows all over the floor. Marta closes her eyes. There is no dignity or privacy left, however hard people try to shield each other.

The smell is overpowering. Some of the men take it in turns to empty the bucket through the narrow slits of windows when the train slows or stops. Those slits are the only place air can filter in and everyone fights to stay near them, suck at the air greedily.

Marta cannot breathe. She cannot breathe. All around her there are moaning bodies pressed up against her. She is going to be sick. The terrible stench fills her nostrils, chokes her, makes her retch. There is nothing but sweat and fear and excrement. Degradation.

I cannot breathe . . . I am going to suffocate . . .

Papa pulls her to him, pulls her to the side of the carriage. She is dizzy; her legs will not hold her up any longer. Papa bends to her, his mouth to her ear.

"Breathe, Marta! Don't hold your breath. Marta, breathe as deep as you can. You will get used to the smell. That's it, breathe. Good girl. Breathe . . . You are all right. We are all together. Come on, come on, child."

The wailing is like Kaddish, an endless, frightened lament. Eventually, people fall asleep, collapse against each other exhausted. The family next to Marta talk to one another in low voices, try to find hope in words of comfort. When the train slows two young boys climb up to peer through the slits to try to see the names of the stations as they pass.

They are leaving behind towns and places and people they once knew. Everyone comes from somewhere. They all had homes and lives and happy times once. The train stops. Quite still. Papa tells Mama it is because of the daylight. Because of the bombing. This train waits for darkness.

Marta listens to the silence as people sleep. Silence in the crowded darkness where each person fingers his own nightmare. Marta is so thirsty her throat swells. To swallow hurts. She can feel the stultifying terror caught from Mama's hand, the abject stillness of Papa. Hanna is almost paralyzed with fear.

She feels an enveloping cloud of terrible helplessness descend. Mama and Papa seem to fade before her eyes, as if, unable to protect her from anything any longer, they are fragmenting and shrinking.

Sometimes the train stops at small stations. They call out, beg for water, for someone to come to take out the dead. But they are invisible. Their cries fall on deaf ears. No one comes. No one dares.

At one station Marta peers through a crack and sees a woman in a red hat standing on a platform. That red hat gives her a shock. Life is going on out there as if nothing terrible is happening. Marta clutches Hanna's hand. She cannot stop shivering. She wants to wake up. She wants to wake up.

On and on into darkness. People begin to die: the baby next to Marta, the old man pushed onto the train last. The sick and the old die of heat and thirst as the stations get fewer and fewer. Then, finally, the grinding of the wheels as the train slows and comes to a halt.

Mama tries hard to rally them all. "The journey is over. We are going to be all right. When we get to the resettlement we will work hard and we will come through this war together. You'll see."

The doors are thrown open; they are blinded by floodlights. Terrible creatures with shaven heads and in striped pajamas leap out of the fog at them. Drive them out of the trucks with whips. Marta clutches Mama and Hanna as they pour off the train, dazed and bewildered. Papa is behind her, everyone is milling and turning, trying to stay together in the chaos and noise.

German SS guards stand waiting for them on the station, holding great dogs on chains. Under the lights they scream and yell orders, but people are too terrified, dazed, and exhausted to move quickly.

The guards walk up and down using their whips, pointing, dividing, choosing. Two lines. They are separating this huge milling crowd into lines. Right lines. Left lines. Groups. Columns. Marta watches carefully. People move, jump, shuffle confusedly or maybe cleverly, from one line to another. People seem to be making split-second decisions. How do they know? Marta wonders.

The old and frail, mothers with small children are all directed right.

"Left line," someone whispers behind them. "You must get into the left line. The right line leads straight to the—" Beside her, Mama turns quickly, stops the woman's words with a small movement of her hand.

Young boys using their wits lie about their age, what work they have done, and are sent left. Women forced to abandon their children have to watch them go to the right, to their deaths, alone. Healthy women beg to die with their children. Some are allowed. Some are beaten and forced to the left, to work.

I, too, would have chosen death.

Mama, Hanna and Marta hold tight to one another, struggle to stay together in the crowd. They look round for Papa but he is no longer behind them. Papa, looking bent and old, is disappearing somewhere else, pushed and carried away in the crowd. Marta screams out, but he is gone, gone, into the confusion and noise. Herded away with a large group of men with skills that are needed, before they can even say good-bye. Gone forever. Papa.

Mama, Hanna and Marta are sent to the left. They are ordered to leave all their possessions on the station platform to be reclaimed later. But they never again see the things Mama so carefully packed for them. They are marched in a group of women healthy enough to walk. They are marched through a gateway under a sign which says "arbeit macht frei"—"Work Makes Free."

Everyone is herded into a large building, a huge bathhouse. They are ordered to take off their clothes and shower in freezing water. They are told to separate any woolen garments they wear from their other clothes. They are disinfected and showered. Their hair is cut off.

Our heads are shaved. We are shaved of all body hair. My long dark hair falls in a great mass onto the floor. Then Hanna's. Then Mama's.

They stand naked, shivering, sick with cold and humiliation. They are thrust dirty, sacklike garments, which rub roughly against their skin. No undergarments. No stockings against the cold. No shoes, just ill-fitting clogs.

Marta thinks there is nothing else the SS can take from them. Ordered to line up once again, they have to shout their names out and they are issued with a number. That number is tattooed on their forearm.

They take our names and they give us back a number. A number branded into our flesh. This is who we are now. We have no hair, no clothes, no identity. We are nameless. I stare at Mama and Hanna and they stare back. The only way we recognize each other is by the horror reflected in our eyes.

"Gran! Gran! Wake up, you're dreaming. Gran? Look, I'm drawing the curtains. Look, look at that sky, it's a beautiful evening."

Lucy throws light back into the room. She turns, sees in Martha's eyes abject terror. Her face is like a ghost, her small body trembling as if she has a fever.

Lucy pulls the eiderdown up over Martha's shoulders, right up to her chin and sits on the edge of the bed and holds her tight, tight to her.

"Gran," she whispers, over and over again, rocking her. "Gran . . . Gran, it's all right, everything's all right. You are safe. You are home. You are safe. You are home . . ."

Martha slowly comes back from the terrible place she has been and struggles to remember Lucy . . . stares up at the young girl. "Oh, darling, darling, I am so, so glad you are here."

She reaches a thin arm up out of the eiderdown and Lucy takes it, turns it gently and presses her mouth to the tiny scar on Martha's left forearm and her tears fall on Martha's arm. When Lucy looks up she sees a fleeting awareness in Martha's eyes.

"I love you, Gran," she whispers.

"And I love you, darling," Martha replies.

Chapter 36

That evening, a subdued, ill-looking Anna appears to say a formal good-bye before driving back to London.

"Please, don't go like this," Barnaby says to her. "Stay the night. Make your peace with Lucy. Go in the morning, Anna. You shouldn't drive when you're upset."

Anna raises her hands abruptly to shut off his words. "Barnaby, I am not upset. I am perfectly all right. Don't fuss. Lucy and I have said all there is to say. I want to get back to London . . ."

She pauses, closes her eyes for a moment as if the subject depresses her beyond words. "You know how I feel about the right care for Martha and Fred, Barnaby. We'll have to talk about it another time. I'm just too tired at the moment. Perhaps without Lucy you'll realize you can't cope."

Barnaby experiences a familiar stab of frustration. Anna is never deflected or swayed once she has made up her mind. He is suddenly glad she is going. Both of them always revert back to their childish positions of attack and defense. Lucy is unfortunately right: Anna always heralds disruption while making him feel guilty at the same time.

She gathers up her expensive bag, scarf, and car keys and says suddenly, "Barnaby, you do realize Fred is ill? That he is probably more in need of medical care than Martha at the moment?"

"Anna, of course I know," Barnaby says quietly. "I'd have to be an idiot not to realize. He made me promise not to worry you and he doesn't want Lucy to know how ill he is. Brian comes in every week unofficially and I am in constant contact with the surgery. It is the only medical monitoring Fred is prepared to accept at the moment. I have to respect his wishes."

Anna stares at him, her hand on the open front door. "Then you will also know he is injecting large doses of morphine into himself to kill the pain, which make him hallucinate."

She stares at his shocked face. "Barnaby, I don't envy you. I'm more than prepared to help with their care. But you must meet me halfway. I've made my feelings clear on what I believe is the best thing for them both."

"Yes, you have, Anna. And I told you I won't discuss that subject with you again. And I meant it."

Anna walks away into the conservatory to say good-bye to Martha and Fred.

"Good-bye, Barnaby," she says as she passes him still standing by the front door. On the doorstep she turns. "By the way, I have decided to sell the plot of land Fred left me. It will release funds that are needed and will enable either Martha or Fred to go into the best home possible. As Fred deteriorates, he will thank me for this, Barnaby." She stands looking at him for a moment. "I suggest you talk to Social Services about a suitable place, or I will have to alert them to the dangers of my parents not being professionally and adequately monitored."

She walks away from him and climbs into her Mercedes and is about to glide down the drive when Barnaby pulls open the door of the Mercedes, startling her.

"How dare you come here and issue threats? How dare you come down and make decisions which will affect the rest of Martha and Fred's lives? You waltz in when it suits you and decide you have the moral right . . ."

Barnaby pauses, takes a deep breath. "If, over my head, you try to contact Social Services or indeed try to sell that parcel of land on the pretext of it being necessary, I will go to Fred's solicitor. It is part of Martha's rose garden and Dad only meant you to sell it when they were dead. I will also make sure I have sole power of attorney. Martha and Fred have never been apart and there is no way I am going to let you ride roughshod over their lives now."

He leans into the car. "This is not about money, Anna. It's about a guilty conscience. It is as if you can't relax until they are both tidied up into a home. Well, Anna, people's lives can't always be pigeonholed into safe compartments. The old do end up with sad, untidy and, to you, possibly useless lives. But there are worse things than being safe. Living your last days as a couple, with people who love you. What could be more important than that?"

Barnaby can't stop. "You work extremely hard, you don't have to have a conscience. I am here because I want to be, Anna. You do not have to feel grateful. But don't try to deprive me of what I want to do because you would like to say to your friends. 'Oh, my parents are in a wonderful home. It costs the earth—I had to sell my inheritance—but it is worth every penny. . . .'"

He is shaking. Anna is very still, staring at the dashboard, not at him. He sees for the first time how exhausted she looks.

He says more quietly. "I have never fought you on anything. But I mean everything I say, Anna. I don't want to make you look silly, but this is my parish, the place where I work and live. I know, through my parishioners, most of the social workers and doctors here. You have not visited Martha and Fred for nearly a year. Do you really think you can achieve the moral high ground? Sound entirely altruistic?"

Barnaby cannot be sure—the light is going—but he thinks Anna might be near to tears. "Look, I am not rubbing it in, Anna, just stating a fact," he says more gently.

Anna turns then and looks at him. For the first time he sees age in her drawn face, and not her beauty.

"Have you finished? Are you going to let me drive to London now, Barnaby?"

"I've finished." Barnaby stands up, takes his hand away from the car door. "I'm sorry you are leaving like this. I think you're very tired and I would be much happier if you drove back in the morning."

Anna smiles tightly, changes in to first gear. "Barnaby, if you don't want the Social Services to take an active interest in your domestic arrangements, I suggest you sort out Fred's drugs. However sentimental you feel about Martha and Fred ending their days together in abject poverty, morphine is not exactly a prescribed drug."

She shuts the car door and drives away without looking at Barnaby. Anna always has to have the last word. Barnaby turns to find his father behind him.

"Sorry old chap, should have told you about the morphine. Don't worry, Brian has taken me in hand." Fred smiles with irony. "Run out of my own little stash and doctors nowadays have to account for every drug they prescribe."

He pats Barnaby's arm. "I think a whisky might hit the spot, don't you?"

They hold their glasses up to each other as Martha sleeps.

"We'll be all right, Dad. We've managed so far."

Fred smiles at his son. "Of course we will. No doubt about it."

Barnaby wonders how many times in his childhood Fred has made Anna's bitter, hostile words more palatable. What is it in Anna that she can never back down, or admit she might be wrong about anything? He wishes he knew.

Anna drives towards the causeway. Lights spring up in the dusk around her like fireflies, increasing her sense of isolation. Orange reflections lie across the black water over which creek birds swoop, giving out mournful cries.

Anna turns off the road into the empty pub car park, drives to the sea wall and sits in the car looking out over the water. She is very still. Something has happened. She feels unreal, as if she is in a mild form of shock. For the first time she no longer knows herself. She never loses control.

She turns and fishes her cigarettes out of her bag, lights one and inhales deeply. She has got to stop this. Her closet smoking is creeping up. She is deadly tired, to the point of exhaustion. She has been drinking during the day and despite sleep and copious amounts of coffee she knows she cannot drive to London tonight.

In a moment she will ring Rudi, tell him she will book into somewhere for the night and set off early tomorrow. It is odd. She is normally reluctant to talk about her feelings; now, when she feels like talking to someone, Rudi is not here.

There is a small commotion on the water and two ducks rise squawking and fly away clumsily with their wings touching the surface. Anna longs to be back in London, away from this stillness, this quiet and beautiful dying of the day. She feels a profound sense of loss and longing that feels unbearable. For one second she understands how it would be possible to walk into those still waters and let the blackness swallow you up. That tiny second feels very powerful. Then it is gone.

Martha and Fred. Gentle people who have never given her anything but love. Suddenly old and frail and needy as if they had got that way overnight, without her noticing. She has not made time to notice the weeks and months of their deterioration. They are slipping away from her, never to be recovered. How easy it was for her to have taken their love for granted, like background music, always there.

Two people she could have asked and now it is too late.

Did something happen when I was born? Or did I come too soon, before you were both ready for children? Why do I dream?

It was the end of the war. Maybe Martha had had no time to get over the loss of her family and the strangeness of a new country. If her conception had been a shock, so early in the marriage, it would account for the distance she and Martha have always had, and her parents' seeming reluctance to talk about her birth or the time they spent in London while the house was being built.

Once, when the nightmares were very bad, Fred carried her back to his study. The room was warm and stuffy and Mahler was playing softly. She curled up on his knee, listening with him as she grew sleepy. The music was exquisitely sad. It had touched and loosened something inside her. It felt as if she were fraying and coming undone, but she did not know why.

She had started to cry, burying her head into Fred's shirt.

He had bent his head to her and his hair, which used to flop when he was younger, fell over her face.

"Can you tell me, Anna, darling, what you dream and then I can send it away?"

This fear of something dark and suffocating edging slowly but surely her way, waking her with a sick jump in the night, making her toss and turn, the face of the thing approaching, the form it will take, the terror of it always shapeless.

"No, if I talk they will get me."

"Who will, my sweet? There is no one here but you and me."

"There is, there is, in the dark whispering when I'm asleep and they don't speak English."

Silence.

Then: "Well, I am your father and I am telling you there is nobody in the dark whispering. It is a dream you have, a very horrible dream. Now, this beautiful piece of music we are listening to makes you sad while you are listening, but when I turn it off, after a little while the sadness you felt in there . . ." he patted her heart, "will fade away, with the music, won't it?"

She nodded.

"Well, these dreams that seem real to you now in the dark are like a piece of music. They will fade too, and the memory of them."

"Promise?"

"I promise."

They did fade. They do. But they always come back.

She looks out onto the dark water. She cannot ever remember seeing the adult Barnaby so angry. As a child she could push the small Barnaby a hell of a long way, but occasionally he would suddenly turn like a small spitfire and let fly at her, fight back. Those were the times Anna knew she had gone too far. She was never punished, but Martha and Fred could not look at her. She felt their hurt and longed for their anger, as if anger would be a signal, proof of their unconditional love.

She knows she has gone too far today. She could not stop. Once she had started she just went on and on. Enough to have a row with Lucy. Why then did she have to start again with Barnaby? She heard herself compounding threats, like a child, that she had no intention of carrying out. Why?

She closes her eyes against the memory of Fred's sad face behind Barnaby, waiting, hovering to protect and comfort. As he always had.

Is she heading for a breakdown? She has frightened herself today. She would despise it in anyone else. Perhaps she should have a word with Alice. Too many big cases, one on top of another. She tries to think when she and Rudi last had more than a snatched long weekend and she cannot.

She lights another cigarette. After this packet she will not buy any more.

Anna draws deeply on her cigarette and stares across the reed beds. Out of the open car window the water slaps against the sea-wall like the sound of small hands clapping.

Fred is dying. Martha no longer recognizes her.

Is this deeply embedded anxiety that is stalking her to do with them? Is it merely the manifestation of her guilt? She has shut them out of her life. Her busy London life. As if without them she feels safer.

Down here, the nebulous fear of her dreams seems closer.

She stubs out her cigarette and starts the car engine. Sleep. All this is due to lack of sleep. She will have to resort to temporary sleeping pills if this goes on, at least until this current case is over. She turns the car round and drives out into the road.

She has always been healthy and she thinks suddenly, I will be perfectly all right as soon as I reach London and get back to work. It is having time to think that is the problem. She picks up speed over the causeway. She is going to have to leave her parents to Barnaby at the moment, whatever her views. She cannot afford to take on any more. She must concentrate on work.

She books into a small hotel in Truro, has a meal and goes straight to bed. She gets up at four o'clock the next morning and has an easy drive back to London. The roads are clear. She has slept well and she feels good.

She plans every minute of the coming day as she drives, feeling the familiar excitement of being in control again. She finds she is humming as she turns into her own road of terraced houses and parks the Mercedes. She smiles, as Rudi, obviously watching for her, opens the front door.

She is home. The Anna of yesterday is conveniently buried and forgotten. As so much of Anna is.

Chapter 37

BERLIN

It is the sight of blossom everywhere, in the gardens and parks and wide suburban roads on the edge of the city, strewn across the pavements like confetti, that takes him back to that house in Poland.

That apple tree in the garden of his childhood would spread huge sprays of blossom, coloring the lawns pink and white. They lived too far out of Warsaw for him to have friends to play often. Friends had to be invited, they could not just appear over the wall. It was the same for the girl.

They both used to climb up into the great branches of the apple tree to hide. They would ride their horses under it, make them stand still, then clamber up into the highest branches while the horses cropped the grass and filled themselves with fallen apples in summer.

Often, in the evenings, the boy would hide from his nurse for hours up in that tree—bored, until he was old enough to meet his German friends. It was as if he had been waiting all his childhood for life to get more interesting, for things to happen. He had never before had the opportunity to make close male friends.

His father was busy building up a successful practice and as a small child he had been left with only Mutti for company. If that little family had not moved next door, he would have been isolated from children his own age until secondary school.

How his father loved that tree. Each winter he would go and check the leaves for infection or insects, place his hand on the great trunk as if it were a friend. The day he had his last conversation with his father, there was a bad storm. He was out riding a small mare through the forest—Tylicz was lame—and the noise of the wind through the trees made her annoyingly jumpy so he came home in a bad mood.

His father sent a message to ask him to go to his study. Mutti was away and the boy supposed his father was taking this opportunity to talk to him alone—a last-ditch attempt to influence his son into his way of thinking.

When he entered the room his father had his back to him. He was looking out on to the garden, at the trees bent in the storm, at the rain lashing the windows, at the apple tree, which was almost in blossom. Spring . . . it must have been spring 1940.

The boy stared at the back of his father's neck. His collar seemed suddenly too big for him, as if he had lost weight. He saw the way the gray wispy hair on the back of his neck curled inside that too large collar, at the way his father's narrow shoulders were bent in a sort of heaviness, a sad bewilderment.

He knew his father had heard him come in. He also knew that he was having difficulty turning to face him, and, amid a spasm of pity for an aging man left behind by events, he felt a surge of satisfaction, a little lurch of power too.

"You wanted to see me?"

His father turned then, trying to smile. The boy watched his face change when he saw he was in uniform. The boy was quite aware of the effect his Hitler Youth uniform would have on his father. It was why he had changed into it. His father stared at him, his smile fading.

"Sit down. Will you have a drink?"

"Thanks." The boy straddled the chair near his desk as insolently as he could, resentful of the way his father could always make him feel.

"I have a meeting in half an hour. I can't stay long."

His father handed him a beer. "I won't keep you long. I have to go to Lodz tomorrow and I wanted to talk to you before I leave. You might be gone before I get back."

"I am awaiting orders," the boy smirked. "So, Father, finally even you, in your reserved occupation, have not been able to avoid joining the glorious Third Reich any longer."

He watched a small tic start in his father's cheek. His father would have liked to slap the smile from his face. "I go to Lodz as a civilian doctor still although, of course, you are quite right. I cannot avoid the inevitable much longer."

The boy took a sip of beer. "Why would you want to, Father?"

"And I ask you the very same question."

"What do you mean?"

"I ask you, why? Why would you want to wear that particular uniform with such pride? Has nothing I believe in, none of the values I tried to instill, had any influence on you whatsoever? Despite your years of insidious domestic and institutionalized anti-Semitism, I expected more of you. Hoped for more. I have waited for you to reject your mother's extreme prejudices, use your intellect.

"Tell me, have you no mind of your own, but absorb Nazi propaganda like a willing sponge? Without question, without any intellectual or moral appraisal at all? You seem to have embraced Nazi ideology with an enthusiasm and vigor I find quite abhorrent."

Angrily, the boy started to get up but his father waved him back into the chair.

"It is not your fault you were born and educated within the shadow of Hitler, with all the influences of fascism, but, I ask you again, are you quite incapable of separating right from wrong?

What you must know is perverse and evil? Please note, I am not talking of finer feelings here: I conclude you do not have any. I am talking about quite basic human instincts."

The boy stared at him coldly. "You should be very careful of what you say, Father. You are a German and you are speaking treason."

His father smiled at him without humor. "Would my son report me to his new Nazi cohorts in Tomaszow?"

"I won't have to report you. Germany is at war and it is our duty to defend our country and all that Germany stands for. You know very well, Father, we have to protect our own interests in the face of an inferior race that threatens to infiltrate and overrun us in all directions. It is not possible to think in terms of *individual* interest. The purity and survival of the German race is what we are up against here."

His father sat down heavily. "Oh, my son, my poor son, if only you could hear yourself. The Jews account for about one percent of the population! This is Poland, not Germany. A defeated Poland. Yes, of course you are a German, but your maternal grandmother was *Polish.* This is where your mother's wealth, this house came from, even if your mother tells it somehow differently." He held his hands up. "I am not questioning you having to be in a uniform—we *are* Germans—what I am questioning is your need to wear *that* uniform."

He put his beer glass down and looked into the boy's eyes. "I ask you to stop and think. Stop now, and make a moral judgment on where you stand in this war before it is too late. You were not part of the German forces who invaded Poland. You have lived here all your life. You have Polish friends. Who do you need to impress with your fervor for fascist uniforms? Yourself? Or the German bully boys you have taken for your friends?"

His father turned away to the window, taking a drink of his beer.

"Of course it might just be that you have worn that uniform for propaganda purposes so often in the last year, they have made a gift of it to you."

The boy jumped up. His father was mocking him. He could feel his eyes blazing, hurting with his fury. *The stupid, senile, treacherous old buzzard was going to end up in prison.* Obviously, he was totally incapable of grasping what they were all fighting for.

"I am proud of this uniform! I am proud to be chosen to wear it. I am a German—why shouldn't I be proud of all that we are achieving? A German is a German whether he lives in Warsaw or Berlin, Father. Don't you read the papers? Don't you see what we are up against? I've told you, if we don't fight for our own German identity we will be swamped. Our blood will be diluted by Jewish blood, Father. There will be no such thing as a pure German."

"Do you really think that everyone back in Germany is a Nazi? I have friends and colleagues in Germany as appalled as I am. There are thousands of normal, thinking people, who have the courage to reject what is happening, despite the hysterical rhetoric, to turn their backs on what they believe to be wrong. Can you really believe those thugs you go around with represent the true German? Neither you nor your mother are *pure German.* In fact I am the only pure German in this house, and the only antifascist."

The boy ignored this remark and marched up and down his father's study, warming to his theme. "Industry, banking, medicine . . . They are everywhere. I'm proud to be part of this new order where we will be able to protect our own interests and our children from disease and poverty. I don't want to be overrun by another race. I want my children born in a safe, clean enviro—"

He stopped. His father was *laughing.* The boy became still like he used to when he was a child, unsure suddenly of what was coming. The laughter was not a nice sound and something in his father's eyes made him squirm. His father swiveled suddenly in his chair and swung round to him. His voice was soft, conversational.

"I presume part of this new order, this cleansing, this safe environment for your children is the public humiliation of Jews in the streets. As well as divesting them of all they have, proclaiming against their very existence, robbing them, you, in your smart shiny uniforms, find it amusing to strip them, cut off their beards and make them dance like monkeys in the street for everyone to jeer at. Oh, great new world! How proud you must be to be a German! Courageous, brave, blond and good! Hitler's idealistic *pure* race."

His father's anger choked him. He closed his eyes for a second, then said so quietly the boy had to bend to hear his words, "I saw you yesterday on the corner of Krakowskie Street."

The sweat suddenly broke out under the boy's shirt.

"Five of you. All in the uniform you are so proud of. Five youths, all tall, fair hair blowing in the wind, just like one of your propaganda films. You were with one short fat *Volksdeutscher,* wearing his red swastika armband with pride. Do you know what you were doing?"

The boy did not answer. He did not look at his father but stared resolutely at the branches of the apple tree being bent against the wind, sending little flakes of white from the unopened blossom whirling to the grass.

"I will tell you what you were all doing." His father's words caught in his throat. "You were making an old man in bare feet leap up and down like a frog. Over and over, on and on, until he fell over in the gutter exhausted. You were all laughing and encouraging the people watching to laugh. I thought, I've made a mistake, that isn't my son. Yes, he has always had a cruel streak as boys sometimes do, but he is not wicked. He is not a weak bully. He is my son who is going to be a medical student."

The boy was silent.

"I *prayed* it wasn't you. But it was. I cannot describe the shame I felt, or the lurching horror of seeing the son I love in a base act of cruelty. I also know that what you did yesterday afternoon is nothing compared to other horrors being heaped upon the Jews of Warsaw by Germans like you."

He spat out those last words and the boy was able to react. "He was trying to beg for bread. He was where he shouldn't have been. He was a dirty old man. We were just having a bit of a laugh, teaching him a lesson."

"For being hungry? For being alive? For being a Jew?" He turned for the door, he had had enough. *"I haven't finished."* His father's voice made him jump. *"Turn and look at me!"*

Despite himself he turned.

"There has always been a frightening coldness about you. For a while I thought it had disappeared with your loneliness when the little family moved next door, when you and the child became friends."

His father came right up to him. "Tell me, how do you think they are managing next door? Now Dr. Oweski is no longer allowed to work with me, or indeed with anyone? How do you imagine the girl and her beautiful mother are going to cope with the ghetto when their time comes, as it surely will? Do you ever think of them having to go out and forage for food in those appalling armbands. Do you?"

"They could leave. They have money. It is possible."

"Is it? You are not answering me. I want to know. How do you think of them, this family, this girl you have known nearly all your life. Are they dirty Jews? Should they too be humiliated? Are they like all the others? Are they social outcasts and a threat to society? Are they due for your institutionalized horrors? What have they taken from Germans, this doctor next door who has never discriminated against any patient, rich or poor, German, Polish or Jew? Come on, answer me, you who have all the answers and no conscience."

The sweat poured down the boy's arms and legs in the hot rough uniform.

"You don't understand. It is . . . Yes, it is unfortunate. But we have to think of the greater good."

His father stood up abruptly, one arm holding on to his desk as if for support. His face was stiff with contempt. "*Unfortunate?* Oh, get out of my sight. I don't want to see you anymore. I don't wish to hear you spouting any more propaganda to cover what you really feel, what you must know to be right. Just remember this. What you do, what you are, will come back to haunt you, for this is only the beginning. One day you will have to face yourself. Now go . . ."

He never spoke to his father again. He knew why he was going to Lodz. He was going to take medicines to the ghetto. He wishes he had told him he was sick in the grass with disgust, with shame, the afternoon he baited the old Jew.

With the help of Mutti's contacts, he was in a German army uniform three weeks later, just before his eighteenth birthday.

He was to do worse, much worse, before he began to question himself. This is why he sits in his comfortable flat in Berlin, old and haunted, as his father warned him he one day would be.

Chapter 38

Lucy sits on the wall outside the church where she can see down the road. The sun is warm on her face and she lifts it to the sky with closed eyes. She can hear seagulls on the roof screaming noisily as they nest, carrying large twigs in their beaks and stuffing them, to Barnaby's annoyance, down the chimney.

A helicopter flies over the coastline and away towards the horizon. The church clock strikes and the dull roar of the ocean reaches her as the helicopter disappears. She is leaving. Tomorrow she will close her eyes and imagine herself still here, sitting on this wall.

She is waiting for Tristan to arrive to take her back with him to London. Excitement flares in little waves, making her feel slightly sick. She cannot sit still; she keeps thinking of things she has forgotten and she runs back into the house to find Barnaby.

Barnaby is amused. Cool Lucy keeps flying to the mirror and redoing her casual ponytail, which is anything but casual, as far as Barnaby can see, with one piece of hair sticking up or falling down at a special angle and needing to be constantly readjusted.

He winks at Kate, who is also driving up to London this weekend to collect the rest of her belongings. She grins at him.

"Lucy is making me feel very, very ancient," she mutters as she passes Barnaby with coffee for Martha and Fred.

"Poor old dear." Barnaby pats her arm as he goes out of the

front door for lunch with the Bishop of Truro, and at that moment Tristan's red car turns in the drive in a great splutter of loose gravel. Barnaby smiles to himself. This is like old times, Tristan is incapable of driving slowly through the gates.

Tristan leaps out and he and Barnaby grasp hands warmly. "Still got the tartmobile, I see," Barnaby says.

Tristan laughs. "I was going to ask you out to lunch, Barnaby. Not sure I will now."

How young he is, Barnaby thinks. How young to be going out to that violent and unpredictable place. "Afraid I'm on my way to have lunch with the bishop, Tris. I'll see you later. Forgive me rushing, but I'm late as always."

Lucy comes flying out, squeaking with joy and Tristan catches her and whirls her round as Barnaby makes a dash for his car. As he reverses he can see Martha inside the house making her way towards the front door. Tristan holds his arms out.

"Martha! Every time I come you are more beautiful."

"Balls!" Martha says fondly, clucking her tongue at him and they all burst out laughing.

Tristan turns to Fred and shakes his hand.

"You taught her that word!" Fred says drily, smiling. "Good to see you, boy."

"Good to see you too. I know it's a bit late but can I take everyone out to lunch?"

"My dear fellow . . ." Fred says vaguely.

Martha says, "Darling, how lovely!"

Lucy is staring at Tristan, consumed by desire. He winks at her. "Luce?"

"It's a great idea, but I don't know whether Kate has already cooked for Gran and Grandpa. Come and meet her."

"Hi," Kate says, and waves her hands over the kitchen table dismissively. "It's only cold chicken, it will keep until tonight. Go, have fun, they will love it."

"Come and join us," Tristan says. "You're very welcome."

"Thanks," she smiles at him, "but I've got to drive to London later, so I'll take this opportunity to get organized."

When they have all disappeared in the red car, which could not possibly have held her too, and the house, flooded in dusty sunlight, is silent, Kate sits for a moment in Martha's chair. She has never been in the house alone before and the feeling is dreamlike, the silence filled with the essence of people living out their lives here.

Kate sits listening to the sound of birds and the rustle of overgrown rose branches brushing against the windowpanes. She watches the sun catching at the peeling paint of the doors, lifts her face to catch the fleeting scent of lemon balm, which is growing in a pot in a corner of the conservatory. Her hands on the faded covers of the chair are almost translucent in sunlight.

Time seems to stop. She feels without substance, as if she is floating. Into this intangible emptiness rises an acute and haunting sadness. Almost unendurable.

Kate thinks suddenly, I am sitting with ghosts of the past. I am sitting with young Fred and Martha. I will never know them, they were different people then, living in a world before I was born. A wave of loss, a faint echo that seems caught forever in the fabric of the house like a muffled lament reaches out to touch Kate, and is gone.

She gets up abruptly, locks the house and walks across the garden and through the overgrown gate. She stands and stares at the little cottage that will soon be hers. She feels the excitement of a child. It is a long time since she had anywhere of her own. The weather is too good to go back to the hotel, too hot to drive. Kate ducks out of the gate again and down to the beach. The sun touches the back of her neck and she takes her shoes off and begins to run towards the distant hum of the sea.

* * *

Tristan drives into St. Ives and down the steep incline to the Beach Café, his and Lucy's favorite place. It is warm enough to sit out, and Martha is enchanted by the little tables set out above the beach. She sits looking at the children below her, happy and distant. Fred, watching her, thinks: it is as if we are all muffled, under water and Martha has given up trying to make out what we are all silently mouthing.

She eats with delight the fish Tristan carefully orders for her.

"Oh, darling, this is lovely."

Tristan is working hard to make this a special treat and Lucy loves him for it. Fred and Martha seem relaxed and happy. The sea, behind them, Quink ink blue, glitters against the warm sand and Lucy knows she can leave for London with the memory of this day. If Barnaby could have come it would have been perfect.

Tristan looks at Martha's face as she stares out at the glittering sea below her and at the small children playing in the waves. He gets up from the table and holds out his hand to her.

"Come with me to the sea. Let's see how cold it is."

Martha looks up and smiles. She likes this tall boy with the floppy fair hair and lopsided grin.

"Oh, darling . . ." She takes his hand and lets Tristan pull her to her feet. They move awkwardly across the heavy sand, arm in arm, and Fred smiles to himself.

"Nice boy." He winks at Lucy, amused by her happiness.

At the sea's edge Tristan bends and rolls up the bottoms of Martha's trousers, lifts her feet one after another and takes her socks and shoes off. He kicks his sandals away and they step gingerly into the small slapping waves.

"Ooh!" Martha gasps, flinching.

"Ye gods!" Tristan yelps.

They stand facing out towards the lighthouse, giggling like children as the waves buffet and drench the bottoms of their trousers.

Watching them, Lucy experiences a stab of pain, is choked

with love. She turns to Fred as the figures in the sea bend to something in the sand. The expression on his face is wistful, lonely. His mouth is pulled in a tight line, as if to prevent it trembling. His eyes are fixed on the figures in the sea. His voice when it comes is just a sigh caught by the distant sound of the sea.

"I miss her. Oh, how I miss her."

Below them, Tristan holds something in the palm of his hand and Martha peers down at it. It is a tiny, frail crab shell intricately decorated in pinpricks. It lies translucent against Tristan's hand. At their feet, lying on the foamy shoreline, there are rows of similar shells as if the occupants had left their coats there while going for a swim. Martha stares at them.

"Like baby skulls," she says suddenly.

Tristan looks at her, startled. "What a horrid analogy, Martha."

The wind suddenly takes the frail crab shell out of Tristan's hand and it blows into the sea, turns upside down like a walnut and is brought again to their feet by a wave.

Lucy runs across the sand towards them. "Is it freezing?"

"Delicious, darling." Martha's words are snatched by the wind and falling waves.

Tristan watches the crab shell nudge his toes before it breaks up and sinks. For a moment a cold shadow, like the wings of a great bird, hovers over him, then is gone.

He turns to Fred and waves, and the old man waves back.

"Get your kit off and swim, I dare you," he says to Lucy, trying to recapture the lightness of the day.

"You must be joking!" she says. "Get your kit off yourself."

Tristan lifts her, squeaking, and pretends he is going to throw her into the sea.

"Gran! Gran! Save me," Lucy yells.

Martha pulls at Tristan's shirt, worried now. "No. No. Naughty boy. Drop her at once."

Tristan roars with laughter. "You make her sound like a bone, Martha!"

He puts Lucy down, and gathers up all their shoes and they walk back across the sand to Fred.

Later that night, after they have made love and are curled up together in Lucy's bed, Lucy tells Tristan about Martha's hidden, secret life contained in the faded red box. Of the childish Polish diaries she cannot read and the letters in German which she can. Of the yellowing photos and the frail brown documents she still has not looked at. Tristan is shocked, but he is not as surprised as Lucy thought he would be.

"It is strange," he tells her. "It's something my father said ages ago. I was telling him how protective Fred was of Martha, long before she started to get Alzheimer's, and he said, 'Naturally, he is,' rather sharply. I asked him what he meant and he told me to use my imagination. I just thought he meant that Martha was Polish and had had to leave her family behind. Perhaps he just guessed . . ."

Lucy leans up on one elbow and presses her mouth to his shoulder, closes her eyes against the memory of her grandfather's letter to his mother.

"My father knew someone who had been at school with Fred. He told him Fred had been a somewhat smug and arrogant boy, typical of his era. He was clever but never worked particularly hard because he knew he was going to inherit."

Tristan strokes Lucy's pale coffee skin distractedly with his finger.

"This man told my father that Fred was incredibly brave in the war, got mentioned in dispatches, all that, but he came back a completely changed and different man."

Lucy gets out of bed and pads naked to the window seat and brings Fred's letter back to Tristan, opens it and hands it to him. As Tristan reads Lucy watches the moon, a pale crescent emerging out of the shadow. Within it she can see the perfect whole reflected in a ghostly light and mirrored again in the water below.

All is quiet. She can hear the silence outside and inside. She hears Tristan swallow, feels his tears suddenly, cold on her bare skin. He scoops her to him, holds her tight against his chest, holds her so tight it hurts.

Over her head he stares at the sliver of moon, which will be shining on Kosovo. And presumably shone on Auschwitz.

Against his heart, Lucy whispers, "Don't ever change, Tris. I love you so, so much. Don't get hurt or change, will you?" Against her hair, Tristan smiles bleakly. Lucy is so young. He wants to say, "Lucy, of course I'll change. Everyone changes, all the time. You are changed by finding Martha's papers. I am changed by reading Fred's letter. *Of course I will change and so will you.*" But he is silent, rocking her gently. Still mesmerized by that eerie moon, he wonders what the next few weeks will bring. He has had many doubts about the futility of refereeing someone else's war, the impossibility of taking on or ever understanding another country's ethnic loathing. But maybe it is purely about a principle. Maybe it just comes down to standing up for what you believe to be morally right. Standing against evil. Because one day you might wake up and it will not be finding a mass grave that breaks your heart, but finding a whole lost life of someone you love.

He thinks of Martha. Martha, Lucy's age, staggering towards him like a bundle of rags in a landscape stripped of all human compassion. He thinks of a young, carefree Fred running to catch her as she falls.

Lucy's body is warm and he turns to bury his head in her hair.

He hasn't told her yet his leave has been canceled.

Chapter 39

I dream of Poland under snow. In my dream our house is still crouched there on the edge of the forest with icicles hanging blue-tinged from the roof. The trees bend under the great weight of snow, which slides off the branches in great plops of muffled sound.

The garden lies silent. Magic. Waiting. I walk across the snow where no one else has walked and my footsteps behind me are like the tiny marks of a bird. When I turn and look at them I feel the smallness of myself in the white and suffocated garden. I stand in wonder at this world in which I feel insignificant in the vast expanse of white. Invisible under the snowy branches of the great firs.

When I see the ocean for the first time—that great swell and rise of blue stretching out forever into the distance, glittering and dazzling in a hundred shades of turquoise—when I see the sea I drown in the blueness of it. I am swallowed whole. It is like snow all over again.

Alone, I run down to the beach, across the rippling, uneven sand full of troughs and ridges made by the beating of the waves. I run through warm pools of left-behind sea to the water's edge. No one is here. Just me on the edge of the ocean where small neat waves curl inward and break at my feet with a soft smack.

I look down and see, in a row along the sea's edge, a line of tiny, oddly marked shells with marks like delicate filigree. I bend and lift one and see with horror it is like a tiny empty baby's skull. It is so light that it blows from my hand back into the sand.

I look up into the curl of the great, green waves in the second before they break and I see the faces of the children in the ghetto. I see my school friends, Berta, Ilsa, and my little cousins, Joshua and Jacob. I catch the faces of Mama and Papa, Aunt Rina and Uncle Horst. They are caught, turning, their eyes watching me in the curve and fall of that great thundering mountain of water.

I watch the sea and I think I see in the patterns of foamy surf tumbling arms and legs thrown together or held up, up in surrender. I turn and run from the waves and when I am hugged by the cliffs, huge seabirds whirl and circle their nests and I jump as the explosion of water hits the rocks with a great crack.

I remember the slow, sure shot that will wing out of nowhere. I will hear again the faint scream like the sound of these strange birds hovering in the air with trembling wings above the cliffs. I will listen for the thud of a body falling on snow, the sick crack of their frail, shaved skulls hitting the frozen earth, breaking open like an egg.

I do not just hear it. I feel that sound with my whole body, a sound I hear forever in the darkness of my dreams. Poland under snow, covering mounds and mounds of bodies, adhering and smothering, with soft, mothlike stillness, curled stiff limbs in a crisp white shroud.

In my hand, culled from the blue sea, the crab shell still lies. Anna will come with Fred and collect them with other shells. She will carefully try to wash away all the sand and fishy smell and bits of seaweed, and dry them in the conservatory on a large tin tray before they go on her dressing table.

But in her room there is always the smell of the sea.

Fred asks Lucy and Tristan to make a bonfire before they leave.

"Burn all that rubbish in the loft."

Tristan suggests that Fred should really go through it first, maybe with Barnaby, and next time they were down they could have a bonfire. Tristan seems so laid-back, so vaguely disinterested, that Fred feels a surge of relief. He thinks maybe it is all right, the children have not been tampering up there in the attic.

It is almost, Lucy thinks, as if Fred had needed some affirmation that he had done the right thing, even if they were not to know why. No way could they destroy all the documents in the trunk. Grandpa's life was in there too.

Lucy makes a sudden decision about what to do with Martha's box and the documents she has taken from the trunk. She wraps them in bubble wrap and places them in a padded envelope. Then she hides everything securely and safely. When Anna is dead she will decide what to do with them. They are a random record of a life Lucy knows nothing of, a little fragment, a snatch of the childhood and growing up of her grandmother.

She and Tristan place them in the hollow, defunct fire surround in her bedroom. If the house burns down they will be lost forever, but Lucy is unable to carry the burden of them with her. She wants to leave them here.

If Tristan wasn't leaving, if she wasn't going to be on her own, maybe she would have taken Gran's childhood diaries and Polish letters with her to London, have them translated. Lucy does not know. She cannot make the pages into fiction. She cannot pretend the horror the pages reveal did not really happen. The knowledge of that reality lies on Lucy's heart like a stone. Somewhere, in a will or note or maybe in her own diaries, she will say where and why she has hidden them again.

Tristan is unhappy about it. "I think you should put everything in the bank or leave them with a solicitor, Lu."

"Maybe I will later, but for the moment I want to leave them here in the cottage. I want to walk away from them, Tris. Perhaps Grandpa should have burned them . . ."

But even as Lucy says the words she knows she does not mean them. She is just being selfish, not wanting to be upset or confront all the issues they bring up. Of course Gramps did the right thing.

"Perhaps I will make sense of it, one day," she says to Tristan, "the silence, the secrets, even if I never understand how those things could have happened to Gran and millions of others like her. It is beyond comprehension, but perhaps I will accept it did happen, when I've grown up a bit."

Tristan smiles, touched as he always is by Lucy's unsophisticated honesty.

Lucy knows that for Anna it is a different thing altogether. They have never got on, but she is not going to let Anna's life be destroyed by finding out the truth at her age. She and Tris have talked about this a lot. How could Anna accept that her father might have been a Nazi?

Lucy goes cold at the thought and Tristan pulls her to him.

"I just don't want to think about it anymore, Tris, I won't have my grandfather taken away. *Fred is my grandfather.* I do not want any of this to be true."

"Lucy, it's OK. It's fine. I understand. Think about the future, think about happy things. Come on, it is going to be so great having you in London when I get back and you are really going to enjoy living up there with your old mate."

Lucy smiles. "I'm going to work really hard while you are away, Tris. I'm going to make the time fly past. On the night you leave for Kosovo I am going to get drunk, blind drunk with Diana. She's invited a few other friends round to the flat, it's all arranged."

"Is it indeed, my little soak. There am I fighting for Queen and country and my woman is transmogrifying into an old lush . . . Ow, that hurt."

"There isn't such a word as transmogrify," Lucy says.

"I'm sure there is and if there isn't there should be. Or do I mean transmute?"

Lucy giggles. "No, you mean metamorphose."

Tristan looks disappointed. "Well, sorry, but I insist on you transmogrifying, it is a much more visual way of imagining you holding your head the next morning. Metamorphose makes me think of sticky caterpillars. I have never been convinced they change into butterflies."

"You're barking, Tris. I don't know how you got into the army."

Tristan can always make her laugh. Maybe life in London is going to be fun, especially when Tris is home again. Lucy is suddenly excited.

Chapter 40

He wakes covered in sweat. His heart thunders with fear. He is back in that terrible, terrible night of screaming. He turns on his side in the dark room, as if to move will banish the images crowding his head. But as soon as he closes his eyes the nightmare lurches back.

He is on horseback. It is dawn, the moment of least resistance. The trucks are lined up. The dogs are muzzled. He lifts his hand to signal in the dark. There is the crack of rifle butts breaking down doors in the cold night air and then the terrible screaming starts as the children are pulled out of their houses, dazed and bewildered. He is frantically shouting orders. He has to strike the mothers trying to hang on to their children. His soldiers have to use their whips before total hysteria breaks out and they lose control.

Bedraggled men and women pour out of the houses into the square, trying to drag their children back, begging, howling and distraught.

This has to be done. It has to be accomplished. He is obeying orders. They do not have enough soldiers and they must beat the women back. The orders are to clear all the Jew babies out of the ghetto.

"The children will be safe," he shouts. "You must obey the declarations. Get back! Get back!"

He wheels his horse round; he has to use his whip to keep a space between the trucks full of the children and the screaming women who scatter before the hoofs. He must not lose control of this situation.

The first trucks, full now, rev up and thunder out of the compound.

He swings his horse to face the wailing crowd. The stench is overpowering. He feels sick with the smell of fear, unwashed flesh and excrement. His horse rears up, nearly unseating him, and in that moment he suddenly sees the girl in the doorway clutching her baby to her, frozen back into the shadows as if she is invisible.

He pushes the nervous horse forward, gently, gently forward. Does she really think he cannot see her hiding her baby there? She is very thin, her face like a death mask. As he urges the horse towards her, her eyes become huge with terror. She takes the baby from her shoulder. Slowly, she raises the baby up towards him. Pulls the bonnet from its head so that he can see the blond curls.

She holds the child out to him. She is pleading with him. She is pleading for this child's life. She looks into his eyes, holds them for only a second. He meets her eyes with growing horror. He knows these eyes. He knows this face.

"Help me," she whispers. "Help me get her to safety."

He turns to look behind him. There are no soldiers near; the last trucks are leaving. He weaves the horse round to mask her from the square. He bends down, across the side of the horse towards her.

"Hide her," he hisses at her. "Get rid of her, get her out of here. All the houses in this road are going to be cleared for resettlement."

The girl's eyes do not leave his face. Then she is gone, she is gone, the girl he once knew, like a shadow. Down into the holes, the sewers, the rooftops, wherever it is they all hide like stinking rats in this godforsaken place.

In his dream the tiny child with the blue eyes is held out towards him. Her eyes locked to his. Wide. Terrified. As if he could save her.

He gets out of bed and goes to get himself a glass of water. It is four o'clock in the morning and the birds are singing. *Open the lid a fraction and you are back in hell.*

In hell, but alive. He has had a life, a successful and fulfilling one. He has been able to shut it all out. *Before. After.*

How many medical lecturers did he know were guilty of war crimes? Doctors, surgeons, teachers, bank managers. It was not that they slipped through the net, it was not that no one knew of their crimes. It was because they were needed by the Western allies to get the administration back on its feet, to return Germany to a semblance of order as quickly as possible.

They were not wicked enough to be tried and imprisoned, but guilty all the same. Some, like him, guilty of following all orders blindly, until they found the courage to question or desert.

He gets up and wanders round the flat. Not all were reformed, or felt they had been wrong. In the sixties he had had an anesthetist who refused to take part in any operation on a Jew. It did not matter if they were American tourists or British matrons. He had a nurse who would not touch anyone with dark skin. There was Mutti, railing against the world in her dilapidated flat. Fascism could be buried, but it did not go away.

He was still young when the war ended. It was easier for him to push things into the dark recesses of his mind. He was not middle-aged with his youth behind him. Germany desperately needed doctors and surgeons. He had seen the mutilated limbs, and that determined the path he would take. He had learned an enormous amount quickly. The end of his training could not have been more different than the beginning.

He was in the hospital, safely in a white coat, when the Red Army swarmed into Berlin. The Russians did not wait to ask you who you were. Anyone in uniform was killed or shipped off to the Gulag. Anyone in an SS uniform or hiding and proved to be an SS officer . . . God help them.

He pours himself a brandy and opens the sliding doors to let in the night air. Berlin falling to the Soviets was the most frightening thing of the whole war. No one was safe. Their tanks mowed down anything in their way. Their men swarmed over the rubble, pulling out anyone they found hiding. They raped and they killed, they looted and they destroyed. The Germans had lost the war and yet they had the temerity to have so much more than the Soviets had at home.

It was impossible to judge Russian reaction. Their soldiers were also capable of amazing and touching acts of humanity. Soviet officers would carry in wounded children and old people to the hospital. They would take food into the ruined houses where children had made makeshift homes.

One Soviet officer ordered him to follow him to a bomb site where a child was trapped by a fallen beam. The boy was still conscious, though barely alive. He opened his hands to the Russian. He had no painkiller left with which to treat the boy. The Russian roared orders and suddenly a medical kit was produced, and soldiers to lift the beam from the boy's legs.

He had to cut the boy's leg away from the beam, which could not be dislodged, even by hefty soldiers. He died, luckily unconscious.

His hands shake, remembering. His first crude operation, culling memory from his father's medical books. He vowed there, in the surreal downfall of Berlin, to become so expert he would never lose a patient if he could help it.

He found Mutti one day in what was left of her flat. She had had the doorway mended. She had swept and cleaned, blocked up windows, made her bed in the one good room. She was smaller and thinner, disheveled, somehow diminished, but very organized. The one thing that was keeping her alive was the knowledge the British were coming.

Berlin was being slowly divided into four: Russian, French, American, British. She was so relieved to be living in the British sector she became almost haughty again.

In the chaos of postwar Germany, the opportunities were immense. People and money poured into Berlin as fast as some, mostly the young with children, left.

He finished his medical studies, qualified with a disparate age group thrown up by war. A third-generation doctor. Forgetting, watching Berlin grow like magic from the rubble. As excited to be in a city as Mutti had been before him. Forgetting. Pretending he was born anew. Having a new and different life.

As the war faded, and the sixties came and West Berlin thrived and relaxed, so did the bad memories.

Did you really think you could get away with it? The past buried. Your conscience so conveniently dismissed?

Raus! Raus! Obey the declarations. Your children will be safe.

You, you have had a long, good life. They had no chance of one.

Chapter 41

Barnaby, walking Homer round the garden, glass of whisky in his hand, notices the sky beyond the garden and over the sea is turning an ominous orange. The long hot days are going to break.

The leaves on the trees hang limp, waiting for the first gale to fly them to the ground. The garden is bleached and dying, just a glimpse of a pink rose among the brambles and bright, brave nasturtiums blazing in clumps, stems clinging along the cracks of the patio like pale worms.

When Lucy left, Barnaby missed her more than he thought possible. It was as if he had borrowed and lived on her energy and youth. He felt plummeted into winter, the years stretching ahead endlessly like elastic. Lucy had always been able to talk to him about anything and she had disappeared to London with something on her mind, and it had worried him.

It was to do with Anna, he had no doubt.

The row between Anna and Lucy carried over the garden, raw and unpleasant. Screamed, unintelligible words caught by the wind reached him and Fred and Martha sitting in the garden, and tore the afternoon apart. He made the day even worse by losing his temper. Despite his anger, Anna's white face haunted him. He wrote her a note, but she hasn't replied.

He hears faint music from the cottage and is cheered. Kate is making it into a home again. Her colors are startling, but warm, as if the rooms have suddenly sprung to life from a deep, musty sleep.

He likes, without knowing why, the thought and feel of her presence beyond the hedge. He is amused at the glimpses of this strange girl, like a bright parrot, lugging driftwood and shells from the beach, to put in corners of the garden in little artistic displays that Lucy would approve of.

With the aid of copious gardening books she is clearing the overgrown garden, conscious that she knows nothing and anxious not to disturb or dig up plants she does not know. Martha, fascinated by Kate, and missing Lucy, will wander over to the cottage where Kate sits her in an old gardening chair, muffled in a rug, and listens to her rambling, jumping conversation.

Barnaby has noticed that Kate's rather abrupt movements and speech are slowing to a more relaxed rhythm. Her bright Indian skirts are gradually being replaced by jeans and shirts, sweaters and shorts. She has a way of wearing clothes that make them look subtly different, with a panache and an eye for color and style Martha loves and admires.

"Darling," she cries, "lovely, lovely color."

Barnaby or Mrs. Biddulph will find Kate's bright sweaters or scarves tucked into Martha's drawers and capacious wardrobe, and guiltily return them. Kate finds it hilarious that an article of clothing discarded at random can disappear so quickly into Martha's small, determined arms.

"She has always adored clothes," Barnaby tells Kate. "Dad could never get her to throw anything away."

"Oh, let them stay in her drawers. I have too many clothes. I love to see her swamped in my sweaters. My aunt keeps sending me things, and I don't need clothes down here."

Barnaby, looking across at the cottage, suddenly realizes he is startlingly attracted to this girl. Kate would laugh her head off if she knew.

* * *

Kate is restless. It is the most wonderful evening. People keep walking past the cottage lugging picnics and throwaway barbecues and cans of beer and bottles of wine. The church door is open and the choir are rehearsing for choral evensong. The music is wonderful. Kate leans over the gate and gazes out over the bent oaks in the graveyard to the water.

Should she go down to the beach with her bottle of wine and sit until the sun goes down and a chill creeps up over the sand? Somehow there is something sad about drinking on your own, especially on your birthday. An exquisite solo starts in the church, a contralto. The sound carries and lifts and dips over the gravestones, rises up to the blood-red sun, and the beauty of it makes Kate shiver. Barnaby comes striding down the church path at that moment and, seeing Kate, crosses the road. He has insisted that Kate has one whole day off a week so Mrs. Biddulph is putting Martha to bed tonight. Kate grins at him.

"Heavenly choir."

Barnaby laughs. "What are you up to, leaning over the gate like an exotic racehorse?"

Kate snorts. "I like the exotic bit. Wish I had the legs of a racehorse. I am debating whether to take a decadent bottle of wine to the beach and sit in the last rays of the sun with Homer."

"Is Homer the most romantic male you can find?"

"'Fraid so."

Barnaby looks at Kate, amused. He recognizes this restlessness. It surfaces suddenly, a need for adult conversation and company.

"I suppose," Kate says carefully, "you haven't got time for a glass of wine?"

"I'd love one. I was cramping choir practice so I came away early. But I haven't got time to go to the beach, Kate. I have to relieve Mrs. B. in a quarter of an hour."

Kate opens the gate for him. "The sun's nearly gone, anyway. Come in."

Inside the kitchen Barnaby sees Kate's cards.

"Kate, it's your birthday! You should have said. You should be out having fun—" He stops. "You can't possibly have met anybody yet to have fun with . . ."

Kate gets the bottle of wine out of the fridge and opens it.

"This should be good. Marjorie, my aunt, in a typically profligate manner, sent six bottles down by courier. Barnaby, I'm quite happy. I'm thirty today. I've done the club, pub scene."

Barnaby spreads his arms in mock horror. "*Thirty!* Oh, definitely past it."

Kate laughs and hands him a glass.

He raises it to her. "Happy Birthday, Kate, and thanks for all you do."

"Come and see what you think of the sitting room. I've finished it," she says awkwardly, picking up her own glass of wine.

Barnaby is amazed at the transformation. "How on earth have you had time to do all this?"

The walls are an apricot yellow and the last rays of the dying sun match the color exactly. There are thin muslin curtains the color of pale tea at the windows that don't block the light. Kate has hung some unusual Indian prints on the walls and a piece of bright batik. Small pieces of driftwood lie on the mantelpiece.

It is very much Kate's room. Lucy's student chaos of many years has disappeared in clean paint. Barnaby stands silent, absorbing it. It exudes a sort of wistful peace. He is touched by the poignancy of the empty room, as if it should, somehow, have a husband or lover. A child. A splay of toys over the polished floorboards.

"It is quite beautiful." He turns to Kate. "Where are your family, Kate? What do they think of you being so far off the beaten track?"

"My parents are dead," she says abruptly, refilling his glass. "I have a brother who lives in France. We're not close."

End of that conversation, Barnaby sees.

"There is Marjorie in London, though." Kate suddenly smiles. "She's mad, but I adore her. She edits the travel magazine I worked for, before I came down here . . ."

Kate suddenly feels self-conscious. Away from Martha and Fred she and Barnaby are suddenly formal with each other, the casual everyday intimacy gone. Barnaby thinks, how pretty this girl is with that spiky black hair beginning to curl round her ears.

"Kate, I'm sorry, I'll have to go and relieve the dragon."

"Of course you do."

"I wonder, if I went and got fish and chips would you come over and eat them with me? Poor substitute for a birthday dinner, but . . ."

Kate is touched. "It's sweet of you, Barnaby, but really, I'm absolutely fine. You don't have to organize a birthday party for me."

She watches disappointment flit across his face. Perhaps he wasn't just being kind. "Unless, you really do fancy fish and chips?"

"I do. Absolute exploitation of your birthday."

Kate laughs. "I'll go and get them while you tackle your dragon."

"As long as you understand it is my treat. I warn you, Martha will probably smell them in her sleep and join us. You know what she is like about chips."

Kate picks up her car keys. "Why not? The more the merrier."

"What brought you to Cornwall, Kate?" Barnaby asks as they take the fish out of the paper.

"A whim. I'm a gypsy at heart."

"I thought you worked on a travel magazine in London?"

"I did, but only for a short time. I thought it might be fun, but I loathed it."

"Lucy said you have a psychology degree."

"I do."

Barnaby places the plates on the table. “Eat, or they will be cold.” He smiles. “Am I prying?”

“Not at all. I’ve spent most of my life working for aid organizations abroad—mainly Africa, but for the last two years I was in Karachi.”

She lifts her wineglass to Barnaby. “Thank you for my supper.”

“A pleasure. That must have been a wonderful experience. What brought you home?”

“My mother was dying.”

“Kate, I’m sorry.” He sees her face and says gently. “How long ago?”

“Six months.”

“You nursed her?”

“I tried to, yes.” She looks at him. “I didn’t go back to India, because . . . it wasn’t possible.” She smiles. “Personal reasons. Can we talk about you now?”

“I am afraid I’m not half as interesting as you.”

“I’ll be the judge of that.”

They both grin at each other over their wineglasses.

“How does it work then, this vicar thing? Where you are sent to, I mean? Can you choose? Do you get any say in the matter?”

Barnaby laughs. “Not really. You can object or have reasons for not wanting to go to a particular parish, but it’s a bit like the army: you accept a posting which is good for your promotion. There is a hierarchy system like any other profession. Of course there are cases which don’t apply. I asked for a parish in Cornwall when it became apparent, through Fred’s letters, that something was wrong with Martha.”

“Where were you before?”

“On a sabbatical. I was teaching in Nepal.”

Kate is intrigued. “And before that?”

“Northern Ireland. Belfast. I was an army padre.”

Kate watches his face as it closes. She wonders what happened out there. "So you came out of the army and dropped out for a while?"

"You could say that." Barnaby holds his wineglass up to her. "A very Happy Birthday, Kate."

He smiles, but not with his eyes. He wants to change the subject.

"Obviously, I wasn't just given this parish on a plate. I was sent to Camborne initially, about twenty miles away, but the old vicar here suddenly had a stroke, by which time I knew I needed to be nearer home than I was. Divine intervention, I think."

"Not just plain old luck."

Barnaby laughs. "Oh no, Kate."

"So, how long have you been here?"

"Four and a half years."

They hear Martha get up and go to the bathroom and Kate is silent, suddenly thinking about what these past years must have been like for Barnaby, watching his mother softly snuffed out, slowly, like a roomful of candles, one by one.

"Do you miss the army life? This must be so different."

"I did. I missed my friends, the comradeship. I am an entirely institutionalized male. I missed the traveling and being able to feel I could contribute, in places like Bosnia, with the young, like Tristan."

He twists his glass of wine round in his hands. "It was great when Lucy came down to do her A levels . . . wonderful to have her next door. Now, can we talk about you again?"

Martha appears suddenly in the doorway in her nightdress with Fred's old gardening coat over it.

"No one told me it was breakfast," she says crossly. "My stomach is crossing its legs."

Barnaby laughs. "That must be painful. Come and sit down, Mum. It's actually supper. Fish and chips. It's Kate's birthday and she didn't tell us."

"Naughty girl," Martha says, eyeing the chips Barnaby is putting on a small plate for her. "My father is snoring."

"*My father,* I think you mean." Barnaby puts the chips in front of her and hands her a fork.

Martha waves it at him. "No, no, *my father.*" She turns to Kate. "My father is a . . . is a . . . he surges, you know."

"Fred was a GP, not a surgeon, Martha." Barnaby and Kate grin at each other over Martha's head.

"No," Martha says firmly. "He used to surge, I know he did."

Barnaby says, "I'll walk you back to your hedge. Thank you for spending your birthday with me, Kate. I enjoyed it."

"So did I. Thanks for asking me."

They are both slightly inebriated and walk carefully across the garden, trying not to bump into each other. No moon tonight and the seabirds are silent.

Kate, thinking of Martha poised on the sofa in dressing gown and slippers demolishing a plate of chips, says quietly, "It's so strange, Barnaby. I feel so much more for Martha than I ever felt for my own mother."

Barnaby looks down at her. Something catches at him, painful and sudden. He takes her hand and smooths it between his own. "How wonderful for Martha. How sad for your mother." He hesitates. "One day, maybe, we'll talk about this?"

Kate smiles. "Maybe. Good night, Barnaby."

Their faces are almost hidden by the night. Barnaby bends and kisses Kate's cheek. "Good night, dear Kate. Happy Birthday. God bless."

He watches her disappear through the little gate, listens as the overhanging branches fall back with a thwack. Then he turns and walks in the dark across the overgrown lawn to the house. It is amazing, he thinks, that human beings always start the most revealing conversations on the point of good-bye.

Lying in bed, Kate closes her eyes and listens to the sudden sharp warbling of seabirds down on the foreshore as the wind gets up. The sound is as comfortable as a Gregorian chant.

She envies Barnaby's close relationship with Martha. She thinks back to what she was doing this time last year. She was in Phuket with Richard. His birthday treat. Was she blissfully happy, or does she just remember it like that? Was she wistful? Was she waiting, even then, for a word of commitment?

The odd thing is, she would not go back a year, even if she could. This time last year she did not even know this family existed. Now she feels her life has slowed to the beat of theirs and she would not have it any other way.

Being adult does not overturn a childhood of longing to be loved. Something relentless and obstinate goes on and on hoping; accepting the manner and loneliness of Dora's death, means letting go of part of the child she will forever be.

Don't carry the shadow of Dora around with you, Kate. Marjorie's voice is firm in the dark.

I'm not. I'm not. Honestly. I'm happy. It is just seeing Martha and Barnaby. I'm thirty. Will I ever have children who lie awake and think of me?

Chapter 42

Hanna no longer goes home every night because of the curfew. Her family have asked Dr. Oweski to keep her away from the streets of Warsaw. She is safer in the country, but Hanna's heart remains turned to the city. The voices of her brothers and sisters rise and fall in her head, bubbling and chattering, like the river after rain.

Papa, disappearing early each day with his medical bag to do what he can on the edges of the city, always tries to bring back some news for Hanna from some member of her large family.

Before the Germans took Warsaw, Hanna used to travel home each night with another Jewish girl and two Polish women who worked in the Saurers' house. The Jewish girl is gone and the Polish girls have long ignored Hanna.

Each time Papa leaves the house Marta and Mama feel a dread in case he does not return. Each journey from the safety of the house is dangerous. The Warsaw streets are full of German soldiers, opportunists and *Volksdeutscher*, but Paul Oweski is a doctor and he refuses to remain safe and cocooned in the country while people are sick and dying.

He has said nothing to Marta or Esther, but he feels it is only a matter of time before they are sent behind the walls into the ghetto. He wishes with all his heart he had sent his wife and child away before it came to this, that he had been firm, instead of hoping for a miracle.

As he leaves the house his heart is heavy. He has heard a rumor and he must find out if it is true. He has learned to walk neither too fast nor too slowly. Sometimes on the outskirts of Warsaw he will take his armband off. He could be a Pole or a German; he is not dark like Marta or Esther. It is a terrible risk if he is stopped, but one he calculates and takes if he needs to travel to a particular place.

It has come to this. I uprooted my family to throw in my lot with a German, who loves Poland as much as I do. I have lost everything: my life's work, my money. I will lose my house and my family could lose their lives. It is not the fault of Saurer that he gains from this. He is as much the victim of circumstances as I am. The bitterness lies in the fact that neither of us is allowed to protect those we love.

It is a chilly spring morning. The mist is hanging over the valley, suffocating all sounds, enclosing the village below them in a thick shroud. Saurer is waiting with his car under the trees and Oweski slides into the passenger seat without a word, his hat pulled low over his face. Neither man speaks for there is nothing to say. They have known each other too long to attempt words. There is work to do, people to help: this is their common aim.

Marta waits. Some days when the valley is in mist, the sun is not strong enough to burn it away and the day slips by in an eerie muffled silence as if the forests and hills are suddenly underwater. Papa is gone so long today. Mama sits by the window sewing and watching. Marta wants to scream as the silver needle flashes in and out, in and out, in those quick nervous little movements. She hates being inside, she aches to ride, to be outside. Spring is here and she feels like a wild trapped thing.

Hanna keeps dropping things and she cannot get the fire to catch. She keeps starting little jobs she has been asked to do, then forgetting and starting another. Marta follows her around finishing them, tidying things away, looking out of the window with longing.

Mama hates her even walking down the garden to the forest now, in case she meets someone from the Saurer household. The few vegetables they have grown in the garden have been stolen in the night. They have run out of flour, so there is no bread.

Papa will bring something back, he always does. Marta assumes the food comes from grateful patients, for each week the Germans reduce the rations for Jews. Some mornings the Oweskis will open their door and find bread or vegetables on the step. Mama will smile faintly and murmur, "It is Heinrich."

Papa will shrug. "Perhaps. Maybe someone from the village."

In the late, heavy afternoon, long before curfew, but when the day is already darkening, Marta, watching, sees the figure of her father beyond the garden, walking home on the other side of the hedge. She rushes to open the door and sees immediately something is wrong. His face has a yellowish tinge, he walks as if he can walk no further, and he carries nothing.

Mama rushes to make him sit, calls to Hanna to bring him a warm drink. He sits heavily in his chair by the fire, neither speaking nor greeting them. For a moment he holds his hand to the flames, which hold no real warmth. The sticks are too new and they give out a pungent, gluey, cloying smell.

He looks up and it is Hanna that he looks at. He takes his tea from her and puts it on the table without drinking. Marta watches the color drain from Hanna's face. She is like a rabbit caught in a searchlight. She cannot move or look from his face.

Papa reaches out for Hanna's hands and he tells her what she already knows in her heart, for the voices of her brothers and sisters in her head have stopped. Have been silent for days.

They have gone, all gone. The door of the tenement where they lived has been battered down. The shabby rooms they once inhabited are strewn with scattered possessions and babies' clothes. Paul Oweski tells poor Hanna only what she has to know. He does not mention the baby's bottle of milk, half empty, on the table where he was being fed. Or the tiny suitcase dropped on the stairs, bursting with cheap childish treasures.

A whole row of houses standing empty and silent. Poor and rotten as bad teeth. The inhabitants taken no one knows where. Except that Paul Oweski has reason to suspect in this case it is not behind the high walls of the ghetto. He holds tight to Hanna's hands and he tells her a lie that she knows is a lie. He tells her that he is sure they are safe in the ghetto and he will find out where they are very soon.

He tells Marta to make up the bed for Hanna in her room. He tells her that from now on the two girls will sleep together for company. Marta and Mama rush to do this, their hearts beating with dread for Hanna and for themselves.

Papa gives Hanna some medicine for the shock and they put her to bed. Marta sits with Hanna in the dusk, listening to the soft, urgent voices of her parents below. Hanna is so still. She lies, face to the window where they laid her, without moving or blinking. Then she closes her eyes.

Marta undresses and gets into her own bed. She is woken in the night by Hanna's soft keening. She is sitting up in the window, frozen, keening a strange, monotonous, rhythmic lament.

Marta gets out of bed and goes to her, stands awkwardly, not knowing what to do. Then suddenly, choked with pity, she bends and holds Hanna's thin body, ashamed that she and the boy ever teased this solemn girl.

"It will be all right," she whispers. "Hanna, it will be all right. Papa will find your family, he will find where they have gone. The ghetto is not far away. Come, come to bed. You are shivering, you are so cold."

But Hanna will not go back to bed. She just rocks back and forth, back and forth on Mama's small bedroom chair. Marta goes and pulls two blankets from the bed, wraps one round Hanna and one round herself, then she pulls another chair to the window and sits close to Hanna so that their arms touch under the blankets.

They look out of the window where a moon sails in and out of dark clouds. Marta watches Hanna's head begin to sag in an exhausted sleep. Her eyelids flutter as if the images of her brothers and sisters, a new child each year, are passing across her closed eyes in a small jerky possession.

Marta, at fifteen, feels suddenly grown up, protective and older than Hanna. Whatever happens, she and Mama and Papa are all together. They will look after Hanna. They will look after each other. She falls asleep watching the clouds move across a blue-shadowed moon.

Chapter 43

He drives to the outskirts of Berlin to go to the funeral of one of his oldest friends. While he is there Hans does his best to persuade him not to return to London. It must be unnerving to see a rational man turn irrational after thirty years. Also dangerous. The last thing Hans wants is for anyone to dig into the past. His father, Mutti's solicitor, grew rich on the past.

The funeral is of an old friend, a man he respected. They had joined the Hitler Youth at the same time. Both had been rebellious, derisive, and bored. As teenagers, it was the most exciting thing that had ever happened in either of their sheltered and provincial lives.

Their world had become suddenly full of exhilarating male camaraderie, excitement, and power. Perhaps this was why their friendship lasted: they both hung on to the memory of a time when they were young and life glittered before them, when anything seemed possible. They were both six foot, blond, strong and athletic. They were the perfect Aryans, boys in love with their own image, an image they were encouraged to cultivate.

As the war progressed, Mutti's tuition was useful. In the dark of night he mouthed her words and Nazi propaganda like a mantra, to drown out any other voice. He learned, with his friend's help, to obey orders—house arrests, clearing the ghetto, *any order*—with maximum efficiency and total detachment. Much as he would have behaved had he been cleaning out Tylicz's stable of horse dung.

Why does he go on lying, even to himself? Memory keeps on throwing up festering fragments of himself, burrowing to the surface like a splinter. He no longer knows what is truth. What he really believed. What he has made himself believe.

It all started as a game of dressing up and playing soldiers, not quite real. At the back of his mind he always thought he could turn his back and go on to medical school; they would always need doctors. But he was sucked, pulled into that rising wave of euphoria. He flew on the crest of that wave and found, like many others, he could not just jump off when things got . . . unpalatable.

There were times he was physically sick. On occasions he found the courage to query an order, and his weakness was noted. He began to be tested by the authorities. Crash. He brought the shutter down, battened it down tightly. No chink of light. He must not think. He must obey orders without question. *Heil Hitler!* He did not recognize his own face in the mirror. Stopped looking.

Now, a lifetime later, he stands beside his friend's grave. Faced with a brutal order, the man beneath the ground taught him the wonderful art of drinking to oblivion. In peacetime they met infrequently. Christmas cards, the odd note. In an unspoken pact they *never* spoke of the war, but kept the tenuous thread of another time and place in their lives, when they were boys, before their worlds fell apart, before they became part of a terrifying, ordered destruction.

At the funeral, on a bright, Berlin summer morning, there are hundreds of mourners, many Jewish, colleagues, friends, Poles, Germans. The dead man's wife, her French family. His friend has spent the last fifty years unremittingly doing good. Did he die content? Did he find peace? Did he feel he had made restitution?

He has no idea what is possible and what is not.

Before him now, in black formal coats and black hats, two respectable small men in spectacles. Probably bald. One a bank manager. One a teacher. He sees only the SS uniform they had once worn.

That night he stands on his balcony, as he does every night, looking out over the darkness of gardens and park. He watches the moving ribbons of cars out on the autobahn. Thousands of small bright lights stretch out before him. Berlin. Home. His mother's house had once stood away on the left of the city.

She raised her fists defiantly at the departing Soviet bombers. Terrified of squatters and thieves, she lived absolutely alone amid a ruined suburbia razed to the ground and still burning.

Leaving the glass doors open, he goes inside and pours himself a whisky, and swivels his comfortable leather chair towards the windows. His mind goes back to the funeral. Jews standing next to ex-Nazis to grieve for the same man. It was not the boy in uniform they had come to pay their respects to, but a man who spent the rest of his life giving his wealth and his time to those who had suffered because of an era he had been part of. A pain starts up in him, lonely and stark, the possibility of something, undefined hope.

The Jewish doctor in Warsaw had undoubtedly saved his father's practice. Without him and his money, his father could not have afforded to expand the clinic. Mutti never saw the irony of her prejudice.

He remembers how drunk he got the day his father was arrested and formally charged with treason, sedition, disloyalty to the Fatherland, and threatened with the Russian front. His father was being punished for refusing to obey orders. At the end of the war he learned exactly what the Nazis had wanted his father to participate in, and paled at the extent of his father's courage.

Mutti had already gone to Germany. She was making preparations to move "home." His parents' marriage was over. He wonders now how long it took his father to realize that the beautiful girl he married had a heart of stone. A heart he had inherited, a coldness he had preferred to his father's gentleness. An innate goodness that he had taken for weakness. Sometimes he wondered if his father had been secretly in love with the beautiful, dark Jewish wife next door.

He wished he knew where his father lay buried. How he died.

After the war, he dreamed often of that empty Warsaw house, where anything left behind would have been stolen, anything movable looted. Before she finally left Poland, Mutti opened his father's safe. There was nothing of any value inside, except his father's personal diaries and copious notes for a book he had been writing. More journals than diaries—his father had kept explicit and controversial notes throughout a war he abhorred. Even before the Germans invaded Poland, his father had been trying to make sense of a world where everything he loved and had valued was fast disappearing.

He did not know why Mutti brought them with her to Germany, but he suspected it was in case there was anything that might have incriminated her, by association. Everyone, at that time, became paranoid. He was grateful that she had given them to him and not thrown them away.

Sitting in bleak lodgings in Berlin in those chaotic postwar years, aching memories of his childhood came flooding back. He sat on the floor and read and reread the words of a man he would never listen to.

His father had written that he believed anti-Semitism was not something that lay dormant to erupt at certain times in history, but an emotion *central,* endemic, to the German people: the whispered fairy stories that start in the cradle; the scornful references throughout childhood, afterwards expressed continually and more radically in schools, colleges, and most institutions, so that a whole population automatically absorbs a little seed of prejudice that lies lodged just under the skin forever.

"Hitler," his father had written, "did not invent anti-Semitism, just fed it judiciously and let it flare out over the land to lick and flicker greedily over Europe like a snake. The Nazis only needed to fan the flame. Instead of expelling a permanently persecuted migrant race they decided to settle the *Judenfrage* (the Jewish Problem) forever. To exterminate a whole race.

"This does not explain to me how ordinary people can condone and willingly slaughter. How is it that people I have known and worked with, liked and respected, can go along happily with the Nazis, and people I have hardly noticed before abhor what is happening, and, at great risk to themselves, help Jews and try to alert the world to what is happening here?"

Before he was sent to his icy death, his father wanted to believe that for thousands of his fellow Germans to subject a whole race to perdition, they had to believe that what they were doing was not *wrong,* but the *lesser* of two evils: saving Germany from obliteration.

Yet how could judgment be suspended on this when in all else a set form of order prevailed? Efficient, institutionalized slaughter. Could former civilized men and women really believe they were purging Germany of vermin, not human beings?

He thinks suddenly: why was my father so surprised? He had only to look back into history. Men have with ease, in the name of religion, territory, race, extinguished, without conscience, the lives of whole tribes. Look at the Balkans.

Semantics. Intellectual juggling. His father, worn out, disillusioned, had been scribbling in order not to believe in the power of evil. In order not to think, *especially of his son,* because it was not just about *collective responsibility.* Each human being has to be answerable to himself, for his own actions in the end, doesn't he?

When the war drew to its humiliating and terrible end, when he saw with merciless clarity what he had been part of, he thought about Germans like his father. What gave them the courage to rebel? How did they summon the bravery and conviction to reject those principles upon which the German culture of that time, and many other cultures, were based? To walk against the vast tide of public opinion and stay stalwart the whole of your life, *never* to be swayed by a lifetime of subtle and insidious prejudice or fear. He could not imagine it. It was beyond his imagination.

He did not have that bravery. He lived his childhood close to a Jewish family so he knew perfectly well, unlike many other soldiers who had never met a Jew before the war, that his mother's wicked stories were all totally unfounded, just medieval folklore. He thought of the one Jew who had been to him a person, a human being, before they were ever a Jew. He thought of that family that must have perished and he slammed the journals shut, closing a whole life he had lived with a shudder. He was looking back on someone he no longer was. He would have put the clock back and tried to save them, if only he could have that time again.

I thought more of you . . . Hoped more of you . . . Waited . . . because of your friendship . . . your knowledge of the goodness of the Oweskis next door.

He brought a shutter crashing down and sealed himself in. He became one of the best surgeons in Berlin. He learned never to let anyone get too close for too long. He lost the ability to feel love.

Had he ever had it? He does not know.

The moths are beating against the glass doors, trying to get into the light. He closes the windows against the dark.

Far away down the years he sees the boy he was, laughing, playing ball with his father. He sees a tiny child held up to him. He hears the voice of the man he buried today, after a long drinking bout: "We use uniforms to hide our souls. Violence to keep us brave. We use guns to mask our terror and doctrine to hide our ignorance. One day we will scream, Stop! No more! Enough! But it will be too late, my friend. We will be drowning in blood and our hands can never be clean."

He was right. *I didn't realize. I was just obeying orders. I was afraid. Honestly, I didn't know what was really happening . . .*

No wonder nobody listened. Nobody heard. They never will. There are too many who still think like Mutti. And that will never change. Fascism feeds on quite ordinary fears.

So it is full circle. He could be wrong. How can he be sure? Refugees were shipped to so many places. Emotions play tricks. But a likeness, so profound as this, does not.

He will return to London. It is just possible that all did not perish.

Chapter 44

Martha sits watching Kate garden. Kate has tucked a rug round her and she can see through the little gate into her own garden. The sun behind the leaves of the copper beech are a flash of deep ruby. The grass no longer smells of high summer, but of autumn crouched, waiting.

The view through the gate reminds Martha of another garden and as she closes her eyes it comes to her. A garden she knew well, a garden she passed on that last day of freedom. But it was spring. She knows it was spring because the apple blossom was out.

Hanna has been gone too long. Far too long. Marta is nervous. She has gone to find bread because she is better at bargaining than Marta or Mama.

Marta pulls on her yellow armband and slips out of the house. She will look for Hanna and she will walk to the village to see how Aunt Ilsa is. Poor Aunt Ilsa, who fled from Tomaszow when Uncle Horst and all the men and young boys were rounded up and taken away.

Marta, like Papa, tries not to walk too quickly or too slowly. She does not want to be conspicuous. She keeps close to the high wall of Dr. Saurer's house where the apple blossom from the great tree is bursting forth in clouds of white and pink. Marta cannot believe now that she ever played under those branches.

The wall dips into a lower hedge and runs towards the gate. As she passes the gate she hears a long, low whistle. She freezes. She knows that commanding whistle and she turns slowly towards the sound.

A young man comes towards her dressed in a German army uniform. She dare not walk past him and stands rooted, watching the figure get nearer and nearer. As he reaches the gate he takes his hat off and makes a mock bow.

"Going somewhere interesting? Lost someone?"

Marta makes herself meet his eyes. "I . . . I was going to visit my aunt. I was looking for Hanna."

"How careless of you to lose her." He laughs. "I don't think we've rounded up any little Jewish girls today." He sees Marta's face. "Forgive me. You should know my sense of humor by now. Come in. One of the servants is finding Hanna bread."

He pushes the gate open and sighs. "God, what a beautiful morning. Come and look at the tree."

Marta knows that Hanna would never willingly enter this garden. She is sure he is lying, but suppose Hanna is here? Reluctantly, Marta moves forward. The gate shuts with a clunk and she stops, afraid.

"Come," he says. "I am not going to eat you. Come and feast your eyes on this blossom, enjoy the green of the garden . . ."

He stops, stares at Marta as if he knows something Marta does not.

"Where is Hanna?" she asks.

"Up at the house. I told you. I sent her up there with the gardener."

He pulls her underneath the great branches of the apple tree and turns her to face him. He is very close and his eyes are a startling and strange blue. They hold her own. For a moment he is the small boy of her childhood. For a moment he is the boy who taught her to ride.

He will taunt but he will not hurt me.

Then something in his eyes changes. Marta tries to back away, knowing she has made a grave mistake, and he catches hold of her.

"Are you afraid of me, my own little Jew girl?" There is sweat on his top lip. He has been drinking.

"I am not afraid of you," she says, suddenly defiant, holding his eyes.

This is a boy I know, she tells herself. We were friends. I have known him all my childhood. I will not be afraid of a uniform. He will not hurt me.

For a moment he hesitates, staring at her. Brave little Matusia. Brave little witch. Then he pulls her to him.

"You are never afraid, Marta. It has always intrigued me, the way I can terrify your little maid, but you refuse to be frightened of me."

Marta is frightened now. "Please . . . I must find Hanna and take her home." She tries to hold herself away from him, her back pressed into the trunk of the tree. But he is not listening, he is looking down at her breasts and the long arc of her neck.

"Beautiful Jew girl," he whispers. "My own little Jew girl. Yes, I feel you belong to this family." He smiles. "Like one of our beautiful horses . . ." He runs his hand down her neck and across her breasts, and Marta can feel him tremble.

"Please . . . let me go."

She tries to push him away, but he pulls her to him and starts to kiss her neck. In panic Marta digs her nails into his back. With a shout he pushes her away and then slaps her. Marta turns to bend under the branches of blossom, to run, but he pulls her back and throws her to the ground and straddles her. He is angry now.

"You can make this hard or easy. I don't care."

Marta is still. This is a German in uniform. A drunk German.

She says without hope, "Please don't do this to me. I have known you all my life."

He stares down at her. A fleeting, hesitant moment as their eyes meet. Then it is gone.

"Yes, and I have wanted you since you were about twelve. I know, I know, Marta, you have always wanted me to touch you. I have felt your body tremble. Mutti says all Jew girls are little whores."

Marta's hand comes up and strikes him across the face. Furious, he hits her back and rips the front of her dress, forces her legs open; pins her to the brown grass, between the roots of the big tree. She lies under the great sky of wavering blossom until it is over. Until the awful heaving and grunting have stopped.

He does not look at her. He rolls off her, buttons himself up and turns his back on her. In too much pain to get up, Marta turns on her side with a smothered groan and pulls her skirt down, biting her lip so she will not cry out.

"You will find your maid waiting in the summerhouse. You must go out of the garden, quickly. Jews are forbidden here." His voice is husky. Distant. He turns suddenly and bends to her. Then he dips his head and moves out from under the blossom.

Small white petals rain down on her and settle in her dark hair.

Suddenly Hanna is with her under the tree and they are crying and holding each other close.

"He made me come into the garden. He said he would find us bread," Hanna keeps saying over and over. "He saw you coming and told me to go up and stay in the summerhouse while he talked to you. There is no one up there, the house is quite empty. It is all right, Matusia . . . It is all right . . . I will take care of you."

Neither Marta nor Hanna tell Mama and Papa. It would kill them. Hanna gently washes Marta and puts her to bed. They do not speak of it ever again. For Papa the final insult would have been the knowledge that he can no longer protect his daughter from anything.

The next day German soldiers come banging on the front door. The Oweskis have three hours to get out of their house. Mama and Papa packed long ago. Mama made them all sew money and jewelry into the linings and hems of their clothes. She gives some of her jewelry and money to Polish neighbors who have been kind to them.

She asks them to keep a box with their personal papers safe until after the war—valueless, but dear to Mama: letters from relations, photos taken out of albums and placed into envelopes, small mementos she could not bear to throw away. Marta adds her own little box, full of childhood diaries, letters, her favorite books. After the war, they will at least have something of their former life. Papa burns all bank statements and business papers he does not want to fall into the wrong hands. He makes copies of birth and marriage certificates, places them in a folder and adds these to the box. He urges their Polish neighbors to look after them until their return.

The neighbors assure them they will keep them safe. They cry a little. Embarrassed, they quickly take the gifts handed to them without meeting Mama's and Papa's eyes.

Mama and Papa and Marta put all the possessions they think they will need on a draga, and a neighbor's horse pulls them slowly to the outskirts of Warsaw. They cross the Vistula over Poniatowskiego Bridge. They ride slowly down Jerusalem Avenue and Marszalkowska Street, past the Saski Gardens, full of trees bursting into flower. Past Krasinski Gardens where everything smells of spring and on into the guarded and closed wall of the ghetto.

Marta does not know she will not see a tree or a blade of grass, or smell a flower for a long, long time. If she had known she would have breathed deeply as they crossed the river, she would have turned to savor the smell of the air outside the wall, so she could live there, walk there in her mind in the dark of cold nights. She would have fixed the color of the last spring flower she saw and remembered exactly the clear blue of that sky. But she did not know.

All she can feel as the horse trots along are the eyes on the draga as it passes through the streets, and the burning sense of shame and humiliation that they are here, exposed, as if they have committed some terrible, unforgivable crime.

Once they are through the gates and have left the outside world behind, time changes and is never the same again. They are allocated one small room for all of them to share. Privacy and finer feelings fly like fleeting memories. Silently they unload their possessions in the dark and stifling room.

No green of grass or shadow of trees.

The next day, a Jewish neighbor, sent into the ghetto after the Oweskis, tells them that as soon as they left their house their Polish neighbors hurried to take their linen and china before all the valuable furniture was carted away by the Nazis. Mama wept. The linen was her grandmother's. The china was priceless.

No shooting buds through soft dark earth. Just people. Bewildered, displaced, hungry, and homeless people dumped by the endless transports that arrive at the gates. Refugees from all over occupied Europe, traumatized, bereft of their belongings, without any means with which to barter, often speaking only a foreign language, they starve and die on the streets.

In the ghetto Papa loses most of his teeth in six months, and much of his strength trying to save lives. Children, orphaned and desperate, beg on the streets. Mama is only thirty-seven but, unused to manual labor as she is, her beautiful, once shiny black hair goes white.

"She used to wear beautiful clothes, such beautiful clothes," Martha says, watching Kate bending to the flowerbed, in a lime-colored linen shirt, and a perfectly cut pair of white shorts. "Absolutely beautiful."

Kate looks up and smiles. "Who did, Martha?"

But Martha is watching Fred coming slowly towards her in his battered Panama, followed by Homer, who is missing Lucy.

"Oh, darling!" she calls out. "How lovely!"

Chapter 45

It is Sunday. London is muted and strangely still. Below Lucy, car doors bang, people shout to each other. There is the smell of cooking. Someone in one of the other flats is frying bacon. Although Diana is asleep in the next room, Lucy feels alone. She is homesick.

She sits up and reaches into the bedside table for Tristan's letters. She has read them so often the airmail paper is creased and beginning to tear. She places them in order beginning with the first postcard.

May 29, 1999
Darling Lu,
Hasty postcard. Will try to post this from airport. Have huge hangover. Colonel insisted we drank at Dinner Night then make out our wills! (Only protocol. No danger, darling.) New uniform bit tight, will have to diet! I love you. Tris.

Prizren
May 30, 1999
Darling Lu,
Too tired to write much. Thought we would have a night's sleep before we flew in, but no such luck. We were ordered into our wagons straightaway. Bloody Colonel! Not funny with a

> *hangover . . . The atmosphere when we arrived was amazing . . . The Albanians welcomed us like conquering heroes. It was quite an experience.*
>
> *The place where we are based is very bleak . . . Everyone seems disorganized and it rains nearly as much as in Cornwall. I will write properly when I have regained sense of humor! Take care, darling. Hope all is well with you. The little cottage and you seem a long time ago already. Love, Tris.*

The phone is ringing in the hall. Lucy hears Diana rush to answer it. She has had a row with her boyfriend.

"Lucy!" she calls, disappointment in her voice. "It's for you. Hurry up, it's Tristan."

Lucy leaps out of bed. "Tris?" she says. "Oh, Tris."

"Hi, Lucy."

His voice sounds different, far away, very tired.

"I had the chance of phoning, so I took it. I've only got a minute."

"Tris, where are you? Are you all right?"

"I'm fine. I'm sitting in a Land Rover in the middle of nowhere."

Lucy listens to the flatness of his voice. His voice is making sounds but his heart is somewhere else. Suddenly, she realizes he is in shock. He has never rung her before. He refused to take a mobile phone.

"Tris. What is it? Something's wrong. Are you hurt? Please tell me."

There is a long silence. Then he says, "I'm not hurt, Lu. I just needed to hear your voice. Talk to me for a moment, tell me about your days. Just boring everyday stuff. Tell me what you have been doing."

Lucy cannot be sure, but she thinks Tristan might be crying. She talks. She tells him about her students, about getting them ready for Milan. She tells him about the film she saw with Diana last night and the frosty little lunch she had with Anna and when he speaks again his voice is more like the old Tristan.

"Thank you, Lu. I have to go now. I love you very much."

"Tris, write to me. Write to me. I'm not a child, I need to know what's happening to you."

"I'll try," he says. And is gone.

Lucy looks out of the window, the day shimmers over the rooftops. It is going to be hot. What will she do with this day? Back at home, Kate is in the cottage, lying in *her* bed and caring for Martha and Fred. For a moment Lucy is tempted to make a dash for Paddington and catch the first train home. She misses Barnaby more than she believed possible. It has been hard watching the hot summer slip by, in a city.

She makes tea and takes it back to bed. She hears again Tristan's flat, expressionless voice, smoothed of all inflection which hides something so terrible he cannot even speak of it.

Lucy gets up again, finds her mobile phone and rings Barnaby. She lies on her bed listening to his voice calming her as he always does.

"Just be there for him, Lucy, cheerful as you can be. He may not want to tell you about whatever it is, at the moment. Write to him of happy and trivial things. Let him know you understand. I'll write to him too. Darling, I'm sorry I must go, I've got nine-thirty Communion. I will ring you tonight."

Ten days later a letter comes for Lucy.

Darling Lucy,

I have been assigned to some sort of UN human rights investigation team. On Sunday when I rang, we had been called into a village. There was a house which had been burned to the ground and in the cellar we found dead women and children. They had all been mutilated before being burned to death. It was sickening, Lucy. Their arms were raised up, caught in death. Young pregnant women and children. Who can hate that much? What sort of people maim and kill the defenseless?

Sorry if I upset you on Sunday. Sorry if this upsets you, but I know you read the papers and you asked me to tell you. Lucy, this is just one example of the horrific atrocities that have been committed out here. The Serbs have a scorched-earth policy. Nearly all the villages here have been razed to the ground. There are millions and millions of displaced people with nothing and nowhere to go.

The atrocity we found was committed by Serbs, but I have no doubt the Albanians would do much the same. We rescued a young Serb boy from some Albanian youths the other day. He was probably only about twelve. Everybody here seems to feed on hate—not surprising after what has happened, but I don't think there is ever going to be any real will to live together. It is all tribal and difficult to comprehend. Not forever, darling. I dream of you and making babies.

Love you, Tris.

Lucy reads this letter twice on the flight to Milan. She has just posted him Bill Bryson's *Notes from a Small Island* and a tape of her and Diana being very silly. She looks out of the window at the earth that is disappearing and hears her own voice. "*Don't change, Tris. Don't ever change.*"

Tristan is already changed. The moment he ran down some cellar steps in a burned-out house in a foreign city will lie in his memory forever.

Chapter 46

Anna finds the humid city unbearable this summer. The hot days slide into one another in an unreal way. The London streets are full of coachloads of perspiring tourists in untidy, flapping lines, like washing. The traffic grinds to a blaring bad-tempered halt. Petrol fumes hover over the city like a smog. Anna is used to a city in summer, used to the traffic and tourists. She does not know why she is so affected by the heat this summer, why London feels so claustrophobic.

Rudi insists it is because they have not had a proper holiday, but Anna has never bothered about holidays, she has just taken short breaks when she can. Rudi is very Germanic about holidays. He does not think of them as a luxury, in the way the English tend to, but as an absolute necessity in order to function efficiently.

He watches Anna in growing alarm. She seems to be winding down like a clock and appears to be losing weight. Often when he wakes at night, she is no longer in bed. It is like seeing an exotic flower slowly fading, losing the natural bloom of health. She seems driven, working long, punishing hours.

As Anna is going through the court lists one day, her dour usher suddenly says, "You are looking tired, madam. Are you going to have a break soon?"

The solicitor with Anna on her current case, looks at her as the usher disappears to find them coffee.

"He's right, Anna. You should take some time off at the end of this trial."

When Anna gets home that night she looks in the mirror. She is not the sort of person people make personal comments to. The lack of tennis shows; so does her loss of appetite. The sun, shining in the world outside the court, has not touched her face for weeks, apart from the occasional Sunday afternoon walk with Rudi.

Anna stares at herself. She does not want to become flabby and old. She wonders about going to a health farm when this trial ends. She wanders in to Rudi, who is cooking steak and tossing salad in the kitchen. She has been working most evenings, if not at her chambers, at her desk at home.

Rudi turns, so delighted to see her that Anna feels a pang of guilt. When did they spend an evening just talking? When did she last ask him about *his* day? When was she not thinking about work?

She has had two long cases in a row and the next one threatens to be political. Anna has made it clear to the CPS that in her professional opinion Stefan Tauber is too old, the length of time too great, the witnesses too ancient and scattered to bring this ill, old Nazi successfully to trial.

"I have," Rudi says, "a good, very cold bottle of dry white wine in the fridge."

"*Utter bliss!* as Lucy would say."

Rudi wipes already glistening glasses and opens and pours the wine.

"Have you seen her lately, darling?" he asks.

"I rang her and we had a quick lunch the week before she left for Milan."

Rudi looks surprised. "Oh, I didn't realize she had gone."

"I thought I told you."

"No." He raises his glass. "To you and the end of this trial."

"Amen to that. Darling, are you busy in October? Perhaps we should try and get away for a few days?"

"I think we need longer than a few days, Anna. I think we should try for at least two weeks somewhere."

Anna is startled. "I can't take that amount of time off, Rudi."

Rudi stops tossing the salad and says evenly, "I run a bank, Anna. If I am tired, I don't run it efficiently, my work suffers, and so do the people around me. Everybody needs to rest, even you."

He sits down opposite her. "Anna, if you have to work the long hours you have been putting in all summer, I would suggest that you are not delegating. There is a limit to the workload any one person can competently do."

Anna is annoyed. "Rudi, this is what happens in big cases. You can delegate in a bank. Yes, I could delegate to my assistant, but in court it is my expertise that is being paid for, my responsibility if things go wrong."

"I would very much like to see my wife for two weeks of the year, away from the court. Is that too much to ask?"

They stare at each other across the table. It is not a row, it is not anything like a row, but it is the nearest to an atmosphere of disagreement, of things hovering, waiting to be said.

"I've felt," Rudi says, "that something has been worrying you all summer. You sleep so badly. Is it your parents? I know your visit there was a shock, but you never talk to me about them. Since you visited them, you have seemed . . . withdrawn. They must be on your mind, Anna."

Anna gets up abruptly. "Rudi, there is nothing to talk about. They are both ill in their different ways. I don't agree with how Barnaby is handling their medical care, but unless I'm in a position to offer practical help, I can't do much about it. I am too involved at work to fight him, much as I would like to."

She smiles at him. "I'm fine, really. Just tired at the moment. Darling, do I have time for a bath before supper?"

"Of course you do."

She moves to him, kisses him on the cheek. He holds on to her for a moment.

"Bear with me, darling. I will try to organize time for a holiday, I promise," Anna says before she goes out of the door.

Rudi pours another glass of wine. He wishes Anna would sometimes just burst into tears. Howl. Lean against him, wilt at the end of a long day. Turn his way in the night when she tosses and turns. Say, "Rudi, can I talk to you?" But he knows she won't. It isn't Anna. Anna seeks an order and perfection in her life that is rarely possible. She expects much of others and so much of herself.

He looks through the doorway into the sitting room where a vase of roses sit, *just so,* on her mahogany desk. He would like to take her another glass of wine and sit on the edge of the bath and say, "Anna, I love you very much and I don't want this civilized, polite marriage. I want you to share things with me, even the CPS case, if it is worrying you. I want to swap companionable gossip. I want to relax with you, slouch on the sofa with you watching some silly film. But life is too busy for that. You do not have time. You are never silly."

He thinks back to the first time he saw her, stunning and vibrant, and knew with absolute certainty that this was the woman he wanted to spend the rest of his life with. He still does; nothing has changed. But he cannot get near her. He lives with her. He loves her. He is sure she loves him. But he cannot get near her.

There have been times when he thinks he has been close. Yet those moments slide away into an invisible wall, as if she scented the danger of disclosure or weakness and retreated.

Rudi gets up and begins to bang the steak. He thinks it is possible Anna is unable to trust anyone with her heart. But he is not going to give up trying.

Chapter 47

One evening while he is walking in Regent's Park he passes a small family of Hasidic Jews coming the other way. They are wearing the striking black mantles and *shtreimel* fur hats. It is such an incongruous and surreal sight, especially on a warm evening, that people stop and stare.

He has never seen Hasidic Jews in London before, and he too turns to watch them. A bearded father, black boots, black coat, black hat, the boy child in a little skullcap and baggy trousers. The girl, about five, in a frilly dress, her hair long and dark and glossy. Tourists like anyone else, he supposes.

He turns away, feeling sick; sits heavily on a bench as the park empties and the sun slides behind the trees. He is back in the garden of the house in Poland, on a summer's day. A small dark little girl in a white dress is standing on the lawn looking at him curiously, but unafraid.

He can hear only the whispering, endless lament within him. Can feel only darkness and sorrow. The horror of remembrance.

If he closes his eyes he can see and almost touch that house on the edge of the forest, smell the pine needles, the horses, the apple blossom in spring. He trembles as he thinks of her first time in his father's garden and her last . . .

Although he no longer saw the little Jewish girl after the Germans invaded, he often thought about her. There was only a garden between them . . . and a thick hedge.

One day I see her maid moving quickly on the road, past the wall of the garden. She sees me and tries to move faster. Her fear suddenly brings out the worst in me. I shout at her to stop.

"Where are you going?"

She cannot answer. She is so terrified of me she just stands there like an idiot.

"Come here," I shout again and point for her to come in the gate. "Don't you have a tongue in your head?"

"I have been down to the village to look for bread."

"Did you find any?"

"No," she whispers. "I am on my way home."

I see her suddenly glance behind her to the road and I catch sight of the dark head of the girl moving past the lower part of the wall.

"Go up to the house. The servants will give you bread. Go on! Move!"

The girl stands afraid, knowing I have seen her mistress.

"Go," I say quietly, "if you know what is good for you. I want to renew an acquaintance."

She passes me in a little frightened run towards the house.

I smile. I whistle softly like I used to in the early mornings outside her window. The girl freezes, turns slowly my way, watches me moving towards her in my dark uniform. I have been drinking all afternoon and I suddenly feel sick. I go to the gate, stare at her in her thin clothes and yellow armband.

"Where are you going?"

"I'm looking for Hanna." She does not look at me, but at the ground. Her frailty, her beauty, touches something in me, makes me angry.

"Come here," I tell her and open the gate and point for her to come in.

She does not move.

"Come on, come in," I say. "I have sent Hanna up to the house to get you bread. Come on, it's a wonderful day."

Still she does not move. Her stubbornness has always annoyed me. She is so pale her lips seem almost blue.

"I'm waiting," I tell her softly.

My little Jew shakes herself, tries to smile as if to give herself courage. She comes to me through the gate. She stares at my uniform and I see how nervous she is. This is the girl who crept out before dawn so we could ride before the sun was up. This is the girl who would tremble if our hands or bodies touched as the light spread over the land.

I remember the day I started to notice that her body was changing, that she was beautiful and no longer a child. I stare at her. She cannot know what is coming for her or her family. I feel a swift and sudden pain. How dare she, how dare she with her tricks make me feel like this?

"Come," I say, "come and look at the garden and my beautiful apple tree." I pull her across the lawn, draw her under the great branches of blossom. I want her. I want her before it is too late. I have to have her. It is my right. My own little Jew girl.

What she will not give me I take under the apple blossom. Then I am suddenly cold sober. I look down at her, at her dark hair floating across the ground full of tiny petals. What have I done? What have I done? I bend to her, try to smooth her clothes down. She curls away from me, draws her legs up. She is just a child, a child. I would undo the moment. I would undo it if I could.

This is the moment that haunts me. This tiny movement, this tiny drawing away like a hurt animal. This is the memory that wakes me in the suffocating blackness of my dreams.

This is why I cannot use names when I remember. People who eat meat do not name those they devour. And what of remembrance? How reliable? Tell yourself the same story long enough and you will believe it. You have to. Twist and turn it this way and that until it is something you can live with.

The next day the family next door were gone. They had a few hours to put their belongings onto a cart before they were herded into the ghetto.

Did she sometimes dream of galloping under bridges of wet leaves, that girl, with the rain falling on her dark hair?

Mutti, arriving home that morning from Germany, took two servants and walked down the garden and into their house with large baskets into which she wrapped all their good china and anything she thought valuable. She had always admired that china.

Afterwards he walked into their empty house and found their private papers, photographs, the girl's diaries, medical notes, scattered around the downstairs room. He found the box they had been packed in. It had the name of their nearest Polish neighbor written on it. He gathered them up, replaced them in the box and sent them to his German bank. At the end of the war he posted them to a Red Cross unit, in case any of the family had survived.

It was that day his first real doubts began. Like a tiny seed, the strength of his convictions slowly began to shrivel. Perhaps he had a little touch of his father in him after all. The sight of Mutti stealing turned his stomach that day. He had to put the plight of the family next door out of his mind. He had to shut a door firmly, make it so that they had never existed.

Now he wants to go back to the place of his childhood, to that house in Poland, to be a boy again, to begin anew.

Chapter 48

The night seems to go on forever. The pain grows and swells, getting steadily worse like a rising tide of water. Fred times himself. An hour, and an hour and then one more before he will call out. He does not want to wake Martha or disturb Barnaby, but he knows he is quite incapable of getting up and walking to his study for morphine.

As day breaks he feels relief. Cold sweat breaks out on his forehead. Soon Barnaby will come. Fred trembles. He has almost reached the end of his endurance.

The day is absolutely still. The trees and shrubs that reach into the long, low window hang immobile, as if waiting, breath held—for my death, Fred thinks with a half-smile.

The sky lightens to a flushed pale glow. Fred can feel the beauty of the morning through his pain, as if the startling, bruised, new day is a part of him. He can hear Martha's gentle breathing beside him. A bird somewhere in the garden sings a low throaty song to the imperceptible movement of leaves. He can feel or think nothing beyond this.

The sky is spreading and brimming, the glow turns to red and Fred feels a sudden peace, as if he knows, when the sun moves up in the sky to fill the room with warmth, the pain will ease. He has a clear sensation of being able to fly and leave this painful body behind and there is such a release in this thought, in this knowledge of flight. But first there is something he must do and he must remember what it is.

Barnaby wakes abruptly, but hearing no movement inside the house he lies for a moment watching a perfect blue sky full of wispy pink clouds. The anxiousness persists and Barnaby gets up, pulls on his dressing gown and opens his parents' bedroom door. Martha is still asleep, lying on her back, her mouth slightly open, snoring softly.

Fred is on his side facing the door, his face is gray and taut. A flicker of relief passes across his eyes as Barnaby opens the door and with panic Barnaby realizes Fred has been lying there waiting for him to come.

"Dad? Why didn't you call out? How long have you been like this?"

Fred whispers. "Top drawer, dear boy, in my desk . . . quickly."

Barnaby turns, runs across the hall to the study and grabs Fred's medical bag out of the drawer. He goes back to Fred and his fingers are trembling as he prepares the needle. Fred tells him what to do, his voice fading with pain. The effect is almost immediate and Fred gives a little sigh of relief as he collapses back on the pillow, eyes closed.

Barnaby watches the pain start to leave Fred's face and he sees what he has not wanted to see before: the color and texture of his father's face. It is waxy with a strange yellow tinge. He places his hand over his father's and the long old fingers curl over his for a moment, bringing a lump to Barnaby's throat.

"Never," Barnaby says with difficulty, "ever lie there in pain without calling out. Dad, it doesn't matter if Mum wakes up. She'll go straight back to sleep again. Promise me, otherwise I'll have to sleep in here like a dormitory."

His father opens one eye. "Heaven forbid," he murmurs drily. "Martha snoring gently is bad enough . . . I promise, I'll call you next time."

"Cup of tea?"

"Love one." Fred is sliding into dizzy, black sleep.

Floating and flying. Floating and flying. Body like a bubble . . . unsure where his body is. No pain. Strange thoughts. Mother with her long hair unbraided and her lady's maid brushing it and brushing it so that the electricity flies off the brush and her hair seems alive, moving, dancing with chestnut lights.

The small child that is Fred stands in the doorway unseen, fascinated, wanting to touch but not daring to enter without Nanny. His mother turns and sees him, bends and holds out her arms, her face lighting up, as he runs to her and throws his arms round her neck. She smells wonderful as she swirls him round. Her great curtain of hair encloses him against her breasts and he wants to stay like this forever, hidden in his mother's hair.

But there is Nanny and there is his father, both suddenly in the doorway—Nanny to take him away; Father to take Mother away, as he always does.

"We are going to be late, Margaret. You must get dressed." His father is watching his wife with amusement.

Nanny says gently, "Come, Frederick. Kiss your mama good night."

He leans back to look into his mother's face. It is sad.

"I love you," she whispers fiercely. "I love you more than anything in the world, and we'll spend time together soon, I promise. Don't cry, darling. Don't let your father see you cry."

She bends to place his feet once more on the ground and hastily wipes his eyes with the edge of her sleeve before walking to the door with him. His father bends to shake his hand.

"Good night, old chap." He looks down on Frederick and says quietly, "Big boys never cry, Frederick."

Big boys never cry.

Fred did not cry when he was sent, a year or two later, to prep school. He did not cry when his best friend died in his arms on the rugby pitch at Eton. Or when Toad, his bull terrier, got run over by a tractor on the estate. He cried when he came upon the starved, frozen, and beaten bodies of the survivors who had been marched away from Auschwitz. In the moment that he stood and wept, he knew many of the values his father had instilled in him were wrong, class-ridden, and bigoted.

When he first drove back to Yorkshire to tell his parents that he was going to bring Martha to England, he believed his parents would feel the same stunned shock and outrage over the terrible atrocities that were coming to light in Hitler's extermination camps, that they would sympathize with the pathetic flood of displaced refugees who had lost families and possessions and lives.

Fred discovered they were only appalled from a distance. As long as it did not affect them, or him, personally. They were careful what they said about Martha but he could tell they were dismayed about him getting involved with "a little Polish refugee."

Fred, sure that he could make his mother understand, if not his father, came up against a solid impenetrable wall of ice.

"You are our eldest son, Fred. You are our heir. You will go on to have your own son, who will inherit all this . . ."

She kissed the top of his head. "Of course you had to help, darling. It was your duty and we are proud of you. But once you have got her safely to England, the little thing will be safe. She must make her own life. There are people who will help her. Of course it's sad, but there are hundreds and hundreds of displaced people, Fred. Are you going to take them all on?"

"No, of course not. Martha is not just another refugee to me. She is a twenty-year-old girl who has lost her entire family. Can you even begin to imagine what that must feel like? I would not bring her to England if I did not want to take responsibility for her. I intend to look after her for the rest of her life."

"You can do that without marrying her, Fred. Don't mistake pity for love. Father and I will help you. Financial provision can be made."

Fred stared at her. "This isn't about money. It is about a human being I happen to love."

"Come on, Freddie, you're young and impulsive," his father said cheerfully, coming into the room. "Quite understandable, in the circumstances. Awful thing to have seen and experienced at your age. Look, old boy, give yourself six months. Sort yourself out with the regiment, then come home. It's time you started to run the estate. Charles is going up to Oxford next year and I am going to need you at home."

Fred looked at his parents as if he were seeing them for the first time—which in a way he was. Home, boarding school, army. Nothing outside these narrow boundaries had ever really affected him. In the moment his eyes were opened he realized there was no going back to whoever he had been before the war. That person did not exist.

He returned to Poland, to the intelligence unit he had been attached to. Martha had been moved to another hospital. She had managed, with her own knowledge and help from the Red Cross, to get in touch with the varying and disparate Polish underground and Resistance movements. Fred set about using his own contacts and the search began.

Martha was able to give a date and a name on the documents of her child, but in the chaos and flood of refugees in postwar Warsaw it was not going to be easy to find out if her child had survived.

Martha, recovering well, was able to leave the hospital, but she would not leave Poland without searching for her child and Fred could not ask her to. Before he was posted back to England he managed to arrange for Martha to stay with Polish friends he had made.

He tried once more to talk to his parents, a last bid to make them understand, because they were his family, and he loved his home and cared about the future of the estate passionately.

"Please listen to what I have to say. I *am* going to marry

Martha. It isn't about pity or feeling responsible. I love her. I know, if you could only meet her, you would love her and see that she is a truly extraordinary person, with great strength and warmth. She is educated and wise . . . Of course, I realize that this is very hard for you both and not what you expected, but the war has changed how I see the world and I think it is a good thing."

His parents stared at him in silence. His mother brought her hands up to her face and her words escaped before she could stop them. They sealed her fate and determined the future of all their lives.

"She's a *Jew,*" she whispered in horror.

Fred never forgot. Love for his mother fled forever like a wild, lost thing.

He turned to go without a word and his father said quietly to his back, "Frederick, I don't want to disinherit you in favor of Charles. You are my eldest son. But if you persist in this with the Jewish woman, I will do so."

Fred turned back. "I would like to ask you one more thing. If Charles inherits and runs the estate, will I be welcome to visit you? To come home, to bring my wife?"

His mother's mouth was trembling, but neither of his parents seemed able to answer and the silence grew and grew into something unendurable, and Fred, having his answer, walked out of the room.

His mother's voice cried out, reached him in the hall as he passed the great gilt mirror. Her voice and his pain caught up with him and were reflected back in his last moments in that great, much-loved house of his childhood.

"If you marry her, you are no longer our son. You are dead to us, dead to us, Frederick."

Fred's footsteps, walking away across the flagstoned hall, echoed to his own grief. *So be it.*

He had already enrolled at medical college, but the sadness, the waste of it all, never left him, and he did not believe that they would keep it up for a lifetime.

He drove down to Cornwall to look at the small manor house his grandfather had left him. He sold off the manor and built his own house, his own place, to face the sea.

Anna was part of the reason he never tried again to breach the gulf with his family. Fred knew, even if his parents ever accepted Martha, he could never explain this withdrawn, frightened, undernourished little girl arriving with Martha, via the Red Cross.

In those first years, they had hidden away in London, anonymous in a big city, recovering, and healing from the war. They kept Anna close to them, taught her at home. They went down to Cornwall for holidays, for long weekends in the cottage until their house was almost finished, until Anna started to speak again.

He wondered sometimes, if he had stayed in Yorkshire, nearer his parents, if they had heard or seen glimpses of him, his wife and children, if they could have kept up their lifetime of steely, relentless unforgiving.

He always hoped they would mellow, as they grew older, not just so they could gain from knowing his wife and children, but because it would mean they understood that they had represented an insidious part of what he and his fellow soldiers had been fighting against.

If they were unable to grasp this principle, when so many people had died for it, he could not feel any regret for not inheriting what they represented. He felt sorrow and shame at their lack of humanity, and an aching sadness for the memory of himself and his mother in childhood and for a place that had been home.

Yet, he would not change a thing in the life he had chosen. He could never have derived the fulfillment in running the estate that he had as a country doctor. Life without Martha would have been half a life. No life. Unthinkable. Martha has been sadness and great joy . . . Not a day has gone by without a small happiness of some sort. Martha can make an ordinary day magic. Each and every day in her life counts. Is a gift.

How lucky, how extraordinarily lucky he has been . . .

Anna. This is what he must tell Barnaby. So important, Anna . . .

A dove is cooing somewhere and Fred sleeps.

Barnaby lets Homer out into the garden and puts the kettle on. He makes Martha her thin slices of bread and butter while it boils. She is awake when he goes back into the room, lying watching the sky.

"Darling, how lovely," she says, as he puts the tray on her bed.

Fred is asleep so he places his tea beside him. "It is," he says to Martha, "the most beautiful day."

Martha looks out of the window. "I really must do some gardening today."

"Good idea," Barnaby says, kissing her. "I'm going to get dressed. See you in a minute."

He goes to the telephone and rings Brian, their GP.

"I'll come straight round before morning surgery. Barnaby, you know I can only make sure he is comfortable?"

"Yes," Barnaby says, and rings his curate to ask him to take Holy Communion for him.

He hurriedly showers and says his own missed morning prayers and goes back to look at his father. Martha is dozing against the pillows, soporific, her face in sunlight. Fred is awake again and tries to smile.

"I think, dear boy, I might have a bit of a lie-in this morning."

Barnaby sees clearly and with shock that Fred is dying; that his father has suddenly found the struggle unequal and is giving up. The mug of tea is cold and a thin creamy veil of milk is forming on the surface.

"That's a very good idea, Dad," he says. "I will bring you the newspaper in bed."

Martha is getting out of bed. "What is it?" she asks anxiously. "What is it?"

Fred opens his eyes. "Nothing at all, M. I just have a bit of a chill . . . going to stay in bed for an hour or so."

Martha stares at him worriedly. "Are you cold? Shall I get another blanket?"

Barnaby gets her into her dressing gown. "Let's leave Dad to sleep. Come and help me feed the birds."

He closes the bedroom door and gets Martha a stale loaf. While she stands at the French windows feeding the birds he finds her clean clothes from the airing cupboard. With relief he hears Kate open the front door. Quickly he explains while Martha is still outside. Kate, upset, takes Martha's clothes from him.

"I'll give Martha a bath, then I'll take her out of the house for as long as possible. You concentrate on your father. Barnaby, I'm so sorry."

Martha comes into the hall and, hearing Kate running a bath, says loudly, "I don't need a bath . . ."

"You do need a bath," Barnaby snaps, and shuts the bathroom door on them both and leans on it for a moment. A refrain is going round and round his head, a childish, panicky one. "Don't leave me, Dad. Don't leave me with this."

Fred is conscious of Barnaby in the room, sitting in Martha's little bedroom chair. "Something I should tell you . . ." But he feels tired and strange. Barnaby's voice floats gently to him. "I'm not going anywhere, Dad."

Poor Anna . . . Fred thinks . . . Poor child . . . should have told her. She was always Martha's cross . . . They have never got on . . . very sad . . .

"Barnaby?"

"I'm here."

"I've made mistakes, Barnaby, misjudgments."

"Can't think of one, Dad."

Fred smiles. "You always were a nice chap." And sleeps again.

Brian calls out and comes in the front door and straight into the room. He stares down at Fred and sighs. "He's not in pain at the moment. He can have another shot in an hour. I'll be back at lunchtime. Barnaby, this is to be expected. I'm amazed he has gone on as long as he has without treatment."

"I know, I know," Barnaby says.

When Brian has gone, Barnaby wanders round the house, feeling numb. Knowing death is approaching is not the same as accepting it when it arrives. Finally, he goes and sits in the little bedroom chair Fred used to read to Martha in, and into the silence of the room he hears the long-ago echo of his father's voice reading Edward Thomas, smells the pipe smoke of Fred's jacket and the faint smell of whisky on his mouth.

> I have mislaid the key. I sniff the spray
> And think of nothing; I see and I hear nothing;
> Yet seem, too, to be listening, lying in wait
> For what I should, yet never can, remember:
> No garden appears, no path, no hoar-green bush
> Of Lad's-love, or Old Man, no child beside,
> Neither father nor mother, nor any playmate;
> Only an avenue, dark, nameless, without end.

He looks up to find his father watching him.

"Should have burned or told, not stayed silent all these years."

"Dad, please don't worry about anything. You're very hot. I'm just going to get a cold cloth."

Fred is rambling. Barnaby gets a cold flannel and bathes Fred's forehead and hands. Then he rings Brian.

"Give him another shot. I'll be round straight after morning surgery."

The bedroom is full of sunlight. Fred is alone.

Somewhere in the hall outside the door he can hear Barnaby's small childish footsteps running up and down and Martha's laughter.

"Come," she calls to the child. "Come, we will go and plant roses and honeysuckle and big fat sunflowers for Barnaby's garden."

Sometimes he wakes in the night to find Martha reading gardening books beside him with a torch.

"Are you happy?" he whispers. "Martha, are you happy with a poor doctor in Cornwall?"

She will raise those great black eyes from the page, marking something with her finger. "Poppies . . ." she muses . . . "I think great papery red poppies . . . Happy?" She stares at him, amazed, her eyes meeting his. "You need to ask me this? I have you, I have everything, everything that I want." She curls into the bed, close to him. "Fred, I have this such happy life. It is enough. You know, it is more than enough. Not just life . . . a *happy* life."

Contentment surfaces. For this life he has lived. For the sun that will move around to touch his face and hands on the bed. In this house he and Martha designed together to catch every last ray of warmth and light. The house they have lived a lifetime in.

He has a wonderful sensation of being able to fly and leave his painful old body behind, and there is such relief in this feeling: the peace of letting go, of riding this wonderful soft wave. The fear of leaving Martha is suddenly gone. His dying has to be his own. Martha's dying cannot be done for her. She began her life without him. Before him she had a life. When he is gone she will have a death. It is how it is. They have lived a lifetime together but must leave separately. It is clear and obvious. No point hanging on.

"I'm just going to give you some more diamorphine, Dad." Barnaby's voice is anxious, gentle.

He is rolling, rolling in high on this wonderful pain-free wave. Somewhere far away he hears the phone ringing. Odd, in the stillness and dizzy bliss of the sea. He struggles for the memory of Martha young. Her face, her excited face as she stares at the mass of iridescent sea running fast in ribbons of froth as the tide turns and the estuary becomes rough. It is the sound as she turns to him, the very first sound of her laughter. It startles Martha as much as it does him—this sound she has forgotten she can make. It bubbles up, cautious and excited, then gathers speed as she swings round and her arms embrace the great curved necklace of warm blue water cradled against white sand. "Here?" she cries. "Here? We are going to live here? Oh, Fred. Oh, Fred."

Her laugh, like a ripple, a childish, infectious giggle, takes on a life of its own and gathers pace like the sudden speed of an incoming wave. Unique, her laughter, all her own, this astonishing wonderful sound.

She stands, arms curled outwards to hold sudden and forgotten joys and a future she never expected. Fred reaches out for her as the huge wave starts to slide downwards.

When Barnaby returns to the bedroom, Fred's death rattle is just beginning. He thanks God he is alone in the house. Glad to hold the thin brave old man as he dies. Glad to howl for a moment in the empty house. Grateful for this quick, kind death.

Chapter 49

Martha peers down at Fred, her face impassive. She is so still it is as if she is frozen, but Barnaby catches the sudden light dying in her eyes. She stands staring at Fred, then she puts out a cautious finger to feel his face, and it is then, as Martha feels his coldness, that she lets out this cry.

It is a sound so guttural, so strange, so foreign, that Barnaby, and Brian standing in the doorway, jump. Martha holds up her hands and chants and the isolating lament rises and hovers in the still room as if it has an entity of its own. To Barnaby it is one of the most chilling sounds he has ever heard.

This is not his mother, it is suddenly an old Polish woman he does not know, making this hair-raising, lingering keening, in a language he does not understand.

"Ahh! Umm . . . mmm . . . naa . . . aaa," Martha cries, rocking on her heels. Like a ritual dance, she bends and bends again. Places her lips on Fred's forehead again and again, leaving her mouth on his skin as she wails. As if she could breathe new life back into him.

"My love . . ." she whispers. "My life . . . Ah . . ."

She kneels on the floor beside Fred and whispers so softly that Barnaby has to bend to catch the breath of her words.

"Only you . . . There has only ever been you . . . Now you too go to join the mountain of the dead . . ."

She stops suddenly, becomes motionless again, as still as Fred. Her small hand rests on his faded pajamas, over his heart, which no longer beats.

Barnaby goes and gently touches her. "Mum, time to go . . ."

Martha stares up at Barnaby. Her eyes are startlingly clear as she says to him, "He came, you see. He came. Your father breathed life into me. Warm, warm life. He brought me and my child here. He gave up his own life so that I might have a life. This, this was your father. There was no one left, only the Englishman. Now he has left me. Barnaby, Barnaby, he has left me . . ."

She reaches out to Barnaby and her grief is raw and desolate. Barnaby, taking her outstretched hands, shivers. He understands all of a sudden the terrible echo down the corridors of his childhood. His world shifts back to the memory of that desolate sound of crying that had no place in the happiness of this house. Unspoken tragedy moved, like wavering shadows across a window.

His mother folding and smoothing, folding and smoothing. Endlessly tidying. Everything always had to be in its set place. Fred would gently go and stop that obsessive folding and smoothing of some ancient garment as if it were still new or valuable. He would take her small twisted hands, smile and bring them to his lips. Distract her, make her laugh.

Suddenly, it is all so starkly clear. Martha angry when he or Anna left food on their plates. The crusts, the unexplained crusts of bread hidden in small pockets of her clothes. A trembling starts up in Barnaby as he and Martha hold each other, rock in the hot and stuffy room.

He has never questioned the truth of what he has been told about his mother. If ever a small doubt edged its way to the surface of his mind, he dismissed it. For why would his parents lie?

He has imagined so many times Martha alone in London waiting to meet Fred, a story told so often in childhood, with added embellishments, it was never questioned. Like a fairy tale, it became a certainty, an unquestioned truth.

Brian leads them both outside and shuts the bedroom door behind him. Out in the hall Kate is standing, white-faced, waiting for Martha. She takes her from Barnaby and leads her quickly into the kitchen as the undertaker knocks on the front door. Barnaby shows him into the bedroom. They cannot leave Fred here in the house with Martha.

When Barnaby comes back, Brian has poured two drinks and they stand in the hall silently listening to Kate's soft voice talking to Martha. On and on, Kate's voice, gently rising and falling, to divert Martha.

Barnaby cannot speak. He cannot meet Brian's eyes. His feelings are so powerful, they frighten him. He wants to run from this house to the beach, to his church, *anywhere.* His breath comes in uneven gasps as he tries to calm himself. Brian puts a hand on his shoulder. He has never seen Barnaby like this. He has always been afraid this would happen one day.

"Auschwitz?" Barnaby's question is rhetorical. Then: "You knew?"

"Yes," Brian says. "I knew. I am her doctor, Barnaby. But it was not a subject I was ever allowed to bring up."

Barnaby downs his drink and places it with shaking fingers onto the small hall table. Brian seeing he is in shock, picks the glass up to refill it. In a sudden sharp movement Barnaby brings his hand down of top of Brian's.

"Why? Why weren't we told? I don't understand. Why the silence? I don't understand, Brian."

"It is what Martha wanted, Barnaby," Brian says gently. "She needed to forget. It is how she survived. How can we even begin to understand? It is quite impossible."

Barnaby stares at him. He is overwhelmed by the knowledge that Martha safe in London and Martha imprisoned in a concentration camp are two entirely different people. A huge part of Martha seems lost to him. What would have enlightened his childhood and brought him closer to understanding his mother has been denied him. It is as if he has been given a sanitized version of Martha's life, not the whole.

He has not been given the chance to love and care for Martha with the depth of meaning that this knowledge of her life would have given him. Martha's life had been shaped by a past he had no idea of and he is angry, so angry not to have known.

"Don't you see, Brian? My mother's life, her childhood, my grandparents, Fred's part in it all—it's gone forever, and Anna and I will never know a part of what we are."

"My dear Barnaby, nothing has changed. Martha did not want you to know a harrowing part of her life. Fred wanted to forget the war. They both concentrated on the future, not the past. The future was you and Anna—"

He stops, seeing Barnaby's face. *Anna.* They stare at one another.

Brian puts his hand on Barnaby's arm. "Barnaby, Fred has just died. You have enough grieving to do. Leave this. Put it away until you are able to cope. You've had more than enough for one day. We'll talk about this, but not now. Can I please give you something to help you sleep tonight?"

Barnaby closes his eyes. "Brian, I'm fine, I don't need pills. Sorry. You must have a surgery, I'm keeping you."

Barnaby wants to be alone and Brian acknowledges there is neither comfort nor a single word he can use at the moment to make him feel any better.

"I'll come round in the morning. But if you or Martha need me, ring, please, just ring. Kate is going to be here to help with Martha?"

"Yes, yes. Thanks, Brian, we're fine."

When he has left Barnaby puts his head round the kitchen door. Martha is glued to the television while Kate cooks her fish fingers. Barnaby stares into the room. It is unnerving, this ability of Martha's to jump lives, like shutting off a computer. What transpired moments ago is wiped out until activated again by a random switch.

"Kate, are you all right for ten minutes or so if I take Homer and get some air?"

"Of course I am, Barnaby. Go."

Martha looks anxious. "Don't be long, darling," she says.

The undertaker has finished. Barnaby and Homer watch as Fred is wheeled out of the bedroom, across the hall and out of the house for the last time. He is lifted carefully into the hearse and Barnaby follows it out of the gates and into the empty road.

He turns and walks down the path to the beach. The sea is rough and there is a high tide. He stares down at the sea.

"Something I should tell you, old chap, made mistakes . . . misjudgments . . ."

Oh, Dad.

"He brought me and my child here . . . He brought me and my child here."

Oh God. Nothing quite what it seemed.

He feels like placing his lips on the glassy water, opening his arms out wide and floating with his head below the surface without thought. Downwards, downwards for a long, long time. This burning sense of shock feels like another, separate death.

Kate moves about the kitchen talking quietly to Martha. She cannot get Barnaby's face out of her mind. He had seemed quietly self-contained when Fred died, now he looks dreadful, wild almost, as if he might hurl himself into the sea.

Kate thinks about Martha's bloodcurdling cry that had burst from the bedroom and filled the house with utter desolation, with such an unearthly, hopeless sorrow that Kate's arms had broken out in goose bumps. It was the loneliest sound she has ever heard. Long after the cry ended, the sadness went on and on reverberating in the air, heavier than silence, making the house thick with misery.

Kate puts some chicken in the oven for Barnaby while Martha eats her fish fingers, knowing he probably won't want to eat. She tries to settle Martha into the sitting room in front of the television with a bowl of ice cream.

"Are you coming to sit with me, darling?" Martha asks Kate anxiously, grabbing her hand.

"I'm just going to put clean sheets on your bed, Martha. I will be back in two minutes. Call if you need me, I'm only next door." Gently she pulls her hand out of Martha's.

"Darling," Martha says worriedly, "don't be long."

Kate walks across the hall and opens the door of Fred and Martha's bedroom and goes inside. She remembers how Dora's room smelled after she died. The sheets on Fred's bed have been folded neatly by the undertaker and the window has been opened wide, but the room still holds an aura of bodily smells, a whiff of death, as if Fred has just left the room.

Martha cannot sleep here. She cannot sleep in the room where Fred has just died. Kate shivers with the memory of death: the finality, the yellow waxiness, the immobility of features, the rigidity of expression behind the way a person dies; the imprint of peace, bitterness, or surprise caught on a face in death, and the immediate moments after it. *Dear Fred.*

She closes the door and goes back across the hall. She goes into the spare room, which doubles as Barnaby's study. It is a small room in the front of the house. It has a huge and beautiful double bed, an armchair full of files, and various items that look as if they might be jumble on the floor. She hesitates. Should she wait to ask Barnaby?

Martha calls out, "I'm tired, darling."

Kate makes up her mind, even if Barnaby does think she is interfering. She makes up the double bed with clean sheets, fills Martha's hot-water bottle and hurries back into the sitting room.

"Your bed's all ready for you, Martha."

"Thank goodness, darling. I'm so tired." She reaches for Kate's hand again, her eyes full of anxiety. She is confused. She knows something is wrong but cannot remember what it is. Kate sits on the sofa beside her and takes her small hand, twisted by arthritis.

"Where is Barnaby?" Martha asks suddenly.

"He's walking Homer. He'll be back any moment."

"Is Fred with him? It's getting dark, you know. Fred should be here."

"Martha, Barnaby knows the path like the back of his hand. Let me help you get undressed and by the time you are in bed he will be home."

Kate gets Martha's night things and they change in the bathroom. Kate does not know if Martha will sleep in a different room. She gets Martha's sleeping pills and gives one to her with a glass of water. She is worried about Barnaby. He seems to have been gone a long time.

"Martha," she says, "will you come and tell me about this beautiful bed in Barnaby's study?"

The spare room looks warm and inviting. Kate has switched the bedside lamp on and the room somehow smells comfortingly of Barnaby. Martha smiles.

"This bed came from the big house. It was the only pretty thing in the house. Isn't it lovely, darling?"

"It's wonderful."

Martha climbs in with a sigh and collapses against the pillows. Kate sits on the bed, relieved.

Martha says softly, with her eyes closed, "We spent so many years in this bed, Fred and I . . ." Her breathing becomes shallow and Kate thinks she has fallen asleep. In the gathering dusk birds sing and the wind gets up. Darkness hovers at the windows and Kate thinks of Barnaby and of Dora's death and how devastated she felt that day. No going back. No second chance.

Martha opens her eyes and looks straight at Kate. "Fred is dead."

"Yes," Kate whispers. "Yes, darling, he is."

Like Lucy used to do, she brings Martha's hand to her cheek and holds it there. Martha closes her eyes again and is very still. She makes no sound, but she is weeping. Kate strokes her hair and feels like weeping too.

When Martha is asleep, Kate looks at the chicken in the oven, then checks Martha once more and goes out into the dusk and across to the church. There is a light on. This is difficult. She is someone who works for Barnaby, a woman he hardly knows. Barnaby is grieving and this might be quite the wrong thing to do.

Homer sits patiently on the porch and thumps his tail when he sees Kate. She opens the catch of the door as quietly as she can, but Barnaby does not turn. He is kneeling in front of the altar, head bent, praying. He has lit the candles on the altar and they flicker over the old mellow stonework and brass plates on the walls.

Kate has not been inside the church before and is astonished by its beauty. This then is Barnaby's little kingdom. She goes and sits in one of the pews and waits. This is a great invasion of his privacy. Kate does not know what to do. He must have heard her come in.

After a minute Barnaby gets up, bows to the crucifix and turns to her.

"Barnaby," she whispers nervously, "I just wondered if you were all right."

He does not answer for a moment then smiles briefly, politely. "Yes. Sorry, Kate, I must come back to the house. You will want to go home."

"I hope I've done the right thing. I made up the double bed in the spare room for Martha. It seemed wrong for her to sleep next to Fred's empty bed."

"Oh, Kate, of course you did the right thing, thank you. It was thoughtless of me to be so long. I'm sorry, I should have been there. I didn't mean to land you with all this."

"You didn't land me with anything. I'm glad to help, Barnaby."

Barnaby starts to snuff the candles out one by one with a long silver snuffer. He looks tired and defeated, rumpled and bewildered like a large bear. Kate longs to comfort him, make him less polite and distant. Make him like he usually is. His acute misery is painful to watch.

"There."

He picks up the church keys from the table at the back of the church and follows her out. Homer gets up relieved and they cross the road and walk up the drive to the lighted house.

Kate says, "Martha's asleep. I gave her a sleeping pill. I've put some supper in the oven for you. You must eat, Barnaby."

Barnaby looks down at her. "You're being very kind."

"No, I'm not."

Barnaby opens the front door and waves Homer in.

In the hall, Kate says suddenly, in a little rush, "I told you my mother died a few months ago. I did this dash home from Karachi, hoping we could make it right between us before she died. We never spoke a word. She spent the last hours of her life watching the door for my brother. I didn't make *any difference at all* by being there. It's quite nice to have another chance of being some real help." Kate stops, suddenly embarrassed. "Sorry. Sorry, I don't know why on earth I am suddenly telling you this. Just . . . the awful finality of someone dying. I know you have hundreds of people in the village who will want to help, but I sort of feel part of this house. I'd like to be there for Martha and for you. I am not being kind, just selfish. I need to do something."

Barnaby, touched, smiles at her. "If it is a question of accepting help from you or my old ladies, there is no contest, Kate. And you *are* part of this house. You have already made a difference to Martha's life, as you did to Fred's, and I thank you for it." Barnaby holds her eyes and Kate sees he means it.

"I'll just check the oven, before I leave you in peace."

She walks away from him into the kitchen and Barnaby goes in to Martha. He is back in a moment. "She's fast asleep. I don't know how long it will last. Is this for me? I hope you're having some with me, Kate? I hate eating alone."

Kate has only laid one place and Barnaby firmly lays another.

"Kate, please stay. I really would appreciate your company. The rest of the evening is going to be spent on the phone, so please eat with me."

He runs his hand through his hair. "I need a drink. What will you have?"

He pours himself a whisky and Kate a glass of wine. They sit at the kitchen table and eat while the moths batter the window outside and Homer sits at Barnaby's elbow, ever hopeful. The wind outside gathers and moves round the house in little gusts that rattle the loose panes. The house feels empty without Fred, as if a clock has stopped.

Barnaby breaks the silence they are both listening to. "Martha and Fred always used to sleep in that vast double bed until Mum began to get dotty. Fred wasn't getting any sleep because she tossed and turned and got in and out of bed so many times in the night. We changed to two single beds. Dad always refused to sleep in a different room."

"Could the double bed go back into her own room now? It might be comforting for Martha and gets rid of the empty single bed sitting there where Fred has always been."

Barnaby smiles, holds his glass up to her. "Kate, you are full of good ideas. This food is delicious, thank you. I feel guilty for suddenly being so hungry."

Kate smiles. "I really don't know why."

Barnaby looks at his watch. "I must ring Anna and try to get Lucy again."

As if on cue the phone rings out jarringly and Kate gathers the empty plates and takes them to the sink. On impulse she pours

Barnaby another whisky, takes it to him in the sitting room and places it by the phone. Barnaby reaches for her hand, smiles and curls his fingers around hers for a moment in thanks.

Martha appears in the kitchen as Kate finishes washing up. She is bewildered and disoriented and Kate takes her to the bathroom and then back to bed.

"Barnaby is on the phone, but he'll be in to see you in a minute. Shall I sit with you for a while?"

"Yes, darling, thank you, but I should like to go home soon."

"And so you shall. This room is only for tonight."

Kate tucks Martha back into bed and climbs on the bed herself and under the eiderdown. Martha smoothes the old eiderdown around Kate as if she is one of her children and they both fall asleep almost immediately.

Barnaby spends the next hour fielding the phone. Thinking Kate must have gone home, he puts his head round the spare room door to check on Martha before he goes to bed and sees that Kate has fallen asleep beside her. He goes and gets a blanket and places it carefully over her. He cannot make out their faces in the dark, but he is comforted and moved by the sight of the young girl and the old woman asleep on the bed, heads close together.

He turns the lights off in a house that he has never known without his father, and falls exhausted into bed and sleeps before he has even formed a prayer.

Martha listens in the dark for the sound of Fred's breathing. It is as familiar as her own. She will slow her own breath down to breathe in time to his. While he breathes beside her she can feel her own heart beat and the pulse of life blood as it flows around her body, keeping her alive. But tonight she can hear nothing. Only silence.

Fred. My name is Fred.

* * *

The frozen earth burns my cheek and eats into my bones. My body is ice and I know if I do not move I will fall asleep and die. All around me lie the mounds of girls, dead, sleeping, and so dying. I try to rub some feeling back into my ankles and somehow I get to my feet. I wobble dizzily and try to take some steps. I do not hear the SS Oberschütze behind me until I feel the rifle butt across my shoulder.

"Down! Get down!"

Sharp, sick pain. I go down like a matchstick and lie still on the frozen earth. The pain in my limbs that began in the hospital burns on the inside of my arms and legs. It feels as if my bones are on fire.

For a moment I stare up at the stars in a cold, clear, black sky. I can hear the hysterical, jumpy shouts of the guards echo repeatedly in the dark. We all know that to lie still on the frozen ground is certain death, but to raise our heads an inch is also death.

"Down, bitch, get down. I'll shoot the next Jew beast to get to their feet."

Why, I wonder, before I lose consciousness again, why do these men feel such hate for girls who cannot hurt them or defend themselves?

I wake suddenly to thin, cold sunlight and silence. Horror fills me, for when I lift my head there are only bodies around me. No one moves. I have been left. I have been left with the dead. I hear my own thin cry of terror in the still air and I crawl painfully away from the dead girl under me and the one lying over my legs.

I, too, am dying. The cold shadow of death hovers over me. It is my nightmare come true. To die alone without another human being near. I hope death comes quickly.

I hear the sound of trucks returning. They are coming back for anyone not yet dead, to kill us. I open my eyes. The truck stops a distance away. Men jump out, but they do not wear German uniforms. They look around them at the mounds and mounds of dead girls near me and they do not move. They are very still, just where they stand.

There is only the silence.

I must get to my feet. I am alive. They must not leave me here. I am alive. I bring my knees up and with one last effort I stand. I wobble and stagger towards the men. I try to make words, to call out, but no sound will come. No sound will come.

The foreign soldiers turn as one and see me. They seem frozen to the earth. I see horror on their faces. I know that I am dirty and full of lice. A tall soldier drops his gun with a clatter and starts to run towards me.

He is making a keening sound up to the sky, a high cry like a bird in distress. He holds his arms out, out towards me, reaches for me as if I am a human being. I hold my arms up towards him as I fall, but the man in the uniform catches me.

"Got you," he says. "I've got you."

He picks me up, turns and starts to run with me back down the road. I can hear a sudden flurry of movement as the soldiers run to check the mounds of bodies for anyone else alive.

I am trying not to lose consciousness. I can feel the frightened beating in the man's chest. I hear him say over and over, "It's all right. It's all right, you're safe. You are safe. We are British soldiers, we're British . . . The bastards. Bastards. Bastards . . ."

He runs with me into a building and he is yelling, "We need help here. We need help. There are more coming, dead, dying, we don't know, hundreds of them. Jesus Christ, they are just young girls, women."

The British soldier's name is Captain Frederick Tremain.

"Fred," he says, as he brings me flowers. "My name is Fred."

Sometimes when I wake in the hospital he is asleep in the chair next to me.

"Live," he whispers when my eyes are closed. "I will you to live."

He is young, with this beautiful and sad face.

Fred. My name is Fred.

Chapter 50

He drives early one morning to the woman's house in a small Volkswagen Polo. He wants to approach her when she is on her own, preferably at home, but he does not know if her husband ever leaves the house before her. A sprinkling of stars dot the still-dark sky and the road is empty.

As he turns into the road he sees the husband come down the steps from the house and walk away from him towards a row of garages. He backs a silver Mercedes sports car out and parks it near the house. The man turns quickly round and faces the way he has come, pulling in between two parked cars.

Looking in his car mirror he sees the woman come down the steps with an overnight bag. She kisses her husband, waves him back into the lighted house and climbs quickly into the car.

He has never before seen her drive in London. She looks stressed and unhappy. After a minute he pulls out and slowly follows the Mercedes. He is not worried about losing it. He is suddenly sure it is heading west. He settles a good way behind her and switches the radio on.

The farther west he drives the darker the sky becomes. He feels odd and suspended as if he has been shot into some alien landscape. Mist and gray cloud meet the tops of green trees, which hang still and limp like a depressing stage set. He has a strange foreboding, a feeling of panic, as if an ending is in sight, but not one he envisaged.

The Mercedes, which has been cruising steadily, turns off the motorway suddenly and into a service station; he turns after her, keeping well behind. She gets out of the low car gracefully. She is effortlessly elegant and holds herself in a way that is familiar to him. Hidden by the car sunscreen he can look at her openly. This is the nearest he has been to her.

Oh, this cold ache of loss.

He does not follow her inside. The rain has stopped and a watery sun emerges as he sits in the car park and questions the sense of what he is doing, as he has done so often these past few months. He closes his eyes against a surge of displacement.

Children run and roll down the wet grass, walk their dogs, play on a slide, call out one to another . . .

I can close my eyes and see the little dark girl in my head, hear her voice as clearly as if it were yesterday. Our running footsteps marked the lawn as we chased around that wild garden, making camps and climbing the trees.

I can remember the feckless Austrian nursemaid who was supposed to watch us and always disappeared with one of the gardeners. I remember how her beautiful mother would stand at the bottom of their garden and call and clap her hands for the girl to come back to the house for a meal or because the sun was going down.

The timid little maid who was frightened of me, frightened of everything. Had cause to be frightened . . .

He had liked frightening her. He still sometimes likes to frighten. He never seems to have lost the knack. Survival perhaps? If you wanted Mutti to love you, you had to be careful to show no weakness. She liked only strong people.

He shivers now in this strange no-man's-land, this stopping-off place between lives. He remembers when he was suddenly no longer a child. When he had to start to make choices.

He knew his father was smuggling food and medical supplies into the ghetto. He did nothing. Later in the war, he discovered that he had also been trying to alert the Allies, the Swiss ambassador, the British, to what was happening to the Jewish population. No one wanted to listen. If only his father had known the Swiss were operating their own racist policies, closing their borders to Jews.

His father compromised everyone's position. Both he and his mother had to distance themselves. Mutti was about to move back to Germany. What his father was doing was treasonable. He could have been shot. Instead, he was offered a way out, a way to save his own life. He refused, preferring to meet an icy, lonely death in a field hospital or in some Siberian wasteland. This is where bravery got you. This is what happened if you could not be ruthless. Treason, is how his father died.

He smiles grimly. He and his mother survived. Mutti. Ruthless, with steely unswerving principles he once admired. Cold to all but him. A fascist until the day she died. He believed he was the only human being she ever loved. His father she betrayed.

Oh, this past, this past that I have put so carefully behind me, a world that is gone. What of my good and challenging life? I have done well. I have been successful. My past was buried safely and deep, until a random, chance sighting of a woman brought back ghosts that woke the dead.

He watches the woman walk back to her car. She is the age of his mistress and no less attractive. It is an interesting, Freudian thought. Always his women have been blonde. Always. City women who would not know the front of a horse from its backside. Looking down he sees the sudden unsteadiness of his fingers resting on the wheel. Did he choose women who would not remind him? Or had Mutti embedded so deeply in his psyche the belief that dark women equals Jewish women, and are forbidden?

He rode in the woods outside Berlin for years until he decided he was too old. The shadow that galloped beside him through the leaves he angrily banished, whipping his horse faster and faster to drown out the sweet sound of laughter.

He lets her drive away while he goes to buy himself a coffee and a sandwich, both surprisingly bearable. Twenty minutes later he is once again settled behind the silver Mercedes as it crosses the Bristol suspension bridge, still heading west, where the sky hangs over the ocean like a bruise.

Chapter 51

Lucy leans back in the airplane and closes her eyes. The plane rises and turns for the coast and Lucy wills the time to melt away, wills herself home, the journey finished. She should have been there. She should have been with Barnaby.

Tears rise in her throat, salty and suffocating, and she desperately thinks of something to distract her. If she starts to cry she will not be able to stop. She opens her eyes and looks out of the window. Below the wheels, wisps of cloud blow like smoke. Below the clouds, layers of buildings, patterns of houses, threads of roads, ribbons of motorway. People in toy cars moving from one point to the next. Everyone going somewhere.

Gramps, with his old tweed jacket with the leather elbows still smelling of pipe tobacco although he gave up years ago. Gramps, sitting in the old squishy chair with the dodgy springs, reading to her as she sat on his knee. The comfort of his smell, the softness of his worn old corduroys. A house filled with the feel of him, even when he has left a room. Safe. Grandpa always made you feel safe, even when he was old.

What will happen to Gran? Martha and Fred have never been apart. Lucy cannot remember a day when both of them were not together in that house. She takes the tray from the stewardess and turns back to the window, moving to shut out the woman in the next seat, the cabin, and the heavy hum of the plane where time is moving so slowly.

Tris, I want you here. I cannot even let you know. By the time my airport postcard reaches you, I will probably be back in Milan.

Lucy slides her hand into the pocket of her rucksack and pulls out Tristan's last letter with the photographs he has sent. Five men in uniform. "Cpl. Taylor. Dave. Me. Sgt. Eliot. Gary."

They are all smiling at the camera, but tiredness hovers like a shadow across faces she remembers looking younger and carefree. Doing the hokey-pokey at the Regimental Summer Ball, yelling at a rugby match, Sandhurst Passing-Out Parade.

Lucy has brought all Tristan's letters with her. She reads them again and again as if each time she will glean something new from them. Sometimes he cannot post them and two come in one envelope.

> *This is me and the boys outside our living quarters. What do you think of the officers' mess? We have tried to improve the concrete bunker by pinning up this bright ethnic rug (requisitioned) over the entrance. Do come inside. See photo two. Now these three camp beds belong to Dave, Gary and me. More rugs on the concrete floor. See lovely photo of you on shelf above bed. (*Playboy *centerfold is Gary's, by the way.)*
>
> *Now, look carefully. Do you see two little beady eyes glowing reddishly on that concrete shelf above the camp beds? In shadow, but curious too? Please meet Raymond Rat! A few nights ago Dave woke up with a terrible scream. Raymond was sitting on his head trying to pinch his digestives. There was total panic as we flailed around in the dark trying to find our torches. (I know, marines we ain't!) Anyway, Raymond proved such a persistent little bugger, visiting every night, that we have made a pet of him and he is honorary, temporary, regimental mascot, doubling as a hot-water bottle as the temperature in this bunkerlike cave dives at night.*

I have to tell you we prefer Raymond to many of the local officials here. This rat at least knows he is a rat . . .

Just one funny story to tell you before I go out on patrol for a few days. I decided to do some washing yesterday and washed a pair of kacks. Looking for somewhere to hang them to dry I went outside where Cpl. Taylor was making a brew. I walked a few yards from him to some barbed wire and hung them up. A hen was pecking under the wire at my feet and I watched her for a moment or two, thinking about a pet hen I had as a child, called Friendi (because she was!) Then I walked back to Cpl. Taylor and as I reached for my mug of tea there was this huge explosion where I had been standing a second ago and the chicken flew skywards in a million pieces taking my kacks with her. Everyone just stared, speechless. I am now called Captain Lucky Kacks.

Lucy looks again at Tristan's photo, brings it up to her face. His mouth is smiling, but his eyes are dark and still. She could have lost Tristan and Gramps all in one go. She shudders and looks at her watch. Rudi has organized her ticket home and a flight straight on to Newquay from Gatwick, and Lucy is grateful. She does not think she could have borne the long train journey home.

The plane turns and begins to descend and Lucy puts Tristan's letter back in the pocket of her rucksack. Barnaby is meeting her at Newquay and she is glad it will be him and not Anna. After the funeral she will write Tris a long, long letter, telling him everything.

Late afternoon sun shines on England and glitters on the sea. In three hours she will be home.

Anna lies in one of the single beds, which are now back in the spare room. She wonders if it is the bed Fred died in. The house is very quiet, only the ticking of the clock in the hall and Homer's heavy breathing coming from the kitchen. It feels like a piece of her is gone, a first fragment of childhood slipping away. When Martha dies Anna will never come back to this house.

Anna cannot cry and the heaviness in her chest is not just grief. There is a separate dread, a nebulous fear that has inched nearer and nearer over the weeks. She cannot shake it away. It remains on the edge of her being like an invisible stalker.

Or a visible one.

She gets out of bed, makes herself a cup of instant coffee and carries it back to bed. It is too early to ring Rudi, to find out if he was able to cancel his meeting in Brussels, and fly down to join her for the funeral. Homer thumps his tail hopefully, thinking it would be nice to keep her company, but Anna does not approve of dogs in bedrooms and gently shuts the door against him.

Just one day to get through, Anna thinks, rubbing her cold feet. Bury my father, then I can leave. Barnaby has organized everything with military precision; there is little for her to do and she hates this. That strange girl in the cottage, Kate, Mrs. Biddulph, and half the women in the village have cleaned and polished the house and filled it with flowers. The Women's Institute have cooked and organized a billion sausage rolls, sandwiches, a tea urn.

There is drink on the sideboard and gleaming glasses. "The doctor" is going to be sent off in style. Anna smiles to herself. People will start with a cup of tea for form's sake, but drinking at funerals is mandatory; even little old ladies feel safe drinking with the vicar.

Anna lies down again and tries once more to sleep. She has drawn the curtains back and light filters into the room. The roof of the cottage, where Lucy is staying with Kate, rises up between the trees. Lucy arrived late last night, exhausted and tearful.

Anna closes her eyes and dozes, floats between sleep and half-sleep. Quite suddenly the faces appear, just like they used to in childhood. Disembodied faces, mouths working, opening in silent screams. Rubbery and blurred like masks, changing shape, eyes bulging with fear, each mask torn off reveals another gray, terrified face. They follow one another into her head until it is crowded and bursting.

Anna opens her eyes abruptly, sweat breaking out all over her body; her heart thunders painfully. The image comes once more as clear as if it is in the room, of hands, many hands passing her small body over the heads of crowds, of hundreds of people, as if she is a parcel.

She sits up, trembling. It was Fred who always came and held her against these nightmares that came swinging in from nowhere. Martha was hopeless—she used to get too distressed hearing Anna scream out. Fred would gently send Martha back to bed, shutting the bedroom door firmly against the fluttering anxiousness that Anna hated.

It was Fred who read to her, told her a story, made her laugh, Fred who banished the demons. Fred was always there, even when she knew she was making the rest of the household utterly miserable with her sharp tongue. Anna cannot remember ever doubting Fred's love, even when he showed disappointment in her for being horrible to Barnaby.

When she was very young, she thought she heard Martha crying in the night, but in the morning she knew she must have been dreaming because Martha was just the same as ever, cheerful and smiling. Before Barnaby was born Martha was very ill. That was when Fred asked her if she would like to go to boarding school like her friends and she had jumped at it. Bored rigid at home with Martha, she had felt totally happy and relieved to be with children of her own age.

When Barnaby was born she was furious. He had no right to come into this world, a boy, sweet and loving and good—revoltingly, sick-makingly good. She disliked him from conception for changing her position in Fred and Martha's lives.

Fred unashamedly adored Barnaby. Martha was triumphant with joy.

"My miracle," she would whisper over the cot when she thought she was alone. "Oh, my perfect little miracle."

Anna, quick and clever, perceived the way Martha touched, talked, and loved this boy child in a way she could never hold or touch Anna. Her tone of voice changed imperceptibly. Her words to her daughter were always loving, but Anna caught the note of a sweet song changing key and her small heart hardened against Martha. Against Barnaby for receiving the soft rhythm of her mother's voice, held in a sure love and joy of him.

And so, Anna thinks now, with wry honesty, are we set like concrete into adulthood. Jealousy becomes second nature. Distrust automatic. Dislike a habit. She gets up once more, pulls on her dressing gown and goes out into the hall. It is still early, but Barnaby is up, waiting for the kettle to boil. He is making Martha her thin slivers of breakfast bread.

He smiles at her. "Proper coffee?"

She nods. "I'll make it."

She reaches for the cafetière from the shelf and tries to say the right thing.

"Everything seems very organized, Barnaby. Well done."

Barnaby grins at her drily. "Funerals are what I do."

Anna smiles bleakly back. "Dad's death, Barnaby? Was it really quick, relatively painless?"

"Anna, he had morphine and he just floated away in a morning. Truly. He—" Barnaby stops abruptly, his face changing as if he has suddenly remembered something.

"What?" Anna asks alarmed. "What is it?"

Barnaby bends and pours hot water over the fresh coffee.

"Nothing, Anna, just . . ." Barnaby is trying to think quickly. "Fred tried to tell me something before he died. He tried twice. It was obviously important to him, but he died before he could speak. I will always wonder what he was going to say, that's all." He watches Anna's face. Hears again Martha's voice. *"He brought me and my child here."*

He stares at Anna as if he is seeing her for the first time and her fear rises up inside her, makes her throat dry.

"Barnaby, why are you looking at me like that? What did Fred say? You must have some inkling of what he wanted to tell you?"

"No."

"I don't believe you. You're like Lucy, I always know when you're lying. Was it about me?"

She can feel her heart thudding in the quiet kitchen. "Was he still annoyed with me for thinking Mum should be in a home?"

"No, no, Anna, you know Fred could never stay cross with anyone."

Barnaby hesitates, seems about to say something, then changes his mind. Anna is here to bury her father; it is not the time to get into this. After the funeral, they will have to talk.

He says truthfully, to gauge her reaction, "I think he was going to tell me something about Martha's life, her past in Poland. Something he thought we ought to know. I wish he had told us before, because Martha is now beyond telling us anything."

Anna pours the coffee into two mugs and says abruptly, "If Martha had wanted us to know she would have told us. She always prided herself on being English. Fred may not have agreed with her total silence about all things Polish, but it was her choice."

She goes to the fridge for milk. "The past is dead, Barnaby, and it should stay that way. Martha decided she was born again when she met Dad. Who the hell are we to decide she should have told us about her childhood, or our Polish grandparents who were probably murdered or displaced to some far-flung place? Mother could never have known what happened to them. No wonder she didn't want to talk about it." Anna picks up her coffee. She is suddenly breathless. "Don't be maudlin, Barnaby. Live your own life. You can't live your life through your parents. None of us can."

She turns away with her mug of coffee and Barnaby, stung, says softly to her back, "Our lives are made up of our parents' and grandparents' lives. We are made of the same genes. We are what *they* made us."

"Balls! Barnaby, we are what we made ourselves."

"You don't believe that!"

Barnaby is angry. "Anna, you and I have no knowledge whatsoever of Martha's family and we know almost nothing about the lives of Fred's family. Yet Dad was one of the kindest, most honorable men I have ever met. Everyone loved him. He was *good.* So, what made him good? He had parents he loved who turned their backs on him for a whole lifetime. You used to ask Fred questions about *his parents* when you knew it hurt him. What is the difference in your curiosity then, or mine now? Or was it the fact that Fred's parents were British and aristocratic that attracted you?"

Anna turns, surprised at Barnaby's long outburst. They both stare at each other across the table.

"You . . . you are a barrister." Barnaby can't stop now. "Isn't the law steeped in the rights of people who want to discover their origins, their true parents? Their rights, their inheritance? *Their identity?* Come on, Anna, you must have had a range of human beings before you with a burning need to discover, fair or foul, something of why they are on this earth? Without knowing our past we are neither entirely rooted in the present nor able to move into the future."

Barnaby stops, startled at himself. Why is he saying all this, when he should be saying something quite else? He waits for Anna to make a crack about sermons. She puts her mug down carefully and leans with her hands gripping the edge of the table towards him.

"Absolute rubbish," she says, in her judge's voice, but Barnaby catches the echo of some other emotion and sees how white her knuckles are. "Barnaby, your energies should be channeled into making a future with someone living rather than trying to discover the past, which is dead." She sighs and says more gently, "Fred is dead, Barnaby. Martha won't be long behind him. What will you have in your life then? *Nothing.* No life apart from the Church. Is knowing what both sets of grandparents were like going to make you happier, more fulfilled? Will those things make a different, happier Barnaby? We make our own lives, despite our antecedents. We make our own lives, Barnaby, good or bad."

Barnaby warms his hands on the coffee mug. He feels like going back to bed. He and Anna cannot seem to have a conversation about anything without arguing.

"We have no idea what Fred was going to say," Anna says, pouring herself more coffee. "It might have been about money, Martha's medication, his will, a hundred things. Both our parents buried their past. For God's sake, respect that. Respect them. The past is dead. It's the future that matters."

She yawns. "It's too early for this. You obviously have too much time to think down here. I'm going to ring Rudi. He didn't know whether he could delay a trip to Brussels to fly down for the funeral. I'm hoping he's managed to."

Anna turns and goes back into her room. Barnaby walks into the conservatory and watches the birds. *The past is dead.* Anna keeps on saying that, but the past can never be dead. He goes back into the kitchen and picks up Martha's tray. Despite the edge of desperation in Anna's voice, as if she is willing her own words true, Barnaby suspects, somewhere, deep inside him, that she is probably right about concentrating on the living. On the future.

Maybe, just let things be. Bury Fred and keep the silence.

Chapter 52

It is like the flutter of a small leaf turning inside her, the lightest feather touch. Beside her Hanna lies asleep, motionless, and Marta resists the urge to wake her.

There it is again. She places her hand on her stomach and the tiny flutter under the skin feels like a butterfly trapped in a curled fist. Marta feels her heart start up in fright. Her limbs feel weak and start to tremble. Hanna must feel this trembling and wake.

But she does not. Hanna, always exhausted, sleeps where she falls like the dead. Marta always has difficulty slowing down for sleep. All the things crammed into her head seem to come alive at night.

In the darkness of the stuffy room, smelling of too many bodies, Marta can make out the shape of her parents' bed. Her father is gently snoring. Mama is probably lying awake too, as still as Marta.

Shame flushes over Marta.

A small voice says, "It wasn't your fault."

Another little voice answers, "You should have been more careful. You knew he was dangerous. Papa warned you to keep away."

She shuts her eyes tight against the dark stifling room. She will go back. She will walk back home now in her head and she will feel calm. She will wake in her own bed. She will remember . . . remember. It is only a few months ago, it is not years and years.

From her bed at home she can watch the sun flush the sky gold and tint small clouds. She can listen to the early stillness, to the swish of the wind through the huge fir, whose branches are like spreading hands, held outwards towards a vivid sky. The waving green hands hold, in their feathery softness, songbirds who nestle among small brown cones and sing out to the new morning.

Marta's heart swells with the excitement of another day. As the sun rises, the great gray trunk of the fir changes color, becomes beige and warm. It is the most beautiful tree in the world.

In her mind, Marta gets out of her bed, throws her wrap round her and tiptoes down the stairs, out through the glass doors and into the garden. Her feet on the damp grass are deliciously icy, so cold among those glistening green blades that she shivers in memory.

No one is up. The silent garden, still sleeping, is all hers. She walks, turning left and right to see how the dew glistens and hangs, bending the shape of each leaf. How the silver cobwebs catch and spread perfect glistening circles between the apple trees.

She stops and turns to look at her small footsteps, which have flattened and bruised the grass, and as the flushed sky settles and pales to a clear blue of another day, Marta's heart soars and sings with the sheer joy of being. The shock of her cold feet suddenly becomes unbearable and she runs back to the house, clutching her wrap, smiling to herself, for she has been the only person in the world to have captured the beginning of this new day.

Her feet across the carpet leave little wet imprints, like the progress of a snail. Sometimes, Papa, up early to check on one of his patients, will catch her and make her sit while he rubs her frozen feet with a towel, bringing the blood back to her toes, chiding her gently, while knowing it will make no difference.

Marta, with tingling feet, runs up the stairs and jumps back into bed and sleeps again instantly. She will ignore Hanna's and Mama's calls if it is not a school day. The image of the garden and all the possibilities of the day will dance behind her eyelids as she sleeps.

Marta does not remember days that were rainy or cloudy or thundery. Here in this room they all share in the ghetto, she remembers only the sun rising gold over the garden and touching her skin. Her chest heaves with loss and with fear. Tears run in a torrent down her cheeks and onto Hanna's sleeping face. She cannot stop them. On and on they flow silently as if they have a life of their own and Hanna, waking in the dark, airless room, turns and places her arm round Marta-instinctively.

Outside this window there is no spread of fir or song of bird, just building after building, crammed and overflowing with frightened, hungry people.

"Ssh," Hanna whispers. "Ssh . . . ss . . . ssh."

Marta takes Hanna's hand and places it on the flutter and pulse and life beat that will become Anna. Hanna gasps, then holds Marta tight, tight against her, two thin girls curled like spoons as if they are still safe in their mother's womb.

"It will be all right. It will be all right, Marta. I will take care of you. We must tell your parents now. It is not your fault. We will take care of you, we will, we will." And Hanna weeps too, for herself and her lost family.

Marta feels again the horror of that afternoon. The betrayal of friendship. The abandonment of hope. She sees and smells those great frothy mouthfuls of pink-tinged apple blossom raining like bitter snow upon her and the boy.

Martha wakes in a different bed, in a different land, in a different life. Yet, the tree, the garden, home, Mama and Papa, are so vivid, so real, as if she can reach out for them and touch a life that is long gone.

There is a door opening, and a gentle voice beside her. She knows this kind man. In a moment she will remember who he is. Where she is.

Barnaby, coming into Martha's bedroom with coffee and thin slices of bread, sees she is weeping. He puts the tray down and goes to her.

"Darling, don't cry. Fred would hate it. You've had such a happy life together. Don't be sad."

But as Martha turns he sees she has been weeping for something quite else, something she has already forgotten. She struggles to focus, to register the present, and Barnaby's heart aches for this daily battle she has with the lapses and leaps of her mind. He helps her to sit up and places the tray on her knees.

"Thank you, darling." She stares at him. "Is Fred walking Homer?"

"No, Mum. Fred died. He died a few days ago. No pain," he says quickly, to deflect her. "That was good, wasn't it?"

Martha's small, twisted hands play with a piece of bread. Her lips tremble. Her eyes are dark and distant as stars.

"The garden is empty again," she says softly. "Quite empty."

As she speaks the grapevine, which brushes the window, shakes, as small blue tits flutter under and over leaves.

"Look," Barnaby says. "Look, darling, the garden is full of birds."

Martha half smiles at the busy flutter of wings among the leaves.

"Yes," she says. "They always come to pinch the last buds when summer is ending."

She turns to him and reaches for his hand. "Fred always promised he would never die first, never leave me alone." She smiles. "As if he could choose, darling, as if he could choose." She rubs Barnaby's hand gently. "Your father was so special."

"Yes," Barnaby says. "He was."

Martha leans back on the pillow and closes her eyes. Barnaby tucks her hand under the covers.

"I'm going to let you go back to sleep, Mum. Kate or Lucy will come in later and help you get dressed in that lovely green dress Fred loved. We are going to bury my father with love and happy memories. We are going to celebrate a happy life. Isn't that the right thing to do?"

Martha turns over on her side as he takes the tray away. She is watching the birds.

"It is absolutely the right thing to do," she says clearly. "And we will do it without . . . without . . . what did he used to call it, darling?" she asks sleepily.

"Without *blubbing.*" Barnaby bends and kisses her forehead.

"Without blubbing." Martha smiles, hearing Fred's voice.

"I love you very much," Barnaby says.

"And I love you. Chip off the old block."

Barnaby laughs and shuts the door.

Lucy and Kate help Martha into her apple-green dress. Fred hated Martha in black and would never let her wear it. They can hear a steady stream of people talking as they pass up the road early to get a seat in the church and there is the constant sound of car doors banging.

How surprised Gramps would be at the whole village turning out, Lucy thinks. Kate had told her Fred's death had been quick and painless. Why do people always say that? As if they could know. This is her first funeral and she is dreading it.

I wish I had rung home last weekend, I meant to. I just didn't.

Lucy leaves Kate to finish dressing Martha and goes out of the room to find Barnaby. He is standing by the open front door with Anna.

"The hearse is going to drive slowly through the village so that people who can't get to the church can pay their last respects. It will be outside the church at twenty past two," he is telling her. "We'll follow the coffin into the church. Philip, the new curate, will start the service and announce the first hymn, then I will take over."

Barnaby is relieved to see Lucy. "Is Martha nearly ready?"

He looks at Lucy's white face and gives her a bearlike hug and she smiles bleakly.

"I know. Grandpa would say, 'No blubbing, chaps.'"

Barnaby smiles at her. "You blub if you feel like it, darling. You won't be the only one."

Anna goes out of the front door abruptly and lights a cigarette. Oh God! Oh dear God, it takes times like these to remember how she hates these sentimental exchanges between Barnaby and Lucy. Lucy has always accused her of being a snob, but there is a colloquial shorthand, a smug collusiveness, about the middle classes she has always loathed. Has she always loathed it, or is it since she married Rudi? It is the same sort of mutual exclusion Martha and her foreign excitability used to make her feel as a child—embarrassed and very irritated.

At this moment she could do with Rudi's wonderful German understatement, but he is flying to Brussels after all. She will have to endure this day on her own. She will leave as soon as she can after the funeral. It might just be possible to be back in London before his night flight gets in.

Martha comes out of her bedroom with Kate, wearing the green dress, looking neat and pressed and vacant.

"Gran. You look delicious." Lucy goes to her, smiling at Kate over her head.

Two undertakers appear at the corner of the drive and nod at Barnaby, watching through the open door.

"Are we all ready?" Barnaby calls.

Anna goes to Martha. "Mum," she says firmly and rather loudly, "this is Dad's funeral we are going to. Do you remember?"

Martha stares at her daughter, unsure who she is exactly, but knowing whoever she is, she has always been bossy.

"Of course," she lies. "Of course I remember."

Barnaby takes Martha's arm and they walk down the drive to the hearse where the coffin, covered in flowers, stands waiting outside the church. Barnaby takes a corner of the coffin and Brian and two churchwardens take the other corners. Lucy puts her hand out for Martha's as the coffin moves forward. Martha's eyes rest on it, unsure.

Her white hair catches in the wind as she shuffles in her funny little lopsided walk, one hand clutching Lucy's, the other thrown slightly, oddly outwards, as if she might lose her balance, or need to catch her fall.

She turns slightly towards the sea and catches a shadow of someone near the oak. It reminds her of something. Someone who used to like to hide behind trees. Someone who liked games that scared.

I stand in the shadow of a thick and ancient oak, twisted and bent by the sea winds, the edges of the leaves permanently burned. Behind me the black water lies on a full tide.

They come suddenly out of the gate and walk across the road to stand by the waiting hearse. Anna Gerstein, a young girl who must be her daughter, the vicar, and a tiny old woman with white hair that is caught and tugged by the wind. She walks strangely, holding tight to the girl, her other hand thrown out for balance. She passes so near and she turns slightly, as if she might sense I am here.

I see the high cheekbones, I see—oh God, I see the right hand with the twisted fingers. It is . . . No, no, it can't be. Marta Oweska? It is not possible. She could not have lived. Dear God in heaven, it is not possible.

In the church Fred lies swathed in bright wreaths that also cover a great sea of floor. Martha, mesmerized by the flowers, the people, the coffin, suddenly remembers clearly and with horror that Fred is dead. It is Fred in that coffin. Fred is dead.

She sits abruptly in the first hymn and Lucy sits with her.

"All is gone," Martha whispers to herself.

"All over now. I shall not stay," she says clearly to Lucy as the hymn ends.

"Oh, Gran, you must." Lucy looks alarmed.

Martha bends towards Lucy. "Fred and I . . . always together. I shall not stay now. Will he know?" She is becoming anxious.

Lucy, suddenly understanding, whispers in her ear, "Gran, of course he will know. Fred will be up there waiting for you, looking at his watch."

Martha smiles, reassured and turns to listen to Barnaby's address.

I am sick. I rush to vomit, away from the gravestones, down the grassy slope towards the water. The sweat is cold, icy all over me. I shake, shake with horror and memory. She has to be dead. Surely, she could not have lived.

I do not see an old lady. I do not see a laughing child on the back of a horse, a girl who feared nothing. I see a broken girl, as she was the last time I saw her. My memory stops. It has to stop here. Now. Now. I must not remember, I must not remember that terrible place.

I am violently sick again and I lean exhausted against the trunk of a tree.

There are tributes from Fred's friends, legendary stories of his absentmindedness: the time he was supposed to have left a woman patient behind a curtain in his surgery, waiting to be examined. He had been rushed out to an emergency and had forgotten all about her. When he returned for evening surgery, there she was, still waiting, fast asleep.

In the faded afternoon, under a bleached gray sky that seamlessly meets a pale ocean, Fred is buried. The earth is replaced over his coffin. Martha's face is utterly still as the earth trickles through her fingers. She knows she is burying Fred. Barnaby is beside her, but it is Anna, standing opposite Martha, the other side of the grave, who sees her mother's face invaded by an anguish of loss, a flash of pain so unbearable Anna gasps. Then it is gone. Nothing.

Lucy walks Martha slowly across the road. At the gate Martha turns suddenly and looks behind her towards the water. There is nobody there.

Chapter 53

He goes into the empty church and the porch door creaks shut behind him. He can feel his heart still beating irregularly from vomiting. There is a cold layer of sweat lying all over the surface of his body, disgusting like the skin of some snake.

It is a tiny church, almost primitive in design. He moves slowly inside, his eyes getting used to the dark. He stares at the brass plaques to the dead, the stained-glass windows, the two altars, the small one to the Virgin Mary. The large Bible is open at the Gospel of St. John. The candles are extinguished, leaving a faint smell of wax. The flowers left here are the large overpowering white lilies that go with death.

He absorbs these things into him as if he can be part of the composition of wood and stone. He moves to the back of the church into the shadows and sits in the empty space. It is very still here. Silent, more powerful than a church full of people.

The sickness will not leave him. It rises from his stomach up into his throat and he has to swallow his own bile. He knows if he vomits violently again he will pass out.

This is shock. This is what happens when you follow something you do not entirely believe in, but become obsessed by. He closes his eyes. Shuts out the memories coming to life behind his eyelids. Shuts out the girl. Shuts out . . .

Marta. Marta alive. The name clings to the roof of his mouth, sticks, for he cannot absorb this, cannot shut out the image of that last time he saw her.

He moves into the shadows and the edges of stone blur with the edges of himself. He feels unreal, insubstantial as he molds with the damp granite and meets the darkness of what he is. This silence is as deep as death. This silence he breathes. This hand on worn smooth wood. This smell of candle wax and flowers, this glimmer of brass.

Out of the dark the crucifix shivers and glints in light from a window. He dare not take his eyes off that frail light in case he is pulled down into emptiness.

He sees the streets of the ghetto where small children huddle to die alone. He sees pinched, frightened faces. Sees the trucks and the whips. Sees the girl in the shadow of a doorway. He smells the fear. His own.

Row upon row of cattle trucks move slowly out of a siding and shunt into an icy night. He sees terror in dark eyes and frantic fingers gripping bundles. He feels again his own horror, which froze into a cruel shutter, which crashed down on all emotions to survive. He drank. He obeyed orders. And drank.

The church creaks. Around him the darkness aches. He can remember the youth he was in a hundred ways and never know the truth. Did I always abhor the violence? Was it fear that made me brutal? Or did I, like a school bully, revel in a whiff of power. His sense of detachment had always been there, since childhood. A vein of cruelty, a thin flaw running like a foreign substance through his makeup.

The darkness nestles. The church is cold. Shadows crouch like cobwebs and reach out for his face. He betrayed his father. He betrayed the family next door. He betrayed himself.

What sort of man is he? He has hummed the tune of a successful life until he knows it by heart. *Until I believed it. Until it was real.* Until he no longer knows the truth of the song he sings. If you are brutal and weep, is it less brutal than indifference or enjoyment in the act? If you spend your whole life healing broken bodies, but are unable to conjure any particular compassion for your patients, is it as good as if you did care? Their bones are good as new. Their gratitude rings true in your ears.

If the challenge of making damaged limbs work is taken for empathy or understanding, in the end, does it matter? Their joy in being whole again is the same joy, whatever you feel for them.

He does not know. He only knows this moment, this pain. This terrible ennui that is engulfing him as he flutters, fragile and elemental as a moth, in the shadows of his life, unable to place a finger on the pulse of what he became, or why.

He has reworked his life so many times, like a thread in a tapestry, all the stitches tight and uniform, neatly worked back and front. No time to think. Just work and women and sleep.

Bury the memory of a boy who grew into a man who wore a dark uniform. A soldier holding a gun, watching frightened, fleeing figures in a fuzzy black-and-white photograph in a history book. That was that life. This is another.

Anna walks away from the chatter, the bonding of funeral memories, the cheerful clink of glasses, the glint of an eye as someone spies someone else still alive whom they thought was dead.

She crosses the garden quickly and a stiff wind from the sea blows her through the small gate to the cottage. She knows the cottage is empty because Kate is helping Lucy with the food. She enters guiltily like a thief. It is her house, but she has no right to be here. It is rented out to someone else and she knows she would be outraged if anyone invaded her privacy.

She has been listening to Lucy telling Kate how, when she was small, Fred would make her things out of wood—small boxes, and little wooden dolls Martha would then dress for her. In a room full of people Anna suddenly remembered how he made the window seat in Lucy's bedroom into a hiding place.

She moves straight upstairs to Lucy's room. She is motivated by instinct, a sudden sureness that Lucy has hidden something from her. She presses the hidden catch, lifts the lid and searches among the innocent debris and worn stuffed animals of Lucy's childhood. She feels a lurch of disappointment when she finds nothing of any interest.

She pauses, catches herself in a rare moment of self-doubt. She does not know exactly what she is looking for, but she feels this burning need to search the cottage.

Lucy's voice echoes in her head, faint, furious, and insistent: *"You are nothing but a nasty-minded little fascist . . . It's in your blood, isn't it? In your very genes."*

Anna closes the window seat and listens. Nothing. No footsteps, only the sound of the wind outside. Anna does not want Kate to catch her trespassing. Why didn't she just ask Kate if she minded her looking for something in the attic?

Anna goes out to the landing and pulls the ladder down. It could be that her memory is faulty, the imagination of a small child caught doing something forbidden and the guilt of that moment forever confused with the discovery of something unpleasant.

She switches the light on, pulls herself up into the attic, crawls once more to the partition and kneels in the dust by Fred's trunk. As last time, fading bills and letters. Many, many letters. Some, Anna sees, for the first time, in Fred's own writing. Returned. How cruel. How bitter that family of his must have been.

Will anyone, she wonders, connected with his family read of his death in the papers and stop for a moment at the familiar name? Grieve for the memory of something wasted and lost? These old school reports, his diaries, the curling brown photographs. Part of Fred. Part of a life he couldn't quite let go of?

Memories he couldn't burn or destroy because this beginning, this childhood, this life, was once his whole existence. A carefree indulgent life, before he even knew Martha existed on this earth. Those first years, that familiar, comforting canvas of childhood was the life he lost forever.

Something lost forever. Anna, kneeling in the dust, feels such a dislocation, such a haunting melancholy, like a snatch of an echo at the end of a dark, distant tunnel. Not quite heard. Never quite captured. But, here, here, snagged on the edge of her consciousness like a tiny piece of fabric held by barbed wire. What was that poem her father used to read to Martha? "Like a half-remembered thing . . ."

As Anna kneels in the shadows, memory of the red box flashes clearly into her mind. There was a box. It was here. Spilling out of it were documents, brown envelopes. Anna's heart thumps. She pulled out a piece of paper, saw her name. She feels a sharp, sick pain and cries out, as a strange, ruined landscape swings out of blackness, full of people moving and moving and moving. Memory flies ahead of her panic and snaps shut like a trapdoor.

The box has been moved. Lucy has moved it. Why? Anna turns off the light, retreats down the ladder and pushes it back up to the ceiling. She brushes herself down, goes back into Lucy's bedroom and stands looking round the room. Lucy was adept as a child at hiding things she would rather Anna did not see. Anna was adept at finding them.

She notices the fireplace, the way the surround does not fit exactly on one side. She goes and pulls gently and it comes away immediately. Inside is a parcel wrapped in bubble wrap.

Anna shakily crouches down but cannot touch the parcel. She can hear her breath, quick and heavy in the small room. She reaches slowly inside for the parcel, pulls it to her and replaces the fire surround.

Standing up, she turns to the window and sees the church is lit up, the stone mellow with yellow light. This cottage, this view. Her first memory?

The church stands like a beacon in the growing dark. It draws her there. She wants to go and sit in its dark stillness, like Fred used to. Like Barnaby always does. Her hands holding the parcel are icy. She is afraid.

She goes out of the cottage, shutting the door carefully behind her and walks across the road to the church.

Chapter 54

When the war began to go badly, I was ordered from my regiment and seconded to a military research institute where I had to work in a laboratory while continuing my medical training. Men with any medical knowledge were being sent to the hospitals and medical units. They were so short of manpower that they were beginning to recruit children into the army.

The department had the tense atmosphere of time running out. As a medical student, I had limited access to the work in progress. I correlated statistics on medical experiments. I was never given an explanation of what the experiments were or the reason for them. I was just told they were crucial to the welfare of serving soldiers.

The head of department, SS-Hauptsturmführer Professor Dr. Mueller, made sure we saw only what was in front of us. The rest was restricted.

When the Soviets began to look unstoppable, I was sent with SS-Sturmbannführer Bruher to Auschwitz. The Red Army were closing in, the camps were about to be dismantled. Mengele and his staff wanted all evidence of medical work completed and brought out. I knew why I had been sent into the hospital. There was suspected typhus and an epidemic of dysentery in the hospital.

Auschwitz. All I had heard was true, but I had chosen not to believe it. Here in this terrible place lay the experimental hospital with the volunteers. Volunteers for statistics I had been analyzing. I did not know how these experiments had been set up. How could I? How could anyone imagine this nightmare, unless they were mad?

All over the camp, there was an air of suppressed panic as evidence was cremated. SS-Sturmbannführer Bruher, terrified of catching typhus, refused to enter the hospital and ordered me inside to collect all relevant documentation, as ordered.

In the hospital women and men were separated. In the room I was taken to I saw only young women and children. Twins. They lay dying in white hospital gowns, in a grim laboratory, on trolleys, bunks, terrified. Waiting.

Until that day, it had just been laboratory work—correlating data, checking facts. Now, in this room, I saw the effect of experimentation on human beings. This was my part, not in saving the great Fatherland, but in the foul experiments going on here and in the hysterical genocide going on in the camp itself.

Auschwitz. A place of foul death, of unimaginable torment. I heard rumors, I saw paperwork pushed past me and I chose not to see and not to hear, because I did not want to believe and because I thought, even if it is true, what can I do?

The Polish doctor on duty was watching my face.

"Go and get these patients' notes," I told him sharply. "I will examine the patients in here to see if they are infected. Do not come back. I do not want any disease to spread."

I looked at the women in this gruesome torture chamber. They were dying, but not of typhus or dysentery. A girl died as I turned her over, as I touched her. Inside the hospital, the women's hair had been allowed to grow. Hair and bones had been measured and documented under strict medical conditions.

It was how I recognized Marta. Her hair. She was lying turned to the wall, knees drawn up, motionless.

I woke up in Auschwitz. I woke up in hell and screamed in my head for my father, who spent his whole life saving lives. It was as if he had foreseen the terrible awakening waiting for me, a punishment for my part in something so evil I would have to suppress the memory of it forever, or go mad. It was as if he were here, beside me, whispering.

"You became immune to thousands of dead. The death of this one will haunt you forever."

I reached for her wrist and found a dull pulse and her eyes flew open in terror, bereft of hope as she turned my way. Her blue lips drew back over her teeth in something far beyond pain. It was freezing, but sweat broke out all over my body and a great wave of dizziness made me cling to the cot.

"It's all right," I heard myself say from a long way away. "Stay very still. No more. No more. I will get you out of here."

Her sunken eyes fixed on me were empty. I did not know if she recognized me.

Trembling, I went back outside and looked at the Polish doctor poring over the medical reports I was to take back to Germany. The doctor's hands shook under my gaze. He too was an inmate. He too wanted to survive.

I told him there could be no more experiments until further notice. The dead must be taken out immediately and the whole ward thoroughly disinfected. With my left hand I fingered the money in my pocket. With my right hand I saluted "Heil Hitler," as I gauged the Polish doctor's level of fear and his willingness to obey the uniform I wore. He knew I was exceeding my authority and rank. Could I distract or bribe him, in the light of a far more terrifying authority than mine?

Outside the hospital, mounds upon mounds of dead were piled on top of each other, frozen in the bitter cold. It would be impossible for anyone to check the identification of the dead. It was my only hope.

In the frenzy of preparation around me, as the SS guards sought to save their own skins, ready to flee before the Red Army arrived, there was a chance that I could get her out of the hospital, back into her block. She could die away from those butchers.

I could not leave her in there alive. I could not leave her to die in that terrible place.

* * *

He wants the silence of this church to swallow him. He wants memory to flee like a hound in front of him, to drop safely back under the dark earth and let him have his fruitful, busy, respectable life back.

Was it only at that moment, in Auschwitz, that he realized he was a war criminal? Silence. He cannot answer.

It is too late for the whispers to haunt him now. He is old. He has lived his whole life saving lives since the war. He has been a skillful and clever surgeon. He has tried to give back . . .

Not true. He was a cold and ambitious doctor who saved many lives but who rarely had a kind word for his patients unless they were young or attractive. He was an excellent diagnostic surgeon who was not afraid to take risks with other people's lives, a man who liked to play God.

Did he save more lives in the second part of his life than he helped to kill in the first? Did he? He trembles now in this small English church, and the man who forgot how to cry fifty years ago, weeps now.

Because of a small old woman who walked behind a coffin in an odd, crooked walk, hands held awkwardly, fingers bent painfully and forever, bones full of arsenic, because of something I took part in.

In memory, I see a girl young and untouched. Innocent. Laughing with excitement on the back of my shiny Tylicz as he rears up on the lawn before the house and even Mutti watches, silent with admiration.

Because I hold the picture of the beautiful Esther Oweska, her hands clapped over her mouth in fear of her daughter falling off the gleaming horse and I see clearly the hardworking, gentle Dr. Oweski, who seemed to see into my soul and know what was to come.

I grieve for the memory I buried, the knowledge I suffocated, of a small child held up to me in the ghetto, eyes huge with fright as her mother begs me to save her before she is sent to Auschwitz.

Despite me, Marta Oweska lived. Had a life. And children.

It is as if he dare not believe the evidence of his own eyes. Exhausted, he feels light-headed. He is disappearing into the fabric of the church. He is being swallowed by time, like a mote of dust, becoming part of the age and timelessness of this church.

He is crouched here like stilled memory, waiting. For reparation? A heart attack? Or the energy just to go home?

Anna pushes the heavy church door open. It has always creaked, ever since she can remember. Before the door clicks shut behind her she hears people in the road and car doors banging and Barnaby's voice calling good-bye. She stands for a moment, her eyes getting used to the dark. Then she walks up the aisle with her parcel and sits in one of the pews.

This is Barnaby's place. The brass plaques of the war dead. The glint of gold cross and candlesticks on the altars, the flags unfurled, the musty smell, the tapestry kneelers, bright and varied, the hard wooden pews, the soundlessness with the door shut.

This place she sits in suddenly has no sides to hold on to. This space she inhabits makes her dizzy as a small gap opens up in her memory and threatens to trap her in a thin crack of remembrance, of some loss that she cannot form into any shape, only feel in the icy coldness of a fear she cannot name. A fear that has always been with her.

Fred could keep this dark thing at bay, he could banish demons as quickly as he could extinguish his pipe. Now he is gone and nothing can stop them.

Here, below the church, Fred used to tell her as a child, on the same piece of headland there once stood a primitive little stone chapel facing the ocean. But the sea encroached and swept away the scattered little cottages and that first church. There is a legend, he told her, that village life lives on under the sea, and when the wind is right you can hear watery voices calling one to another.

Later men sowed marram grass and changed the movement of the sea by creating sand dunes. The feeling of time arrested lives on, Anna thinks. Is this why Barnaby is at peace here? She feels the box heavy on her lap, the bubble wrap soft against her fingers. The church, still and dark, gathers itself around her like a heavy woolen cloak and Anna cannot move, feels she will never move again. She becomes conscious suddenly of not being alone. In the silence she hears a movement, a tentative rustle in the back of the church, someone breathing in the dark behind her. The hairs rise on the back of her neck. Anna turns, her heart thumping, to see a tall, thin old man coming out of the shadows as if she has conjured him from darkness. She freezes, gathers herself for flight, conscious that he is between her and the door. In the dark, she cannot see his face properly. He holds his hand up at her fear.

"Please, please, don't be afraid. I am sorry, so sorry to startle you."

He speaks with a German accent and Anna, staring into the dark folds of the church behind him, answers him automatically in German without thinking.

"Who are you?"

The man stands quite still, but does not reply. There is silence as they both stare towards each other.

Then Anna says, "The church is usually locked at this time. I was just leaving."

"It is a most beautiful church," the man says.

Anna moves across the pews to avoid passing him and reaches the door.

He follows her and as she hesitates, hand on the heavy brass door handle, he says, "I am glad of this moment in a church. To be reminded of someone and something that was once good; people I never knew existed."

Anna pushes the door open, blinks in the sudden light and turns to look at him. His face is tanned. His hair, gray, almost white, is receding. She meets his eyes. They are the most startling blue and they hold hers with a moment's strange intensity. Anna, hand on the heavy latch of the church door, stands motionless. Meets her own eyes. Stares at her own reflection.

She opens her mouth as if she wants to call out in another language, high and loud and guttural, things she cannot cry in English, words she does not know, fearful, foreign and eerie to her ears, as if Martha is crying through her and someone else is in her head.

"Good night." The man turns his eyes away from her abruptly. "I am so sorry I startled you."

He is gone, walking quickly away into the night which is swooping down to meet the sea, the dusk divided by a thin white ribbon of the ocean.

Ice-blue eyes glimpsed in a crowded courtroom. A figure walking away from her. An early morning shadow alone on a London street.

Anna shuts the church door. She cannot lock it. Barnaby has the key. When she reaches the road the stranger has gone.

Chapter 55

The ground is frozen. In the blocks, the tiers of cots where we lie cramped together are like cages. There has not been a selection for weeks and there are hundreds of women in here, huddled together for warmth like animals pushed into a barn.

All summer the smell of mud has clung to us, carried in from the fields, sticking to our legs, filling our nostrils sickeningly, because we cannot get clean. Now the ground is frozen and our feet freeze. Today the girl digging next to me bent to feel her foot and a toe broke off in her hand. She did not feel anything.

Next to me on the pallet, I feel Mama's bones digging into me. I move closer. She is so frail, so thin. She cannot last much longer outside. I have to try to get her on an inside work detail. But how? I have nothing to barter with. She will not leave me. She wants us to stay together. I think if I were not here she would let herself die, but she wants to see that I live. She cannot bear what happened to Hanna.

"Mama?" I whisper.

But Mama is asleep and at the other side of her someone else lies where once poor Hanna slept.

Two days ago a woman went to the Kapo and asked for proper shoes for our feet. Our clothes are inadequate for the bitter cold, threadbare. Most of us could not keep the wooden clogs on, our feet were so cold. We are dying so fast that we have now been issued shoes of a sort, so that we can keep working. I think often of those clothes and shoes Mama packed for us. How we could have done with them now.

I hardly raise my head anymore when someone dies in the fields, in the washroom, or at roll call. In the morning I will try, somehow, to get Mama in the laundry, or on sewing duties. I must get her inside work, even if it means she has to sort out the clothes of those who have gone to the gas chambers.

She must close her mind. She must not let herself think. Just keep warm. Just keep alive. I want Mama to live. I do not want her to freeze to death, to drop suddenly, where she digs.

This morning there is a special roll call, earlier than usual. The SS guards are jumpy and nervous; there is going to be some sort of selection. Rumors fly round, but no one knows. For hours we stand in the cold of a bitter early morning, shivering. When people drop dead they are dragged away from where they fall to join the growing heap of frozen bodies.

Nothing happens. It is so, so cold. We are counted and counted again, formed into lines, separated, formed into different lines.

"What is happening?" I whisper to a Hungarian woman from our block.

"I heard the doctor is coming. Dr. Mengele. For volunteers for the infirmary."

A selection is going on. I see now that certain women are being segregated from the others. It is not like a normal selection. The young and healthy are being picked out of the lines. Why are they being selected?

Anything is better than the fields, but I am afraid. Mama will not be picked and we must stay together. We must get inside.

"I heard," the woman next to me whispers, "that those who 'volunteer,' get clean, warm clothes and proper food."

"Is it inside work?"

"I think it is inside the infirmary."

I see that young women, sisters, and twins are formed into a different group. Dr. Mengele arrives and stands with the SS guards. Some twins are discarded when they reach the top of the queue. Some are selected. Slowly the line moves forward. Mengele's eyes fall on me. He points. He selects me from the rest of the line and I join the others. I look for Mama. I cannot see her.

Suddenly, from the back of the other line I hear Mama cry out. She runs out of her line, runs forward towards the SS guards. She is pleading, she is begging them. She offers herself instead of me. She falls to the ground and touches the heel of an SS officer's boot in supplication.

"Take me. Take me, not my child."

I stand frozen, terrified. As the fear twists and grabs my stomach, the guards drag Mama away without pity, swat her like a fly, club her with their rifle butts, screaming for my life.

I never saw Mama again. You must never even touch the heel of an SS officer's boot. It is useless to beg. You must never ever draw attention to yourself in Auschwitz. Mama knew what I did not. Mengele wanted twins and the young and healthy for the experimental hospital.

If I had known what was going to happen I would have run like Hanna for the electric fence.

Kate, stacking the last of the hired cups and saucers in the kitchen, jumps as she hears Martha's thin blood-curdling cry. She runs across the hall and into Martha's room. Martha is having another nightmare.

"Martha, wake up. Wake up, you're dreaming." Kate shakes her gently, horrified by the look on her face. "Wake up. Martha, open your eyes. Look, I've put the light on. There. It's Kate. You are in your own bed. You are safely at home. It's Kate, Martha. Martha, wake up."

Martha slowly wakes up, blinks and stares at Kate. Her eyes seem dead and the expression on her face frightens Kate.

"Oh, Martha, don't tremble. You are so, so cold," she says anxiously, leaning forward and touching her arm. "I'll do you another hot-water bottle. Please don't cry, Martha, it was just a bad dream."

Martha's small hand clings to Kate's arm. "Don't leave me, darling. Stay here. Leave the light on."

"I won't leave you. Just a minute . . ."

Gently she removes Martha's hand from her own and goes to put the electric heater on. She switches the television on low, climbs onto the bed beside Martha and takes her hand. The trembling is easing, but Martha is still cold.

"Where is . . . you know?" she whispers.

"Barnaby is locking up the church. Lucy is taking Homer for his last walk and I am not sure where Anna is. Maybe she is at the cottage, or with Lucy. They will all be back soon, Martha, and they will be in to say good night."

Martha is silent, watching the flickering images on the screen. Then she turns to Kate.

"Fred? Did we . . . ? There were lots of people. Was I dreaming?"

"No, Martha. Fred's funeral was this afternoon. So many people came. The church was overflowing. He was very much loved, wasn't he?"

Martha smiles. "Oh, yes, darling, everyone loved Fred. Tell me all about it."

Kate sits on the bed and tells Martha about the women from the WI, and about her friends in the village who came back to the house. She tells her about the flowers, literally hundreds of them, some of which Barnaby has sent on to the old people's home and the hospital.

She tells her that so many people came back to the house after the service that they ran out of food and Mrs. Trelawney, who was manning the tea urn, was shocked at how much wine was consumed, which made the second tea urn totally redundant.

Martha giggles. "Mrs. Trelawney is a strict Methodist, darling. You must tell Fred when he gets back. He once offered her a gin and tonic when she came on village hall business and she thought he was an alcoholic."

Kate laughs. "I bet you have lots of good stories, living in the village so long, Martha."

"Oh, I do, darling, but sometimes I forget." She pauses. "So many of the people I know are dead." She closes her eyes. "Tired, darling."

Kate stays until Martha's breathing changes. She hears Barnaby come in the front door and she gets off the bed and turns the television off. Then, leaving the light on, she goes out to him.

"Martha had a bad dream. She's all right now."

"Kate," Barnaby says, "you look exhausted. Go straight to bed."

Kate smiles. "I'm fine, Barnaby. Good night."

She walks towards the front door and Barnaby reaches out and stops her, bends and kisses her cheek.

"Kate, you've been marvelous. Thank you for today. Thank you for being here."

"I'm glad I was. Don't thank me."

She meets his eyes, then bends her head suddenly and hugs him. For a moment they stand very still in the dark hall, holding each other at the end of this long, sad day. Then Barnaby kisses her forehead.

"Good night, dear Kate."

Kate crosses the garden where lights burn in the cottage. Away over the trees an owl hoots, the very first one she has heard here. There were only seven people at her mother's funeral and no celebration of a happy life.

The house sleeps. Outside the wind has dropped and the trees are still. A fox streaks across the garden and Eric, the cat, watching in the bushes, flicks his tail in excitement. The moon sails in and out of fast-moving clouds, and the sound of the sea reaches the cottage.

Only two lights burn. One is in the house where Anna sits up in the narrow single bed with the box open beside her, Martha's letters and diaries spread out around her. Browning photographs slide out of envelopes. Martha's letters in German tremble in her hands. She separates documents: those in German, which she can read; those in Polish, which she will have to have translated.

Out of a brown envelope she lifts a crude yellow star, a small empty pouch, a torn identity card. A pair of glasses. Red Cross documents with strange headings: "Zegota," "Centos," "Social Welfare Department of the Municipal Administration of Warsaw." Another identity card, different name. A small Polish travel book.

Anna is cold and slides down the bed. Her hands lie on the covers, over Fred's diaries. Over the pouch that once held crumbs. She does not sleep.

The other light glows through the hedge from the cottage, where Lucy lies on her side with the bedside light on, reading Tristan's letters from Kosovo.

Chapter 56

From the top of Trencom she can see both coastlines. To her right, the sweep of beige sand stretching away in a smooth curve edged by frothy waves. In the distance the lighthouse, clear and near today. On her left St. Michael's Mount rises out of a rough inky sea like a magic volcanic eruption, not quite real.

She clambers onto the flat boulders and wedges herself into the shelf and shelter of the rocks so that she can sit with her legs straight out, hidden. She wriggles her body until her shape molds with the warm rounded contours of the stones underneath her.

The flats of her hands balance her and she can feel beneath her splayed fingers the heat lying on the surface of the boulder she sits on. This place has a wild, primitive appeal: the archaeological wonder of the vast formation of rocks, the mystery of age, the strange beauty of their height and power. Far below her a long white ribbon of moving sheep makes its way across a field to a gate where a farmer is emptying feed. The top of a tractor passes along the hedge and the smell of farmyard reaches her as she sits looking down from her eagle's height.

Underneath her spread hands, lying on stone, she can feel the different layers and skins that make up the surface of the boulders. The tips of her fingers touch the lacy edging of gray, dried lichen, colorless moss, grains of stone, dust, grass and tiny particles of crystal that catch the setting sun.

All these worn layers she feels under the very edges of her hands, all the gray and almost-blue faded fragments that make up the boulders where she sits. Where other people have sat and stood, changing the texture and color of the surface of stone that have been here for thousands of years.

The sky is catching fire, flaring and spreading before her so that the figures below become black and white against the exaggerated colors of this dying day. Below her, in a moment, in the farm buildings, in the little row of isolated cottages crouched, nestling into the hill, the lights will come on, one by one igniting her loneliness out here in the coming dark.

Martha. Martha, always leaving a small light burning in a dark house.

There, the first light comes on now in the little dark cottage as it loses the sun. She is out here feeling the first bite of cold as the wind rises and the sun goes down. She is looking in on lighted windows. This is how people feel in a big city when it is still afternoon but the shop lights spring on and they are not yet safely home. A little pang of leftover, primitive fear, the need to be back in a safe cave. Block the entrance with a boulder. There, no one can get in.

She shakes herself. Why is she thinking these things?

The sheep leave their huddle and form a thin, ragged ribbon back up the field to their shelters. She is thinking these things because Martha must have felt like this her whole life. Looking in on lighted windows of strange houses. Knowing however much she hurries in the encroaching dark, she can never reach her home again.

Opening a front door, calling out, "I'm home," while her heart is thudding with remembrance of another doorway, other lighted rooms, where a different people greet her in a language as familiar and safe as laughter. A place that is gone forever. A place she can never find.

Martha suddenly talking too brightly, gesturing too wildly,

hugging a little too hard. Making things right in her heart. Folding and tidying. Saving and smoothing. Crooning lullabies to the cat. Suddenly, inexplicably, crying without sound.

You were embarrassed. You sneered. You left the room. Went to do your homework. Excused her to your friends, raised your prim little eyebrows to the sky. "She is Polish . . .," you'd shrug. "My mother is Polish," as if it were some strange, eccentric disease.

You couldn't feel close. You never felt close.

The sun has nearly gone. She must go back down the hill before dark comes. There is no one to hear her. It is all right. Everyone is down there in their lighted houses having tea. She did not know it was possible to cry like this, to feel such grief.

She turns and gets awkwardly to her feet, stands against the last strip and flicker of crimson in the sky, and the steep world below her, sharply beneath her, swings dizzily.

"Why?" she screams to the coming night. "Why didn't you tell me? Why? I didn't understand! How could I? You should have told me. I had a right to know. I had a right to know who I am and who you were."

Her cry echoes and shivers over the fading landscape, hovers in pockets of air, swoops and dips in the curve and hollows like the shadows of birds' wings and then is still. Swallowed forever, the knowledge of who she is. Forever hidden and lost in the fields and stones, hedgerow and boulders, trees and skies, disappearing deep into the damp earth. Gone, a trace only in dreams she can never quite catch, and memories like brushing against a spider's web.

She stumbles back down the hill, not caring what she looks like or who sees her. She turns one last time to the layer upon layer of stones springing out of the earth, framed stark against a slither of orange along the edge of the horizon and she whispers, "I'm sorry. I'm sorry, Martha. Forgive me. Forgive me. I didn't know."

As Anna nears the road she sees a familiar car and Barnaby standing beside it in the dusk, looking anxious. She sees suddenly he is beginning to look like Fred and is comforted. She went to his room when she had finished reading in the first glimmer of dawn and handed him the box of Martha's things.

"This is the past you were looking for, Barnaby."

Then she disappeared out into the still dark morning, numb, and has stayed out all day.

Barnaby opens the passenger side for her. "You look frozen, get in quickly." He gets into the car and turns to her. "Anna, we've been so worried about you. Lucy is in a terrible state. Then I remembered you used to come here as a child."

Anna looks at him. He is pale too.

"I don't want to talk about *anything,* Barnaby."

Barnaby hears the break in her voice. "Anna, we don't have to. All you need at the moment is food and sleep. Let's get you home . . ." He stops. "Oh, Anna."

"I'm not crying," she says crossly. "I'm not, Barnaby. It's . . . you sound just like Fred."

Chapter 57

The following day Lucy wakes early. She is worrying about Anna, about Tristan, about everything. The sun has crept up over the horizon and reached the gravestones. She gets up, goes to the small window and looks out at the familiar shadows, the pattern of trees and the still water beyond.

She pulls on jeans and a sweater and lets herself quietly out into the dawn. She moves across the road and over the Cornish hedge into the graveyard. She walks towards the water and looks beyond the grass, to where the seabirds run and lilt softly on the pebbly foreshore.

Her hands curve round her stomach. She is pregnant. Anna will think she has done this on purpose, but Lucy is as surprised as anyone.

She thinks about her letters from Tristan. The cheerful, carefree soldier who flew out to Kosovo three months ago has disappeared into a man who is facing the aftermath of one tribe trying to obliterate the other from the face of the earth.

Darling Lu,

This barbaric place often makes me think of Martha. It is difficult to think about normal everyday things anymore when we are confronted daily with the result of unimaginable evil and hate. How did people like your gran manage to survive? To go on and lead happy lives? That is what I have been wondering.

The Serbs have burned down most of the Catholic churches. A French soldier told me a smelting works had been taken over by the Serbs as a garrison and detention center, the ovens used as a crematorium with reportedly hundreds of bodies burned there.

I don't know whether this is true but there are mass graves everywhere. Yesterday, we found an old Serbian woman who was hiding in her house from a group of Albanians who had decided to burn her alive. They were furious with us for arresting them. They could not see why we prevented them "getting rid of a Serb."

You know the depressing thing, Lu? We are not going to make an iota of difference here. We can't change anything. Eventually the Albanians are going to stop being grateful and hate us for preventing them doing to the Serbs what was done to them. My faith is wobbling, I have to tell you. I wrote to Barnaby—did he get the letter?

Do you know what I think about when it all gets to me? I think of Martha standing in the shallows with me, giggling. Isn't the human spirit amazing? It endures, survives unimaginable things. And I think of you, my exotic little half-Italian and beg you not to fall in love with a Dago bottom pincher . . .

Lucy is sad, for Tristan's loss of innocence, for his first doubts in his belief in the basic goodness of human beings, and for the things he is having to see. But there is a steady sureness growing, as if this new life inside her is giving her a sudden acute awareness of the cycle of things: the coming to an end of Fred's and Martha's lives, but the irrefutable continuation in the life she is carrying. A part of Martha, and, as far as she is concerned, a part of Fred.

She walks round the church as the sun edges over the horizon. Tristan is making a difference. They all are. He has to go on believing that. We have to believe in good, Tris. We have to believe we can make a difference or there is no point in going on.

The day is quite still as she moves round under the trees towards the sea. She hears the crack of a twig in the clear morning air, the sound of a foot carefully placed behind her.

She turns to the close darkness of trees behind her, feels a jerk of terror as a shadow dislodges itself from the shelter of branches and moves towards her. Homer starts to growl a warning low in his throat.

Lucy hesitates, blinded by the sun edging over the harbor. A man is coming towards her, his features blurred by the sun in her eyes. He holds his hands out to her, calls out to her in German.

"Go away. Who are you? Keep away from me!" Lucy cries, her arms automatically curling round her stomach to protect herself. The gate is behind him. She could run and jump over the high wall, but . . . the baby.

The man has nearly reached her. Still she cannot make out his face, but he says in a breathless voice, heavily accented, "Please, please, don't be afraid of me. I have no intention of hurting you. I just need to talk to you. Please, I am sorry. I did not mean to frighten you."

Lucy turns from the sun and when the light blobs in her eyes have faded she can see in front of her a tall, old man, distinguished-looking, but agitated. He is staring at her in a curious way. She shivers. Homer goes on rumbling warnings in his throat and Lucy wants to run fast away from this man.

"What do you want? Who are you?"

Still he stares at her with that strange concentration, as if he wants her face to be imprinted forever on his mind.

"I would like, if it is possible, to speak with your mother and your grandmother."

"Who are you?" Lucy asks again. He looks ill.

He opens his mouth as if to reply but no sound comes. He rocks slightly on his feet. Lucy trembles.

"Do you know my grandmother?" she asks, fighting a horrible, surreal panic.

"Yes," he says. "Once, I knew your grandmother."

"And Anna, my mother?"

"I met her yesterday in your church."

"What do you want with us? Why won't you tell me your name?"

He does not answer.

Suddenly, Anna is coming, running up the path. She calls out to Lucy and the man turns towards her. Anna and the man stand quite still, facing each other.

Lucy has never seen her mother so pale or afraid. Her eyes never leave the man's face. Lucy moves quickly over to her and Anna, surprisingly, reaches for her hand and holds it. She is shaking.

"Tell me your name and what you want with us. You have been following me, I realize that now," Anna says.

"My name is Kurt Saurer."

Lucy draws in her breath. *Saurer.* She clutches Anna's hand.

"I believe I am your father, Anna."

"Anna's father is dead," Lucy cries out. "We've just buried him."

Anna's face is like a mask; all blood drains from it. She meets the man's eyes, holds them. Her voice is dead.

"Yes," she says. "I think you probably are. It was your name on that birth certificate."

The man sways, begins to fall and crumples at their feet, as Barnaby comes running up the path towards them.

The man sits at the breakfast table in the conservatory clutching a mug of steaming, sweet tea Barnaby has made. Anna, Barnaby, and Lucy watch him in silence.

"I am sorry. I have never, ever passed out before." He looks down at his hands holding the mug, then up at Anna.

"I first saw you when you came to lecture at the Free University, Berlin. There was also a photograph of you in the newspaper." He puts his tea down on the table and reaches into the inside pocket of his jacket, finds his wallet and takes out a small photograph, which he hands to Anna. "This was my mother."

Anna leans forward to take it; peers down at a photograph that could be her.

The man says, "I had not thought about the war, I had not thought about the past until I saw you. I buried deep the knowledge of . . . I had to know if you could be my daughter."

Anna says quietly, "Do you realize my mother is still alive? That she is in this house?"

He nods. "I did not even consider she could be alive. I did not know until the day before yesterday, when you buried your father. It was a terrible shock." His mouth trembles. "You see, I thought you must be adopted, brought to England by some relative."

Barnaby gets up and stands behind Anna.

"Anna and I know almost nothing of our mother's past. She has never spoken of it. She has Alzheimer's disease now. Until the day before yesterday, when Anna found Martha's box of papers, she believed Fred was her father. You talk of shock . . ."

"I am sorry. My being here is difficult, I know this."

"Yes," Anna says. "It is. But necessary, I think." She turns to Barnaby. "I'm worried Martha will be awake soon. This feels wrong, somehow."

"Mum, Gran is fast asleep. I've just been in." Lucy turns to the man. "You were a Nazi, weren't you?"

"Yes, I was. I cannot undo what I did or what I was. I am not going to try. I do not use excuses, except to say there was a climate that pulled many of us in for a time."

He looks at Anna. "Since the war, I have spent my time as a doctor, like your father, like Marta's father, and like my own father."

"Tell me about my mother," Anna says. "Tell me how you are my father. According to her papers, my mother was in the Warsaw ghetto from the age of sixteen. At eighteen she was in Auschwitz.

How can you be my father? Why is your name on that strange birth certificate? I don't understand."

Kurt lifts his hand and strokes his hair nervously. How will he tell this story? How will he make it palatable, in any way believable, to Anna and her family, these hostile people watching him so closely? He has never envisaged talking to anyone but Anna. Why do the others not go and leave them together?

"My family lived next door to Dr. Oweski, his wife, Esther, and Marta, in the countryside near Warsaw. When we were children, my father and Marta's father set up a clinic. They were at university together and had remained friends. My father was German, but my mother had Polish blood. I used to play with Marta when we were small. We were good friends. Marta and I both had a passion for horses. I taught her to ride."

He pauses, sips his tea, watches Anna light up a cigarette, but her eyes never leave his face. "Then we grew up, saw each other less frequently. The war came, Poland was invaded. I had to join the army. Things were bad for the Oweskis, for all Jews."

The stillness of Anna, Barnaby, and Lucy is unnerving. He looks up, he does not want to continue.

Anna's voice is cold. "Go on," she says.

Her face is a mask behind which she hides the terror of hearing the truth. Lucy moves imperceptibly so that she leans gently on Anna as if to protect her.

"I saw Marta one last time before the family were sent to the ghetto. We talked together in the garden of my house where we had once played. It was wrong of me—she was very young—but we had always been friends. Anna, this is how you came to be, though I did not know it."

He looks up at Anna and he is trembling, his face white and pinched, his eyes too bright, too tense, waiting. Anna stares back, hostile.

She wants to cry out, "I don't think so. Oh, I don't think that is how I came to be . . . A little Jewish girl of sixteen, with a Nazi, willingly? I don't think so, Kurt Saurer." But she says instead, "Was that the last time you saw her?"

Kurt hesitates. "I saw her again, in the ghetto. She—" He stops but they are waiting for his words. "She . . . held up a child to me from a doorway. She pulled the bonnet from a small child to show me she was fair. They were taking the children that day. I . . . I told her to hide the child, get the child out of the ghetto. Make her disappear." To keep his hands steady he wraps them round the mug and still they tremble. "I do not know how, but she managed to get you out, to save you, Anna, most probably through the Polish underground. There were agencies that helped to get children out of the ghetto. Sometimes they were given German identities, sent to German and Polish homes. I am sorry, I do not know any more."

He brings his hand to his face, a long hand with the little finger missing.

"I taught myself to forget. I could not know if the child she held up was even hers. Anna, I am sorry, I never thought about that day until I caught a glimpse of you through an open door in the university, studied the photograph of you in the paper. Then the nightmares, the terrible memories began all over again. I had to find out. I had to know."

Anna is slowly dissolving. Where did I go? Who looked after me? How did I survive? I will never know. Never.

Staring at this German, her natural father, she sees herself for a second in the cold blue of his eyes. Herself in a stranger. Herself in all he does not say. What he cannot say. What he does not know.

The bitter disappointment at his inability to tell her the whole story of who she is and what happened to her, the shock of the last few hours, tips Anna slowly into no-man's-land. Something starts to break inside her.

"Your nightmares!" she whispers. "At least you know the origin

and reason for yours. I will never know. Never, never!" Anna's pain is terrible to watch.

"I am sorry. I am so, so, sorry."

Barnaby, still standing behind Anna, protectively wraps his arms around her. He is angry. He loathes this man talking about Martha, destroying Anna. No one has the right to try to salve their conscience through another human being.

Lucy is furious. "You shouldn't have come. You should have stayed away. What have you achieved by coming here except disrupting my mother's whole life?"

There is a noise from the door and Martha appears. She cannot understand what is going on, but she can still gauge atmosphere. Lucy turns quickly and tries to turn Martha back into the kitchen.

"Cup of tea, Gran?"

"Thank you, darling." She stares at Kurt. "How do you do? I'm Martha Tremain."

Kurt gets up and bows. "How do you do?"

He wants to look into Marta's face, but is afraid. "I will leave you to have your breakfast."

Martha goes on staring. "Do I know you?"

Kurt looks up at her still-beautiful face. "Once. Once, a long, long, time ago we knew each other."

Martha is silent. A small sliver of memory comes out of the darkness.

"You are German?"

"I am."

"What is your name?"

The man hesitates.

"Gran, he has to go. Let's make some tea."

Martha ignores Lucy and goes nearer. Kurt, unsure what to do, holds his hands out in front of him in a nervous little gesture and then holds the edges of his jacket.

Martha sees the blueness of his eyes and the missing finger. She sees the tall, good-looking man and has a flash of searing memory, a glimpse from another life.

"Kurt Saurer," she says. "Tylicz bit your finger off."

Kurt smiles. "It is a long time to remember that."

"Yes. It was your own fault."

"It was, Marta."

He looks into her eyes, eyes that have grown dim but cannot extinguish the essence of Martha or an amusement he recognizes.

"I must leave you to your family."

"I will walk you to the door."

"Thank you."

Martha turns in her old cardigan with her nightdress showing beneath and, ignoring her stunned family, leads Kurt out of the room, firmly waving Lucy out of the way.

At the front door Kurt says, "I am so very glad I have seen you again." He pauses. "I did not know you lived, Marta. I did not know you survived."

Martha looks up at him surprised. "*But you saved me.* You got me out of there. Mama and Hanna died, but you saved me. I could walk. I walked out of the gates . . . a long way . . . Fred found me. *I lived.*"

"I wish I had known. How I wish I had known. Good-bye, Marta."

"Good-bye."

He opens the front door and walks out into the morning. He cannot look back.

At the gate, he hears running footsteps. It is Lucy.

"I want to ask you not to come back. I don't want you upsetting my mother again. She can't take it."

Kurt reaches into his pocket and takes out a card. Holds it out.

"If you or your mother ever need to ask me anything, here is my address. I do not seek forgiveness from you, or understanding. There can be none. I am not proud of having been a Nazi. But I exist and I have lived another life since the war. Please, take this.

There may be a time when Anna needs to know more. Or a time when you do."

He looks into her face, at her hand curled round her stomach. "I am your grandfather, Lucy."

Lucy hesitates, then, reluctantly, hand shaking, she takes it and watches him turn and walk away down the drive. A frail old man with Anna's eyes.

He had no right to come. No right at all.

Chapter 58

Barnaby leaves Lucy in the house dozing in front of the television. She wants to stay near Anna and Martha. He walks under a full moon over to the cottage. The air is cold and his legs feel wobbly as if he has been swimming. Kate opens the cottage door, takes one look at him and goes and pours him a huge glass of red wine.

Barnaby reaches for her suddenly, holds her tight against him without speaking. His sadness is tangible and Kate is silent, her arms wound round his waist. Barnaby lets her go, takes the glass of wine and smiles.

"Kate, I honestly don't know what I would have done without you, especially these last forty-eight hours."

The day has slid by in a strange, slow unreality. Anna took pills, slept. Lucy hovered, looked after Martha, continually checked on Anna. He took a Communion service, did a hospital visit, could not concentrate.

He and Lucy tried to talk to Anna, but she had retreated into herself, unable to react to anything anymore. Lucy cooked a meal only Martha ate. Barnaby, worried about Anna, eventually rang Brian, who came round to the house pretending it was a social visit, but Anna remained monosyllabic. Brian left some tranquilizers with Barnaby for her, but thought it unlikely she would take them.

"Shock," he said. "Anna is in shock. She has just closed down for a while. Leave her, Barnaby, just let her sleep, for the moment."

Lucy, washing up the supper things, said to Barnaby, "I wish she would get angry or bitter. I can't bear her like this. Gran and Grandpa were right. She should never have found out. It's my fault, Barnaby. I should have burned those things. I should have sent the German packing."

Coming into the kitchen, Anna said quietly, "No, Lucy. You're wrong, I had to know. I had to find out why I've had nightmares all my life. I'll be all right. I'm going to bed now. I'm going to go to bed with Martha."

"Anna," Barnaby said gently, "have you spoken to Rudi?"

Anna turned tiredly at the door. "He is stuck in Brussels, Barnaby. It is not something I want to talk about on the phone."

"No, but he would be a good person to understand, Anna."

"Yes, and I will talk to him, when he is home." She smiled. "Good night, Barnaby."

Barnaby says now to Kate, "I have just watched the disintegration of someone I have known all my life. It is a terrible thing to see, Kate, a terrible thing."

Kate picks up the bottle of wine and leads him into the sitting room.

"I know it's still summer, but it seemed so cold suddenly I lit a fire."

Barnaby sits in the shapeless armchair that has always been in this room and looks at her.

"Kate, I'm sorry. I shouldn't really have come. I'll depress you. I just wanted to be with you." He drains his wineglass.

Kate pours him more. "You won't depress me," she says softly. "I'm glad you came."

Barnaby stares at her. Kate has a way of looking at him, saying things sometimes, that make his heart do an almost forgotten flip of excitement. Kate, staring back, puts down her glass of wine and goes over to him. Bends and kisses him. He puts a hand up to her cheek and holds her to his mouth, kisses and kisses her back. Feels her face under his large hand grow warm. Wants to leap up and press her to him.

Drawing away from him, Kate says, "Barnaby, let's just go to bed." She takes his hands to pull him out of the chair.

Barnaby is startled. "Kate, dear Kate, it's sweet of you to want to be my comforter. I did not come over to . . . I just had a need to be with you, that's why I came over."

Kate, kneeling by his chair, looks up at him. "Sorry, Barnaby. It's probably never entered your head, but I've fantasized so long about getting you into my bed. I thought . . ." She stops, looking young and pink and embarrassed.

Barnaby, astonished, stares at her, then bursts out laughing. "Good heavens! Have you? I'm afraid it *has* entered my head. I think you know perfectly well how attractive I find you, but I'm too old for you, dear Kate."

Kate grins at him in that way she has, then links his hands between her own. "I think there are times for talking and times when you don't. I think we should just go to bed and lie together in the dark, Barnaby, where I can hold you. Unless, of course, you find me totally repellent?"

Barnaby smiles. "*Totally.* Isn't it obvious? Kate, you're lovely. I long to go to bed with you, but—"

"Come on." Kate takes Barnaby's glass. "We'll see who's too old. I have another bottle of wine I think we might take up with us."

Barnaby watches Kate undress in the dusk without any self-consciousness, as only the young can. Her body is neat and tanned. Sexy but unthreatening to an almost celibate vicar. When she disappears to the bathroom, he undresses quickly and gets between the cool sheets.

For a second he is reminded of another dusk, of a time when he made love to someone who was not his. When he broke his vows and let so many people down. Clouds paler than the night scud past the squares of window and the night birds echo over the water as sad as the memory of that hopeless lost love set in a backdrop of violence.

Kate patters back, smelling sweet, and gets into bed beside him. He reaches for her.

"Oh, Kate," he says, "I have had very unvicarish thoughts about you."

Kate laughs and rolls on top of him and he holds her young body to him with a soaring feeling of euphoria, light-headedness, and desire.

He wakes in the night as Kate sleeps beside him and is reminded again of a love that cut like a knife. He knows he must rein himself in, not expose himself, belly up, to middle-age hurt or ridicule.

Kate, waking, asks, "What is it, Barnaby?"

Barnaby pulls her to him under the covers. "It's hard to talk about," he says. "Because I never have. When I was in Northern Ireland everyone thought I left the army because the Irish nurse I was engaged to was caught in a bomb explosion and killed. The truth is, both Isabel and I were on the rebound, two desperate souls brought together. Even if she had lived, the poor girl and I would never have married."

He closes his eyes and absorbs the wonderful warmth of Kate's body. The desire that rises up in him makes him want to tell her quickly, as if in the telling he can move on, make love to her again and lose the guilt of that other time.

"I was madly in love with a friend's wife. A fellow officer. Obsessed."

Kate stirs against him. "And she with you?" she asks.

"Yes. I betrayed that friend, Kate. It was a long time before we actually had an affair. But the betrayal was from the first moment

I did not walk away. They were posted back home. Their marriage survived, but not before she tried to commit suicide."

"Because she loved you."

"Yes."

"But surely it would have been better for them both if they had divorced?"

"They were both strict Catholics. She must have been in an awful state to even contemplate suicide. He adored her and she was fond of him. She wanted to do what was right."

"Even if they both were unhappy for the rest of their lives?"

"But they weren't, you see. They have two children now. Their marriage survived. They are happy. Later, many years later, she was able to write and tell me this."

"So why have you still got a conscience?"

"Because of the grief I caused by not having the moral courage to walk away, especially when I was in a position of trust."

Barnaby smiles suddenly into Kate's hair. "Why on earth am I telling you this when I could be making love to you?"

Kate lifts her head. "Because you needed to tell me so you can let it go. Now you can draw a line under that time and forget it." She kisses his nose.

"How wise you are," Barnaby says, "for such an unconventional little thing."

Kate grins. "You are not quite such a goody-goody as I imagined, Barnaby Tremain."

Lucy lies on the sofa with Homer beside her smelling like sawdust, and writes to Tristan.

Darling Tris,

I miss you so much it hurts. It sounds so horrendous out there. You sound sad and cold and tired and there is nothing I can do to comfort you. I wish I could phone or e-mail you and I have no idea how long letters take to reach you.

Tris, you've got to keep safe. Please, please don't take any risks, please don't be a hero. I've read about the Albanians rioting. I can't cope if anything happens to you. Life is shitty just at the moment. Grandpa has died. I flew back to England for the funeral and I am here in Cornwall with Barnaby. Mother is here too.

Tris, Anna found the letters and things we hid in my bedroom, and then, you won't believe this, Kurt Saurer, her German father, turned up. He traced her somehow, wanting acknowledgment or to lay ghosts, I don't know, insensitive bastard, so you can imagine Mum is in shock. It is horrible to see her sort of diminished. There are times when I thought I hated her, but I don't. She has always been so strong, unwavering. To see her wobble is unnerving; makes me feel small, like a child again.

Tris, you know that last evening in the cottage before we left? Remember! Well, I'm pregnant (three months). Hope this is a pleasant shock! I am telling you now, in a letter, to give you something to hold hard to in the bad times, so you know you do make a difference and to make sure you come home safely to me. I will tell you everything that has happened in detail later.

I love and miss you so, so much,

Lucy

Lucy puts the pen and paper on the floor and turns on her side, an arm thrown over the dog. "Stop snoring, you old fleabag."

Through the huge plate-glass windows that lead to the conservatory she sees a new moon shining on the cherry tree and casting buttery shadows over the overgrown lawn, across the trees and along the high hedge that hides the road. She can hear the roar of the sea beyond the graveyard and the familiar, haunting sound of curlews.

She thinks suddenly of the sad and dignified old face of the German.

"I am your grandfather, Lucy."

If Martha could not conjure anger from her muddled soul, has she any right?

These sounds, this house, this sofa where she has lain so often in childhood, her head on Martha's lap, is her *safe house.* Because of Martha. Because of Fred. Because of their happiness together, which has always filled the house like endless summer. Despite shadows and vague echoes that sometimes hung in the air like sea mist, her grandparents have given her a childhood full of time and love.

Lucy is too tired to think clearly, but if only she can get Anna to focus here, on the home of her childhood, the home Martha made for her, maybe she can let go of memories she can never, ever capture. She will regain her sense of self. She will see that this home, this first place of her real life, is the only place that matters.

Chapter 59

It is Anna. Martha wakes and Anna is with her in the dark.

"Darling," Martha says, "what is it? Why are you crying?"

But Anna cannot answer and Martha cannot bear her pain. She takes Anna's hand and holds it to her cheek, tries to cover her with the eiderdown because she is shivering, because she is so cold.

"Sleep, Anna, sleep," Martha whispers. "Mama is here. I am here."

Mama is here. But her baby is starving. She has no milk. Her milk is gone. Papa bends over her in the dark room.

"Marta," he whispers. "Marta, I have milk."

His face is cold from the bitter chill outside. His face is drawn. He has become so old.

"How?" Marta whispers. "How did you get it, Papa?"

"Give me the child." He takes the baby from Marta and from him Anna takes the milk, slowly, so slowly.

"Enough for now," he says, and kisses the top of the baby's head.

"She is so small," Marta says. "Will she live?"

Papa smiles and hands her back. "She is a fighter," he says. "Tiny, but look at her grip."

Marta holds the baby close to keep her warm and when she looks up Papa is staring at her.

"A child with a child," he says, with that quiver in his voice that means he loves her.

As the child grows Marta makes her a velvet necklet to hold crusts of bread. The child has to suck them they are so hard; she has to lick her fingers to hold the crumbs. Children dig under the wall, creep out at night to steal. Sometimes they are shot or captured. It does not stop them. They are starving.

After two years, Papa is skeletal. He gives what little food he finds to Marta, Hanna, and Mama. They cannot get him to eat properly and his teeth have fallen out. Sometimes there is a parcel. Papa says it comes from Dr. Saurer.

Anna, on that morning of screaming, half light, half dark, in the hushed slurred moments of half sleep before dawn, Papa rushes to the window.

"Quick," he says, "quickly, Marta, come with me. They are taking the children. They are rounding up the children."

Papa and Marta run down the stairs towards the cellars, but everyone else is running too—running and pushing, screaming in panic, knocking each other down, pulling and pushing their children ahead of them.

Papa is pulled away from Marta, gone in a surge of bodies.

"Up," he shouts, and points to the stairs. "Up, we will try the roof, Marta." But Marta cannot move. She is afraid of this rush and panic of people. She holds her child tight, tight to her and the child's thin arms are clutched around her neck.

Marta smells her hair and the still-baby skin. She backs into the shadows by a door, crouches, holds the child until the shouts and the shots and sound of the whips and the screaming move slowly away.

Marta hears the trucks start up, and the terrible surge of wailing begins and echoes in the empty street. Then, a sudden and strange silence. She gets up, the child's face still buried in her shoulder. She opens the door and stands in the shadowy doorway as the trucks full of children rev up and move away.

They make no sound. The children make no sound. Passive, they stand there so still, looking back, holding on to the rails of the trucks.

There is a point beyond fear, Marta learns later, when body and mind can no longer react. Or is it hope? A brief, innocent and pure belief in better things before an understanding of evil?

Suddenly, out of nowhere, a German on a horse comes wheeling round the corner. He sees Marta and she stands in the doorway, frozen with fear, as he swings his horse round towards her. The child whimpers, a tiny sound.

Nearer he comes, the horse's hoofs loud in the deserted street. Nearer and nearer until Marta can see his face. She stares and the horse whinnies and she knows for sure.

Marta takes the child's arms from around her neck. She pulls her bonnet from her head and she turns the child that is Anna round in her arms to face him. She holds her out to the German on the horse. He stares back, looks into Marta's face and then the child's. Marta sees shock. He whips the horse round across the road so that they are hidden from the departing trucks, Marta and the child.

Marta holds Anna up, up in her aching arms and the blond curls move in the cold wind. She looks into the German's eyes. She begs. She begs him with all that she is for this child's life.

The moment seems endless as he bends across Tylicz to peer into their faces. Then he whispers, "Hide her, get rid of her, get her out of here. All the houses in this road are going to be cleared for resettlement."

Then he is gone. Just the echoing sound of horse's hoofs in the cold morning air. Marta goes back inside and Papa finds her, takes Anna from Marta and holds the child to him, tight, tight.

Martha is dreaming, moaning softly in her sleep, turning this way and that. What does she dream? What does she remember? Anna wonders.

The old go back in time. Childhood becomes clearer than something they did yesterday. Anna is getting warmer under the eiderdown. She cannot remember the last time she was this near to Martha. She smells vaguely of lavender and the baby powder the carers use.

The house is still. Barnaby and Lucy must have gone to bed. Outside the large windows a new moon hangs in the sky, making the room light. Small branches knock gently against the glass. Martha's room. The room she has shared with Fred nearly all her married life.

Anna wants her childhood back. She wants to start again and be different. She closes her eyes against the memory of the things she constantly inflicted on this family. Cuckoo in the nest. She feels a growing dislocation that will not go away. Will not leave her.

I need time, Anna thinks, time for this. I am no longer the person I was. I am not even the age I was.

The trembling starts again, deep inside her very bones, as if her body cannot cope with this shock. Anna has never ever felt like this before and it terrifies her. She has no idea how her mind or her body are going to react any longer. She moves down in the bed and at that moment the door opens and a little slither of light fills the room.

It is Lucy, in sexless, baggy pajamas, carrying a mug of tea and a hot-water bottle. She looks about eleven. She puts the tea down on the bedside table and pushes the hot-water bottle under the eiderdown next to Anna.

"Are you all right?" she whispers.

"Yes," Anna whispers back automatically.

Lucy sits on the bed. "No you're not, Mum. You must feel like you are in the middle of a nightmare and just want to wake up and find everything's normal."

Anna half sits up and sips her tea. "Thank you for this, Lucy. Go to bed, darling, it's late."

Tears spring to Lucy's eyes. She gets off the bed and stands awkwardly.

"Mum, you are the bravest person I know. You are just like Grandpa. You never make a fuss." She bends and kisses her mother quickly and makes for the door.

"Lucy," Anna calls softly.

"Yes."

"Thank you."

As the door closes Anna pulls the hot-water bottle to her and tries to fall in with the rhythm of Martha's breathing. She is like her father. What a lovely thing to say.

Martha sleeps and dreams again, but turns sometimes in her sleep and touches Anna, feels the warmth of Anna's body with the back of her hand. Martha dreams of long-forgotten things, held by sheer will to the furthermost reaches of her mind.

She dreams of her life with her child, closeted in the dank room with her parents and Hanna. The baby that lived despite everything. The child they could all keep alive because they were able to work. As long as they were useful, they could evade the transports. This child was the last thing they all shared together. The warmth of Anna's small body kept Marta going.

As hunger growled in her stomach and her limbs grew shaky and weak, Marta would whisper stories of hope to the baby. She would tell her of the garden at home where the grass met the edges of the forest. She would tell her of the chickens and the cat they once had. Of the horses, sleek and shiny, she learned to ride, but now hardly dared let herself think about.

In her head, Marta would go back over and over again, galloping, galloping away, with the wind loosening her hair, the excitement bubbling up inside her in great whoops and rises of pleasure.

The figure who had always been beside her, their horses neck and neck, had become a painful shadow. Like a child coloring over a face that betrayed, so Martha made him shadow. But he would not stay a shadow. Would not fade.

She tried to obliterate the memory of him from the joy and freedom of those rides, those times when she was truly free of the restrictions of being a girl, an only child, in an expectant Jewish family.

The boy, who was difficult and wild, showed her there were other ways to live and feel. Marta knew he liked her because she had the courage to challenge him, and an intellect that questioned everything and learned quickly.

She knew she would be matched with a suitable Jewish boy, despite the fact they were religiously unobservant Jews. She knew that if it had not been for Papa, her freedom would have been curtailed by her mother long before. These years had to be stored like treasures in a drawer.

The small boy, who could be cruel, turned into a strutting teenager in a dreaded uniform. A man who grew to love the power of fear. After the Germans invaded, he became cold, calculating, and dangerous. So why could she not banish him from her mind? Why wouldn't he become shadow?

On the day he raped her under the apple tree, why did she remember his face immediately afterwards, as he sobered up? The horror of what he had done. His hands lifting her against the trunk of the tree, trembling, trying to do up the buttons of her dress, staring at her, white-faced. Wanting to smooth her hair before she flinched away from him, turned painfully into the fallen apple blossom.

Why did she remember this as if it excused him? These thoughts she has not been able to tell anybody, ever.

Martha moans and tosses in her sleep.

Because she had to make the place inside her heal, because of Anna and because . . .

"Mother," Anna whispers, tapping her arm gently. "Mother, you're dreaming."

Martha opens her eyes, comes from some faraway place. Does not recognize Anna. Turns again to sleep.

"Papa," she says, "we have to get the child out. They are going to come back. These houses, this street is scheduled for resettlement."

Hanna and Mama stop what they are doing. They all know what this means.

"Who told you this, Marta?" Her father's voice is urgent.

"The German on horseback. He told me to hide her, get her out. I recognized Tylicz, Papa."

Her father is silent. The room is still. Then Papa picks up his coat and goes to the door. "I must organize a meeting. Jacob must contact the underground. We must get out the children that are left. As many as possible."

In the dark cellar her child wants to scream. She clings to Marta, is terrified of the huge man with the beard who is going to carry her down into the slimy blackness where the smell makes her sick.

Anna has been tied to his back so she does not fall off.

"Anna, Anna, you must not cry. You must not make a sound. Do you hear Mama? You must be silent. You must not cry or say a word."

The child, strapped to the broad back of the man, whimpers, clings to the black hair growing over his collar. Her lower lip wobbles but she makes no sound. Her eyes are riveted to Marta's face, begging her not to send her away with this man, down into the darkness.

Marta presses her cheek against her child's face. She dare not weep.

"You will be safe. You will be safe, my darling. Soon, I will come. Go with Jacob. Mama will come soon."

Slowly, as my heart breaks, you disappear with Jacob down the manhole and into the sewers, to crawl through the filth, to slide inch by inch through the maze of underground tunnels. On and on Jacob will crawl on his stomach. Inch by inch men carry silent, petrified children down the stinking sewer pipes, until you are all on the other side of the wall.

Silently, I turn away from you disappearing down that foul hole, and Hanna and I hold each other and we weep for the loss of you, the warmth of your small body. It is the only way out of here, Anna. The only way you might live.

Where were you taken, my Anna? To what sort of safety? I will never know. I will never know what those years did to you.

Martha turns, faces Anna in the dark, reaches out a hand to touch her, struggles to hold on to this vivid dream.

Did Papa find you? No, no . . . Dr. Saurer told Papa to put his name on the little record of your birth we made. If you were taken, a baby with German blood might survive . . . We never thought that Germany would lose the war . . . I put these papers in your pouch round your neck . . .

Anna, my Anna, when they found you, you had a Polish name. A little girl with white hair, who would not speak. We saw so many children, so many sad children. Like luggage, waiting to be collected . . .

You were starving. You rejected me. From that first moment you rejected me. How could you know I did not betray you? When I sent you away you were only two—a baby still. How could all memory of me not die inside you?

Anna, who can never bear a door closed on a small room. Who could never play hide-and-seek. Who goes pale at the thought of traveling underground. Who had to train herself to fly on a plane. Who never trusted another human being again. What happened to you?

You were torn from me and came back a stranger. Grew into a girl with a little sharp tongue. Mama will come soon. How long did you wait? How long before hope died?

Anna sleeps heavily beside Martha. She can feel the warmth of her mother's body in the bed and, feverish, she floats to another place where her mother held her tight.

A connection is made by their warm touching bodies, a collective memory that has not been broken. Martha and Anna merge into one another in the night. Anna is as close to her mother as she was in the womb.

A crack of memory opens . . . Anna has the sensation of being trapped . . .

A feeling of rising panic. She must not cry or make a sound. She gags and is sick on the big man's collar. The terrible smell, the fumes make her dizzy. On and on he crawls and Anna clings so that she will not fall off into the filthy water. Every now and then at a junction of tunnels the man stands up and a hole is opened above them and they gulp fresh air. Then they crawl on again and Anna can see the feet of the man in front and hear the breathing of the bigger child behind her, and the man behind him.

Mama will come soon.

Suddenly, the tunnel ends. A small opening is revealed. She is taken from the man's back and handed up through the hole to a woman. Another man stands guard in the empty road with a gun.

"Hurry," he says. "Hurry, we've only got five minutes. You're late, you're late."

Child after child is pulled up through the hole and the woman clutches them, runs with them to a truck, which has its engine running. She pushes them in, hurriedly, one on top of the other. Anna watches the children behind her still emerging, still being pushed up. Then there is a piercing whistle and a child half in, half out of the hole is pushed abruptly down, the cover is banged shut and two men run for the truck, which is already moving away.

As it gathers speed Anna can smell the sweat and the fear. She sees the crying face of the small boy caught half in and half out of the hole, pushed back into the tunnel and she wants to cry. Mama will come. She will come.

Everything familiar is gone. Loss and fear make her rock the ache away. There have always been so many people to hold her close. So many soft voices have crooned her to sleep in the dark. All snatched away. No arms ever hold her so close again.

There is a place with a spicy smell where they sing in a language she does not know and perform strange prayer rituals. There is the deafening, frightening noise of planes up in the dark sky. Dead bodies of nuns and children lie still on the hard cold ground, beside her.

Buildings burn, great flames leap upwards to the sky. There is choking smoke that suffocates.

One house, another and another—always moving on. So many families, so much fear. So many rules and punishments. She must speak only German. Never ever feeling safe. Mama does not come. Mama does not come and Anna gives up hoping. Forgets.

If ever, ever she dares feel secure or happy, tries to open her small heart to anyone, she is moved on or they disappear suddenly to the sound of marching feet. Once, when the soldiers came, she and a small boy were hastily hidden in a cupboard. It was two days before anyone found them.

Memory, long buried in silence, clams shut. Anna, distressed, wakes.

Martha is staring at her, wide awake.

"I wonder who I am," Anna whispers.

"You are Anna, darling. You are Anna."

"Yes, Mother, I am Anna." Anna smiles reassuringly.

"You've come home?"

"For a little while."

"How lovely, darling."

"Mother," Anna asks, without hope, "do you remember what happened to me in the war, when I was a baby?"

Martha looks puzzled. "You were here at home with me."

"No, Mother, in Poland. In the war. Before we came here. Do you remember anything? Do you know where I went?"

Martha is confused. "I get muddled, darling." She reaches out and pats Anna's hand. "You're home now, that's all that matters, isn't it?"

Anna takes Martha's hand. "Yes, of course, that's all that matters. Shall I make us some tea?"

"Oh, darling, that would be lovely. You will come back and have it with me?"

"Of course I will."

It is six-thirty. Anna pads quietly out into the hall. Lucy lies fast asleep on the sofa with Homer, who opens one eye and dares Anna to challenge him. Barnaby's door is open and the bed has not been slept in. Anna, surprised, smiles. Barnaby is getting a life.

She takes the tea tray with thin bread and butter back to Martha and climbs back into bed.

Martha says suddenly, "He saved you."

Startled, Anna says, "Who did?"

"Kurt Saurer. He warned us. We got you out of the ghetto in time, before we were sent to Auschwitz. You would have been killed, Anna. You would have died if I had kept you with me."

Anna shivers, cannot speak. *If only, only, you had told me.*

Martha struggles once more to hang on to what she is trying to say. "He, he was a Nazi, but before that, we were friends. We grew up together. Kurt got me out of that hospital. He got me out. He was lucky not to be shot."

"How, Mother?"

Martha looks at Anna. Her eyes are devoid of any emotion, but she says clearly, "Money. He bribed . . . the doctor to say I was dead . . . He got me back to the block . . . He threatened . . . said, the Russians were coming." She holds her small twisted hands out suddenly to Anna as if asking for understanding. "I lived. Kurt Saurer gave me life. He saved my life, Anna. To save one life is to save many. He got me out of that place. Kurt Saurer got me out of hell."

Martha is trembling now, her eyes hold a shocking, undiminished terror.

Anna pushes the tray of tea away, leaps out of the bed and goes round to her mother, hugging her fiercely.

"Enough, Mother, enough. You must not think about it anymore. It's gone, I won't ever ask you anything again, I promise."

Martha and Anna rock together, back and forth, back and forth.

"I understand," Anna whispers, as she strokes Martha's white hair. "You had to forget. You had to. Oh, Martha, you became this Englishwoman, and I never understood. Forgive me. Dear God, forgive me."

The sun reaches them on the bed, flooding the big windows of Martha's room.

Anna holds her away. "Would you like your tea before it gets cold?"

Martha leans back on the pillows. "Thank you, darling."

They drink their tea looking out over the garden.

"What was it Fred used to say when he did not want to tell us something, was losing an argument or wanted to change the subject?" Anna asks, after a moment. "Something about butterflies?"

Martha laughs, wags her finger in the way Fred used to do to the children when he was pretending to be cross, but trying not to laugh. "Butterflies. Yes, something about butterflies. Fred used to say it when he thought you or Barnaby were telling fibs or exaggerating." Martha holds her face to the sun and closes her eyes. "'Butterflies can hear their wings.' Was that it, darling?"

Anna smiles, hearing Fred's voice. The sun shines on windows that need cleaning and on a summer garden that is fading, a garden Martha started from a field.

"Actually, I think it was, 'Butterflies can hear *the sound* of their wings,'" Anna murmurs, literal as always.

Chapter 60

From Lucy's old bed in the cottage, Kate and Barnaby lie watching the early morning light tinge the water in dancing, silver sparks. Kate turns to Barnaby and grins. "In my wildest dreams I never thought I would end up in bed with a vicar."

Barnaby smiles down at her. "Is that a complaint?"

"Oh, no," Kate says softly. "Noo . . ." She grins at him. "Can't understand how you've avoided being snapped up by one of the numerous single ladies of the village."

"Unfortunately," Barnaby sighs, "I am only pursued by largish widows who woo me with homemade pasties."

Kate laughs, then props herself up on one elbow. "I'm thinking about Anna, Barnaby. Is she going to be all right? Should you be over there?"

Barnaby sighs. "Yes, I should. Rudi rang me last night after Anna had gone to bed. He had just flown in. He's driving down today. Kurt Saurer has been following Anna around London. Rudi has been making his own inquiries. He thought Saurer was to do with Anna investigating a case of some war criminal for the CPS."

"What about Kurt Saurer? How do you feel about him, Barnaby?"

"It doesn't matter how I feel. My parents haven't changed. But for Anna—"

"And Lucy?"

"As far as Lucy is concerned, Fred was her grandfather, end of story."

Kate throws a kimono over her naked body in a quick practiced arc. Barnaby stares at her as he gets out of bed and pulls his clothes on.

"How lovely you are. How lucky I am. I like your hair growing longer."

Kate touches it. "When I got back from India it was down to my waist. I cut it all off at Glastonbury with friends. I went a bit mad, had the nose ring done and a small butterfly tattoo."

"So I noticed." Barnaby is laughing. "Why?"

"The nose ring was a mistake, something I instantly regretted, but it has been an interesting experiment because of people's extreme reactions. The tattoo I like. When I'm old I will remember a time when I was young. The hair? Well, women cut their hair off when they are sad or angry. It's something they do, a sort of penance for unhappiness or when they want to be someone else." Kate grins at Barnaby's face. "I've lost you?"

Barnaby reaches out and takes a piece of her hair between his finger and thumb. "You've totally lost me. I am just a simple vicar. Women are a mystery."

"Simple, my foot! You are one very, very sexy vicar," Kate says in a way that makes Barnaby shiver.

"As a child," Barnaby says, pulling Kate to him, "Anna used to have the most appalling nightmares. Fred was the only one who could calm her down. It was very distressing."

Barnaby stops, remembering also the thin distant echoes of what he now knows were Martha's birdlike cries. This was why Fred had sent them both to boarding school—to protect their childhood, to protect Martha. Living away from home makes a small but measurable distance between children and their parents.

He places his hand on the warmth of Kate's neck, the soaring feeling of love rising in his throat, making him swallow.

"Now, of course," he says after a minute, "everyone has counseling, and therapy is available. But then, after the war, people just muddled on, comforting each other."

Kate leans back to see his face. It is sad.

"Anna must always have had memories, flashbacks," Barnaby goes on. "She was such a spiky, sharp-tongued little girl. She could upset everybody in a moment. If only I had understood, Kate."

He hesitates, struggling with himself, his sense of loyalty. "I was so angry when Fred died, so upset that I had never been told what really happened to Martha. I still feel this . . . this burning regret that Anna and I were not brought up with the truth."

He turns to the window, where the sun is reaching into the little room. Kate, watching him, knows she must try to find the right words. "Barnaby?" She turns Barnaby to face her, holding on to his arms, feeling her own familiar anger.

"My mother carried her heavy little burden of guilt for the whole of her life, dragging it along behind her like a great sack of potatoes. And boy, did my father and I have to know about it. She made my brother into a living shrine, dedicated to the memory of her brothers and her beloved father who had died or been imprisoned in the war." She takes a deep shaky breath as Barnaby listens. "We all knew about *my* mother's past, what her family suffered, how many died. We were never allowed to forget it. Not for one minute. Her guilt for leaving Holland with my grandmother for England in the early 1930s, before things even started to get bad, stayed with her for her whole life. She married a gentile and then made his life a misery because he wasn't a Jew.

"She did not have a happy life and neither did we, Barnaby. Yet, it was all there for her to grab, if she had wanted it. Sweet husband, a totally loving man. No money worries. Lovely house. Two healthy, bright children. But she was incapable of love or joy in anything except my brother.

"But your mother isn't like that. Martha still embraces all things with wonder and joy. She is still capable of giving happiness and love. No one can even *begin* to understand what it was like for

Martha. How can anyone understand a horror that is totally and utterly incomprehensible? Martha needed her silence. Let the past go now. It is *this life* that Martha made for you that is important."

Kate stops, suddenly near to tears. "Sorry. Sorry, who am I to . . . ? I've no right . . . I'm talking too much."

"Kate, you are making perfect sense."

Barnaby looks out on to his church, lying among the twisted oaks, immutable, ageless, a lasting monument to faith. He suddenly wants to be inside there with his familiar God. A God he can worship with known rhythmic rituals as comforting and somnambulant as a faint medieval chant.

He feels afraid of the speed and strength of his feelings for this woman.

"I hope these moments with you are not a dream," he says, almost to himself, staring across the graveyard to the water.

"They aren't a dream. They're real, Barnaby."

Kate goes to him standing in the window. "But I'm a gypsy. It's early days. I don't know . . ."

Kate too is afraid of hurt, of getting it wrong again.

Barnaby turns and puts his finger over her mouth with a smile.

"Of course you don't know. You are young, with your whole life before you. Of course you don't know."

He bends to kiss her. "I treasure this time with you, Kate."

Kate reaches up and places her cheek against his. "Oh, so do I. Go, go, dearest Barnaby. You must see how they are at the house."

They go down the stairs and as Kate opens the back door on to a new day, she murmurs to his retreating back, to his footsteps walking away from her over the wet grass, "Most improbable, thee and me, but very real."

At the gate Barnaby turns and looks at Kate's exotic little figure in the kimono standing on the step, and laughs. Very improbable. But deliciously exciting.

Chapter 61

As the Mercedes purrs towards London, Rudi puts on some Bach. Every now and then he reaches out to touch Anna as if she has been ill and is convalescing. Anna is moved. It is as if the dynamics of their relationship have subtly shifted. As if her vulnerability makes her someone other than the woman he married and he is enjoying being allowed to show how he feels for the first time.

She thinks of the surprising strength of Lucy, who is staying one more day before catching the train back to London. She closes her eyes and listens to the music, glad the countryside is flashing past. Glad she is returning home with Rudi, to all that remains good, familiar, and routine. She will talk to him about Kurt Saurer. But not yet. He will understand the anomalies of the past, the time it takes to let go of it.

It is enough to be in this warm car with the man she loves. A man who loves her, with a quiet strength she is only beginning to understand. Anna leans back, her tiredness making the air hum.

She accepts now that her memory will stay forever locked. She has only shadowy, fleeting images. Things she has read or been told, mingle with dreams, which will go on surfacing, but can never be unraveled.

It feels as if a thing that has hidden in dark corners all her life and stalked her all summer has just jumped out. Life can never be the same again. Yet she is here in this car with Rudi. She has survived. The world has not come to an end.

She thinks about Lucy and the baby and the growing respect she has for her daughter, as if she is seeing Lucy for the first time as an adult.

She thinks about that boy of Lucy's, facing ethnic hatred so strong there is no room for anything else. In a place where boundaries are blurred. Where good people are hard to separate from bad. Where years of propaganda and prejudice leave layers and layers of loathing, touching everybody with evil.

She remembers Rudi once telling her that people of his generation in Germany rarely asked their fathers what they did in the war. She thinks of the time one of Rudi's sons slammed a taxi door too hard and the driver muttered angrily, "Bloody Germans."

How ashamed she was at his rudeness and at the boys' startled faces. Xenophobia whipped up by a tiny thing. Colleagues who turn out to be hidden racists. People always surprise you.

She thinks wryly how instinctively German she has always felt. How comfortable she is with the language and the people. Being with Rudi is like coming home from a long journey. Everything right. Everything falling into place. She cannot imagine life without him. She has never realized the power of her feelings. She has never told him. Anna smiles suddenly, opens her eyes.

Rudi turns, startled. "What is it?"

"I was just thinking of Barnaby. Barnaby and Kate. I would never have put those two together in a hundred years."

Rudi laughs. "I picked up the sexual chemistry immediately."

"Did you? Good heavens, Rudi. Well, good heavens." Anna is speechless.

"Will it work between them, do you think?" Rudi asks. "There is a hell of an age gap."

Anna considers it. "I might be wrong," she says, "but I think it might. I have a feeling Kate will go away and then come back to him." She starts to laugh. "Who would have thought Barnaby would fall in love with someone not much older than Lucy?"

Anna laughs and laughs and suddenly she is crying. It feels a blessed relief.

Rudi steers the car into a rest area and reaches for her. "Darling Anna, you are going to be all right. You are going to be fine."

Anna closes her eyes. "I hope so, Rudi. I hope so."

Rudi bends round to the backseat and pulls some papers out of his briefcase.

"I was going to wait until we got home, but I think this will interest you. I contacted a friend of mine who wrote a book after the war, about the bravery of women who worked for various Polish underground movements. They were virtually unrecognized, until the children they rescued grew up and could tell their stories."

He places the pages on Anna's knee. "There was Zegota, which was the Council for Aid to Jews. They smuggled thousands of children from the ghetto and hid them in normal homes.

"There was a woman working in the Social Welfare Department of the Municipal Administration of Warsaw called Irena Sendlerowa. She used her position to give financial help, to smuggle food and assistance to many Jews. She formed a network of people she trusted and they issued hundreds of false documents with forged signatures, because obviously no one Jewish was entitled to assistance."

Anna stares down at the pages. "The envelope with my birth certificate had that name on the front, Rudi."

"I know. Barnaby told me."

He places his hand on the back of her neck and rubs it gently with his finger.

"I have only had time to find out a tiny amount so far. But this is how you most probably got out of the ghetto, Anna. It tells you here how they smuggled children out in the underground corridors and then placed them in families, orphanages, and convents."

Anna leans back against his hand and shuts her eyes again.

"I know," Rudi says, "we can never really know what happened to you, my beloved Anna, but this is a clue. I have no doubt that the same agencies helped to find you, for Fred and Martha, after the war."

Anna is so still, Rudi wonders if he has done the right thing. Then she opens her eyes and gently folds the pages.

"I have spent a lot of time telling Barnaby to look forward, not back. Lecturing him on the importance of the future." She smiles wanly. "And I was right. Thank you for finding this, Rudi. It is important. It places me somewhere. And I can do some research, when I'm ready."

She turns in the car seat and meets his eyes. "I am four years older than the woman you married. I am not the same woman, Rudi. I am someone else."

"You are exactly the same successful, beautiful woman you ever were." He smiles. "I could not love you more, or be happier than I am. You are Anna, my wife. And now I am going to drive you home."

Anna brings his hand to her lips and holds it there, tight to her mouth, in a gesture so unlike her, so full of love, Rudi closes his eyes hard against the tears that spring to his eyes.

Kate, coming into the bedroom with Martha's hot chocolate, eyes Martha's nightdress suspiciously. "Martha, how many pairs of tights have you got on under there? You look like a pumpkin."

Martha looks down at herself. "A pumpking?"

She meets Kate's eyes and they both start to giggle.

"Hanna, darling, I'm a pumpking."

Kate puts the mug down, before she spills it. "Martha, let's get some of those clothes off, you'll expire."

Kate begins to peel five pairs of tights from Martha's thin legs, and numerous other strange garments. She is incredulous. How is it possible for Martha to get all these layers on? With each layer she peels off, she and Martha get more and more hysterical, until they both collapse on the bed convulsed with laughter, surrounded by pools of odd garments.

Barnaby, opening the front door after putting Lucy on the night sleeper, stops and listens to the infectious sound of women laughing. Martha, hastily tucked back into bed, is sitting up, flushed and happy, holding a drink.

"What's this, a midnight feast?" Barnaby smiles at the sight of them both looking vaguely guilty and sees what looks like Martha's entire wardrobe on the floor.

"I had supper in bed," Martha says happily.

Kate grins at Barnaby, winks at Martha and leads him out of the door.

"What's going on? I can't leave you two harpies together for two minutes. Lucy gave Martha supper and put her to bed before we left for the station," Barnaby says.

"I know. Only she got up again, four times. Every time I put her to bed she got up again. She said she was hungry so I made her scrambled egg."

Barnaby laughs. "She will burst. Sorry, Kate."

"Don't you dare apologize," Kate says vehemently, going back to Martha.

"We've had a whale of a time."

"Great fun, darling." Martha is nearly asleep.

Kate turns Martha's light out. "Good night, Martha, sleep tight."

"And you, darling, sleep tight. See you in the morning."

"See you in the morning."

Kate hugs Barnaby's arm as she passes the end of the bed and his face lights up.

Martha, seeing this, says, "I love Hanna. She is so pretty."

"Isn't she just? Good night, Mum. God bless."

"God bless, Barnaby darling." Like a child she is almost asleep as she talks.

His plane is delayed for one hour. As he sits and watches the people moving round the terminal, he is suddenly glad it is done, over with. He can go home. Did he do a bad or a good thing in coming? He does not know. What he does know is *Marta lived.*

In Switzerland there is a bank account where his father put Dr. Oweski's money in safekeeping. He can now return it. It is Marta's. When Mutti died he put the Oweski's china in the Swiss bank too. He could not bear to see it. His mother had never known about the money.

He does not think he will ever return to England. In his heart he wishes he had not come. Never known for sure. The pain of seeing his daughter, who has his eyes, his lips, his way of holding her head and Mutti's way of standing; the expression of contempt on his granddaughter's face, hurts.

Every time I close my eyes I see the child held out to me as I sit up on that great horse and I feel a haunting sense of loss for a life lived without me.

Anna puts down the telephone and then redials for a taxi.

"Rudi," she calls, "there is something I have to do. I won't be long."

Rudi comes into the room looking anxious. "What is it? Let me come with you. Has something happened?"

"No," Anna says. "Nothing. Rudi, I'm perfectly all right. It is just something I must do on my own. I'll tell you later. Let's meet for lunch. Usual place?" She goes to kiss him. "Don't worry, please. It is just something I have to do."

Anna runs down the stairs and jumps into the taxi, glancing at her watch. She tries to relax. She is not used to being impulsive. She is used to weighing odds. If she is too late, then it is meant to be. If not, she will find the words.

The taxi drops her and she runs into the airport and looks up at the screen with the departure times. Has he already been called? She moves towards the Berlin check-in desk, but cannot see him. Suddenly he sees her and gets to his feet slowly, like a sleepwalker.

Anna stands breathing heavily, a little way from him.

"Martha may be muddled about this, but I don't think so. She told me you saved my life and later hers. She told me she owed you her life. I don't know if this makes up for the other things you did in the war. Only you know this. She told me . . . She told me that you were friends as children. I got the feeling, I don't know . . . that she could never hate you despite what you did. I do not really understand."

I shake. I wish I could tell the woman standing in front of me what I have never dared to admit to anyone. I loved Marta from the first moment I saw her. A small dark child, unafraid of anybody. Ready, like me, to try any and every adventure, to burst out of her narrow life. And I was terrified of this feeling that grew and grew, this love. The feeling that Mutti suspected and beat out of me. With Matusia I could be myself. I did not have to prove anything. We had different lives, and yet, as children, for a brief time, we were soul mates.

He looks at his daughter. It does not excuse anything, only makes his betrayal worse. She is watching him with his eyes.

"Maybe you have condemned yourself all these years," she says. "Maybe in remembrance you have made yourself all bad. Martha told me that to save one life is to save many. Whatever you have done, you gave my mother her happy, fulfilled life."

She holds out her hand. "Good-bye. Lucy gave me your card." She pauses. "It is too early to know how I feel or how Lucy will feel, but later, maybe there will be things we will want to ask you . . ."

He takes her hand. "Later, perhaps," he says.

Then quickly he lets her hand go. "It means much that you came. Thank you."

"Good-bye," she says again, meeting his eyes, looking carefully into his face, as if to remember it. Then she turns and walks away. Very straight. A tall, fair woman with long slim legs and a walk that makes people turn. *This is Anna. My daughter. To come took great courage.*

His flight is being called. He is going home.

In remembrance, have I softened the edges of what I did and what I became in order to live with myself? To explain to a family I never had, how it is that they exist?

Chapter 62

LONDON, 1946

Sitting in a black taxi. Still unsteady with freedom. Sitting with this tall, kind English soldier who has never seemed a stranger. Everywhere buildings bombed, and shells of houses.

People walk free. No one stops them. Men and women in uniforms who do not look threatening, but comforting. There, back there, the taxi passes a park. Huge great plane trees. Sweeping green leaves touching the ground. Blossom bursting into new life. People sit under those trees. Children run about. Babies? Yes, babies.

Marta's eyes are riveted to those babies. Men throw those babies up, up into the air. But they catch them. They hold them tight and safe. There is not a yellow star to be seen. Nowhere.

Marta is shaking with this new and sudden knowledge of a world order that might contain hope. She turns to the man who has brought her here and he smiles. His eyes hold all that he has seen and all that Marta has experienced.

They rest on the small rigid child next to Marta, holding herself in, away from all contact with them. Her cold blue eyes look straight ahead, her face is impassive, registering no emotion at all. She has not spoken a word in any language.

The man speaks to the child in English, gently, not expecting her to understand or to answer. His words wash over the child like small warm waves. Marta meets his eyes. He holds them steadily. In that unflinching moment, Marta knows he is not going to walk away from them. He is not going to abandon them in this strange new country. He is going to be there, always.

CORNWALL, 1999

Martha wakes to the stillness of a morning. A blackbird sings. Just one. Over and over. The birdbath overflows with night rain. Martha thinks she can smell lavender. In a moment Fred will bring tea on a small lacquer tray. On the tray will be her favorite cup, thin as the petals of the poppies she grows in the flowerbed down by the hedge.

Fred will sit on the bed before early morning surgery and he will say to her as he does every morning, "What will you do today, darling?"

She will shiver with anticipation. In her head she is already walking the dew-damp grass, checking every plant, every new bud in the garden.

At lunchtime she will sit in the garden and write letters to Anna and Barnaby away at university and school. She will doze in the hot sun and when she sees the tide full behind the trees, a sepia photograph, the water like mercury, shimmering on the turn of the tide, she will walk with Puck down to the sea.

The larks will rise vertically out of the marram grass, which smells warm like mown hay. Fishing boats chug home through the mist, glide in on the glassy evening tide, engines throbbing, voices carrying over the blue shush and beat of the ocean. Sounds as familiar as breathing.

When she returns to the house Fred will be home from evening surgery, smiling, waiting as he always does. Fred will be home. Martha, smiling, closes her eyes, sighs. "Such a happy life," she murmurs. "Such a very happy life."

* * *

Kate and the nurse lay Martha out together. Silent, moving swiftly, working as one. This is Kate's own separate and private homage. This is the last rite and act of love she can ever do for Martha.

They wash her small body with cloths dipped in lavender water, Kate and the nurse. They take from the drawer her favorite cotton nightdress. They make the bed with her best linen. They brush her white, sparse hair and position her thin arms and tiny hands before they stiffen.

They call Barnaby, sitting very still in the hall listening to the tick of the grandfather clock and the sound of church bells coming from the floodlit church. He moves into the room. Martha's face is still beautiful. The wonderful angles of her cheekbones are like a smudged sketch, without expression. She has faded away and the spirit of her is gone. She no longer radiates all that she was and will always be to Barnaby. This tiny Polish woman who became his mother.

The nurse leaves the room and Barnaby reaches out instinctively for Kate and draws her to him. Her hand is warm and her hair smells of flowers. His eyes are fixed on Martha's face, but he has a sudden flash of Anna walking with Rudi through a shady park somewhere. Of Lucy, in Milan, sitting in an outside café with plants trailing down the walls behind her. Her hands are curled around her stomach as she feels the kick of new life starting up within her.

The future is this. These things.

Somewhere, far away down on the estuary, the warbling high note of curlews like the note of an uncaptured song. Then silence.